Five out of Five stars: "In the Shadows of the Gods is well-written and entertaining. Author John Raines has created a rich fantasy landscape full of magic and a plot that is well-paced and able to hold the reader's attention. The characters are the best part of the book. Few of the characters fall neatly into the category of good or evil ... Fans of high fantasy will find a worthy quest In The Shadows of the Gods and will likely turn the last page anxious for more. "

—ForeWord Clarion Reviews

IN THE SHADOWS OF THE GODS

The Rise of the Guard

By John F. Raines

iUniverse, Inc.
Bloomington

In the Shadows of the Gods

The Rise of the Guard

iUniverse books may be ordered through booksellers or by contacting:

iUniverse
1663 Liberty Drive
Bloomington, IN 47403
www.iuniverse.com
1-800-Authors (1-800-288-4677)

Because of the dynamic nature of the Internet, any Web addresses or links contained in this book may have changed since publication and may no longer be valid. The views expressed in this work are solely those of the author and do not necessarily reflect the views of the publisher, and the publisher hereby disclaims any responsibility for them.

ISBN: 978-1-4502-4532-6 (sc)
ISBN: 978-1-4502-4533-3 (ebook)
ISBN: 978-1-4502-4534-0 (dj)

Library of Congress Control Number: 2010913915

Printed in the United States of America

iUniverse rev. date: 4/14/2011

For my God and for my family,
because they were always there for me, even when I drove
them away.

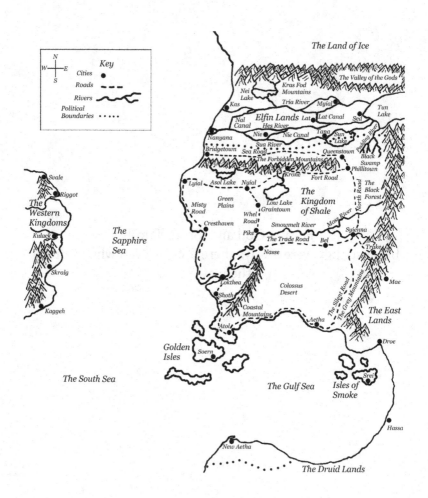

On Hybrids

It is a troubled time. The might of the Kingdom of Shale is spread thin as a marauding group calling themselves the Rogues has begun launching raids across the kingdom. The elves to the north have also made small incursions into the kingdom's land, raiding the odd settlements around Bridgetown; but fortunately, the memory of their losses against the terrible walls of the dread fortress Krone still stands strong in their minds, and they fear open war with our kind.

The Rogues, however, are proving a more dangerous and cunning enemy than we feared. Their assassins are of great renown. King Leon Shale has had numerous attempts on his life, and many of his kin have died at the Rogues' hands. It is clear the Rogues will not stop until the order of the land has fallen and chaos grips the kingdom, as it did before the rise of the Kingdom of Shale.

This will not happen. I have made sure of it. My creations shall become the bane of the enemies of the Kingdom of Shale. After countless years of study, and after enduring much criticism for my work, I have finally achieved my goal: I have honed the magic that will allow me to bind creatures by body and mind. I now have the ability to create hybrids, creatures produced of a magical blending between man and mythical beast. They are everything I dreamed of and more, with power and strength beyond any of the heroes of old. These creations shall be unstoppable at the head of the king's army, and no assassin shall have a hope of coming near the king with the hybrids standing guard over him.

I have given my creations to King Leon for his protection or for his conquests—whichever he chooses. They are now being called the Royal Guard, and they will decimate any who try to oppose the king.

There are fourteen in all—each one different,

and each one powerful. There is the troll, the merman, the phoenix, the griffin, the manticore, the sasquatch, the gremlin, the werewolf, the drake, the harpy, the basilisk, the unicorn, the golem, and the one all the others have taken to calling Demon. As for exactly what Demon is, I do not know rightly. In my quest to find suitable creatures for this experiment, I found a strange being held fast in a hunter's trap. It was a gaunt creature with leathery wings and a mouth that stuck out from its face, similar to that of a cat. I have had some postulate that it may have been one of the last gargoyles, but there is little more than guesswork to support this.

Each Guard brings special traits from his or her other half. Jinx, the harpy, is capable of bewitching others to do her will, while Pyre, the phoenix, can surround himself with flames. These magically imbued abilities make the Guard members dangerous foes, but when they combine their abilities, they become an army unto themselves.

The merman, dubbed Mer by his comrades,

has become an adept healer, and Silver, the unicorn, has often demonstrated his prowess at attack magic. Howl, the werewolf, and Blade, the griffin, have both shown exceptional skill in swordsmanship, while Crash and Crunch, the sasquatch and troll, are both capable of sending grown men flying through the air with their tremendous strikes. Together, the Royal Guard members shall make the armies of the Kingdom of Shale unstoppable. These creatures will soon be ready to take their rightful place in Shale Castle, protecting the king from any harm that could befall him and leading his armies to glorious victory.

My creations shall buy me great fame in the Kingdom of Shale, and I am certain my name shall be spoken with the same honor as the great heroes of the past. Head Magician Marcus shall at last be forced to accept my greatness and raise me to a high position of honor among the mages of Castle Shale.

These are the accounts of Halifin, the soon-to-be hero of Shale.

Chapter One

A man in a hooded tunic clung to the walls of Castle Shale, slowly scaling the mammoth structure. The night concealed him as he clambered up toward the top of the keep, scrambling from statues to windows on the glassy stone. His muscles burned from the exertion, and sweat clung to his brow as he steadily climbed higher, all the while praying within his head that no one would take notice.

He had studied the castle long and hard, and he knew the dangers of getting caught. There were warriors within Castle Shale the likes of which no other castle contained, and though this man was confident in his sword arm, he had no desire to test his mettle against them: especially without his sword.

The air grew damp as the night went on, and from the west he saw clouds rolling in his direction.

Curses! he thought as he redoubled his climbing efforts. *If these walls are this difficult to scale dry, how impossible will they be wet?*

Even without the rain, the walls were smooth and slippery, made from a dark stone built so tightly together it seemed like a solid sheet of obsidian colored rock. If it were not for the many windows and gargoyles built into the structure, he wouldn't have been able to climb an inch up the wall.

Is this mission worth the danger of this climb? he wondered as he almost lost his footing for what seemed the thousandth time. He paused a moment, giving himself the smallest of breaks. *Of course it is. Justice will always be worth it.*

He climbed on, ignoring his aching fingers and arms until finally he was hanging just below the battlements. He was glad to have climbed without the extra weight of his sword, but as he reached the top, he wished for the blade again.

He sensed them before he heard them: three guards patrolling along the roof of the keep. Worse, he sensed that these were no ordinary guards—these guards had wings.

Hybrids! I can't fight all of them! I'll have to wait until I have an opening to sneak by. I can't let them keep me from my goal! He glanced back at the clouds apprehensively. *If the gods are good, I won't have to hang here while the rains drench me.*

As the clouds grew closer and darker, he became increasingly certain that the gods would not be good. He prepared himself for a night of absolute misery.

Blade stood on the ramparts of the keep of Castle Shale. He wore his Royal Guard armor, as every member of the Royal Guard did while on duty—except for their assassin, Shadow. The heavily plated armor, made with the finest steel, was just light enough for the Guard members with wings to fly. The helmets had all been designed after the creatures they were magically intertwined with. Blade's helmet had a nose guard like that of a griffin's beak, and Pyre's armor had a phoenix engraved into the breastplate, which glowed red as he burned.

Blade glanced at Jinx and Pyre, who patrolled the battlements as well. The fliers were always the ones who patrolled the ramparts around the base of the tall tower, which rose high out of the castle keep and had many smaller towers reaching out from it to dizzying heights. The offshoot towers first ran parallel with the ground before angling sharply toward the sky, giving the tower a look reminiscent both of a tree and a trident. It was the fliers who patrolled here, for if they saw an assassin they could immediately take wing to intercept him.

Beyond the outer walls of the castle was the capital city of Syienna. The city was near the center of the Kingdom of Shale, which extended for well over a hundred miles in whatever direction they might travel. Here the hybrids resided, guarding Castle Shale, where King Leon Shale sat upon his mighty throne to rule his kingdom.

Their job here was not a particularly difficult one, simply a tedious one. For the many months they had lived in Castle Shale, the Guard had not caught wind of so much as a rumor of an attempt on the king's life. Regardless, though, they had all served countless hours of patrol duty. The only thing that piqued their interest in their assignment was the castle itself—which, fortunately, was quite large and offered much potential for exploration.

Below Blade was the large courtyard between the keep and the outer wall, filled with many different types of plants— some exotic, like the bright red dragon's-tongue flowers, and some not, like the many oaks and firs. Winding through the lush gardens below were dozens of pathways and streams, fed by the Snowmelt River, which forked around the castle like a living moat. Below, the garden fountains spluttered and splashed water from the river up into the sky in glittering cascades, both for aesthetics and to provide extra water to some of the thirstier plants in the gardens.

Beyond the courtyard was the outer wall that surrounded the entire castle. The wall was at least sixty feet high and was built in jagged angles that formed a stone star encompassing Castle Shale. Blade doubted whether anyone, hostile or otherwise, would ever be able to get past those immense walls unnoticed, let alone penetrate the castle itself. The walls were constantly manned by at least two hundred archers, who kept a wary eye on the streets and comparatively quaint buildings of Syienna, which tangled around the castle like briars about a rose.

The city had been founded there, at the foot of the castle, because of the protection Castle Shale had provided during the chaotic age before the rise of the Kingdom of Shale, during the reign of King Leon the Conqueror, some four hundred years ago. Beyond the walls, the vast city stretched out for miles in each direction. Syienna was massive—the largest city in the kingdom and possibly the world.

Trade from all over the lands came through Syienna, making it a rich melting pot of cultures. Merchants with strange accents and even elves were a common sight within the borders of the city. The hillsides surrounding the city were guarded by two large fortresses, Fort Freeman (named so because King Leon the Conqueror had freed every slave who toiled over it) and Fort Dread, which had been King Jeremiah the Builder's attempt to rival the ancient fort of Krone (It was well agreed that he had failed miserably). Each fort was capable of repelling an advancing army if need be. Both had a garrison of nearly five hundred troops, and sometimes more, all of whom had been trained in archery. Indeed, Syienna, and to a greater extent, Castle Shale, were among the safest places in the entire kingdom.

It is precisely the last place that the Royal Guard is needed, Blade thought miserably.

Blade glanced again at Jinx and Pyre, who still patrolled along the ramparts of the keep. He also knew Crunch, Crash, and Howl were undoubtedly within the castle, looking for any assassins who might be skulking around down there. Shadow was, of course, secretly following King Leon the Meek himself, as he always did, ensuring no one could harm the king.

The Guard worked shifts of seven at a time, while the other seven trained and relaxed. Shadow, however, usually was forced to work nearly twice as much as his comrades, for the King felt insecure when he wasn't being guarded by his "invisible warrior," as he had come to call Shadow. Shadow was barely given time to eat or sleep. Tragically, this so-called invisible warrior liked nothing more than to shut himself up within the walls of his room and study who knew what in those large, dusty tomes he was always reading and scribbling in. Shadow was a mystery, even to Blade. He rarely talked, and the few glimpses anyone got of him in his room were always of Shadow either meditating or reading from his strange books.

And Silver is probably out in Syienna, boasting, gambling, and bartering any wealth he came across for whatever catches his fancy. Blade smiled as he imagined Silver, with his shimmering hair and metallic eyes, bragging to anyone who would listen in his cavalier way. Silver was the least disciplined of the Guard by far. The unicorn-man had trouble completing all of his duties—especially the ones he considered boring; which was a category that seemed to include every duty he was assigned in Castle Shale. Even when Silver was on duty, he talked a lot, and took many unscheduled "breaks." He was sometimes scolded for his behavior, but he never did listen.

And why would he? Blade thought. *After all, who would ever be foolish enough to try to punish a hybrid?* Every hybrid could wield more magic than any but the best trained human, not to mention a hybrid's vastly superior speed and strength. A human would be a fool to start a fight with any of them without at least ten good fighters supporting him.

Blade and the two others looked down at the gardens between the castle and the main wall. The moonlight trickled down, softly illuminating the grounds and glinting off the river and fountain water as clouds from the distant coast began to roll across the sky, choking the light of the stars and soon even beginning to strangle the moon.

Blade didn't mind. He could see well in the dark, for he

had a griffin's eyes—golden irises, slitted pupils, and all. His eyes swept over the courtyard, searching for any signs of enemy movement.

No movement ... as always, no movement.

He looked over at Jinx as she passed by; she responded with an apathetic smile. Her golden, feathery hair flowed out onto her shoulders from under her helmet, which curved along her brow and descended to her nose like a widow's peak. Her helmet had harpy wings engraved with gold leaf running along the sides of it. Jinx leaned on her spear like a walking stick as she marched, marking every other step with a wooden clunk as the butt struck the ground.

"Good night for a stroll, wouldn't you say?" Blade asked sarcastically. Jinx didn't deign to answer the question. She gave Blade a halfhearted grin and continued on her way, her golden wings ruffling in the breeze as her downy hair curled behind her in the ever-strengthening breeze.

Jinx sighed in frustration after she passed Blade, who marched off in the other direction after she walked by. *Our talents are being utterly wasted on guarding a man whom no one seems to want dead.*

She was eager for an assassin, just so she could do some sort of fighting. She hated this boredom more than anything else about the job, and her opinions were mirrored by everyone in the Guard; even quiet Shadow had voiced his displeasure several times.

No Rogues had attacked Syienna since they had arrived, but then again, no Rogues had ever attacked Syienna *before* they had arrived.

The Royal Guard is without a doubt guarding the place in the Kingdom of Shale that requires guarding the least. Only

Krone, the ancient and terrible fortress far to the north, was considered more secure than Castle Shale.

However, the security of Syienna did not seem to spread toward the numerous small towns and farming villages dotting the surrounding plains. Reports of attack after attack came in from the hundreds of refugees who had fled their burned homesteads. The Rogues were a new kind of enemy—one that neither the King nor his generals were used to fighting. The Rogues were well organized, striking quickly and most often on horseback before falling back into hiding with remarkable speed. They fought hard, and apparently were skilled tacticians. Many rumors came of brilliant maneuvers, strict battlefield discipline, and near-miraculous victories.

Meanwhile, in the safety of Castle Shale, the hybrids rotted away. No enemy lurked to hone their skills on; no one for them to test their mettle against. None of the humans would train with the hybrids, for they were too afraid of them. All the Royal Guard could do in these most chaotic of times was to sit in the castle and listen to all the stories of adventure and war happening all around them.

Suddenly, as if the gods themselves were mocking their guard duty, the clouds overhead began to shower them with rain. Jinx could not imagine a worse way for the night to carry on.

❀ * ❀ * ❀

Pyre grit his teeth as the rain began to fall. He looked miserably over at Jinx, who looked up to the sky and scowled with irritation as a fat drop plopped onto her nose. She cursed lightly under her breath as drops began to plink off their armor.

Pyre walked over to Jinx, leaned his back on the ramparts, and sighed. "We've wasted yet another day. If the king didn't coop us up here, we—"

7

"You know already that I agree with you." Jinx, too, leaned against the wall as she spoke, resting her spear on her shoulder. "I hate this patrol duty more than most—except perhaps Silver, and maybe Shadow."

"This isn't what we were designed for," Blade said as he walked past. He wouldn't stop to join them. Even though he did hate guard duty, he always forced himself to do the job well. After all, as he often said, he had nothing much better to do.

"Beyond a doubt," Pyre said, raising his voice over the increasing the rain. "We have trained our entire lives to be perfect warriors, and King Leon the Meek uses us to guard a castle that already has a garrison of two thousand men."

"Not in the castle itself," Jinx corrected.

"But in the forts out there." He motioned toward the dark forts in the hills. "They're close enough to be considered a garrison. Why must I defend myself? You know my point. Enough fortifications await here to repel an army of ten thousand Rogues. What business do we have here? By all rights, we should be out roaming around, fighting the enemies of the kingdom wherever they should be. But instead, our king insists he needs us here like a child insists he needs his blanket."

"The garrison may be able to stop ten thousand," Blade said as he passed them again, "but Rogue assassins have already proven they can sneak past a full garrison and kill their target before any even know they are there. He wants to ensure his safety." It seemed even the dutiful Blade had decided not to walk the entire length of the massive ramparts.

"No, there is more behind this," Pyre decided. "We must be missing something. What fool stays his strongest soldiers while enemies eviscerate his kingdom?" Lightning branched out over the horizon, and thunder boomed across the fertile plains and valleys of Shale County.

That's not good, Pyre thought.

"One would think Shadow, at least, would be sent forth," Jinx added. "After all, who else could find and slay the Rogue leaders?"

"I would be willing to give the task a try," Blade said wryly as he passed a third time. He seemed to figure this part of the wall deserved as much guarding as anywhere else.

"True ... but then, any one of us would," Jinx said as she looked at the sky. "After all, no matter how bad it got, it could not be nearly as miserable as this guard duty!" The sky responded to her complaints with a gust of wind and more rain.

"This storm is growing dangerous," Pyre said as lightning flashed, this time much closer to the castle. The thunder boomed with menacing volume, and the group began to eye each other's metal suits apprehensively.

"Jinx," Pyre said, "would you ask the king if we may come down? We couldn't see anyone moving in all this rain anyway, and I certainly do not relish the thought of being struck by lightning."

"Must it be me?" Jinx asked rhetorically. She knew quite well why it had to be her, but she hated talking to the king.

"Of course. Who else can bewitch King Leon?" Blade stated the obvious as he passed.

"I would leave on my own," Pyre explained, "but I know that the overly honor-bound one here won't leave without permission," Pyre jerked his head toward Blade as he spoke. "It just wouldn't be right to leave him to die alone."

"What you may call overly honor-bound, I call having a sense of duty and discipline for battle," Blade retorted over his shoulder.

"Discipline for battle?" Jinx asked.

"I will be less likely to run like you cowards will."

"Perhaps if you live long enough to see a battle, that is," Jinx called back. She sighed reluctantly as she looked again toward the foreboding sky, which cracked again with lightning. "Well,

I should go convince the king. In the meantime, you two get indoors. I don't want you struck dead before I return."

Pyre laughed. "And suddenly, it's almost as if I have a mother!"

"Please," Blade said, starting for the door to the tower stairwell. "How would you even know what a mother is like?"

"Oh, what's this?" Jinx teased Blade. "What happened to your unwavering discipline?"

"I am disciplined, not suicidal. I know when to retreat..." Lightning cracked high above their heads like a long whip, striking a flagpole on the tower. "... and now seems to be a perfect time."

Jinx walked down a long, torch-lit corridor; occasionally, lightning flashes brightened the hallway through the large stained-glass windows. The walls about her were like the rest of the castle: made of strange black stone set so closely together that it created the appearance of a smooth, unbroken surface.

The odd tapestry and painting decorated the walls, but here, away from the great hall, less effort had been made in making the castle feel grand. The only other decoration was a red carpet that led to the throne room, which lay behind two massive metal doors that loomed ahead. Two golden-armored, elite guards stood at either side of those doors, holding halberds bearing the king's standard of a crown wreathed in ivy.

Lightning flashed, and the eerie blue light gleamed off the blades of the halberds and the golden-plated armor of the elite guards. The standards cast shadows at odd angles as the light streamed in from the many windows lining the hall, giving the doors an ethereal look. It was an effect that the strange castle somehow seemed to magnify of its own accord.

Jinx glanced at the old walls as she stepped toward the door. They were ancient—ancient beyond her reckoning. She didn't know much about the kingdom or any of the lands surrounding it. Halifin had never instructed the Guard on the history of the land they were protecting, but even so, Jinx had heard much about Castle Shale in conversations between the humans. It was one of the great mysteries of the land, along with the mystical fortress far away called Krone, which supposedly was protected by magic more ancient than the hills themselves. From what Jinx had gathered, Castle Shale had been ancient even long before the Shale Dynasty had been formed. Its old name, the name few called it now, was Tretia—which she had learned from Shadow was Arignese, a language now long dead, for "House of the Gods."

She brushed her hand against the old stonework as she paused to admire the craftsmanship.

I wonder who first built this massive stronghold. The stone was of a strange quality. Most human buildings she'd seen were made of rough stone, but the stone forming the walls and keep of Castle Shale were smooth—glossy, even, as if the whole castle had a fresh layer of polish. The stones were strong, too—completely unaffected by the ravages time dealt to most everything in this world. *It's almost as if the castle itself is immortal.*

Her armor clanked as she once more took step after step through the massive hall. Castle Shale dwarfed everything around it, casting its protective shadow over the city of Syienna. The castle had to stand at least twenty stories high at its tallest tower, and it was probably half a mile across. Jinx couldn't imagine any army overrunning it; she couldn't even imagine any army building it.

Lightning flashed through the window again, bathing the door and guards with another wave of eerie light. The elite guards stood motionless as she stepped by, only the standards waving in the slight breeze of her wake. However, from behind the eye slits of their armor, she could see them watching her suspiciously. They knew her well enough to let her pass, but no human in the castle knew a hybrid well enough to trust them.

She ignored their stares and walked up to the door. Before entering, she paused a moment, closed her eyes, and concentrated. Bewitching a person could be quite difficult at times, especially when the person was as unpredictable as the king. She somewhat suspected that he might be half mad, but as impertinent as hybrids were allowed to be, not even they would risk giving this thought voice.

She slowly opened the door to peek her head through. The king looked up from a book he was reading and beckoned her to enter with a pleasant smile and a nod from his graying head. Jinx was his favorite member of the Guard, except perhaps for Shadow. It was a sentiment she had earned predominantly by her appearance. Jinx was considered a beauty by the humans. Her angular jaw and brilliant green eyes, coupled with her exotic featherlike hair and golden wings, made Jinx an object of desire within Castle Shale. The guards and king alike of the castle would often stare at her in ways that made her uncomfortable. She was the only Guard member, other than Howl or maybe Freeze, who could merit a stare from the humans inspired by a feeling besides suspicion or fear.

Jinx glanced around the room as she entered, trying to find Shadow; she knew he was there somewhere. She looked at all the dark corners, her eyes straining for any sign of him along the the walls and ceiling. It was a difficult task. The room was immense, rising high above her head, and was only lit by several candle-covered chandeliers. Large tapestries hung from the walls, and a red velvet curtain hung around the king's throne, allowing him to only be seen from the doorway.

"Searching for my invisible warrior?" the king asked amused as he toyed with a jewel-covered ring on his finger. He had a graying beard, and his narrow body was covered with jewelry. Atop his head rested a large, golden crown studded with as many jewels as could be fitted. He wore a flowing purple robe made from some sort of animal skin; all she knew about it was that whatever the robe was made of, its short, violet fur was so soft it put velvet to shame. On his fingers were numerous rings—one for each county in the Kingdom of Shale. She knew that the blue ring was for Lokthea County and its many docks and harbors; and she knew green was for Shale County and its many farms and pastures; but the others she had yet to learn. The Guard had so far been taught very little of the outside world and its geography. All they knew was that they were in Castle Shale and they were defending King Leon Shale and his heirs—and most likely would be for the rest of their existence.

"I am. I do not think he's in here, my lord," she said playfully. "Perhaps he snuck away for a nap?"

"Do you think so?" the king asked with mock surprise. "Well, you should turn around, then."

Jinx whipped around and found herself staring at the large metal doors leading to the hallway.

"Are you entirely certain that you even know where he is?" she asked as she turned back around and found herself face-to-face with Shadow. She let out a small gasp of surprise. "I might have expected that," she told the gremlin-man with a smile. "How do you do that? It's as if you appear by magic."

He turned slightly red and mumbled something about reading the target's movement before he flew off to hide once again, his dark, leathery wings moving him quietly through the air. Even though she watched him go, she was surprised at how hard he was to see as he moved into the shadows. He seemed to melt into the surroundings, a shadow among shadows.

"He's aptly named," she muttered to herself as she stepped toward the throne.

Jinx had always had a soft spot for the shy assassin. She enjoyed trying to get him to talk, even though he was most times reluctant to. He maintained a constant distance; he didn't even wear the Guard armor. He said he didn't like it, as the clanking metal made sneaking too difficult. He wore a hardened leather cuirass, wool pants, and canvas boots stuffed with padding and soled with a strange bark for grip. In those boots, Shadow could step quieter than a cat.

Jinx came to the foot of the throne, where the red carpet halted at the bottom of the large stairs leading up to the ornate chair, and bowed to the king. She couldn't help but feel the imposing aura of his seat of power. The back of the golden throne branched forth like sun rays. The armrests were formed to look like griffins seated alongside the king, their stern eyes glaring down at where Jinx stood.

Jinx knelt on one knee as she spoke, focusing her mind on the king. "Your Majesty, we cannot see anything in the storm, and we fear the lightning may strike us. We request permission to go off duty."

He thought for a moment, unaware of her efforts to assail his will. He smiled with a strange grin and said, "You have! You Guard have earned a break. Tell everyone they have the night to do as they will." His voice sounded almost as if he were inebriated.

"You are most kind, Your Majesty," Jinx said as she rose to her feet, smiling to herself at a job well done. She turned and moved for the door as the king returned to his book, that odd smile still plastered on his face. *Perhaps I overdid it with the bewitchment?*

As she left, she tried to find Shadow, searching the rafters above. She saw nothing. He had moved since she saw him last, and she had no idea where he was.

She felt a little disappointed as she opened the door and

entered the hallway. She was surprised to see Shadow walking casually in the direction of his private quarters at the far end of the castle.

"Shadow!" she called and ran to him. He turned around and waited, fidgeting. He seemed to never know what to do with himself when he wasn't sneaking about. He tried putting his arms at his sides, but abandoned that in favor of folding them at his chest. He soon gave up on that, too, and went to fiddling with the hilt of his dirk, staring at it as if it were the most interesting thing in the world.

"Where are you off to?" she asked, giving him a sweet smile as she approached. She noticed he had covered his skin lightly with fire soot, allowing him to blend better with the walls. It seemed to make his whole person, from the tips of his shaggy, raven black hair down to the soles of his gray boots, blend together, like a smeared charcoal portrait. His face was somewhat handsome, with a slender jaw and tall forehead—the latter mostly hidden by his hair. His eyes were timid, with irises nearly as black as his hair. His long, willowy fingers drummed nervously on the handle of his dirk; he licked his lips as he tried unsuccessfully to return Jinx's pleasant smile.

"I'm, uh taking my ... leave." He stumbled over the words. "I'm still ... uh, part of the Guard, right?" he asked, almost as if uncertain himself.

She smiled. "Of course! You are with us 'til you die."

"Let's uh ... hope that's not, anytime uh ... soon." It was the closest thing Shadow had to a joke.

Jinx laughed. "Don't we all? Would you care to keep me company while I find the others? I need to tell them they have the night free, and I'd rather not wander these depressing halls alone."

He looked uneasy and licked his lips nervously again. He glanced in the direction of his room almost longingly and then looked back at Jinx with a sigh.

Am I really that much of a chore for him? Jinx wondered. "Um, are you sure ... you, uh ... want to talk to ... to me?"

"Why wouldn't I?" she asked. "Of course, you do not have to come. It's not an order or anything like that, but I'd much prefer it if you came." She focused her mind on bewitching his.

He grinned—one of the few times she had ever seen him smiling naturally. "You, um, you know you can't ... bewitch me."

She felt slightly embarrassed at being caught; nevertheless, she pressed on with her request. "Come. I'll be terribly bored if you don't come with me. Not to mention I have been training with you my whole life, and I barely know you. You owe me at least this slight attempt at friendship."

He turned his eyes to the stained-glass windows, and his face flushed with embarrassment.

Jinx groaned inwardly. *Why did I mention his social problems? Idiot!* "So, will you accompany me?"

He looked back to her with a weary sigh and slowly nodded. She wished he would say something.

They walked in silence toward where Pyre and Blade waited. Jinx tried to think of something to say, anything at all, but no words seemed to come. There was only one thing about him she felt certain he would enjoy talking about.

"I have never seen anyone sneak quite like you can," Jinx offered. "How do you do it?"

He breathed hard, as if preparing for a strenuous exercise. "I, um ... I just, uh, try to keep to the ... uh, shadows. Try to stay ... um ..."—he swallowed hard—"behind." Having forgotten to breathe, he had run out of breath as he spoke, his words wilting away like dying flowers. He quickly shut his mouth, and his face turned red even under the soot. He looked away from Jinx, presumably in an attempt to hide his blushing from her.

Why is it so hard to talk to him? She tried to think of another topic to discuss, but her mind was blank. She glanced at Shadow and decided to go with the first thing her glance caught.

"May I see your dirk?" she asked. He nodded, unsheathed it, and handed it to her. The blade had been darkened in smoke and looked oily from the mysterious poison that he coated it in. She compared it to the point on the end of her spear; it looked a little sharper. The edge curved as it traveled from the hilt, coming to a sharp point where the razor edge met with the dull, straight side at the tip of the blade. At the pommel of the weapon was a sharp point that could be used in very close combat. "It's nice," she said.

He mumbled something along the lines of "thank you" and sheathed it. The only noise in the hallway was that of rain plastering the stained-glass windows and Jinx's armor clanking with her steps.

"Sure is coming down hard, isn't it?" she asked. He looked at the windows and nodded.

Suddenly, Sinister came walking out of the stairway on his way to see the king. The basilisk man saw the two walking together, and his thin lips pulled back into a cruel grin, exposing small fangs where his canine teeth should have been.

"Ah, Jinx, Shadow. I assume your Guard duty is going well? So are you guarding each other's lips from dryness, then?" He looked pleased with himself as he watched Shadow look away with an awkward cough.

He always takes a sick pleasure in mocking Shadow. Jinx strongly disliked Sinister for it.

"Why, Sinister? Are you jealous because I would kiss him a thousand times before I would even dream of touching those poisoned lips?"

"Oh, of course you would! With your infatuations clearly for pathetic little gremlins like Shadow, how could you possibly love a real warrior like me?" Shadow turned a bit redder, but kept quiet, his brow furrowing almost imperceptibly. Sinister looked especially smug with himself, grinning like a predator standing over his prey.

"You disgusting worm! Halifin should have left your sadistic hide to rot in the orphanage he took you from."

"Ooh!" Sinister said delightedly. "It seems I am not the only one with fangs, am I?"

Jinx sighed with irritation. "Why am I even trading words with the weakest member of the Guard? You are not even worth the air you breathe." She tried to pass him, but Sinister grabbed her arm and threw her back.

"Weakest, am I?" he asked menacingly. His eyes seemed to bulge and his expression turned to a scowl. "Would you like to put that to the test?"

"I do not have time for your insecurities, worm," she said, trying to walk by again. He lunged forward and grabbed her by the chin. He held her face next to his and stared into her eyes with his crimson eyes.

"Look into my eyes and call me weak." His irises seemed to be swirling red orbs set in his pale face. She felt the strength leach from her limbs and felt as if her blood had turned to frost.

Suddenly, a soot-covered hand clamped down over Sinister's eyes, and another grabbed the wrist that clutched Jinx's neck, wrenching it upward with a vicious twist. Sinister gave out a cry of pain and went onto his tiptoes to try to relieve the strain on his wrist—the wrist that Shadow held tightly locked.

Shadow's eyes had lost their timid look, replaced instead by fury. Shadow led Sinister away from Jinx forcefully by his wrist as she fell to her knees, shaky from looking at those eyes.

Sinister made meek attempts to strike Shadow, but after

every attempt, Shadow tweaked his opponent's wrist cruelly, making him flinch and cry out softly in pain.

"Don't you ever use your powers on another member of the Guard," Shadow said darkly, "or I swear I'll cut your throat ear to ear then and there." He twisted Sinister's wrist more as with his free hand he pulled out his dirk and held it to Sinister's throat. Shadow leaned in closer and whispered, "Especially her."

He shoved Sinister's wrist up into his armpit, pinning it there against Sinister's armor. Then he tripped him, slamming the basilisk man into the red carpet with a great clatter.

Jinx looked up to see Shadow helping her back to her feet by her arm. He obviously felt uncomfortable looking into her eyes, for he averted his gaze to her shoulder while he helped her up.

"Thank you," she said embarrassed. "I ... I guess I did not expect him to do that."

"He, uh, should not have, uh, done that. Don't be ... embarrassed. He was a friend, and you, uh, you trusted ... his judgment," Shadow said, looking as uncomfortable as usual.

Jinx looked down at Sinister, who was trying unsuccessfully to free his sore wrist from his armpit, before turning back to her companion. "You are quite a mystery, Shadow. If I were to meet you on the street, I would never sense you were a great warrior. How are you so confident in battle, but so shy in everyday life?"

He cleared his throat and shrugged. "I would not ... uh, say I am a great warrior—" Shadow began.

"You are right about that, weakling!" Sinister hissed as he hoisted himself up by his free hand and ran down the hallway.

Shadow watched Sinister run away. The basilisk-man was still trying to pull his wrist out from his armpit even as he fled. *If he ever attacks her again, I'll do much worse to him.*

"You certainly wedged it in tight," Jinx said with a tinge of glee in her tone and a smirk on her lips.

"He won't, uh, be able to get it ... out ... um, out himself," Shadow said, almost allowing a grin to form on his lips as well. He had never much liked Sinister, mainly because Sinister always tried to bully him, mistaking him for a weak target. It was strange—Shadow always felt so self-conscious, so meek, when he was talking with people, but those feelings completely disappeared when he fought or while he was sneaking.

"Well, we should keep going; we still must tell the others that they have the night off." Jinx resumed walking down the hall, still somewhat shaky after her stare into the basilisk's eyes. Shadow nodded and followed her down the hallway. He couldn't help but notice how much noise her armor made as she moved. *How do the other members stand those cumbersome things? All they do is slow you down and reveal to everyone where you are.*

"So, what are your thoughts on the Rogue situation?" Jinx asked.

She is still trying to force me to talk. "I don't know, it, um, looks like, it, uh, it is serious," Shadow said, only because he felt obligated to talk.

"Yes, I suppose one could call it serious. I just can't believe they are keeping us here while the Rogues run around killing whomever they wish. If the rumors are true, we are exactly what the kingdom needs in the army right now."

"Yeah."

"I feel especially bad for you," Jinx said, turning to see Shadow's reaction.

He looked at the windows and asked, "Why?"

"Because you are the one who has the least chance of

leaving this place, yet you would be able to do the most damage to the Rogues."

"Maybe," Shadow conceded.

"Maybe? Definitely! You would be an invisible killer who could target their leaders and follow them back to their camps. I wonder where they are hiding, anyway?"

"My guess, is, um ... the Forbidden Mountains."

"What makes you say that?"

"That's where I'd ... hide." He cleared his throat nervously. He always felt people were judging him when he stated an opinion.

"Guess it makes sense," Jinx said, turning onto the stairway leading to the upper ramparts. "And if anyone knew what they were talking about with hiding, it would be you."

Suddenly, Blade and Pyre both leaped out and roared from around the corner. Jinx jumped back, spear at ready, and Shadow's hand gripped his dagger's hilt, the timidity leaving his eyes.

"Scared you," Pyre said with a triumphant grin.

"You ..." Jinx began angrily, but despite her annoyance, she couldn't help but laugh.

"We scared you stiff," Blade added with a grin of his own.

"So what's the king's decree?" Pyre asked. "Are we free to go? Is that why you brought Shadow?"

"No," Jinx replied coolly. "The king said you have to fly around in the clouds 'til the Sky God makes right the mistake of your creation."

"Harsh," Blade said dryly.

"That is a tough decree," Pyre chimed in

"Tough but fair," Jinx added.

"Is Shadow doomed to our fate, too?" Blade turned to Shadow, narrowing his eyes in feigned suspicion. "You took a nap while on guard, didn't you?"

"No, I ... uh, was given time off," Shadow said truthfully.

21

"Oh, well, someone at least has the king's favor." Blade began to sound bored with the jesting.

"Certainly seems our friend is getting special treatment," Pyre joked. "While us poor souls are doomed to fly in a lightning storm, the spoiled Shadow sips wine and toasts with the king!"

"No, you, um, have time off, uh ... too. Everyone does," Shadow said seriously. He knew they were joking, but he didn't find it funny.

"So Shadow just killed the joke," Jinx said as she playfully pushed Shadow. He grinned, as he knew he should, though he cleared his throat with annoyance. He didn't like being pushed.

"It was already dead," Blade assured her.

"There was some life to it yet," Pyre insisted. A look from Blade told him just how much life Blade thought was left to it. "Fine," Pyre amended. "It was dead."

"Quite."

"You feeling hungry?" Pyre patted his steel-covered stomach as he spoke.

"I could go for some pork, or a fine duck with a good pint of ale," Blade said as they descended the stairs.

"How about gruel from the mess hall?"

"Well, not quite duck, but it'll do for now."

Jinx called after the two, "If you spot the others, let them know that they're off duty."

"Please," Blade called back over his shoulder. "They're already off duty—or off guarding the wine cellars to the fullest extent."

"Wouldn't surprise me if Blade's right," Jinx said with a smile.

Shadow didn't respond. He stared up the stairs intently, his eyes and ears alert.

What was that noise?

"Well, we should go look for the others."

"Did you hear that?" Shadow asked. Jinx seemed to stiffen at the tone of his voice.

"Hear what?" she asked tersely.

"It sounded like the door opened and closed."

"What?" Jinx asked, gripping her spear tighter.

"I heard the storm rise and then fall," Shadow said warily, not stumbling on a single word.

Jinx listened for a little while but heard nothing. "Most likely it was nothing. Besides, how would someone get onto the roof in this weather?"

"That's what worries me."

Jinx grinned. "This castle can play tricks with one's mind. Most likely it was nothing."

Shadow stood still and stared up the stairs. He was about to go look, when he remembered that he had leave from guard duty.

I've done enough already. I'll let this one by, he thought. He turned away and said, "Yeah, it was probably ... um, nothing."

"Come on," Jinx said with a light tug at his arm.

As they descended, a hooded figure in a drenched black and white tunic breathed a sigh of relief from where he stood by the door to the roof. He relaxed his grip on a wooden spar with a razor-sharp blade sticking out of it. The razor protruded between his fingers as a blade knuckle.

Luck favors me tonight, but blazes! That was too close.

He sighed nervously as he slowly descended the stairs after them, making sure to stay behind the curve of the stairway and out of sight. He stepped lightly, hardly daring to breathe, as he followed the hybrids down.

After he heard the door shut down below, he silently descended the rest of the stairs and cautiously peered out the door. After he saw the two go around a corner, he left the stairway and headed in the opposite direction, away from the king.

Chapter Two

Howl patrolled the hallways of Castle Shale. He rested his ornate scimitar on his shoulder as he strolled, aimlessly searching for anything amiss. While on patrol, he never sheathed his weapon. Partially, he always wanted to be ready for an attack, but mostly, he liked the glances of admiration the humans gave his weapon.

He walked down hallway after hallway, marveling at their vacancy as his dark eyes scanned the stone corridors. Most of the humans were at a party for a retiring man. The human had helped to keep the castle secure for fifty-five years, and the king had decided to let him live out the rest of his days somewhere else.

Howl imagined the event must be bittersweet for the guard in question, but to the rest of the garrison, it was a chance to gather in revelry with a fine pint of ale. Almost every guard was there—whether they were supposed to be or not. Crunch and Crash were there, clanking tankards together and boasting of feats still yet undone. Those two were as inseparable as Pyre and Blade.

Howl wandered through the halls, hearing clearly all of the festivities echoing through the castle from the mess hall. He had very acute hearing and smell from his werewolf half. Normally, he could hear even the rats scurrying along their little pathways, but today it was hard to hear anything but the drunken rabble and the harpers in the mess hall. He wished he could be there, but he knew he would get into trouble for being caught away from his post. It was a concern Crash and Crunch didn't seem to share. Even now he heard Crash's booming laughter bounce through the halls, deeper than any human voice.

His ears pricked as he heard voices up ahead. Jinx and Shadow came around the corner; amazingly, the pair were talking up a storm—at least by Shadow's standards. Shadow looked exasperated, probably from all the talking. Jinx was well-known for her ability to talk for hours, and Shadow was well-known for taking hours to do any talking.

It's not a favorable situation for him, Howl thought with a grin.

When Howl approached, Jinx motioned to him and said, "Ah, Howl, we have been searching for you. Tell me, do you wish to attend the feast?"

Howl snorted curtly. "Must you ask?"

"Well, one can never truly be certain until one—"

Howl cut her off. "Yes. But I see no way you could rescue me from this guard duty."

Jinx straightened with an air of indignation. "Well, good sir, if you are going to interrupt me and treat a lady of my esteem with such rudeness, perhaps it would be best for me to simply leave you here to rot in these halls."

Howl cast his eyes to Shadow. "What is she supposed to tell me?"

"You uh ... have ... well."

"Ugh." Jinx grunted with annoyance. "Using my spectacular abilities, I spoke with the king, and I—"

"Freed me from guard duty?" Howl asked with an expectant grin.

"Perhaps," Jinx admitted reluctantly.

Howl looked toward Shadow. "Well?"

Shadow looked to Jinx, who was eying Howl with a bitter gaze. Shadow turned back to Howl with another rare smile. "Perhaps."

Howl raised an eyebrow in amusement, while Jinx gave Shadow a warm smile and a nod.

"I suppose I should accept that as a yes?" Howl muttered.

"Accept it as you will. Shadow and I have further business to attend to."

Howl rolled his eyes. "Are you going to play these games the whole night?"

"Perhaps not. If you were to apologize for your rudeness, I may be swayed to reason."

Such ridiculousness I must endure … "Apologies. I did not intend to be so rude."

Jinx smiled triumphantly. "Then, yes—you are off duty."

"Why did I bother asking? I knew already."

"Would you also know where Crunch and Crash are?"

"They are feasting with the humans," Howl said with a grin as he heard a fresh wave of Crash's laughter. *He becomes giddy after a few pints of mead,* he remembered.

"And where is that?"

"The mess hall. All you need to do is follow the smell of ale. Follow me if you like," Howl said as he spun his glittering scimitar deftly and then sheathed it. "I want to see this human party."

They headed toward the mess hall, following the scents and sounds of the festivities. Howl strode confidently ahead, while Jinx hummed a favorite poem to herself, and Shadow grew ever more uneasy at the growing clamor.

Howl stopped suddenly. He pointed toward the ground. "What is that?" His finger pointed toward wet footprints in the rug heading from the throne-room hallway.

"I don't know," Jinx said dispassionately. "Perhaps it is Pyre, or Blade. They were wet."

"No," Shadow said as he crouched down by the footprints, running his fingers over the wet tracks. "They weren't this wet. These footsteps have just come out of the rain. These aren't the look of armored feet, either."

"Whoever made these, the tracks will lead to him," Howl growled. He stepped after the trail. It led through several hallways, growing fainter as the person grew drier.

"Something's not right," Howl said as he paused, listening intently.

Howl stood up straight, and his body trembled. His jaw began to jut out like a wolf's, and small, gray hairs grew over his body. Claws grew out from his fingernails as he felt the strength of his wolf form flow into him. He tossed his helmet aside with distaste as his head morphed. The helm, shaped like the upper half of a wolf's head, clattered across the floor as the werewolf warrior finished his transformation.

He dropped to all fours and bolted down the hallway. Shadow and Jinx gave chase, following him desperately through doorway after doorway in the labyrinth halls of Castle Shale. Finally, they broke into a room and came to a stop within a mage's private quarters. He must have been a very influential mage, for the room was large, was well stocked with furniture and potions equipment, and was one of the comparatively few rooms with a window overlooking the courtyard.

Within the room, a hooded man held a young mage by the neck, a razor held between his fingers just inches from the mage's eye.

"Where is it?" the hooded man demanded.

"It does not exist—I swear it!" the mage cried pitifully. "It is just a myth!"

"Unhand him!" Jinx demanded, holding her spear at ready. Shadow drew his dirk, and Howl unsheathed his scimitar, curling his lip and growling as he did.

The hooded man turned to face them, his blade still held uncomfortably close to the mage. He wore a tunic with black sleeves and leggings. The chest was half white and half black, with a dragon set in the center—white on black, and black on white with orange eyes. A black hood covered half his face so that only his chin was visible. He swept gracefully behind the mage and held his razor so tight against his victim's neck that blood trickled onto the mage's green robes.

"A myth? You mean like hybrids?" he asked the mage calmly.

"Put him down!" Jinx yelled, stepping forward.

"Take another step closer, and the mage dies," the hooded man said forcefully.

"You don't want to kill him," Jinx said smoothly, focusing all her bewitching strength on his mind. "What you want is to leave here in peace."

"You mean in pieces?" the man said with a snort. "But everyone leaves in peace if the mage talks. Don't use your bewitching on me. It is irritating."

"What do you wish to know?" Jinx asked, recovering quickly from her surprise at being caught in her magic.

"I want to know a secret, and I do not think you know it, so if you do not mind, I would like to resume my conversation."

"The Relic Sword does not exist!" the mage cried out in near panic.

"Say that again, and I will slit your throat," the hooded man hissed angrily. "You think you are the only one who knows? I will not fail. Spare me the time of hunting down others and talk. And you don't move another step!" The hooded man pointed suddenly to Shadow, who had been slowly flanking him. Shadow halted, surprised at being caught. The man hadn't even been looking in his direction.

"What is going on in here? Why is everyone shouting?" Silver approached the door casually, still dressed in the cloth he had worn to town. He was pulling his shimmering silver hair into a ponytail behind his head as he stepped into the room. His usual smirk dropped off his face as he took in the scene. "Assassin!" he exclaimed as he drew his rapier.

"You are impossibly outnumbered, outdone, and trapped," Jinx warned. "Yield."

The hooded man smiled. "So you imagine."

"We do not wish to kill you, but we will," Silver said threateningly. "Yield."

"Put your weapons up and back out of the door, before someone is injured," the hooded man answered.

"We won't be." Silver raised his hand. He grabbed the man with his mind, securing tightly all of his limbs as he began to lift him off the ground.

The hooded man laughed. "Am I meant to fear you, hybrid?" He raised his own hand, and his feet lowered back to the floor. Silver gaped in shock as his own power was overcome by this stranger. The hooded figure jerked his hand, and Silver flew bodily out of the room, the door snapping shut behind him. "My odds improve."

Fear gripped Jinx. Not one of the Guard could defeat Silver's magic; most could barely block it.

"Give up!" she yelled nervously. Even Howl's growls sounded uncertain.

"Not likely," the man said. The door shuddered as Silver pounded against it.

During the commotion, Shadow had inched steadily closer. He was within blade's reach now, and the hooded man was still oblivious to him. Shadow lunged, his blade poised to cut the man's neck. The hooded figure leaped back as he shoved the mage forward, pushing them both out of the path of the dirk, which cut a rip into the hood of the man's tunic.

The man grabbed Shadow's hand and slammed it against the wall. Shadow cried out in pain as his dirk clattered to the floor. Jinx charged forward to Shadow's aid, stabbing with her spear, while Howl roared and pounced into the air, the scimitar poised over his head to kill.

The stranger slid past Jinx's spear and grabbed her by the face. With a shove, he pushed Jinx into the flying Howl.

Howl yelped in surprise as he crashed into Jinx, falling with her in a jumble.

Shadow picked up his dirk and turned to face the hooded man with a throwing knife ready. To his surprise, the man jumped through a stained-glass window with the screaming mage thrown over his shoulder.

Shadow rushed forward and watched the two fall several stories before splashing into the choppy moat.

Suddenly, Silver burst through the door with a yell.

"Where is he?" he roared.

"The courtyard," Shadow said, watching the hooded man drag the mage forcefully from the moat. Jinx lifted herself up groggily and grew wide-eyed at the blood pooling around her.

"Where did he cut you?" Silver asked nervously.

"I ... I don't know!" Jinx said in a panic, looking herself over for cuts.

They heard a whine. In the corner was Howl—with Jinx's spear embedded into his leg. The blade had sunk a good two inches into his thigh between two plates of armor.

"Howl!" Jinx screamed as came to his aide. "Go find Mer!" Silver waited for no second bidding before he darted through the door.

"Shadow, you ..." She found herself speaking to a broken window. She ran to it, but fruitlessly. She couldn't have seen a wounded drake flying out in the storm. She turned her attention back to Howl, who gripped the spear in his clawed hands and, with a yelp of pain, yanked it from his leg as blood spilled from the wound.

The alarm bell rang; Silver had gotten the word out. Soon after, Silver, Mer, Crunch, and Crash ran into the room.

"What happened?" Crash growled fiercely, ale still strong on his breath. The brown fur that covered the sasquatchman's body was matted with food and drink, along with his armor, but despite that, every inch of his six-foot-nine frame looked ready to battle.

Crunch's squashed troll features surveyed the upended furniture while he held his mace ready. Mer stepped past them all, the light fish scales on his arms shimmering with the same greenish hue as his hair, while his blue, watery eyes locked instantly on Howl.

"Go," Jinx said, "and search the courtyard for a hooded man with a mage ... or for Shadow," she added. "Mer, you need to heal Howl."

The others ran out of the room to search the grounds, while Mer eyed the situation in the room.

"This is a deep gash. It will take perhaps an hour of healing, but I should be able to finish in one sitting," he said with his soothing voice as he sat down. He laid his hands on the gash and focused, his long, greenish hair obscuring his shimmering, partially scaled face. Jinx couldn't see the cut closing, but the blood flow began to stem.

She stepped out of the room and stood watch over it. She didn't want anyone interrupting Mer; she already felt guilty enough for Howl's injury without allowing someone to hinder the healing. Her underestimation of the hooded man was at fault for Howl's wound, and she knew it. If only she had been fast enough to duck away from him, Howl could have sliced him clean through! Instead, Howl had been impaled on her spear.

She sank down to the floor and pulled her helmet off. Her weakness had caused this. She shook her head in disgust.

No! This was that cursed man's fault! What did he want, anyway? Why risk life and limb to badger a mage about something called the Relic Sword? What is the Relic Sword? She had never heard of it. Her thoughts roamed to how he had entered the castle. His footprints had led from the throne-room hallway. *Why go through there? It would have been much faster to head straight from the main gate to the mage's room, unless ... unless he didn't come from the main gate!* She remembered Shadow hearing a door close in the stairway to the roof.

"Stupid!" she scolded herself.

The assassin must have been waiting there a long time, waiting for the guard to leave. So he had passed by the throne room and ... *King Leon!*

Cold fear gripped her stomach. The king had had only humans guarding him, and this assassin was powerful. He could have dispatched everyone in the throne room in minutes before he moved onto the mage.

She got up and paced back and forth nervously. Had the Guard failed solely because of her? She wanted to retch. She ran her fingers through her downy hair as worries gnawed away at her. An hour ago, she would have given anything to have an assassin attack the castle ... but then, she had never imagined the assassin would succeed.

Sting, Freeze, and twenty human guards came running down the hallway toward the mage's room in a clamor of armored strides.

Jinx barred their path. "You cannot enter—not 'til Mer comes out."

"What? Why?" Freeze asked impatiently, her stern, dark eyes seeming to bore holes through Jinx from under her helm, which was engraved with flying drakes. "There is an assassin loose! Let us in!"

"He jumped through the window. Howl and Mer are in there. Howl has been wounded."

"Wounded? The cur!" Sting's shaggy manticore face scowled, and his venomous tail twitched. "How badly?"

"Mer says he will survive, but is the king ... is the king safe?"

"The king is in hiding with Rocky, Pyre, and Blade to protect him. This assassin will have to return to his masters empty-handed," Freeze declared proudly.

Jinx breathed a sigh of relief. "Thank the gods. Perhaps he had no mind to attack the king. He questioned a mage about something called the Relic Sword. Have you ever heard of it?"

"No," Freeze said curtly while Sting shook his shaggy head and clacked his sharp claws together restlessly.

"Where has the assassin run to?" Freeze asked.

"He is in the courtyard somewhere. Crash, Crunch, and Silver are scouring the grounds for him now. I pray Crash rips him apart when he finds him," Jinx fumed.

"He had better not before I get there," Freeze said. "I want my steel to taste this assassin's blood. Come, Sting—we have a human to hunt." Freeze led the group back the way they had come, and Jinx watched them depart. Twenty minutes ago, she would have gone with them, but now? Now she felt as if she would do more harm than good.

Crash walked through the gardens the only way he knew how: plowing through anything and everything in his way.

"Do you wish him to constantly know where we are, or are your steps just encumbered with drink?" Silver asked scornfully as he slipped through the numerous plants silently.

"Sneaking is for Shadow," Crash said. "Let the cur find me, and I will make him regret his own birth."

"I as well," Crunch added.

"This cur you seek sent me spinning head over heels from the room. Do not make my mistake of underestimating this assassin," Silver persisted.

"Come, assassin!" Crash shouted out to the darkness. "Show me! Are you more than I can handle? Stand and face me!" Crash held his battle-ax at the ready as he called out into the night. His challenge was greeted by the sound of the slackening rainfall. A few gusts still blew, tossing the shrubs and grasses playfully from side to side in the imposing darkness.

"This assassin seems to be in want for courage," Crunch said as he swept his mace through bushes near where Crash stood. "A pity. I would have enjoyed crushing his skull."

"He is an assassin," Silver said. "The shadows are his only ally here. He will not abandon them lightly. It is on us to flush him from them." He raised his hand, and a brilliant white flame burst forth from his palm, dispelling the surrounding shadows. Silver scanned the area to no avail. The courtyard, with its many trees, bushes, hedges, fountains, and plants, offered hundreds of places for an assassin to hide.

"If we had a flier, this would be easier," Crash said as he leaned his ax on his shoulder.

"If I see one, I'll ask him for aid," Silver said with annoyance. "'Til then, the search continues."

"Or at least someone who can see well in the dark," Crunch added as he stepped over the well-manicured grounds.

"Where is Shadow? He can do both."

"If I see him, then I'll know; 'til then, my guess is no better than yours," Silver said as he shined his light into dark corners.

The others moved on in relative silence, except the snap of branches as Crash and Crunch pushed through seemingly every bush they could. Silver rolled his eyes with irritation. He knew the assassin would see his light long before he heard their din, but he found their clumsiness annoying. Worse still were Crash's calls to duel the assassin, which he repeated whenever he grew frustrated with the search.

"What's that?" Crunch motioned toward many small lights that twinkled through the trees.

"Looks to be torches. Perhaps another search party?" Crash said as he stood alongside Crunch.

"Are you friend or foe?" Silver called out.

"Friend, you dolt," Freeze's haughty voice called back from across the grounds.

"Were you expecting an assassin to carry so many torches?" Sting's voice came mockingly.

"A good point." Crunch chuckled.

"Better careful than dead, fools!" Crash shouted back defensively.

Freeze and Sting strolled up with twenty-five soldiers. Each of the humans stood wide-eyed in the darkness, whispering stories of an assassin stronger than the hybrids.

Silver addressed Freeze. "We have found nothing so far. How goes your search?"

"It goes slowly. The humans are terrified, and the darkness is thick." She glanced to the white flame Silver still held in his hand. "Though I see this you have already noticed."

"We have," Silver said.

Crash grunted in frustration. "Why do we stand here like fools? There is an assassin who needs slaying."

"He is not going anywhere in a hurry," Silver said. "The wall guards will spot him if he attempts an escape. He is here, and we will find him."

"The moment we have him," Crash said, "I will cleave his sorry hide like a butcher."

"That will certainly solve our problems conclusively," Sting said sarcastically. "But then again, were we to take him alive, we may discover who it is he works for."

Freeze smiled at the prospect. "That way we could send this assassin's head back to his foul master."

"Your empty words get us nowhere," Crash growled. "If you cowards will not brave the search, I shall go without you."

"Big, hairy fool," Sting said as he watched Crash move into the darkness.

"This from the man with a lion's mane?" Crunch asked before following Crash.

"At least he is not a fool," Freeze said as she turned an eye on Sting.

"And I'm not very big, for that matter," Sting laughed.

"I suppose we shouldn't let them die alone," Silver said dryly, staring after Crash and Crunch's large silhouettes. He glanced back to Freeze. "Send your humans out in groups of three to scour the grounds. Sting can search with me while you see what you can from the air, Freeze."

Freeze raised an eyebrow beneath her helm. "That sounded oddly like an order."

"Argue my authority later. For now, just hunt the assassin."

She smiled coyly. "Trust me, I will."

"Hunt, or argue?" Sting asked.

"Both." She looked back to the group of humans. "Do as he said."

One of the guards complained, "The assassin fought three hybrids, what chance have three humans against him?"

"You either fight him, or you fight me," Freeze said as she drew her katana in an elegant sweep. "Choose wisely."

With quiet murmurs of discontent, the humans formed themselves into groups, with each group including one or two torch bearers.

"They chose wisely, it seems," Sting said with a grin.

Silver chuckled. "I would not want to cross blades with a half-crazy drake-woman, either."

"And woe to this assassin if he finds himself crossing my blade," Freeze said before she took to the air with a strong gust of wind.

Humans and hybrids alike spread out in their groups, searching by torchlight and firelight for any signs of the assassin or the kidnapped mage. Crash and Crunch both continued to search clumsily through the dark gardens, while Crash occasionally called out his challenge to the assassin. Freeze flew above, sweeping over the gardens, trying to pierce the treetops and darkness alike with her sharp eyes. The humans searched reluctantly, their numerous groups staying within close proximity of one another as they clung to the comfort of their numbers. Silver and Sting broke away from the main group, searching in the darkest, most secluded corners they could find by the light of the flame Silver held in his palm.

"He's here!" a human voice shrieked in the darkness. The humans scattered, running in terror with cries of fear and pleas for mercy. Freeze swooped down toward the area the humans had fled, landing in the darkness but seeing no assailant. Silver and Sting turned and sprinted nimbly toward the commotion as Crash and Crunch tore through scrubs and bushes shouting war cries at the top of their lungs.

"Where is he?" Freeze shouted as she turned to face every shape and sound she saw and imagined in the swirling darkness.

"I have you, cur!" Crash's voice rang out in the darkness, followed shortly by the crack of wood on skull.

"Did the assassin have wings?" Crunch asked as he knelt down next to the body Crash had struck with the butt of his ax. Sting, Silver, and Freeze ran to the two colossal warriors and stopped as the light from Silver's hand illuminated the scene.

"Oh, no," Freeze said in horror. Blood dripped from the hilt of Crash's massive battle-ax down onto Shadow, who bled onto the grass from a large gash in his forehead.

"You fool, Crash!" Silver shouted. "Look before you kill things!"

"No ... I ... I didn't know!" Crash's stunned voice came in stammers.

"Please be alive," Sting muttered as he knelt beside his friend, placing a clawed hand over the deep cut to staunch the bleeding. "Do not be dead. Unconscious. Please be unconscious." He put his other hand to Shadow's lips.

"Well?" Crash asked nervously.

Sting sighed in relief. "He breathes."

"Perhaps not for long, if his wounds are untended," Silver said as he too knelt down, his worry evident in his silvery eyes.

"He has more injuries!" Freeze exclaimed. "These bruises were not made by Crash." She ran her finger gently over reddening bruises on Shadow's face.

"His cuirass ..." Crunch motioned toward Shadow's leather-clad chest. "It's dented."

"He needs healing, now," Sting said sharply. "We can ask him of his injuries once he is not on the verge of death."

Silver nodded. "Crash, carry him to the infirmary."

"I swear I did not see who it was in the darkness, Silver," Crash said as he stared at Shadow's battered body. "I thought he was lying on the ground to hide from me!"

"I know," Silver said calmly. "It is fortunate for us you did not use the blade to dispatch him."

"I ... I wanted to take him alive."

"Good thing," Sting said as he lifted Shadow's body toward Crash. "Now carry him to the castle, before your good deed is rendered useless."

Crash nodded solemnly. Stooping down, he lifted Shadow's limp body gingerly.

"Freeze, guard them back to the castle," Silver said as he stood up once more.

"You are not captain. You have no right to order me about like a minion, Silver."

Silver exploded at her: "Will you stand here and bicker with me, or will you do something useful?"

She scowled darkly. "Mark me, Silver: it will not be long before it is you who is taking orders from me!"

"Marked. Now go."

Sting stood next to Silver as Crash departed with Shadow

draped in his arms and Freeze marched alongside with her weapon drawn.

"Poor Shadow ..." Sting said softly as he shook his head. "... that was the work of the assassin, wasn't it?"

Silver sighed deeply. "Who else? And we have lost him. He has escaped."

"You think?"

"I know. He came in undetected; I am sure he had a way out planned, and Shadow would not have emerged from hiding unless he had no other option."

"Will you still search?" Sting asked.

"Of course," Silver said as he turned back toward the dark gardens. "At last I have a job worth doing. I'll not waste it."

"And who knows?" Crunch said, still watching the others head to the castle. "Maybe you are wrong."

"Let's hope," Sting muttered. "I want revenge."

Chapter Three

hadow awoke in the infirmary.

What happened? he wondered as his body slowly acquainted him with his many pains.

He sifted through the bits and fragments of his memories of the previous night. He remembered an assassin breaking into the castle. He remembered the assassin escaping into the gardens. He remembered following the assassin. Brief flashes of hand-to-hand combat with the hooded man flashed through his mind—then the sound of his bones breaking. He remembered crawling in the darkness toward light and human voices. He was forgetting something, though. How had he come to the infirmary?

Gingerly, he reached to his forehead and felt a partially healed scab beneath his fingers running from his right eyebrow to his temple. All he recalled was a flash of pain and the sound of screams, but what had happened?

He sat up in his bed, wincing slightly as his bruised and beaten body protested. An elderly nurse in white robes looked up from where she was smoothing out the wrinkles of a bedspread.

"He has awakened," she more squawked than said.

Pyre, Jinx, Crash, and Sting stood up. They had been sitting on the floor with their backs to the stone wall out of Shadow's sight. Shadow wondered if they had been there the whole night. They were all out of their armor, wearing casual cloth instead.

"How do you feel, Shadow?" Pyre asked.

Shadow shrugged and mumbled, "Better."

Jinx smiled. "Better than what? A butchered animal? You have been beaten half to death."

"Better is better than worse, I suppose," Sting mused.

"What happened?" Shadow asked.

"I ... I mistook you for the enemy," Crash admitted. Shadow ran his finger along the scab on his forehead once more.

Sting chuckled, "If you are wondering why your head is still on your shoulders, it is because he struck you with the butt of his ax."

"You are fortunate you are a hybrid," Pyre said. "Mer was with Howl, but the humans have mostly healed you. The majority of the magicians have been casting security spells over the castle, but the king ordered several to attend to you."

Jinx smirked and said, "He wants his invisible warrior back as soon as possible it would seem. You should see how often he looks over his back without you there to look at it for him."

Crash tugged at his tight-fitting clothes uncomfortably. "I am sorry, Shadow. I did not know it was you."

"No ... uh, I do not ... do not mind," Shadow struggled to say. "All is forgiven."

Crash nodded solemnly.

"What happened to you, Shadow?" Jinx asked. "Where did you go after the assassin leaped from the window?"

"I ... I was foolish. I thought ... well, I thought maybe I could ... follow, uh, him. I failed."

"We all failed last night," Jinx said. "Let us thank the gods no one died for that failure."

"The mage?" Pyre reminded her.

"Kidnapped, not slain," Sting reminded him.

"Where did the assassin escape from?" Crash asked.

Shadow gave a painful shrug. "I ... well, I did not ... I ... he ..." He sighed with frustration. "He knew ... knew I was, uh, there. I did not ... did not follow him ... long."

"Something was not right about that man," Jinx said. "How did he see you creeping toward him? I barely noticed you in the room."

The door of the infirmary creaked open, and Howl walked in with his leg completely healed. Like the others, he was dressed in plain cloth, though he looked much more natural in it than any of them.

"Greetings, Howl," Sting said. "Your leg is well again, I take it?"

"It is." Howl grinned, stamping it a few times on the stone floor to demonstrate. "Can the same be said for our shy assassin?"

"Not as of yet, I fear," Jinx said. "But soon, or so the humans would have us believe."

"He will be well by tomorrow morning," the elderly nurse said matter-of-factly.

Howl nodded. "That answers that, I suppose."

Sting smirked. "I suppose our human allies cannot be expected to heal nearly as quickly as Mer. I am not surprised, though; they are only human."

The nurse gave him a glare that could have soured honey, but said nothing.

"How, uh, how is ... the king?" Shadow dreaded the answer.

"Fortunately healthy," Pyre answered, "if not a measure more paranoid than before."

"If he can, in fact, be more paranoid than he was before," Crash grumbled.

Jinx shook her head sadly. "If he would not send us out to fight the Rogues before last night, we haven't a hope of it now."

"Maybe," Howl said, "but perhaps now that the Rogues have brought the fight to the king he will respond in kind."

"The Rogues have been fighting the kingdom long before this," Jinx replied. "Our king didn't respond then; why should he now?"

"This is an attack closer to home," Pyre said with a shrug. "It may shake the king into action."

Sting laughed, but his mirth held a note of self-pity. "I would guess from the king's history that not much will change after this but the number of guards garrisoned. Not much hope in dreaming for anything else, but still, I suppose a manticore-man can dream, can he not?"

"I hate to break up this meeting," Howl said, "but Silver has said he has found who he wanted to speak with here in this very castle."

"He is in this castle?" Jinx asked with surprise.

"In the tallest tower," Howl answered. "Apparently, Silver has the news from an influential magician."

"Who, uh, do you… mean? Are you, um, searching for… for Marcus?" Shadow asked. The others gaped at him in amazement.

"You knew Marcus was here?" Jinx's surprise was clear. "I thought his whereabouts were meant to be some closely guarded secret!"

Shadow seemed to wilt under their collective stares. "I … uh. I just, well, I read things, and you hear talking, uh … sometimes."

Sting grinned mischievously. "There is much more to our gremlin than meets the eye, it would seem."

"Come. Silver is not known for his patience," Howl warned, "and I imagine I have stayed longer than he would like. He may seek Marcus without us if we delay more."

"Be well soon, Shadow," Jinx said, gripping his shoulder lightly. He smiled and nodded in return. They each said their good-byes to Shadow, and some even said them to the cantankerous old nurse before they left.

"You hybrid types could stand to learn some proper manners," the old woman mumbled to Shadow as she continued her work. Shadow's reply was to lie back in his bed and think over everything he could of the previous night. Even lying in bed, waiting to be healed, he refused to be useless.

Why would this man go to all this trouble just to ask about the Relic Sword?

"Did you wage a small war while you searched, or did you simply nap the time away?" Silver asked, his irritation clear, as Jinx, Howl, Sting, and Pyre approached where he stood in a secluded corner of the mess room. Crash had informed them that he had no interest in meeting a bitter old man, even if he was the most powerful magician in the land, and had taken his leave.

"I apologize for my lateness, Silver," Howl said insincerely. "I stopped to give Shadow my regards. Sorry if that has inconvenienced you in any way."

"Do not act self righteous with me, you—" Silver began.

Jinx cut him off. "Do not act like a captain or a king with us. You are neither. Howl was allowed to take as much time as he wished. If you wanted us so quickly, you could have searched for us yourself."

Silver dismissed the argument with a wave of his hand. "We have wasted enough time already to bicker like this."

Sting whispered into Jinx's ear as Silver walked toward the door, "That's the closest I have ever seen Silver to admitting he was wrong." She smiled to herself as they followed after Silver.

They walked to the winding stairway that led up to the

tallest tower and began their long ascent. It was the main tower that rose up from the center of the keep, rising high above everything around it. One could search all of Shale County and find nothing taller until they reached the distant foothills of the Grey Mountains. The stairs seemed to be infinite, and Jinx stopped counting them at 133, though they were not yet halfway up the tower.

At last, they reached the top and came to a heavy oaken door. Silver did not so much as rap a knuckle against the door before he shouldered through it. Inside was a luxurious room filled with elegant furniture. Tomes lined the bookshelves, and windows all around the circular walls let natural light stream into the room. An older man sat in a well-stuffed chair before a solid wooden desk, reading from a massive text in front of him. His white hair was pulled back into a ponytail, and his skin was unnaturally pale. He tapped the edge of the book he read with long, thin fingers well decorated with rings of many different types of metals and jewels. His gray eyes had a stern, noble look to them. He looked up calmly and silently appraised his unexpected guests before speaking.

"Would you be Halifin's mongrels, then?"

"We are hybrids of the Royal Guard," Silver said confidently, though his breath was weak from the climb. "We wish to ask you some questions."

"I am not some oracle you may ask your idiotic questions to whenever the whim takes you. Be gone. I have business to attend to."

"Such as your book?" Silver said impertinently. Marcus's eyes narrowed.

"Last night's assassin was a strange man with much control over magic," Jinx said.

"Was he?" Marcus asked coldly. "Well, then, you know more than I do. I have heard little of last night's incidents."

"He was a powerful magician," Sting said.

"So she already said."

"He was remarkably fast," Howl added.

"Spell-swords are not as uncommon as you might believe."

"He could see our assassin, even while not looking at him," Jinx said. "It was as if he saw with more than his eyes."

Marcus opened his mouth, but then paused. He looked to Jinx. "What did you say?"

"He could see our assassin. I have never seen another warrior able to detect Shadow so easily."

"Yes ... there are spells to allow oneself better perceptions," Marcus mused. "What was the look of this assassin?"

Howl offered, "He wore a dark tunic with a dragon set on the chest. I did not see much of his face; he wore a low hood."

"His description interests you?" Silver asked.

"No more than most," Marcus said as he returned to his book.

"He sought information on something called the Relic Sword. Have you heard of it?" Silver pressed.

"I have. It is a myth—a story concocted years ago to entertain children."

"He seemed to believe it real enough," Jinx observed. "He risked life and limb to capture a mage from the castle."

"I am aware. The mage was my son," Marcus said, his voice devoid of emotion.

"I am sorry, sir," Pyre said courteously. "We will reclaim him as soon as we can."

Marcus simply shrugged. "He is no great loss. There never was much more to him than disappointment."

"Where is the Relic Sword located?" Silver asked bluntly.

"It is naught but a myth, hybrid," Marcus responded scornfully.

"Humor me."

Marcus looked up from his book again. "No."

"Have you any pressing reason to withhold the information?" Silver asked.

"I do not think the king would enjoy his Guard flying out on some wild goose chase," Marcus answered before returning to his book.

"Even if the Sword is myth, its location will be where our assassin will go next."

Marcus thought for a long moment. "I have a compromise. Convince the king to allow me access to the dread fort Krone, and I shall tell you where the Relic Sword is."

"That hardly seems a fair trade," Sting snorted.

"But that is the trade. Take it or leave it as you will—that is your choice."

"At least tell us what the Relic Sword is," Jinx pressed.

"It is something you do not want your enemy to possess," Marcus said, glancing up from his book with a grin. "Now, go—I have wasted enough time on you unnatural creatures already."

"We have more to ask," Silver said.

"Then ask it after you have done what I have asked," Marcus said, his smirk not yet gone. "I am sure you will not have too much difficulty convincing the king to allow me what I seek." He glanced at Jinx as he spoke.

Silver sighed as he clenched his fist. "If you refuse to aid us, we will leave."

"The king will hear of your disloyalty," Howl added with a growl.

"I am glad to hear it," Marcus said as the hybrids went back to the long stairway. "Give the king my fondest regards as well."

Silver slammed the door shut angrily.

The moment the door closed behind the hybrids, Marcus

sprang from his chair with surprising agility for a man his age.

"Those idiots!" he said, fury in his voice. He stormed to a bookshelf, grabbed a crystal, and sat down at a small table.

He put his hand over the crystal and closed his eyes in concentration. It began to glow, and out of the jagged top, a face appeared: that of a woman with burning red hair and brilliant blue eyes.

"You call, my lord?" the woman asked.

"He was just here," Marcus simmered. "Where are you now?"

"There? At the castle?" she asked with clear surprise.

"Where else, you fool? Where are you?"

She blushed. "We are in Lokthea," she admitted.

"You're a hundred miles away."

"There were strong evidences that he was coming here to attack the Academy," she said in a defensive tone.

"Oh? And what were these evidences?" Marcus asked with clear skepticism.

"We ... we found a journal that said he was coming here."

"A journal!" Marcus scorned. "He fooled you as easily as he fooled that dimwitted master of his!" He sank his face into his hand. "Why must I deal with such incompetence?"

"We will find him, my lord. I swore to it."

"He is more than your match, Bloodmane. That much is all too clear now."

"We will find the traitor, my lord," she repeated, ignoring Marcus's observation. "We will slay him for his crimes."

"See that you do."

"We will not fail, not again—" she began, but Marcus waved his hand over the crystal. It went dark as her words faded.

"Curse him." He leaned back in his seat, deep in concentration. "So you are my opponent now, cursed one?

So be it. I thought you were smart. I thought you would find your freedom in some distant land, but if you wish to war, if you wish to have your grave here, I shall oblige you." He put his hand over the crystal again.

A voice came out of the sharp rock, but no image.

"What is it now, Marcus?" asked the voice of a middle-aged man, deep and gruff.

"You know well enough. How did you help him, Frederick?"

"Help who?" Frederick asked, confused.

"Do not feign ignorance; I know you aided him," Marcus said with an even temper. "He stole into the castle only last night. He spoke of the Relics."

"Ah!" Frederick said knowingly. "Him."

"Yes, him," Marcus agreed humorlessly.

"If it consoles you, I did not free him. He came to me."

"You think me fool enough not to know how my own men desert me?"

Frederick chuckled. "You were always thorough, if nothing else."

"Helping him was foolish, Frederick. You should have slain him the moment you laid eyes upon him."

"Why should I do that when it seems we have common goals?"

"You do not have common goals, you fool of a Rogue. He would see this world bathed in flames."

"That is not exactly how he puts it."

"That is how it is. He seeks to undo all that I have accomplished, to bring chaos where I have brought order. He seeks to put in motion that which took me decades to halt."

"Your cryptic words mean nothing to me, Marcus. He seeks the fall of the Kingdom of Shale, as do I. We have common goals."

"You will rue your goals before the end."

"And you will rue your choices. Are you done, or do you have more to moan about?"

"Did you give him the fancy new tunic?" Marcus asked.

"I did. He looked cold."

"He fooled you. He does not get cold, not him."

Frederick laughed. "Clearly he is a monster for pretending to be cold."

"No, he is a monster for being unable to be cold. When you next see him, tell me, and we can bring him down together."

"You and I are not allies, Marcus, not anymore—and we never will be again. Thank your betrayal for that. When I see him, I shall congratulate him for a successful mission."

"He will be the death of you all."

"Or just you. He is not fond of you, Marcus, and he knows much more about you than I think you would like."

"What did you tell him of me?"

"Enough. He knows what you have done more than most people, and he knows who you are connected with ... at least, he knows who I know you are connected with."

Marcus smirked to himself. "Allies change often, Frederick."

"I already knew that, *comrade.*" The last word dripped with sarcasm.

"I did what had to be done," Marcus said dispassionately.

"And so I do what must be done now. I pray we do not meet on the battlefield, Marcus. As corrupt as you have become since the wars, I still do not relish the thought of slaying you."

Marcus laughed. "How touching. Perhaps when you are captured and stand before the gallows, I will convince the king to let you live an extra day or two."

"We both know you would not spare the effort." The crystal dimmed once more, and Frederick's voice was gone.

"Where are they?" the hooded man yelled as he threw the mage against a wall. The mage's face was bruised, and he had several cuts, as well as bloodied nostrils.

"Don't hurt me!" he cried as he fell to the floor.

"Get up, dog!" the hooded figure said as he hoisted his hostage back up.

"Do not touch me!" the mage shouted, pushing his hands toward the hooded figure. The hooded man calmly waved his hand, sweeping away the mage's attack with ease. The hooded man thrust his hand forward, and the mage lifted off the ground. The mage rose high against the wall of the dank, dark cave until he was pinned against the ceiling.

"You do not wish me to touch you? So be it; we will do it your way." He clenched his fist, and the mage's arm straightened until his elbow was hyper-extended. "Where are the relics?"

"I swear to you, they do not exist!" the mage wailed piteously. "It is an old myth that my father once told me!"

"I do not care whether you think they are myth!" The hooded man was fast losing patience for the sniveling mage. "Simply tell me where they are kept in the myth!"

"I will not!" the mage said defiantly.

"Why not? You do not have to endure this! Speak!"

"My father warned that if I ever told anyone, he would kill me!" the mage said with terror in his eyes.

"I will kill you if you do not! Now speak!"

"No! It will activate the curse if I do!" the mage pleaded.

"Where is it?" the hooded figure said coldly.

"Tun Lake."

"Liar!" the hooded man shouted.

"Please! Do not make me do this!"

"For years, my kind have been repressed by your people. For years, they dealt with injustices wrought upon them simply for who they are! No longer. I will free them, and a disgusting little vermin like yourself will not stop me. Where are the Relics?"

"I do not care about your kind!" the mage said. "I will say nothing!"

"Then you will die, and I will find another." The mage's neck began to slowly twist.

"What are you doing?" he choked out as his neck twisted farther and farther, every second drawing closer to the breaking point. "Stop! Stop it now! Please!" Still his head continued to turn. "Do not slay me!" The hooded man did not stop. "No! I will tell!" His head stopped turning. "I know not where the relics are hidden, but I know where the map is. Please believe me: my father never told me the locations of the relics. The map is in the main temple of Aetha, in the altar." His words dissolved into screams of pain as the curse took effect.

"Now we have the truth," the hooded figure said. He dropped his arm, and with it fell the screaming mage. The mage clutched his ears and writhed on the ground in agony.

The hooded figure turned to leave, but stopped at the cave entrance. He looked back at the writhing mage. He sighed, shook his head, and turned back into the cave.

"Fool that I am," he muttered as he knelt down beside the mage and put his hands on the mage's head. His fingers tensed tightly and his jaw clenched as he wrestled with the curse.

Slowly, the mage stopped writhing and took his hands from his ears. He wiped tears from his eyes as his body relaxed.

"How ... how did you do that?" the mage asked.

"I know the curse," the hooded figure said as he stood up and turned to leave the cave.

"But ... why did you do it?" the mage asked softly.

Chapter Four

Silver, Jinx, Sting, and Howl wasted no time in venting their anger after leaving Marcus's room.

Silver especially was beside himself with fury: "Curse the wretched old man! I pray he dies in his sleep!"

"Perhaps he is right," Howl said more calmly as they walked down the many stairs. "Perhaps the Relic Sword is nothing more than myth."

"Why, then, did the assassin risk his life to break into the castle?" Jinx asked.

Howl shrugged. "The Relic Sword might have been a diversion of his true intentions."

"But the mage spoke its name, not the assassin," Jinx persisted. "And even if it is so, it gives that old man no excuse for using us for his personal gains."

"Tell the king to not let him set foot within a mile of any fort," Sting said to Jinx.

"Who does he think we are?" Jinx asked, paying Sting little attention. "His slaves to do his bidding? Any other human so vile, and I should have skewered him there and then."

"… and tell the king to lock him in the dungeons," Sting continued nonetheless. "That'd be a fitting place for the old villain—"

"Anyway one looks at it," Howl interrupted, "he's of no use to us. Best to forget the event in its entirety and search elsewhere for answers."

"... or dress him in motley and bells. Let him dress the fool if he wishes to act it," Sting added just as bitterly.

"Why is it you are so keen on defending that old man?" Silver asked Howl angrily.

"I do not defend him." Howl scowled. "I simply do not let his words get the best of me. You would do well to remember your discipline, Silver, before you forget it entirely."

"Better undisciplined than a traitor," Silver grumbled.

"Traitor, am I?" Howl's hand strayed to his scimitar. Silver glimpsed Howl's hand and stopped where he stood, a ball of fire appearing in his open palm.

"Draw, wolf—if you have courage enough."

Jinx interposed herself between them. "Enough! We have powerful enough enemies without turning on one another." Neither stood down. "Are you no better than Sinister?"

"What do you mean?" Howl asked.

"Sinister attacked me in the throne hallway. Will you betray your friendships as easily as he?"

"He attacked you?" they both asked in unison. She smiled to herself.

"Were it not for Shadow," Jinx said aloud, "he might have slain me there."

"The cur!" Silver roared.

"He shall have a taste of my claws for this, Jinx, I swear to you," Howl growled as he let go of his scimitar to continue his descent.

"You are too good at that," Sting whispered to Jinx from behind a smile as he passed.

"At what?"

"Manipulation."

"It was no lie," she said defensively. "He did attack me."

"I have no doubt that he did; I just find it odd that you failed to mention this injustice until now—until you needed them to have a common enemy."

Silver and Howl continued to rage against Sinister, each

surpassing the other's punishment for such a heinous treason to the Royal Guard. As the steps went on, their anger waned. Soon, they were planning how to bypass Marcus to discover the truth of the Relic Sword. Howl wanted to dispatch Shadow to find the lost mage, while Silver was in favor of hunting down every last relative, friend, and acquaintance Marcus had ever had.

"After all," Silver reasoned, "even if they know nothing, we may still use them to ransom the information from Marcus."

Sting suggested scouring the castle's extensive library for clues, but both waved a dismissive hand at him, declaring the idea to be simply voicing the obvious.

"Funny that they bicker as much as they do," Jinx muttered to Sting. "They are so much alike in so many ways."

"Oh, they differ quite a bit," Sting argued, "... just not in pride."

At last they reached the bottom of the long stairs. Howl and Silver parted ways, each bound for different means to the same goal.

"They may be tireless, but I hunger after so many steps," Sting said as he watched them go. "Would you care to join me in the mess hall?"

Jinx thought for a moment. "I would rather pay a visit to Shadow. I do not yet hunger enough for castle gruel."

Sting nodded. "I suppose I shall have to dine alone, then. Oh, the sorrow of solitude!"

Jinx gave his shoulder a rough shove. "Your guilt is wasted on me. Go, enjoy your meal."

Sting grinned his knowing smile. "I shall. Enjoy your gremlin, my lady."

"Is there meant to be hidden meaning in your words?" she asked bluntly.

"If the meaning were secret, why would I tell you?" He walked off in the direction of the mess hall.

Jinx shook her head, wondering about Sting's words as she turned toward the infirmary. She found Shadow exactly where she left him, except now his eyes were shut and his chest rose and fell softly with each slumbering breath. She stepped toward his bed, and instantly his eyes shot open.

"On edge, are you?" She laughed. He sat up, blinking his sleep from his eyes.

"Where is ... are the others?" he asked.

"Silver and Howl are trying to root out mages and relatives while Sting is heading to the mess hall. Do you want me to come back another time? You look tired."

"No." He shook his head to drive in the point. "I am fine. How ... what ... um, did Marcus ..."

"Tell us?" she finished for him. He nodded in reply. "Nothing of use. We're no closer to discovering the Relic Sword for our efforts."

"Ah, you ... uh, asked about, um, the Relic Sword?"

"Yes. The mage said something about a Relic Sword, I believe."

Shadow thought for a moment. "I ... I've been, uh, thinking it ... as important."

Jinx shrugged. "Marcus doesn't, it seems. He said it was a myth for children. The old goat told us he would not tell us about it unless we did the impossible for him."

"I ... I think ... I, well, maybe not the same ... but, I know ..."

"Know what?" Jinx asked.

"Relic story." His words sent a thrill through her spine.

"You know where the Relic Sword is hidden?"

"No." Her spirits fell again. "I know of, well ... well, of ... er, a map."

"Like a treasure map?" He nodded. "Where is it? How did you hear of it?"

"I ... I ... I steal books, sometimes." His face turned a deep crimson. "I give them back," he added quickly. "No one notices … mostly. But, I get … well, I learn much, sometimes from …"—he looked over Jinx's shoulder to see if the nurse was nearby—"… forbidden books." His voice was a barely audible whisper.

"Where do the books say the map is?" she asked excitedly.

"Books … books did not, uh, say. Just spoke of … Relics. Three of them. All pieces of … uh … of the … uh, sword."

"The sword is in three pieces?"

Shadow nodded. "Well … at least legend, uh, says so."

"So how do you know where the map is?"

"Aetha. The map is … it is … is uh, in Aetha. In the ruins," he said evasively.

"Where did you hear this from?" she asked. He cleared his throat uncomfortably.

"You … you will tell no one?" he asked.

"What have you been doing? This is worse than stealing books, isn't it?" He nodded. "How do you know?" she pressed.

"Will you tell?"

She paused long. "No," she said. "I swear, this does not leave my lips."

"I heard it from the mage," Shadow said quietly.

"He did not say where it was, did he?"

"Not his voice." Shadow looked even more uncomfortable than usual. "His … mind."

"What?" This time a cold shock went through Jinx's spine. "You … you can read minds? No—that's impossible! You must have imagined it." Shadow shook his head. "Have you done this before?" He nodded. "On me?" He shook his head. "How?"

He licked his lips nervously. "Forbidden … books. Not, not in them. There were … well, there were close things. Not this, though," he mumbled softly.

"You figured out how to read—"

"Shhh!" he warned her.

"—how to read minds?" she continued more softly. He nodded. "And you are certain Aetha is where the map is?" He nodded again.

"The ... uh ... the mage. He could think of, um, little else."

"You are certain?" she asked. "Aetha?" He nodded again.

"I could ... I could see it. Coast, ruined buildings, temple, all of it." Jinx opened her mouth, but he cut her off. "I am certain."

"Have the magicians heal you soon, Shadow. We have a mission to Aetha to plan," Jinx said confidently.

It did not take Jinx long to gather the members of the Royal Guard who were not on duty and not injured. She found Silver badgering a young mage about Marcus's friends, relatives, and everyone in between, getting nothing more than a stammered "I don't know!" in return. Howl, she found in the library, his nose in an old book of legends that seemed to be yielding as many answers as Silver's mage. Sting was asleep in his quarters, while Crash, Crunch, and Pyre were sparring with each other in the gardens, each speckled with bruises.

When she told each of them in turn what Shadow had said, most raised an eyebrow skeptically, but were willing to believe it if it gave them the chance to leave the castle. Freeze, they had found patrolling the halls alongside Rocky, both of whom were inclined to accompany them to speak with the king.

Passing by the elite guards standing on either side of the doors, the hybrids entered the throne room and knelt before the king. The king sat nervously on his golden throne, his eyes never seeming to remain on one thing for long. Demon stood next to him, his bow drawn and strung; an arrow waited, already notched to the string. Blade stood in full armor by the door, his long sword sheathed and his hand always on the hilt.

"Your Majesty," Pyre said, "we bring word of the assassin."

The king raised an eyebrow. "What word do you bring?"

"We know where it is he is heading," Jinx said as she prepared her mind to bewitch.

"Where is that?"

"To Aetha, my lord."

"Aetha?" Blade asked skeptically. "That city has been abandoned hundreds of years."

"What makes you think he is bound for Aetha?" the king asked.

"I found the location of the Relic Sword in the library," Howl lied. "It is in Aetha."

"And you are sure the assassin will be going there?" the king asked.

"He said he would stop at nothing to find the Sword," Jinx also lied. "And he said he was heading south. It all points to Aetha."

"He said this?" the king asked. "Why have you not spoken of it before?"

"My king did not ask," Jinx explained. "It did not seem important at the time."

Freeze spoke next. "If you send us, my lord, we will find this assassin, and we will hear from his own lips who sent him here and where his masters hide."

"But my guard is already so few. Who could I send without risking my life?"

"Every moment you allow this assassin to roam free, you risk your life more and more, my lord," Silver said. "Send us out, and we will rid you of this menace forever."

The king looked less than certain. "But if you are wrong, I shall be exposed more than ever." He shook his head resolutely.

"No, my safety is too high a concern to risk it chasing after some assassin and his sword."

"Your Grace," Howl pressed, "if what I read of the Sword is true, we must do whatever is possible to keep it from falling into this assassin's hands. He has defeated three of us already, and the Sword is fabled to be the most powerful magical weapon in the land. It is said that with it, a common man could move mountains and defeat armies. It is not a weapon I should want my enemy to have."

"Especially an enemy as powerful as he," Silver agreed.

"Send me, my lord," Blade said. "Demon can guard you just as well without me, and my wings can carry me to Aetha before the assassin has a hope of reaching the city. I may even be able to bring the Sword back to you, along with the assassin's head."

"He will need help," Freeze added. "The assassin has fought three of us at once; we shall want at least four to fight him. Send me, my lord."

"Send me as well, lord," Jinx said. "And Shadow."

"Hold steady," the king said, raising a hand against their offers. "I have not even decided whether to send you or not."

"But my lord, you cannot afford not to send us." Jinx fixed every ounce of focus on the king's mind.

"It … it is?" he asked groggily, that strange smile appearing on his lips.

"Yes, my lord. It is most important to your well-being. Here, we can only wait while your enemies grow stronger. If you send us out, we can end them before they have a chance to harm you."

"I …" The king trailed off as his face reflected the depth of his thought. "I suppose that makes sense." He nodded slowly. "But … what … what … who should I send?"

Jinx smiled. It was almost too easy. "You should send your fliers, my lord. They can intercept the assassin the quickest."

"They could …" he agreed.

"My lord, you will want to send walkers as well," Silver said. "The assassin has proved himself far too powerful already; we must not underestimate him again."

"The fliers should be enough," Jinx said. Silver shot her an icy glare.

"Safe is better than sorry," Silver argued. "My lord, send me, Howl, Crash, and Crunch, and we shall slay the assassin with ease and win you this magic sword."

Freeze spoke bluntly. "You would only serve to slow us down. We need the speed of the fliers, and they cannot wait while you and the others come toddling down the road on horseback."

Silver shot her glare as well. "And here I once thought I had allies ..."

"I have decided," the king said, rising regally from his throne, though his grin from Jinx's bewitchment still remained plastered on his face. "I dare not send more than needs to be sent, lest I risk any harm to my own well-being."

"Heroic of you," Jinx heard Howl murmur beneath his breath.

"I will send four fliers. Jinx, Blade, and Freeze shall go to the ruins of Aetha and slay the assassin there."

Howl glanced to Jinx, a look of amusement on his face.

"My lord ..." Jinx said, choosing her words carefully. "... that is but three of us."

The king thought for a moment before a look of surprise flashed across his face. "Oh, of course." He shook his head slightly. "I cannot seem to think straight at the moment." He closed his eyes and shook his head again. "Those three and ..." He looked around the room carefully. His eyes landed on Demon, standing just to his right. "... and you." He pointed to Demon.

"I am honored, my lord." Demon bowed his head respectfully.

"My lord is most wise," Jinx said, though Demon was not

the flier she had hoped the king would pick. "But my lord, the assassin has already shown he can defeat four of us. Perhaps it would be wise to send another. An assassin, perhaps, to fight an assassin?"

"A fantastic idea!" The king beamed. "But ... where could we find an assassin on such short notice?"

"There is always Shadow, my lord," Blade said from the back of the room.

"Shadow would be most helpful," Jinx agreed.

"So would I," Pyre grumbled.

"And I," Silver complained.

"Shadow?" the king mused. "No, I have much too dire a need of him. Who else to guard me from the darkness?"

"There is always Sinister, my lord," Howl said with a grin. "He has shown himself quite capable of attacking unexpectedly. He could easily ambush any would-be assassins."

The king looked unsure. "He would have to guard me night and day; would he be up to the responsibilities?"

"He is." Howl's grin turned positively malicious. "In fact, he will volunteer for the duty." His thumb ran along the hilt of his scimitar. "I am certain of it."

Jinx focused her mind on the king, pressing down on his will with everything she had. "Sinister would be a perfectly suitable replacement, my lord. I would be willing to say he is probably a better match for the job than Shadow is."

The king's smile curled into a hopelessly foolish grin. "I ..." he began, but seemed to think better of it. "Well, what has this Shadow really done for me anyway?" He shrugged casually. "Nothing I can remember. Out with the old, in with the new, I say. Send me this Sinister."

"You are most gracious, my lord," Jinx said.

"If only you had counsel as wise as your decrees," Silver muttered bitterly.

"Yes, I know. I think I shall take the name King Leon the Wise. That has a good ring to it."

"It most certainly does, my lord," Howl agreed. "Now, might I take my leave? I look forward to informing Sinister of his newest duties."

"I could send a castle page to him," the king said helpfully.

"You are too gracious, my lord, but I wish to tell him in person. I would like to see the look on his face when I tell him of his new position."

"Very well. You are all excused. Make haste, my warriors, and bring an end to my enemies!"

"We live to serve, my lord," Jinx said as she rose. She smiled proudly on her way out. Though Silver glared at her and Pyre frowned bitterly at being left behind, she did not especially mind their anger—least of all Silver's. She was too excited to pay them any heed. She was about to embark on the first real adventure of her life.

Chapter Five

Soon all five hybrids chosen by the king were flying south—four shining stars and the black spot that was Shadow cruising across the sky.

Shadow savored the feel of the wind as it washed over him. He had only finished his healing that morning, but even so, he had to slow down to allow the others to keep up while in their heavy armor.

He shook his head. *Why do they wear those cumbersome things? My dirk would penetrate through it as easily as chain mail, and it makes them so slow.*

He continued to fly onward at a leisurely pace, while the others panted and strained to keep up with him. Only Demon, with his comparatively lighter armor and wooden bow, could match him at a sprint, but it would not be long before even Demon's weight would slow him down, and Shadow would speed ahead.

Shadow hadn't been happy with the nature of their departure, so he felt no qualms at letting the others suffer a little to keep pace with him. Though he was glad to be on the mission, the division that ensued had been terrible. Silver had been near shrieking at Jinx, calling her a traitor and a false friend. Blade had had to come between them, reminding them both that they were on the same side, though that only succeeded in allowing them to vent their anger on him. Blade bore it nobly, chastising them now and again as if they were children while they had roared at him like lions.

Crash also had his pride wounded by the rejection, but rather than storming with fury, he had taken to sulking, avoiding speaking with any of the fliers, and embarking on long walks in secluded places. Crunch, always more amiable than Crash, had congratulated Shadow on his assignment, at least, but other than that, Crunch had said little more than Crash—and given looks just as sour.

Sinister had been the worst for Shadow. Howl had been less than gallant in his persuasion, and in the end, his scimitar had been at Sinister's throat before the latter accepted Shadow's old duties. Worse, Howl made it painfully obvious that it was Sinister's treatment of Jinx and Shadow that had brought him the extra work. In the last hours prior to the departure, Sinister had taken every opportunity to annoy, frustrate, and humiliate Shadow, which in turn had earned him a share of Jinx's fury, which only seemed to delight him more.

Then, an hour before departure, the king had inquired why Sinister was standing guard over him instead of Shadow and had claimed not to remember giving Shadow leave to go. It took Jinx the full hour to convince the king all over again to let Shadow go, as he was much more obstinate than usual. Shadow could sense that a magician had put a ward against Jinx's persuasion of the king, though luckily, Jinx was much more than its match.

When Shadow voiced these thoughts to Howl, the werewolf had shaken his head angrily and said, "The work of Marcus, no doubt—curse that old man!"

As bad as the departure had been, the trip was proving to be quite enjoyable for Shadow. The constant roar of the wind eliminated the opportunity for small talk everyone seemed to love so much and he abhorred so greatly, and the fresh air and sunshine were worth more to him than all the luxuries and tapestries of Castle Shale. Shadow had seen little of the Kingdom of Shale outside of Castle Shale, and so far, he liked what he saw.

Rolling hills stretched beneath him, covered with the pasture and farmland that surrounded the capital city of Syienna. Wild herds of bison wandered along the green fields, and domesticated sheep moved sluggishly as the shepherd horsemen and their dogs herded them toward watering holes.

The hybrids sailed high over many streams with trees flourishing along their moist banks against the treeless grasslands like fingers of the mountain forests reaching out into the plains. They passed over the Snowmelt River, which rushed along a winding, twisting course through the hills, past Syienna, and to the sea. Many a riverboat sailed up and down its length, carrying goods from the small farm towns to the docks at Syienna and to the massive wharfs in distant, coastal Lokthea. To the southeast, the blue silhouettes of the Grey Mountains loomed on the horizon, veiling the true height of the white capped peaks surrounding Trake.

They crossed over the bustling Trade Road, which followed a straight course from Lokthea, to Syienna, to Trake. Caravans, travelers, and wagon trains seemed as small as ants below them as the humans inched toward their destinations with goods to barter and trade.

Farther south they traveled, until they were following the pale outline of the ancient and forgotten Silent Road. No travelers wandered the ghostly highway anymore—not since the glory of Aetha had been snuffed out mysteriously long ago.

Hours they had flown, and the sun began to set in the west. Only the red fingers of twilight lit the sky when they halted for camp.

Shadow landed lightly by the side of the Silent Road, with the others thumping clumsily into the ground around him. Shadow stretched his wings and breathed deeply of the cool night air while the others collapsed, sweat steaming from the gaps in their armor.

"Sometimes, Shadow," Jinx panted, "I think ... you may have something there ... about not wearing armor."

Shadow smiled in response before he unpacked the bundle of wood he had carried to make a fire. He knew they wouldn't be passing by any kind of woods until they reached the Gulf Sea.

Even Demon was gasping: "He will ... be wanting it ... the second we get ... into any kind of fight."

"And you will ... be wanting ... a proper sword," Blade said, motioning toward Demon's hunting knife. He pulled a deep breath. "But then, I suppose life is a string of trade-offs ... isn't it?"

They made camp there, lying on the yellow, dried grass of the fields, surrounded by scrubs and the occasional yips of coyotes. They were close to the Colossus Desert, which formed between the Grey Mountains and the Coastal Mountains, far to the west. The air was far more arid here than in Syienna, and the night air grew surprisingly cold.

Demon shot an antelope, and they cooked what they could of it over Shadow's small fire before the coals cooled. Blade tried feeding the fire with scrub twigs, but the weak flame and the acrid smoke soon made him surrender the fight for warmth with a few frustrated curses.

"Should have brought Pyre," he grunted. "He's like a walking campfire."

They got what little sleep they could in the chilly night. Shadow roused them at dawn, and they once more followed the ghostly outline of the Silent Road. In the distance, Shadow could see the grasslands' end and the beginnings of the wastes of the Colossus Desert. To the east, the grasslands climbed up the foothills of the Grey Mountains until they broke against the heavily timbered slopes of the mountains themselves—and eventually even those slopes broke against the snow caps of the jagged peaks.

They flew through most of the day, pausing now and again

to stretch sore wings, until they could just see a blue line on the horizon darker than the blue of the sky.

The Gulf Sea, Shadow thought triumphantly. *It's still far away, yes, but Aetha is just up the coast. We'll be there by sundown.*

Meager clouds rose from the Gulf Sea, which wandered in far enough to cool and water the coast, leaving the desert farther inland scorched and dry as ever. Small trees grew alongside the scrubs and grasses as craggy, crumbling rocks stabbed up from beneath the grass and soil.

They flew to the Gulf Sea, all of them landing to marvel at the endless expanse of water before them.

"That is a big lake," Jinx said with awe as waves crashed along the sand below the cliffs that rose a hundred feet from the water.

"Smells salty," Demon said with a few tentative whiffs. Seagulls shrieked at the intruders as the birds sailed through the air and chased each other about the sands. Piles of kelp and smooth driftwood lay littered over the beaches. The sea hissed and foamed as it swirled among brightly colored tide pools.

"I read … but …" Shadow said over his twisted tongue, made worse by his awe. "It does no justice," he finally got out.

They paused, making a meal of antelope strips and some local roots, berries, and herbs that Shadow swore were not poisonous. The others regarded the herbs warily, but it made for a hearty meal as they enjoyed the sights of their new surroundings.

Soon they were flying west along the coast, toward the ruins of Aetha. Not until tinges of twilight again filled the sky did they see the dark outline of the once magnificent city, still many miles away from them. Calling on the reserves of their endurance, the Guard members pressed toward their far-off destination.

Finally, they arrived, landing under the light of the rising nearly full-moon at the city gates, the frame of which was still standing, though the gates themselves were nowhere to be found. Shadow saw numerous breaches in the ruined walls, and his gremlin eyes saw clearly that there was something very strange, and entirely unsettling, about the breaches.

I need to examine this city closely. Something is not right. He patiently waited for his friends to recover as he devoured the walls with his eyes.

"What exactly are we looking for?" Demon asked. "All I know is there is some sword we do not wish an assassin to have."

"No sword here," Shadow said calmly. "Only a map."

"Great—he has lost his stutter." Blade had trained long with Shadow; he knew what that meant. "When should I expect the fighting to commence?"

Shadow took a few steps toward the gates, but otherwise said nothing.

"So where is this map?" Demon inquired while stringing his bow.

"In the temple. We should find it quickly," Shadow said with a glance back to them.

"What caused Aetha's abandonment?" Blade asked.

Demon shrugged. "Famine? Plague? Could be anything."

"It feels … unwelcoming," Jinx said, looking at the gates. The massive structure towered over them menacingly, its dark gray stone bleak in the soft moonlight. Cracks and fissures could be seen all up and down the archway, but some other trait gave them an eerie feel: they seemed too smooth, too rounded for natural stonework.

"That is because it has been dead for centuries," Blade said callously. "It is jealous of our life. Unwelcoming or not, it is only old stone, and it will suffer us to camp within the walls."

Freeze voiced her discontent. "I would rather camp elsewhere. I do not trust the feel of this place."

Demon agreed: "The sooner we are done here, the better."

"We will search the city at first light," Blade said. "So why not camp within the city?"

"We should search," Shadow said. He glanced back to them. "Now."

"Are you mad?" Freeze's voice was tense. "I'm not searching there 'til we have proper light."

"Daylight would benefit us, Shadow," Blade said.

"So will the darkness."

"I am not wandering around a city I do not know in the dead of night," Demon said. "You are a fool to want to."

"You see in the dark. What is the difference?" Shadow asked calmly.

"The difference is, in the dark ... we ... well, there ... there is a greater risk of—" Blade began.

"—ghosts?" Shadow's mirth was barely detectable on his voice.

"—ambush," Blade countered. "And bandits."

"I am searching. Tonight. Alone, if need be."

"You do not have any claim to the Sword if you find it," Freeze warned him.

"There's no sword here: only a map," Shadow reminded her.

Blade cut in, "It does not matter who gets the Sword, just so long as that assassin dies."

"Please!" Freeze exclaimed. "He wants it for himself. Why else does he search while none of us are willing? Likely, come morning, he will say the map got up and fled the city of its own accord."

Shadow spoke humorlessly. "If I wanted it that badly, I could slit your throats as you sleep."

Jinx piped up quickly. "Trust, I think, is the best strategy here. If we turn on each other, the assassin wins already."

"Then tell him to wait for morning," Freeze said. Shadow just smiled at her before he turned and walked into the inky blackness. *If you wish to stop me, come stop me.*

"Cur!" Freeze called after him.

"I still see him," Shadow heard Blade say as he walked away.

You won't for long. Shadow strode fearlessly beneath the yawning gates. Within the walls was a large plaza. At one time, people had bustled through these gates, eager for the trade and the grandeur that the city offered. Now, the massive square was more ruined than the gates, its stone blackened and cracked, and all grandeur replaced by ominous decay. Where once proud men and noble lords had stood, weeds rose, twisting from the fissures in the stonework.

Streets branched off in every direction, twisting and winding through the buildings, but for one large main street, which cut straight toward the heart of the city, toward a distant, massive structure that Shadow assumed was the temple he had read about. He knew the map lay within.

"He should not go alone," he heard Jinx say.

"I am not going with him. Do you want to?" Freeze glowered.

"If you are all too cowardly, then yes." Shadow was surprised. He had thought they would all hunker down for the night to await the comfort of the sun.

Maybe she is braver than the rest, he thought. *Or maybe she feels for you like you do for her,* his mind responded. He blushed at the mere notion. *She doesn't want someone as shy and clumsy with words as I am. She is nice to me because she pities me, not because she loves me. Don't be a fool, Shadow. She would be better off with someone like Blade, or Silver.*

"Fine, follow him, then," Blade said. "We will camp just

inside the gates. There is enough wood about for a fire; you should have no problem finding us."

Demon promised, "If we are attacked, we will give you a shout, and I will loose a fire arrow into the sky."

"We will cry out if we see anyone as well," Jinx said to them before she began to jog after Shadow, her footsteps heavy, and her armor clanking with each stride.

I could tell where she was even if I couldn't see in the dark, Shadow thought uneasily, though he waited for her just inside the gates. He did not like the notion of being heard everywhere they tramped through the city. There still seemed to be something amiss with the old ruins—something odd in the way the buildings silhouetted against the sky, though he could not yet tell what it was.

"Shadow?" Jinx called out to the blackness as she passed beneath the looming gate.

"Here." Shadow appeared suddenly by her side.

Jinx started nervously. *How does he do that?* Then she remembered how dark it was. *Crash could probably have caught me unaware.*

"Must you always startle me?" she asked with a relieved laugh. He shrugged and shifted his weight from foot to foot. *Ever the talkative one.* She could not blame him, though. Words seemed ill-suited to the deathly quiet that reigned in the city. She looked up to the moon. The moon glowed brightly in the sky, but it did little to illuminate the ruins. *It's as if the stone devours the light before it even reaches it.*

"We should be moving," Shadow said abruptly as he glanced back through the gates. Jinx couldn't see, but she could hear the others coming their way.

Blade was intent on camping within the gate.

Why? she wondered. *That seems like begging any bandits*

here to attack ... though maybe that is exactly what he wants. Blade had never been skittish about facing an enemy; he vastly preferred to bring the fight sooner rather than later.

"Of course. Lead the way," she said with a smile. She remembered that he could probably not see her face in the darkness. "At least there do not appear to be any ghosts." She only half laughed, and Shadow didn't at all. She wished he had—or that he had at least said something.

Anything to break the dread of this place. She didn't feel right. The sense of being unwelcome had only grown stronger within the gates—and with each footfall. "Where should we search first?" Jinx asked with a nervous swallow.

"I don't know," Shadow said absentmindedly. He was staring at the buildings intently. Jinx could barely make out even their shape in the dim moonlight, but she could see that something was strange about them.

"Would the temple probably be at the center of the city?" she asked, regretting her words the moment she spoke. With every step they took into the city, the dread increased.

"I do not like this," he said suddenly.

"What?" she asked as she gripped her spear tighter.

"The buildings. They are not ... right. They are not ruined. They are melted."

Jinx stepped close, and sure enough, she saw the stone buildings were melted and cooled into the shape of flowing stone. Whatever had destroyed these buildings had burned with such an intense heat that it had liquefied the stone itself.

What in the name of the gods could do this? Not all the buildings were completely melted; some even still had doors and windows. Others, however, were barely more than solidified pools lying on the ground.

"What could do this?" Her heart was in her mouth, though she hid her fear from Shadow. *There is something not natural here.*

"Perhaps the Relic Sword. It was said to contain mythical powers," Shadow said. "The legends say it came from the red lands in the east." He turned his head and paused. He stared for a while before he began anew. "Long ago, before the Elf Wars, the Kingdom of Shale fought some terrible power with it."

"What did they fight with it?" *Distract me!*

"Books did not say. They called it the Scourge. It said the Scourge threatened to destroy all of mankind—until the Relic Sword. With the Relic Sword, our champion was able to lead humanity to victory. During the War of the Scourge, thousands upon thousands of people died to the 'purging flames,' as the books put it."

"What happened?"

"Humanity's champion began to win battles, again and again, though those who fought with him paid a bitter price. He ..." Again Shadow paused, and his whole body tensed.

"What is it?" *Don't let there be fighting. How can I fight when I can barely see the road? How can I fight when I feel so frightened?*

He shook his head. "Nothing. Just the darkness. It plays tricks on my eyes."

"So how did the Scourge end?" *Keep talking. This silence is as oppressive as the darkness.*

"Apparently, the Scourge was slowly driven back, little by little, inch by inch, battle by battle." Shadow's body tensed again. *Why in blazes does he keep doing that?* "Until all that remained of it lay in the Forbidden Mountains, in an ancient and evil fortress, into which even our champion could not break." His voice was beginning to strain, and she could catch the tiniest hint of fear in his tone. *So you feel it, too?*

"So, instead, the champion raised a magical barrier—a ward against the Scourge that imprisoned them for all eternity in the Forbidden Mountains. The champion, realizing the power of the Sword could be misused—both because it could give a man the strength to defeat armies and because it was the key to releasing the Scourge—hid it away. He divided it into three pieces and hid them throughout the land. The map was hidden here, in case the Scourge should ever escape and the Sword was needed again. It is said many an adventurer has sought the map, and all went mad upon entering the city."

I can see why! I feel half mad already. "That is an interesting story. Lucky for us, it is likely mostly myth." *I hope.*

"Something is wrong." His voice was pure steel, and his hand clasped his dirk. *Oh, gods, what horror could be hunting us from the darkness?*

"Do you see anything?"

"Shadows. Dark spots even against the darkness. I feel a fear like nothing I've ever known." She could hear his voice waver. "What foul sorcery is this?"

"How many are there?" All she saw were varying pitches of blackness and the starry sky above.

"Many. But the shadows ... they disappear as I look upon them. They dance in the corner of my eyes." He paused. "And there is malice behind them." His voice was near a whisper.

And just like that, Jinx knew exactly what Shadow saw. In the corners of her vision, small spots, pitch black even against the blackness of the buildings, darted and danced away from her eyes. She could sense the hate. *My spear does nothing against fleeting shadows.*

"Did your book say what drove the adventurers mad?" Her voice was little more than a croaking whisper.

Shadow paused so long that she thought he may be too afraid to answer, before his voice came, thin and wavering. "Death itself."

From far off, they heard a cry that sent cold fear shooting through them. It came from the gates, from Blade's camp, though no fire arrow pierced the sky.

"Are they under attack?" Jinx asked. The prospect of her friends being in danger lent her courage.

"Are we?" Shadow asked. "They are all around us, Jinx, and they grow bolder. They do not flee from my vision."

"We need to know what this is, Shadow." Her voice quavered as she spoke, but her mind was made up. "You must be my eyes. Tell me what happens, and if for a second this grows dangerous, you fly."

"What are you doing?"

"I am a hybrid. I will not fear this dark magic. I will face it."

Shadow swallowed hard and looked into the darkness. "You do not see it as I do. You do not see the horror. There is something terrible here, Jinx. Something terrible happened."

"I see the shadows well enough."

"But you do not see their thoughts." His voice shook with fear. "You do not see the fire, and you cannot feel the hate … or the agony."

She felt another cold stab of fear. *Might be I'll feel it soon enough.* "Be my eyes, Shadow. Tell me when to fly."

He shook visibly, but he nodded in the darkness. *I have never seen him half so scared. I have never been half so scared. What is this darkness? There is only one way to find out.*

"You!" She pointed to a shadow that loomed in her vision. "Show yourself."

The shadow stopped abruptly. A whisper chilled the air, high-pitched and shrieking, like a rusty hinge.

"I was called." The shadow rose from the street it marred.

Shadow gave a choked cry of fear as it rose. "Gods be good," he whimpered.

"What is it?" Jinx asked urgently, holding her spear tightly as the shadow before her formed the silhouette of a man. *What is this magic?*

"I was called." The whisper chilled her to her soul. The silhouette stepped toward her, advancing in clumsy, shambling steps, but even its heaviest footfalls made no noise against the silent night.

"Stay away!" Shadow's voice seemed to explode through the still air. *There's not even a breeze in this cursed city!*

"I was called." The figure stumbled forward, its features still hidden from Jinx by the darkness. For that, she was glad.

"Away!" Shadow hurled a throwing knife at it. It did not even flinch; it just stepped closer, and closer, and closer …

"I was called." *The voice is terror itself!*

"Back!" Jinx warned, her spear at the ready.

"I shall drink your mind." The figure drew close, reaching out toward her as it stepped into spear range.

"Die!" Jinx shrieked, stabbing viciously with her spear. The razor tip passed clear through the body without the slightest resistance.

"Give me the warmth of your blood," it whispered as it stepped farther into her spear, groping for her face. It grew close enough for her to see it, and she recoiled in horror.

Gods be good!

It was a man, but could be barely recognized as one. His skin was charred, blistered, and covered with massive burns. Flesh hung like rags from his arms, and beneath the blackened skin, she could count his bones. His face had been burned away, and only dark sockets stared at her where eyes had once been.

"Your soul is mine!" he whispered again, though the lips did not move. *What devilry is this?*

"Fly! Fly, Shadow!"

Shadow needed no second bidding. He leaped off the ground,

extending his wings into the cool night air, and flew toward the camp.

Jinx!

He looked back and saw Jinx close on his heels, her wings beating furiously and her face pale with fear. He breathed a sigh of relief, though his heart still raced. He had never felt a terror that intense; it was a nightmare realized.

He landed before the gate with a cry of dismay. The plaza was completely empty, with only a dead fire to mark where the others had been. Jinx landed next to him.

"Where are they?" she asked.

They fled! They left us to the dead!

"I do not know! I cannot see them!" Shadow looked frantically about for some sign from the others.

"They must be here somewhere!" Jinx cried out hysterically. She screamed into the night. "Freeze! Blade! Demon! Someone answer!"

Shadow had torn the scene apart with his eyes to no avail when he felt a cold malice behind him. He turned, and his blood froze. The burned man had followed, and he was not alone.

"Jinx, he's back ... and there are many with him."

"What? Where?" she screamed. He pointed down the road.

Surely you can feel them as well as I? He felt their pain lance through his head. Images of flame raining from the sky, of screams, and pain ... pain ... pain! He screamed to the sky as he fell to the dirt. *How can anything hurt so badly?*

"Shadow!" Jinx knelt beside him. "Demon! Blade! Where are you? Freeze!" Jinx was nearly sobbing. Shadow forced it all—the pain, the fire, the screams, everything—out of his mind.

She needs you! his mind shrieked. *She needs you to be strong, to fight for her! Not collapse next to her like a cripple!*

He looked to the ranks of burned people filling the plaza. *Do something! They attack the mind, you fool—defend yourself!*

"Stay!" he shouted with more authority than he had known his voice had. He cast a ward—a defensive spell he had made to protect his mind from attack.

To his surprise, the mob of burned creatures listened. Every one of them paused, some in midstep, for just a moment before they broke through the ward and continued their march.

With moonlight glinting off his armor, Blade dropped from the sky behind Shadow and Jinx.

"Follow, quickly!" He took to the air, with Jinx and Shadow hurrying after.

He led them east along the coast, back along the Silent Road, to a nearby beach with a steep cliff face that towered above the high tide surging below it. Up in the cliff was a natural cave, with the red glow of firelight seeping from it. As they entered, both Freeze and Demon jumped up from where they had been sitting beside a small campfire, clutching their weapons.

"Thank the gods!" Freeze exclaimed in relief. "You are safe!"

Demon stared into the fire, his eyes full of fear. "When they attacked, we feared the worst for you. We cried out, but I did not even have a moment to light the fire arrow. They swarmed over our camp, attacking the fire with jet black blades and whispers."

"What happened to you?" Blade asked.

"Near the same." Jinx shuddered at the thought.

"They moved in the darkness," Shadow said. "Jinx challenged one … and … and it …"

"It answered," Jinx finished for him. "By the gods, how I wish it hadn't."

"We were attacked similarly," Blade said. "Demon saw them moving about the buildings as he built the fire. We watched carefully, and when the flame took to the wood, it was like the gates of the gods were thrown open. The dead came swarming forward, and the whispers! The horrible whispers, some talking of flames and mutilation, others talking of hunger, and of thirst for our minds. They sucked the flame right out of the wood—and might have done worse to us, had we had not fled."

"My knife ..." Shadow said, shaking his head in disbelief. "It ... it went ... it cut him through ... but it didn't. He kept walking, and Jinx ... Jinx stabbed it, but it only came forward, through her spear."

Demon nodded knowingly. "I put an arrow through one. Waste of time. He did not even stumble. It was as if they were made of dust; anything solid passes right through."

"And the images ..." Shadow went on as if Demon had not spoken. *Oh gods, the images!* "Like nothing ... nothing I ever knew."

"Images? What images?" Blade asked.

"Fire. Pain. Agony. Screams. It hurt so badly, and I could see the fire, falling on our heads in streams and rivers. Dark shapes swooped through the air, and the fear ... the fear was unbearable."

A long silence passed while the hybrids stared into the fire, remembering their own horrors.

How can I face that again? How can I stand against something so dark, so terrible? He looked over to Jinx. Her eyes were wide, and her jaw was clenched. Her hand shook gently as it gripped her spear shaft. His gaze swept the cave, noting the fear etched on all of his companions' faces—even Blade's. *I can do it for them. I have to.*

"Get by the fire," Blade said, snapping the silence like a dry twig. "It makes you feel better."

"We should never have camped in that city, Blade!" Accusation dripped from Freeze's words. "Gods curse you! You should have listened to me." Blade did not deny her;

he only stared into the flames. "And you!" she whirled on Shadow. "You are worst of all! You stirred the darkness from where it slept! You brought this on us! You could have killed us! You—"

"Stop it!" Jinx's voice cut her short. "You do no good laying blame on others, and your reluctance was hardly borne of wisdom, coward."

"Coward?" Freeze bristled. "I should slay you for even hinting such a thing!"

"Shall we let the assassin kill even one of us?" Blade asked softly. "Or shall we do it all for him?" He looked up to Freeze. "You are right to blame me. I was reckless and careless, but Shadow was only doing his job—what we all should have been doing. Blame me all you will, if it makes you feel better."

Freeze said nothing, her eyes staring furiously into the flames.

"We should keep a watch at all times," Demon warned. "Perhaps they can attack us here."

"There is no way I shall have rest tonight," Jinx said. "I can take the first watch. I could take the entire watch myself, if needed."

"As could I," Blade said as he shuddered. "I can still hear those cursed whispers in my mind."

Shadow spoke resolutely. "I will take first watch. The darkness hides nothing from me, and I can sense them before I see them."

Demon sighed. "If you wish it, I have no complaints. The rest of us should stay and try to get some sort of sleep."

"Our weapons did nothing," Jinx said with a shake of her head. "My spear did not even touch it. What can we do but run from them?"

"Steel is useless," Shadow said as he stepped to the opening of the cave. "But I may be able to fight them. I doubt I have the strength, but I must try." He stepped outside and flew into the darkness.

"I would not want to trade places with him," Shadow heard Demon muttering as he departed. "I would fight a thousand living assassins before I would cross the dead."

The rest of the night passed uneventfully, though restlessly. Shadow had been relieved from his watch near midnight, but found no sleep until the first light of dawn. He awoke late in the morning with the fire down to embers. Blade was trying to stoke it back to life to roast a sea bird Demon had felled.

Freeze sat next to the fire, her eyes fatigued, but her sharp face still intense.

"So what is our next move?" Freeze asked, eying the bird hungrily.

Blade just shook his head as he turned the bird over the fire.

"We have to ..." Shadow said before he became aware they were staring at him. His face reddened. "To ... go back. Back to the ... the ... city."

"Well, you can lead the way, but do not expect me to follow," Demon said as he ran an oiled rag over his yew bow.

"We must ... go. We must, must ... get the map."

"He is right," Jinx said. She had been standing the last watch, but now she stood at the entrance of the cave.

"I know," Blade agreed. "But I also know I do not want to set foot in that city."

"No one does," Shadow said. "But ... still."

Freeze shifted where she sat. "Anything Shadow can do, I can as well. I'll enter the city with you." Her words sounded braver than her voice.

"I can go as well," Jinx said. "We know what to expect now, and daylight will help."

"What about the assassin?" Demon asked. "We need some kind of watch for him."

Blade sighed. "I know. I have been thinking it over all through the night. I think I know what to do, but it is asking much from you, Shadow."

How much? Shadow wondered. "What … what is it?"

"You said last night you could fight them?"

"I think … well … maybe."

Jinx smiled. "That's how Shadow says yes."

"Shadow, there are two ways into Aetha: the east road and the west road. Our assassin could come from either. We need to watch both—"

"You are sending him into the city alone?" Jinx cut him off.

"None of us can fight them. We are wasted against them and would only serve as a hindrance to Shadow."

"Or as rescue. What happens should they seize him? No one will be there to help."

"I can do it," Shadow said quietly. The others did not seem to listen.

"How would we help him, were we there? Arrows and swords do nothing!" Demon argued.

"Sending him alone is near suicide."

Blade countered, "Sending all of us leaves us exposed to the assassin and as possible victims of the dead!"

"But …"

"I will do it," Shadow said louder.

"Shadow, it is too dangerous—" Jinx started.

"I can … get, uh, the map. I can."

"How?"

"Forbidden knowledge." He smiled at her. *Trust me. I made them pause last night. I can do this. I have to.*

"It sounds like it is settled," Freeze said, her relief palpable.

"I still dislike it," Jinx muttered.

"Jinx, if you did accompany Shadow, what would you do to help?" Blade asked, his voice cutting.

"I … I would guard his back."

"I can sense them. They are cold," Shadow said. "I will survive. I will be fine."

Jinx looked at him distrustfully. "If you die, I will kill you, Shadow."

A small grin crossed Blade's face. "It is settled, then."

Shadow stood atop the ruined walls of the city. The damage from whatever fires had fallen on the city was clearer in the light of the sun.

So much destruction. Not one building had been missed. Mounds of melted rock and partially melted homes were all that was left of the once-thriving metropolis, but for a massive building at the center of the city. The building likely had once been rectangular in shape, but since the fires, the corners had been rounded, and the roof dipped.

Even so, Shadow could see the black, yawning doorway into the temple from where he stood. *It's so close. If I can just hold them off for but a few moments, maybe …*

Even then, his prospects of surviving seemed meager. Once he was in the temple, he would be trapped. He flew a wide circle around the city, but for all his efforts, he saw no entrances to the temple but the main door.

No sneaky way out, then.

He flew back to the main gate.

Perhaps if I move stealthily through the streets, they will not see me until I am at the temple? He grimaced at the thought. It did not seem likely to him. Whatever this power was, it was not natural. He doubted it saw by natural means.

He looked to the buildings surrounding the temple. They were larger than the other buildings in the city, though still dwarfs compared to the temple. They surrounded a large plaza that lay before the temple.

Perhaps I can fly to those buildings. If nothing attacks, I might be able to try for the temple. He could think of nothing better to try.

His wings beat against the air as he rose above the city. He flew high, hoping the distance might give him some forewarning of an attack. Into the center of the city he flew. As the buildings beneath him passed by, his feeling of dread increased. It was as if his fear swallowed each inch of the city he traversed, growing and growing.

Images of fire shot through his head.

Focus! Do not let them in. He fought, pressing the images from his mind, only to have more flood in again; it was like trying to hold back a river with his hands.

Suddenly, crippling pain shot through his body. Every inch of him felt as if it were burning with the flames in his mind. He cried out in agony as he plummeted from the air.

I am going to die. The ground grew larger and larger as the wind whistled by.

No! Focus, and you will live! He forced the flames from his mind, and the pain left with it. His wings opened, catching him just before he met the tops of the melted roofs. He flew hastily away from the temple and landed again on the gates.

Much too close, he thought as he panted from the pain, the fear, and the exertion. *I think from now on, I walk.*

Freeze and Demon sat watching the eastern side of the Silent Road. The road was more than living up to its name. So far, not even a sea bird had flown by. The most exciting event of the morning had been a cricket leaping onto Freeze's knee. She was unimpressed.

This is near as bad as guard duty, she thought glumly. *Less comfortable, too.* She looked toward the sun, which burned brightly—and worse, blisteringly—above her head. Beneath her armor, sweat was already beginning to trickle down her back. *This will be a long day.*

The shade of the twiggy tree she sat under did little to help, but it was the best she could find on their hill overlooking where the Silent Road bent north. The hill was covered in brush and small, wiry trees with waxy leaves as small as fingernails. No fruit grew on the branches but a terribly bitter nut.

From their vantage point, they could see down the road for nearly a mile before it curved around another hill to the north. Immediately to their north, they could see mile upon mile of hilly terrain, which Demon scanned thoroughly with his sharp eyes. He had yet to see anything either, it seemed, for he had yet to say a word.

Freeze sighed. *Boring, boring, boring...*

She drew in the dirt next to her. She sketched a stick-figure bandit robbing a carriage and then herself next to him, taking his head off with a single blow.

"Patience truly is not your strength, is it?" Demon asked as he sat watching the road, an arrow notched to his bow.

"I was born to fight," Freeze said with a shrug.

"Sometimes one must wait for the fight."

"Only when one is unwilling to seek it." Freeze sighed again. "This is cowardice. Why sit in the hot sun when we could be flying, hunting our foe?"

"The element of surprise. One tends to lose it when one charges headlong in."

"Element of surprise?" Freeze laughed. "A coward's weapon. A warrior is unafraid to stand and fight."

"I am sure there are many dead people who agree."

Freeze snorted her reply. *Spoken like a true coward. Why are we so afraid of this assassin, anyway? He is but a man, and we are hybrids.*

She wondered about the assassin's attack on the castle. How had he done it? How could a human scale the ramparts in a storm, sneak by the garrison, and then fight four hybrids at once?

"Wait, three," she muttered to herself.

"Three what?" Demon asked, not taking his eyes from the road.

"Three none of your businesses."

He rolled his eyes but didn't respond otherwise.

But still, no human was the match for three hybrids, be he skilled in magic or not. Ten humans didn't stand a chance against a hybrid; one human against three was basically suicide.

Wasn't Howl injured by Jinx's spear? She smiled to herself.

"Oopsies," she muttered again. Demon glanced back but this time didn't bother inquiring.

And it makes sense why the assassin is seeking the Sword! If he were powerful enough to defeat three hybrids, why would he need the Sword? It would be like a full man eating more food. He would need the Sword only if he were as weak as the other humans. If he were as strong as three hybrids, what more could the sword possibly gain him? It suddenly struck her that full men often gorged themselves if they had the means to. How else would some of those rich lords get so rotund?

Still ... she rationalized. *He didn't actually wound any of us. Jinx and the others were lying to protect their dignity. It must be. He can't be any stronger than any of the guards at Castle Shale, and I could best them with my mind alone.*

She thought about Shadow's injuries. *Shadow never was much of a fighter, anyway. That's probably why he was so eager to find the Sword last night—or at least the map, anyway. He can't fight, so he wants to get hold of something that will make it so he can.* She smiled to herself again. *I already can fight. They should give the Sword to me; I'd be the best with it. Blade, or Howl, or Silver will probably end up getting it, though—that's if Jinx doesn't wheedle it out of the king first.* She frowned. *I'd practically have to slay the assassin single-handedly to convince them I deserve the—*

An idea broke into her head: *If I defeat the assassin, I*

would look as if I were stronger than Howl, Jinx, and Shadow put together! Then they would have to give the Sword to me! Who wouldn't? I'd be worth three of the others already! She smiled greedily at the thought of holding the Sword. She would be so powerful, the king himself would be terrified to cross her! *And this is my one chance to make it all happen.*

She stood up and stretched. "I think I shall take a quick flight—scout the countryside a bit."

Demon glanced back at her. "Wouldn't it be best to stay together?"

"Do you want to come?"

"No. My wings are sore enough from the journey already."

"Then stay here. I will be back soon."

"I do not like the idea of splitting up. What if harm should come to one of us? Who would warn the others?"

"No harm shall come. I will just take a quick look and ..." She paused, and looked about uncomfortably, as if there might be invisible listeners. "... and I need some privacy." He just looked at her coldly. "To relieve myself," she added. His look did not change.

"Just don't engage him if you find him. We have the best chance of bringing him down together."

"Of course! You think me stupid enough to fight him alone after all those spectacular horror stories we've heard?" she asked as she lifted herself into the air.

"Just promise not to be as stupid as usual," Demon called after her.

All too easy, she thought haughtily as she sped along the road, flying high to see as much as possible. Farther north she flew, covering mile after mile of road. Her stiff wings ached in defiance as she pushed them farther, doing her best to ignore them and enjoy the cool air around her. Farther she flew, until she felt as if she had traveled half the way back to Castle Shale. She was near to abandoning her quest when, with a spike of excitement, she sighted what she was looking for: a lone figure several miles down the road making its way toward Aetha.

Only one man would walk this road. She raced toward him, drawing her katana in anticipation.

The figure seemed to spot her and stood, waiting expectantly, as she approached.

But I cannot be more than a speck in the sky to him! She had to admit, if this was the assassin, his perceptions at least were strong. As she grew closer, she saw it was in fact a hooded man wearing a black traveler's cloak. It was him; it had to be.

She landed hard only about twenty feet from him and blew down a gust of air to stir as much dust as possible. *Time to be intimidating.*

The assassin stood there, his hand on the hilt of a short sword buckled to his waist, waiting calmly for the dust to settle.

"I have been waiting for this moment," Freeze said darkly as she stood up straight slowly, pulling her best maniacal expression.

"I cannot say I wanted to find you here. Hmm," he mused. "I don't recognize you from the castle. You must have been one of the sluggards attending the feast instead of fighting me." He had the gall to laugh. "Well met, even if it is a late meeting."

"Laughter? From a man standing in the hour of his death? What strangeness is this?"

"Death lost its sway over me many, many years ago," he said coolly.

"Before I slay you, I wish to know: what did you want with the Sword?"

"And before I slay you, I will give you this one chance to yield to me," he said confidently. "I do suggest you take it."

"You must be jesting!" It was Freeze's turn to laugh.

"I do not jest with drunken, half-wit guards. Mocking them is simply too easy to be anything but cruel."

"I will ignore that insolence, because I am still curious. What did you want with the Relic Sword?"

"Justice. To right the wrongs my people have had to endure for the sake of your people's unending pride—or the people you fight for, at least."

"Is this one-man quest to topple a kingdom worth your life?" Freeze asked. *Why won't he show fear? He should be showing fear by now.*

He shrugged. "It is worth yours, at least."

"You are an arrogant one, aren't you? You were lucky with my comrades, but you will not be so lucky with me," Freeze said menacingly as she stirred up more dust with her wings.

"Will we finally get to fighting, then?" he asked as he drew his short sword. The blade was polished to an unnatural mirror shine.

"Not a very stealthy blade for an assassin," Freeze said.

"Assassin?" he asked, confused. "When did I become an assassin? Besides, this is for stealth." He pulled his blade knuckle out from his belt, holding it in his other hand.

"Whatever you are, you will bleed on my steel!" *Now he will quake and run. He can't have the stomach to fight me.*

"We shall see." He raised his blades in a defensive stance.

That's it? Run, you fool—I am beyond you! He did not run. He stood, and what little she could see of his face looked serene and calm.

"Time to die!" Freeze charged forward, wielding her blade in both hands as she slashed down with all her might. Her blade tasted only air as he nimbly dodged past her cut and stood waiting. She attacked once more, cutting at him again and again as their swords kissed with the clang of steel on steel with each slash. Over and over, he deflected her blows, and then he struck her sword aside and slashed with astounding speed with the knuckle blade. Freeze dodged to the side, the razor just nicking her cheek.

"Fool!" she shrieked and attacked with a flurry of swift, powerful blows, her katana singing through the air as he blocked and dodged each blow with smooth, precise maneuvers. As she prepared to strike again, he crossed blades with her and slipped past her sword. He grabbed her sword arm and pulled her back, tripping her with his leg as she went. As she fell forward, he ran his shimmering blade along her leg. The sword cut through her armor with unnatural ease and carved deep into her skin.

She slashed from the ground. He jumped back, missing her blade by a hairsbreadth. He stood by and let her get to her feet, his sword held at ease by his side.

Kill him now! She ran forward and swung the blade over her head, cutting down toward his neck. He blocked overhead, stepped in, and stabbed her with his knuckle blade, but it glanced off her armor.

As he stepped away from her, she lashed out again. He ducked under the blade and kicked her legs out from under her before he rolled back to his feet. Once more he waited patiently for her to stand.

How is he so fast? It is like he sees what I am doing before I even move! She surged back to her feet with a shove of her wings and attacked telekinetically. The grass flattened as her wave swept toward him and stopped before his outstretched hand. *Who is this?*

"Still think it was luck?" He was hardly even out of breath. Freeze was panting hard with exertion and rage. *He is human! How can I be losing?*

"The fight is not done yet!" She slashed out, roaring in rage as he blocked yet again. *His defense is impenetrable!*

She stabbed, but he brushed her sword aside with his and moved past her blade. He elbowed her face, snapping her head back and causing her to stumble. He moved swiftly into an advantaged position. He grabbed her and spun out and away from her as he wrapped his arm around her head, getting ready to throw her to the ground over his hip.

No, you don't! She charged forward, tackling him and pulling herself from his grip as he twisted to face her. They fell together, landing with a thud. Freeze pinned him to the ground.

He grabbed her sword hand. She leaned back and then hurled her weight down with an offhand punch that struck him hard on the cheek. The steel gauntlets bit into his skin, and blood trickled down his face. He tried to turn her, but she pinned him back down. She punched again, but he shielded his face with his arm. She struck his body: once, twice, three times, driving her weight behind each blow, and grinning with each satisfying thud. He slashed the knuckle blade at her face. She leaned back to dodge it, when he twisted violently and rolled her over. Immediately, he scrambled to his feet, stabbing the knuckle blade deep into a gap in her armor at the shoulder as he did.

She felt the cold blade cut her deep. He stood with his sword held low by his side yet again while he waited for her to rise, not even bothering to dab at the blood running down his cheek. She slowly rose, wincing as she moved her damaged arm.

"My fight is not with you," he told her. "Yield, and I shall let you go."

"I do not yield to assassins!" She lunged after him with a fierce slash. He brushed the blade aside and lunged forward. He put his arm around her neck and kneed her ribs powerfully. He struck so hard that the metal guard over his knee dented her armor; she felt herself bruising.

Before she had any time to recover, he pulled her over his hip, throwing her back onto the ground. He planted his knee on her chest, pinning her, and held his sword against her neck while his other hand gripped her sword hand tightly.

Freeze was pinned completely. She tried to blast him off her magically, but again, he blocked the attack.

No! I cannot have lost to him!

"A pity you did not yield. I don't relish the thought of killing you," he said, a tinge of remorse creeping into his voice. He lifted his sword up, the point poised to stab down into her neck, and then he paused.

She glimpsed his eyes from beneath the hood. She saw reluctance in them, but then she saw something else.

What color are they?

"You have red eyes," she spat up at him. Suddenly, he flipped his sword around and brought the pommel down on her head. The force of the blow knocked her helmet off and sent stars bursting through her vision. He let her hand loose, and she felt the weight of his knee lessen.

He thinks I'm defeated.

She swung at him, but he was still too close to her for the blade to catch him flush. Instead, the hilt caught his rib, the blade cutting a shallow wound into his shoulder. The blow knocked him off her, sending him rolling into the grass with a grunt of pain.

She pushed herself to her feet with her wings, charging him despite the stars still bursting across her vision.

This ends now! She raised her sword high above her head and slashed down at his prone form. At the last moment, he twisted and parried her sword aside. With a roar, he thrust his hand forward. His magical wave threw Freeze back nearly twenty feet before she crashed into the earth with a great clatter of armor.

He rolled his weight onto his shoulders, and arching his back, he lurched forward, throwing himself straight to his feet. Freeze pulled herself up less gracefully. Her breath came in ragged gasps; her arms and legs ached, and her armor felt like a furnace.

I can't keep this up much longer. Fear jolted her body as she realized the truth of the words.

"Last chance. My fight is not with you, drake, and I am clearly the better fighter. Yield."

"I am not beaten yet," Freeze said, mustering what confidence she had left.

"I will not be stopped—not now, not by you. I will do what I must to see this through, no matter the cost."

"Then come pay it."

"Meet your death, fool."

They charged, swords raised to meet in battle once more. With a war cry, Freeze slashed at him with all her might. He dropped to his knees and leaned back beneath her blade as he slid between her feet. He thrust both his hands forward, throwing her with a wave of telekinesis that sent her flying into the air. He rose to his feet and focused on her; she could feel his mind gripping her. It hurled her back toward the ground.

This will hurt! She slammed into the dirt with a thud and the sound of metal grinding against metal. Her sword flew from her hand as her head snapped back into the hard-packed soil. The world went black.

"Not so easy when we fight back, is it?" the hooded man asked, and his strained voice betrayed his anger. "Arrogant fool." He cleaned the blood from his blades and sheathed them. He touched the cut on his cheek and saw the blood on his finger. He sighed angrily and took out a cloth to wipe the blood away. He reached down and felt his aching ribs before he tore a strip from his cloth to bandage his shoulder.

Freeze slowly opened her eyes and saw blurry grass gradually come into focus. She rose shakily to her feet, feeling pain all over. She stumbled over to her katana and gripped it again. The hooded man watched her silently.

He shook his head. "You have courage, woman; I cannot deny you that. But know when you are beaten. Surrender your weapon, and this ends now."

She moved into a defensive stance and stood waiting for him.

"Why do you insist on making me kill you?" he growled.

She responded with a smile and stood waiting for him.

He drew his blades. "If you truly insist, then let us finish this."

He circled her while she pivoted, following his every step. He lunged suddenly with a stab; she blocked and answered with a slash. He stepped back and circled once more. Again and again, he lunged without warning, and Freeze parried his attacks away.

He is exhausting me, she realized as she felt her strength draining away. Her limbs ached, and each move was slower than the one before it.

Suddenly he rushed in, his sword swept her blade aside, and he slashed her face again with the knuckle blade. He put a foot behind her, and threw her over his hip; she crashed into the ground face down. He posted his knee on her back and held his sword up, ready to stab down at her exposed neck.

She closed her eyes, waiting for the end to come; nothing happened. She glanced back and saw him looking south, up into the sky. She saw with surprise that he had paused in mid-motion with his sword halfway in its sheath.

Why won't he kill me?

He slowly drew his blade again, though she could see that his eyes were not on her. The cold point rested on the back of her neck. She heard a rush of wind and the thump of feet on the dirt.

"Release her!" Demon's voice had never sounded more beautiful. She twisted and saw Demon standing no more than thirty feet away, his bow pulled back to full draw and a black arrow pointed at the assassin's heart.

"Do not make me kill her," the assassin said coldly.

"Release her, or your black heart will get an arrow to match!" Demon shouted.

"If I die, she dies," the man said as he leaned just slightly on his sword. Freeze felt the point prick her skin; a thin line of blood ran down her neck.

"Free her, and no one dies," Demon said.

"No one but me?" the assassin asked calmly.

"I can guarantee you imprisonment instead of the gallows."

Again, the assassin laughed. "I prefer death to the horrors that would await me in the dungeons of Castle Shale."

"Shoot him!" Freeze yelled with what little breath she could muster with his knee on her back.

"Put up the bow, and no one comes to harm," the hooded figure said.

"Let her up, and drop your weapons, and no one has to die!" Demon shouted, pulling the arrow back farther.

"Agreed," the hooded man said as he stood up suddenly, tossing his sword at his feet.

"Wh-what?" Demon stammered with astonishment.

"Demon, slay hi—" Before Freeze had finished, the man reached his hand forward, and Demon's arrow snapped in two. Demon looked in dismay at the useless weapon in his hands.

"Now we fight on my terms," the hooded man said as his sword lifted itself off the ground and into his waiting hand. As he stepped over Freeze, he thrust his free hand out, and Freeze was hurled through the air, thudding into the hillside. Her head collided with the dirt. Again, stars exploded in her eyes.

"Arm yourself, man," she heard the assassin say. She heard footsteps and the sound of beating wings before the world went dark once more.

Chapter Six

yre, Rocky, Silver, Crash, and Howl sat in the mess hall together, appraising the castle gruel. Silver made a disgusted face as he watched the gray slop swirl about his spoon.

"They presume to call this food?" he asked, pushing the bowl away in disgust.

"It is not so bad as that," Howl said between bites.

"Anything tastes good to a werewolf. You could eat your own hair and not think ill of it," Silver said. Howl shrugged and went back to his gruel.

"Complaining only makes it worse," Rocky grumbled under his breath. The large golem hybrid ran his stone-covered finger through the hot gruel as easily as though it were tepid bathwater.

Golems can't even taste anything, yet he dares lecture me for complaining? Silver groused to himself.

Pyre sat stirring the gruel with his spoon, staring at the gray, clumpy meal with a blank expression.

"Looks like Pyre agrees with me about the gruel," Silver observed.

"No." Pyre shook his head. "I was imagining leaving the castle."

"Imagining is likely the closest we'll get to that," Crash said between mouthfuls of gruel. "At least as long as good King Leon has command over us."

Howl spoke around his spoon. "If Jinx were here, maybe there would be a chance for it."

"If Jinx had bothered herself to bring us, we wouldn't need to imagine at all." *She didn't even try to bring us. She even suggested we stay! Traitor.* Silver frowned. "I suppose we just aren't as special as our winged brethren."

"You complain?" Pyre asked. "By all rights, I should be with them, I have wings like any of them, and I could kill Shadow nine times of ten in any straight fight. The only reason I'm here is because Jinx favors Shadow."

"We're here, though, aren't we?" Rocky asked. "And complaining isn't gaining you anything."

He is doing it again! "And who exactly named you lord of all complaining?"

Rocky shrugged his stone shoulders. "The gods, I suppose."

"The gods gave you nothing but that dense rock you call a brain." Rocky didn't rise to the insult; he just kept working diligently at the gruel.

"How do you think the assassin made it into the castle?" Crash asked.

"I would hazard a guess," Silver said, "that his near-impossible understanding of magic helped."

"How was he so powerful?" Crash asked. "You'd think the Order of Magicians would keep close track of who in their order was capable of such abilities."

"Maybe he was not a magician," Howl suggested. "Maybe he was a warlock."

"What is a warlock?" Pyre asked.

Something Howl just made up, Silver thought.

"It is like dark magic, only I heard that warlocks can be more powerful than magicians," Howl said with a shrug.

"What a pile of refuse," Silver scoffed. "If warlocks are more powerful than magicians, why aren't the warlocks in the king's army? Not to mention, why aren't there more warlocks than mages?"

"Because of what the powers cost," Howl said calmly. "Maybe none of it is true ... but then, none of us would have thought the Relic Sword story would be true before the assassin came."

"I still do not think the Relic Sword story is true," Silver grumbled.

"What does the power cost?" Crash asked.

"Warlocks draw their power from draining their soul," Howl answered. "They get strength through the void that was once their soul. They say that they remove it through the eyes, so their eyes turn red."

"Where did you hear this?" Crash asked.

"I heard a mage talking about it," Howl said. "There's supposed to be a large group of them near Trake."

"Rumors rarely have any credence to them," Silver said. "It's probably just some vampires that were mistaken for something else."

"Vampires? What are you talking about?" Sting asked as he walked up to the table.

"Ask Howl," Silver said. *He's the one who believes these lunacies. Next he will be telling me the gods and demons actually once fought in the Valley of the Gods.*

"We are talking about warlocks," Howl explained. When Sting looked at him quizzically, Howl elaborated: "The magicians who draw their power from removing their soul?"

"I've never heard of them," Sting said as he sat down next to Pyre.

"No one here has," Silver said as he slid his bowl of gruel toward Sting. "You will make better use of this than I will."

"Sounds like a wives' tale to me." Sting took the bowl and smelled it cautiously.

"Ask Marcus about it, or maybe Halifin could tell you,"

Howl said defensively before he took an extra sloppy bite of gruel just for Silver. Silver curled his lip in disgust.

"Silver, you handle blood better than gruel," Sting said before he began to devour Silver's bowl.

"Blood is a bit more appetizing than this," Silver said.

"We are agreed there," Howl said with a wolfish grin.

"So have you heard the news?" Sting asked between bites of gruel.

"Anything from Aetha?" Pyre asked.

"Yes," Sting said sarcastically, "apparently the ruined buildings have sent us a plea for rat poison; they're up to their ears in the little devils."

"How droll, Sting," Pyre mumbled insincerely as he returned his attention to swirling the gruel.

"What is it, actually?" Silver asked.

"Apparently the Rogues raided Trake. They broke through the gates, fought off the garrison, and made off with weapons, armor, and every horse in the stables."

Rocky broke his stoic silence: "How could they attack something so large?"

Sting shrugged. "I do not know, but they did. And what's more, I hear there were at least a thousand Rogues in the attack."

"What of the city?" Crash asked.

"Burned buildings, dead sons, stolen steel, and lost horses," Sting said.

"Our enemies multiply, steal our weapons, and sabotage us, and our king sits on his throne and withholds his strongest warriors," Silver said with disgust. *This madman will be the doom of our kingdom.*

"Maybe not," Sting said. "I heard the raid frightened him greatly. Maybe that will prompt him to unleash us."

"We should have been unleashed long ago," Rocky said.

"Is that complaining I hear?" Silver asked with a grin.

Rocky once more failed to rise to the insult. *He knows I would destroy him in an argument.*

Howl spoke grimly. "Please—every time the king gets more frightened, he draws us closer. We won't be stepping out of this castle unless we escape it."

"I would not mind a little escaping," Crash said.

"Is that the sound of treason I hear?" Sinister asked as he approached. "The king would be most interested to hear of this."

Oh, not you! "Ugh, not you," Silver complained loudly. "I should have thought you would keep hiding from us after your embarrassing fight with Shadow."

"He caught me off guard!" Sinister hissed defensively.

Crash smashed his fists into the table with such force that it cracked. "You ever attack another Guard member, and I will personally cut your arms off." The bustling mess hall grew as silent as a tomb as the soldiers took time away from their gruel to watch the commotion.

Sinister turned scarlet. He opened his mouth to say something, seemed to think better of it, and walked away toward the food line.

Coward. Won't even talk back to stronger opponents. Next time he bullies Shadow, I'll give him a taste of bullying myself.

"Wow, Crash, how did Shadow survive your smack to the head?" Sting asked with a laugh as he looked over the damaged table. "Look at this crack! And this table is cedar!"

"I did not hit Shadow very hard," Crash said humorlessly as he returned to his meal.

"At least you frightened the snake away," Pyre said spitefully with a glance at Sinister.

"I've never liked him much. Can you believe he actually attacked Jinx?" Crash shook his head in disgust.

"I can," Howl said with a grin. "He cannot stand the attention Shadow gets from her."

"What do you mean?" Sting asked.

"Please—he is mad for Jinx. He stinks of infatuation. You can see it with all those lengthy stares he gives her, and how he bristles when she talks to Shadow. He's infatuated and he's not the type of person to stand by and let her choose who she wants." Howl kept his eyes on Sinister as the latter pushed his way past the humans waiting in line to get straight to the front. "He's too much of a tyrant to let anyone get between him and his desires."

"Well," Crash growled, "if he is not careful, his desires will land my ax right between his eyes."

"Do you think he will really tell the king about what we said—about the escaping?" Silver asked. *I certainly wouldn't put it past him. Why must I be surrounded by treacherous friends?*

"Sure, but the king isn't going to execute us over it," Howl said. "Especially if we aren't here when he learns of it."

A bell tolled three times in long, resonating tones. Every human in the mess stood up reluctantly.

"Well, friends," Crash said as he stood, "It would seem it is time to stop dreaming and to begin our watch."

"Speak for yourself," Sting said with a grin. "That bell marks my break."

"I'll be sure to tell King Leon how diligently you guarded his gruel," Silver said.

Howl patrolled the castle once again.

I'm guarding a nearly invincible castle and a king no one seems to care to kill. He shook his head as he wound his way through the black hallways. It was late in the afternoon, so, by the king's command, the upper levels of the castle were nearly devoid of people. Only those with messages for the king or with the direst of needs were allowed to pass the golden guards below. The king had Howl guarding these levels because of his strong senses, which allowed him to hear and smell nearly anyone moving through the halls.

"First Trake, and now Bel? This kingdom is falling into shambles." A voice echoed off the walls.

"Was it another attack, then?" another voice asked. It was the young voice of a castle page Howl had heard many times before. He often led nobles and generals through the winding halls to the throne room.

"What do you think? Rogues have been raiding all around Shale County for months now. It's just they have never seized a city before."

"They seized Bel? I have cousins there!"

"Pray that they got out, boy. Who knows what has happened to them if they didn't."

"Maybe the Rogues left the city already. Maybe they just stayed for a little while. Maybe everything is all right again."

"I wouldn't count on it, boy. The Rogues are trapped in the city by General Nathan's men."

"Will he be able to get them out of the city?"

The man laughed. "Napping Nathan? Not likely. The man has the competence of a goat. That's why I need to speak with the king. We can't let all ten thousand men get bogged down in a lengthy siege. He needs to storm those walls."

Their voices drifted away in the labyrinth of hallways and rooms. Howl sighed. His enemies were so close to him—not more than fifty miles down Trade Road. But he was chained up in the castle, rotting to death.

I'm not a wolf here; I am just a trained dog. Perhaps I should escape this place. He shook his head at the thought. *That's foolish even to think about.*

He continued on his patrol, looking around the castle, sticking his head into odd rooms, and twirling his sword every now and again in an idle attempt to entertain himself. Suddenly, a familiar smell reached his nostrils.

What is Silver doing up here? He followed the smell, sniffing his way to a door by the outer wall.

He looked into a room and saw Silver lazing about on a cushy couch, spinning a very expensive-looking globe as he looked nonchalantly around the room.

"Howl, I'm glad you came," Silver said casually as he looked over the numerous books set into the shelves along the wall.

This room must belong to some high ranking mage, Howl thought to himself. It even had large windows that light streamed through, giving the room a welcoming feel. *A feel so welcoming that Silver didn't think twice about inviting himself in, it seems.*

"So how is your guard duty?" Silver asked.

"Tedious and boring. How's yours?"

"Splendidly boring as well."

"I heard something interesting not long ago, though," Howl offered.

"Oh? Do tell. Take a seat—the chairs are well stuffed, and you must be tired after all that patrol."

"It would seem that Bel has been seized by Rogues," Howl said as he sat down. His armor creaked as he came to a relaxed position. "Why must I wear this cursed metal skin? My blade is the only defense I need."

"Interesting," Silver mused. "I have come to feel almost naked without my armor. But could we get back to Bel?"

"The city is under siege by the King's Army, and I suppose the walls are soon to be stormed. That is all I know, except that the general in charge is incompetent as a goat."

"A goat? Well, that's more competent than most the humans I've seen."

Howl laughed. "Certainly more reasonable than Marcus, anyway."

"That is for certain," Silver said as he gave the globe another spin.

"What brings you up here, Silver?"

"A hybrid needs a reason to come visit with his good friend?"

"We argue more than we act as friends, Silver."

"A good argument can make a friendship stronger."

What in the world is he trying to get at? "I'll ask again bluntly: why are you here?"

"Admittedly, I had initially hoped to elude you in the cavernous, empty space up here ..."

Howl laughed again. "I could smell unicorn across the county."

"So it seems. Now, however, I am glad you came."

"I am still going to kick you off this level."

"Hear me out first. How sincere were you when you said you would like to escape this afternoon?"

He can't be serious. "We have all thought it before. You are not actually considering it, are you?"

"Bel is ... what? A one, maybe two-day march from here?"

"More like two." *He is serious. I should be more resistant to this idea. Why aren't I?*

"The humans could use our help, you know. I would venture a guess that the Guard alone could dislodge those Rogues from the walls."

Howl snorted. "Perhaps, but only if King Leon let us more than a hundred yards from the castle."

"Just think of the damage we could do leading the King's Army into battle. The morale boost alone could be the difference between victory and defeat."

"We would be whipped bloody just for stepping outside the city limits."

"Have you ever been afraid of a human's whip?"

Howl paused. "Not in a long time, no."

"It would be irresponsible of us not to go," Silver said seriously. "Our king's enemies are so close at hand; we cannot allow them to come close enough to harm our beloved king."

Howl's lips pulled back into a slow smile. "Silver, you just may have something there. What kind of Royal Guard would we be to let this threat stand so close to our royal subject?"

"A sorry excuse for a Royal Guard, that's what kind we would be."

"I do not want to be known as a sorry excuse." *Am I really going along with this?*

"Nor do I."

"It would seem our hands are tied. We simply must remove these invaders. But who would we bring?" *I can't let this go on. Before long, I'll actually be doing it.*

Silver smiled broadly. "I am glad you see things as I do. I have a few in mind." He rose, giving the globe a final spin that nearly toppled it. "Shall we go ask them if they will be joining us?"

"You really are serious about this, aren't you?"

Silver smiled coolly. "As serious as an invasion of Rogues."

I guess I am going along with this. "And as serious as I am. After my guard duty is over, I will find you."

Silver walked to the door. "Why not come now? This level is so large and empty; no one would notice your absence for a few minutes."

Howl looked at him warily a moment. "Gods be good, Silver—when did you become so persuasive?"

Crash wandered aimlessly through the great hall of Castle Shale. It was the first room one entered from the main gate of the castle, and it was designed to reflect the wealth and power of the Kingdom of Shale.

The room was enormous, decorated along the walls

with intricate tapestries depicting glorious moments from the kingdom's past. The roof was painted with images from mythology. There Crash could see the Fire God kneeling defeated before the Sky God. He saw pictures of the war between the gods and the demons, and between humans and ogres. In the very center of the ceiling was the image of the Sky God sparing the last demon—an act that had made him a traitor and outcast to the rest of the gods. The ceiling was painted with remarkable skill, created by a painter who predated any known painters. The paintings, like the castle itself, had come before the Kingdom of Shale—before the history and records of the kingdom began.

Hanging from the ceiling and casting light upon the multitude of ancient paintings and tapestries were brilliant chandeliers made of clear crystal, which scattered the light of their lanterns about the room. A thick, red carpet ran along the floor of the great hall, leading up a massive flight of stairs to a grand indoor balcony. Only through this balcony could the rest of the castle be reached through numerous doors and passageways carved into the wall behind the balcony. This made the balcony a critical choke point, and lining each side of the enormous staircase, standing on every other stair, was an elite human guard at rigid attention, each armored in shining, gold-colored plate armor with blue capes. They held halberds tightly against their shoulders, and only those they recognized, or who bore one of the king's signet rings, could pass by them unhindered.

The spectacle of the room was truly awe inspiring, and people came from all distant lands to Castle Shale to see the great hall. Because of this, it was a rare day indeed that the hall was not teeming with commoners and wealthy tradesmen alike, each gawking at the splendors of the castle. The sound of their voices reverberated off the walls as they looked over the intricate tapestries and paintings, as well as the remarkable architecture. The tapestries were especially eye-catching; the thinnest of threads had been woven together to create an image so detailed that it became a window into the past.

Crash liked this room. He enjoyed the grandeur, and he was fond of the crowds—or, more close to the mark, the noise of the crowds. He found he could often think better with the soft background sound of numerous voices, and he loved listening in on the lives of the people outside of the castle.

If only I could leave these walls, he thought longingly.

He looked at the many pictures depicting battle and peace alike, of triumphs both of mortal and immortal, and imagined himself there, slaying vampires alongside Nath the Slayer or besieging cities with King Leon the Conqueror, the first of the Shale dynasty. He pictured himself charging hordes of invading elves in the Great Elf Wars and beheading ogres while the gods and demons dueled and their titans clashed with a fury that scarred the land. He saw the faces of the greatest heroes of the land, and he wanted nothing more than to be one of them.

He glanced at the balcony and saw Howl and Silver descending the stairs, speaking in whispers among themselves and keeping a wary eye on the elite guards standing at attention around them.

What are they doing here? Aren't they supposed to be on duty? I wonder what they whisper about. His curiosity aroused, Crash made his way over to them, the humans around him making a wide berth for the armored, hairy giant.

"What are you two discussing so privately?" Crash asked as he fell in step with them when they reached the bottom of the stairs.

"Follow," was all Howl said. They walked into the crowds, where no one would have a hope of hearing what was being discussed between them over the noise of the surrounding people.

"What is it? It must be dangerous to need such secrecy."

"It is a matter of treason—should it be explained the wrong way, anyway," Silver explained.

"We are planning on making an unscheduled excursion," Howl said quietly.

"Bring me along. I have always been a supporter of unscheduled excursions."

"We know," Silver said. "But what of Crunch? Will he be as eager as you?"

"More so, if that is possible. The troll has been wanting out since we first got here."

"I share that feeling," Howl muttered.

"Where is this excursion bound for? Will we be coming back?"

"Bel," Howl answered. "The city has been seized by Rogues, and we are bound to seize it back."

"I do not know if we shall be returning afterward." Silver shrugged nonchalantly. "I suppose that will depend on how much we miss the others."

"What if the others are forced to hunt us?"

Howl gave a snort of contempt. "That only happens if King Leon has enough courage to send his Guard after us."

"And even then," Silver added, "they are more likely to join us than kill us."

"We are not leaving for good as of yet, but if we find we like the new-found freedom, well ..." Howl grinned savagely. "... then we may just have to."

"Freedom?" Crash mused. "I think I like the sound of that. I will tell Crunch of the plans."

"See that no one else hears," Silver said sternly. "Not even another hybrid."

"Especially Sinister," Howl added.

"Do you think me a fool? No one will know."

"We had to make sure," Howl reminded him.

"I remember subtlety not exactly being your strong

point in the courtyards while we hunted the assassin," Silver muttered.

"Some situations call for subtlety, others not so much. I can tell the difference."

"Good to hear."

"So who else will be coming on this excursion of ours?"

"We have thought a flier might be handy," Howl said.

"Pyre, then?"

"He has yet to agree—or even be asked, for that matter, but I expect he shall be as keen as you are."

"I don't think he can be as keen as me," Crash said with a glance at the tapestries around him. His eyes settled on the image of a broad-shouldered warrior who grinned casually as he leaned on his enormous battle-ax, Steel Wind. He was Deln, a warrior who had led King Darien's men to victory against the elves well over a hundred years ago. He was a legend—a warrior who had brought strength and stability to the kingdom against nearly impossible odds—a warrior like Crash wanted to be.

"Why aren't you doing anything about Bel?" an elderly woman from the crowd screamed at them. The room grew silent as the crowd turned to watch. "My daughter and her babe lost her home, lost her husband, lost everything! And you," she shrieked, "you who claim to protect the kingdom stand here in this castle and do nothing!"

"Ma'am," Howl said quietly. "We are doing what we can. It's the king you want to talk to. He—"

"It is not right!" the woman wailed as two golden guards silently grabbed her by the arms and pulled her kicking and screaming from the castle. "People are dying! It's not right!"

The hybrids watched her go silently. *The world needs another Deln,* Crash thought. *I shall give it to them.*

"Plan this thing thoroughly," Crash whispered to the others. "We cannot fail."

Pyre stood in the castle library, looking over the names of the books. He leaned against the wall and toyed with the pommel of his broadsword.

This place is so boring. He hummed a tune he had memorized as he looked from volume to volume, tome to tome, and scroll to scroll. *They even have boring names.* The titles read along the lines of *The Effects of Magic on Humans, Eye of Newt and Other Fake Ingredients, Tactics and Warfare, Gods and Demons, Elfin Myths,* and many, many more.

The library, like nearly everything else in the castle, was enormous. Bookshelves towered up to the ceiling, completely stuffed with tomes, stories, scrolls, and manuscripts. Here was cataloged all the knowledge and wisdom of the land. One could spend a lifetime reading through the vast volumes of writing here and still not complete every book. Librarians and mages moved through the corridors, climbing up tall ladders to reach the knowledge stored on the upper shelves of the massive bookcases.

How do they know where each book goes? There wasn't any perceivable ordering system that he could note; yet, those seeking books never seemed to take long to find one.

He sighed with boredom. He missed Blade.

At least when things got boring, we could always keep each other entertained with jokes and sparring. Pyre stretched out his wings and yawned, drawing many glances from the humans in the room. The librarians especially eyed him nervously. *They know I'm a phoenix.* He smiled. *They can't be happy to have a creature of fire wandering around their dried paper volumes.* Pyre smiled at them, even giving one especially cantankerous-looking old man a wave. He received an icy glare in return before the man returned to his books.

Cheery fellow, Pyre thought to himself as he went back to looking through the thousands of books. *Shadow would be in paradise here. I wonder how often he comes here? I never see him wandering around ... but then again, would I see him even if he were?*

"Enjoying yourself much?" Silver asked as he leaned beside him on the wall.

"Not especially, no. Aren't you supposed to be on duty somewhere?" Silver pulled a wry smile. "Right," Pyre answered his own question. "That's never stopped you wandering around before."

"Not in the least—nor has it kept me from scheming, it seems." Silver held up a folded piece of parchment.

"And what is this?" Pyre took the parchment but didn't unfold it.

"It's too quiet here." Silver leaned closer and whispered. "Too easy for eavesdroppers. Read it, and then burn it. It shouldn't be too hard for you to figure out how." Silver pulled away from the wall and began to walk away. "Tell me your decision someplace private."

Pyre watched him go. *This can only be one thing.* He looked at the folded parchment. *This has been too long in coming.*

He opened the note and glanced at the letters scrawled along it.

> *Bel*
> *Two days' time*
> *Kill Rogues, be heroes*
> *You're an idiot if you don't come*
> *Tell anyone and we will beat you senseless.*
>
> *Sincerely,*
> *Anonymous*

Pyre smiled as he read.

Silver is quite the eloquent writer, Pyre thought to himself, amused.

He crumpled up the note and looked around to make sure no one had seen him reading it. When he was satisfied that no one had, he held the note tightly in his fist. Smoke drifted out of his fingers before he let the ashes of the letter fall to the ground. His secret safe, Pyre looked out the western window toward Bel and smiled while the librarians stared, horrified, at the smoke still rising around him.

Chapter Seven

*T*he hooded man lay in the grass, motionless, hardly daring to draw breath. The others had come quickly after he had dispatched the drake and chased off the gargoyle. He had been surprised at how few they were.

Just four? There must be more. They must be searching for the map, or perhaps waiting to ambush me—or both. He glanced back toward the road. He sensed that the griffin was flying protectively around the others, who were carrying the unconscious drake along the Silent Road.

The hooded man kept still, his cloak pulled over him. He had covered his cloak with grasses and twigs to help him hide whenever the griffin passed too close for comfort. He had proceeded in this manner for the last hour, crawling as the griffin flew away from him and hiding as he flew over.

This is better than fighting all the way to the city, I suppose. He didn't believe a word of it. *Well, better than being dead, anyway.*

His mind sensed the griffin flying away from him. He glanced from under his hood to make sure; he always did, though his mind had never yet led him wrong. It could see more clearly than his eyes could, yet he had still not learned to trust it completely.

Sure enough, just as his mind had seen, the griffin was flying south, away from him. He began to crawl with all speed. He had always been a fast crawler; on his hands and knees, he could go almost as fast as a man jogged.

He kept close watch on the griffin as he circled, and as soon as his mind told him that the griffin was turning toward him, he pressed his chest into the dirt and waited once more.

What I would give to be invisible!

Again he paused for the griffin to pass, and again he peeked beneath his hood to make sure he was safe before crawling his way toward the city, until again the griffin flew over.

Maybe I should kill him one of these times, he thought bitterly. *I may even slay him before the others butcher me.*

Hours passed of crawling through the grass before he finally saw the city from the top of a hill.

Aetha. It looks just as it did in my memories, even without the fire. He paused and studied the wall from his vantage point. Most of the wall was near as solid as Castle Shale itself, but for a few areas where the melted wall dipped low. He hoped that those dips were low enough to hoist himself over, but it was difficult to tell from this distance. He continued his crawl, moving toward the lowest dip in the wall he could spot, still pausing for the ever-circling griffin. An area of barren, blackened earth stretching nearly forty feet across lay between him and the wall,.

Grass, twigs, and a cloak won't help me here.

His mind saw that the griffin was flying away from him. A quick glance with his eyes confirmed this.

Now's as good as later, I suppose. He rose to his feet, and bolted toward the city as fast as his legs could carry him. He covered the desolate area quickly, the charred earth cracking beneath his footsteps.

That wall still looks pretty tall, he thought nervously as the melted wall loomed over him. He leaped regardless, throwing himself against the stone. His fingers grasped the edge of the solidified structure, and he pulled himself up onto the wall. His mind saw the griffin wheel around, flying straight toward him.

I should have killed him! he thought as he dropped down into the street. He hit the ground, rolling to his feet before he sprinted down one of the small alleyways.

I need somewhere to hide! He turned a corner in the road and then, a bit farther down the street, slipped into a house that had only superficial damage. He crouched in a dark corner by the door, knuckle blade and sword drawn.

He waited. No one came. No footsteps and no wingbeats could be heard against the eerie silence of the ruined city.

Did he lose me that easily? He peeked his head out the door. The sky was empty but for a few clouds

Why would he abandon the chase so soon? Do they already have the map? Am I walking into a trap? What does this mean? He cautiously stepped outside to get a better look at the sky. His mind swept over the landscape. There was the griffin, circling the others again.

Did I simply imagine he saw me? No! He flew right at me—I would swear to it. Why would he let me into the city so easily? He looked up and down the street. *How did these buildings become so damaged? The fire in my dreams did not burn hot enough to do this. Had a fire before my dreams destroyed the city? And why do I feel so nervous?*

His mind scoured the street. His whole body stiffened as his mind sensed a hazy cloud of magic moving down the street toward him. As he tried to focus on it, images of flames, fire, and death jumped through his mind.

What is this sorcery—some kind of guardian?

He did not wait for an answer. He turned and sprinted away, making his way toward the massive temple at the center of the city.

Shadow stood on the main road. Sweat beaded on his forehead, his eyes drooped from fatigue, and his breathing was labored, but for all this, the slightest of grins lay on his face. Before him, the dead stood, silent and motionless, their hollow eyes staring at him.

"Your power is fear," he said to none of them in particular. Images of fire and death pierced his mind, but he did not flinch away from it. "You have nothing but threats of fire and pain."

"Come. Come and find out." Their rasping whispers echoed against the buildings lining the streets.

Shadow walked forward, his smirk still on his face. *You have vexed me the entire day, but victory at last is mine.*

Closer he stepped toward the dead crowd as they hemmed in around him from all sides, rising from the street and stepping out of the walls of the houses to surround him. They closed the circle, their charred hands groping for him as their feet slapped soundlessly against the street.

As the nearest burned man reached out toward Shadow, he stared fearlessly into its hollow eyes.

Fire and screams rained from the sky in his thoughts, but he stood strong before them. He focused his mind against the burned man assailing him, and with a strangled gurgle, the man stepped away from Shadow and fell to his knees. The crowd pressed toward Shadow, and Shadow walked through them calmly, submitting any that stood against him.

The hooded man walked quietly through the streets. His heart raced as the strange clouds of magic moved all about him, rising from the streets themselves. Though his eyes saw nothing, his mind was surrounded in a nearly impenetrable fog of magic as indistinct shapes moved in the mist.

What is this?

He stopped where he stood. The air had grown cold, and

the figures in the mist were growing more distinct with every step he took toward the interior of the city.

There is no retreat. There is no defeat. If I die, let it be fighting for my cause. Let it be at the hands of some guardian barring my way.

"If we are to fight," he called out, "let us simply get it over with."

Before his eyes, dark figures rose from the street, their skin blackened and charred, and their eyes hollow.

He drew his sword and prepared the strongest spell he could think of. "What is this?"

The burned men stood still, the sound of their rasping whispers filling the narrow street like a wave.

"We defend this place, the site of man's doom. But your blood, we can sense what is in your blood. We are here because of the blood of both your ancestors. It is through the ancient magic of your new blood that we are here, and through the new magic of your old blood that we are enslaved. We have sinned against the gods and men. If we help you, perhaps we shall atone. We will take you to the map."

What kind of dark magic binds souls to this world? "How do you know of my blood?"

"We know many things. We know your mind. We see what we could not see in our skin, but explanations take time. We do not have this. The fearless one has broken us. He walks uninhibited to your goal. He will destroy it. We have seen this in his thoughts."

"Why do you help me? What do you gain from this?"

"Atonement. We are dead men who guard this city by a spell. But the magic did not foresee our humanity; it did not account for our will. We can choose which side to fight for. But hurry, we will turn on you soon. We must."

What do they do when they turn on me? But did I come this far just to flee the unknown? "Take me to the map."

"Go to the temple. We will do for you what we may." As

the sound of their whispers faded, the multitude of burned bodies dissipated like ash back into the street and houses.

Only one way to tell if these strange guardians are telling me the truth ... He took off running down the street. The streets themselves were a winding labyrinth, leading this way before curving suddenly that way and ending in a dead end. After his fourth wrong turn, he cursed under his breath and hauled himself onto the roof of a nearby house. Leaping from rooftop to rooftop, he made his way toward the ruined temple, and the dark, warped doorway that seemed to beckon to him.

He landed in the plaza that surrounded the temple, his feet running before they even hit the ground. *My enemies have wings. Open ground favors them.*

He sensed what he feared: he looked over his shoulder and saw two Guard members flying toward him. *I must reach the door before them! I cannot let this fearless one destroy the map!* He ran yet faster, practically sailing through the door with the winged hybrids close behind him. He could sense it was the harpy and the griffin.

Inside the temple was a massive hall. In the center was an altar that stood solemn atop a raised floor several stories high, with stairs that wound up to the top. Statues along the walls crumbled from fire damage and old age, while towering pillars stubbornly held aloft the drooping roof.

A tall ceiling! Of course it's a tall ceiling! They will still be able to fly over my head with this ceiling!

He looked back and saw that the Guards had made it through the door just a moment after him, both with their weapons drawn and their expressions grim. They wasted no time giving chase. High above the floor they flew, weaving around pillars as they closed in on their prey.

Fast as my feet are, I cannot hope to outrun wings! His thoughts did not stop him from trying.

The harpy and griffin both swooped down, their wings tucked close, with spear poised to skewer and sword to cut.

Will I die here in this forsaken place so early in my quest? The harpy was almost upon him when burned men leaped from the floor, their cracked and blistered hands reaching for her as their whispers echoed about the hall.

"Gods protect us!" the griffin cried out in horror as both the hybrids veered away, nearly slamming into the pillars in their desperation to flee the dead.

Now is my only chance! The hooded man could see the door his destiny lay behind: a door that led to an altar once kept behind closed doors to all but the highest of priests. He could see a dead man standing next to the door, motioning him toward it. His feet bore him with speed he did not know he had.

The griffin and the harpy clutched at their heads, their faces twisted in agony as they plummeted to the ground. The dead swarmed around them, their horrible rasping whispers filling the room like a storm.

They will do the same to me when they turn on me, he thought uncomfortably.

He shouldered his way through the door. The gremlin stood before the altar, opening the last fold of the map. Dead men surrounded him, but when they tried to grab him, they fell to their knees before him and backed away meekly. The room was small, the walls and ceiling cramped around the altar.

My map! He will destroy it! "Put it down!"

The gremlin jumped and turned with surprise. His jaw clenched, his eyes hardened, and his fingers clamped down on the fragile leather map.

"Release it!" the hooded man again demanded.

"You will never have it." The gremlin gripped the map and wrenched it viciously.

No! The hooded man lifted his hands, wrapping the map

with his mind, holding it together as the gremlin attempted to destroy it.

"You cannot hold it forever!" the gremlin roared, taking his attention from the map.

Now or never! The hooded man pulled hard with his mind, yanking the map from the gremlin's hands and into his own.

"I should kill you for what you tried," he said as he tucked the map into his tunic. "If only I had time for such—" He stopped abruptly as images of fire and pain speared his mind and the dead standing in the room lunged at him. He turned and bolted through the door as fast as he could.

They've turned on me!

Shadow stepped out of the altar room, watching as the hooded assassin sprinted, his cloak trailing in the wind behind him as hordes of burned bodies surged after him like a flood of the dead. The hooded man let his cloak fall from his shoulders and gripped his head while he ran. Shadow knew all too well the kinds of thoughts that lanced his mind.

Shadow allowed himself a grin at the spectacle. *Even he, with all of his magical power, fears the dead.*

He looked to his left. Jinx and Blade cowered on the floor, surrounded by dead men. Their eyes were wide, the expressions on their pale faces the picture of mental anguish. Shadow felt the dead again trying to conquer his mind, and as always, he focused against it, knowing that behind him, a dead man fell to his knees, defeated.

He walked to Jinx and Blade calmly, staring fearlessly at his friends' dead tormentors.

"Leave them, or I will crush you."

The dead turned to face him, their hollow eyes staring at him. He focused his mind against one as fiercely as he could and watched it writhe on the floor before breaking apart like ash. The others stepped away from Blade and Jinx and fell willingly into the floor.

"How … how did you …?" Jinx asked, her eyes still wide as she picked herself up. Blade shook visibly from fear as he stumbled to his feet.

"My sword … did nothing. And the images! Oh gods save us, the images!"

"Come," Shadow said softly. "We have an assassin who needs slaying."

❈ * ❈ * ❈

The hooded man jumped down from the wall, falling clumsily onto the blackened ground outside the city. His breath came in ragged gasps as those terrible images, sounds, and senses faded from his mind.

I'm safe … Even his thoughts felt ragged. *I survived. I almost went mad, but I survived. I have the map.*

He leaned back against the wall and tried to recover any breath he could.

He sensed them before he saw them: three hybrids flying through the air toward the wall. It would not be long before they spotted him, and twigs and grasses on his cloak would not be enough to hide him even if he still had his cloak.

Can't they let me escape? Have I not endured enough to have earned this map? Have I yet more to pay for its knowledge?

They spotted him quickly, and the three Guards—the griffin, the harpy, and the gremlin—landed in a semicircle around him, trapping him against the wall.

"The map, if you please!" the griffin demanded.

"It is yours, if you can shed enough of my blood to earn it," he said as he rose to face them. *Perhaps they can.*

"We have you, fool," the harpy said. "You are on foot, and we fly. You are but one man, and we three hybrids. There is nothing but grass for dozens of miles to hide you. If we do not kill you here, we will later."

"Do what you must, and I shall do what I must," he said, as he walked toward them, drawing his sword. *Do I walk to my death?*

"Do you wish to die, assassin?" the gremlin asked.

"Someday—and my name is not assassin; my name is Cearon." *I am as ready for this as ever. Why delay?*

Cearon swung his sword hard at the griffin, who struck the blade aside and slashed at Cearon's head. Cearon ducked under the blade and grabbed the griffin's leg, slashing ineffectively at the armor with the knuckle blade as he yanked up, throwing the griffin to the ground.

The other two lunged at him. The harpy stabbed with her spear, and the gremlin slashed with his dirk. Cearon swept the harpy's spear aside and blocked the gremlin's dirk magically. He elbowed the harpy in the face, knocking her to the ground. The gremlin rushed to her aid, but a wave of telekinesis blasted the gremlin away.

I am actually winning.

The griffin was on his feet, his sword slashing through the air. Cearon parried the blow and slashed at the griffin with his razor. The griffin blocked it with a gauntlet and slammed his wing hard into Cearon's stomach, knocking him off his feet. He fell but quickly rolled to his feet, barely missing the sword the griffin plunged into the dirt after him.

The griffin wrenched the blade free, attacking again, as the harpy stabbed from where she had risen. Cearon blocked the sword and magically threw the spear aside. He stabbed at the griffin, who parried the thrust to the side. Cearon grabbed him, intending to throw him, when he sensed the dirk thrusting at his back. He knocked the griffin magically to the ground and stepped aside, narrowly dodging the dirk.

The gremlin slashed again at Cearon. He dodged and grabbed the gremlin's arm, wrenching it hard. Cearon sensed the spear stabbing at him; he kneed the gremlin in a nerve on his thigh and spun him toward the spear. The harpy pulled the spear to the side, missing the gremlin as the griffin came back at Cearon.

Come one at a time, and let me kill you already! he thought in frustration.

The griffin slashed, but Cearon blocked and threw the griffin's legs out from under him with magic. He slashed downward when he sensed the harpy's spear aimed at his back. He dodged the spear, stepping over the griffin as he did. The griffin twisted and slashed as Cearon passed.

His blade! He stopped the sword magically as it cut into his shin. It chipped into the bone, but didn't take the leg off.

Cearon hissed with pain as the harpy lunged forward, stabbing. He deflected the point to the side. He stepped toward her along the haft when she swung out with the spear butt. He ducked barely beneath it, but she swung the butt back and crashed the end into his head. Stars burst through his vision as the blow knocked him off his feet.

This is it. This is where I die, he thought. *If I must, let me die with my sword piercing one of their hearts!*

Cearon let out a groan and tried to get to his feet. He sensed the griffin's blade slashing down at his back. With a startled grunt, Cearon rolled as fast as he could. The cold steel cut deep into his left shoulder as he tumbled at the harpy's feet.

With a war cry, she stabbed down at him.

Move or die! he heard his master's voice scream from the past. He rolled into her shins, barely missing the spear point. She stumbled back before kicking him in the ribs. He felt bones crunch beneath her metal shoe.

He screamed, this time with rage, as he cut at the harpy's legs. She jumped back, but the sword cut through her greaves with the unnatural ease he had spent years enchanting into the blade. She screamed as his sword sliced her flesh.

"Jinx!" the griffin had his sword poised above his head to cut down at Cearon as he turned his attention to his wounded comrade.

End him! Or you die! His master's hated voice filled his mind again, driving him on.

Cearon twisted around, stabbing up at the griffin with the speed of desperation. The griffin swung his blade to counter, but he was too slow. Cearon felt his sword point pierce through the plate armor with the grind of metal on metal. The blade stabbed deep into the griffin's gut.

The griffin made no noise—no cry of pain or surprise. He only looked down at the sword protruding from his side. Cearon jerked the blade back and rolled wobbly to his feet. The griffin fell to his knees.

"Blade!" the harpy shrieked.

The gremlin charged at Cearon as he tried to escape.

Let me flee! Magic poured from his hand. A wall of telekinesis slammed into the gremlin, who managed a look of surprise before he crashed violently into the wall of Aetha.

Run! Run before they can finish you! Cearon's strides were hobbled from his wounds, but still he was fleet of foot. His adrenaline hid his pain from him as he sprinted across the barren land. He rose up over the hill, sensing no one chasing him. He staggered over the crest of the hill, his ears hearing the griffin calling after him, but his mind taking no note of it. *One foot and then the other: do this enough, and you will reach freedom. No rest. Run.*

Pain slowly wound its way through his body. He grit his jaw as his ribs throbbed, his shoulder bled, his head spun with dizziness, and his shin screamed with agony every step he took.

Curse them! How much must I endure for this fight for freedom? He glanced at the blood oozing from his shoulder.

The potion! He stopped, dropped to one knee, and reached for a potion on his belt.

No! He growled with frustration as he realized the fragile glass vial had shattered in the fight. He mopped up as much of the solution off his tunic as possible and rubbed it on the cut. He felt it burn, and he clenched his knuckles as the wound slowly scabbed over. He tore the strip of drenched cloth from his tunic and tied it about his wounded shin. He clenched his jaw and suppressed a hiss of pain as the wound slowly healed.

Hopefully that will keep me from bleeding to death, he thought before he began his hobbled jog again, wincing with every left step.

I must keep going. I must escape. If they catch me, I die. I do not have what it takes to fight them again—not even one. He gave a desperate grunt of pain as he forced himself on. The hurt let him know he was still alive, still fighting, and it was a small price to pay for what he was fighting for.

Jinx ran to Blade and caught him just before he fell from his knees to the ground. His face grew white, and fear bulged his eyes.

"How ... how dire a wound?" He managed to say through gritted teeth.

Jinx looked down at the bloody hole in his armor. It was about two inches wide.

Dire, she thought, but said, "It looks minor. I ... I think you will be fine."

"You are a terrible liar," Blade grunted.

"I need to take off the breastplate to see how bad it is," she said. *It must be bad.*

As gently as possible, she unlatched the heavy steel-plated armor and pulled it off. He wore a satin undershirt beneath the armor; sweat had drenched the top, and blood was already soaking into the bottom from the cut in his side. *Oh no; it is deep.*

Blade kept his eyes on the sky. "Well?"

"Keep your hand here," Jinx said as she put Blade's hand over the wound. "Press down, and staunch the blood flow. I shall get Demon—he should have stabilized Freeze by now. He will heal this. He can stop the bleeding, at least. Shadow, help him ..." she said, glancing over to Shadow. He was lying with his shoulders propped against the wall, his jaw hanging open and his eyes glazed over.

No! Not you as well!

"Shadow!" she screamed as she ran to him. His face was bleeding from nose and chin, but she felt his heart throbbing strongly in his breast. She exhaled her relief.

"I will be back soon with Demon—I swear it," she said as she took off flying toward the cave. Over the rush of the wind, she heard Blade shout to the assassin.

"Run, you coward! I swear to it, if I survive, you will die by my sword! I swear by my honor, by my comrades, and by the gods!"

Demon flew clumsily through the air as he followed Jinx back to where Shadow and Blade lay.

Why must I be the only one of us with a grasp on healing magic? If only Mer were here. Demon landed even more clumsily than he was flying, falling into a lump of leathery wings and armor. With great effort, he picked himself up and staggered over to Blade. *I am already so fatigued from healing Freeze's wounds. What hope have I here?*

Blade's face was pale, and blood was pooling around him. He shivered now and again, clutching his hand to the wound as tightly as his feeble strength allowed. Shadow lay unconscious, still against the wall.

129

"Can you heal him?" Jinx gasped.

"I ... hope," Demon responded, panting even harder than she was.

If I don't, he dies, he thought grimly. With that thought, Demon pulled Blade's nearly limp hand from the wound and put his own hand over the gash. Demon focused every ounce of his mind as he strained any last energy he had into Blade's wound.

Slowly, agonizingly slowly, the blood flow slackened. As the wound scabbed over, Demon collapsed onto his back, too tired to do anything more.

Did I do it? His exhausted mind tried to recall. *I think I did. I can't remember,* he thought as sleep gently filled his mind

"Blade, are you well?" Jinx asked softly.

Blade swallowed hard and gingerly ran his fingers along the scab. "It's ... it's stopped, I think."

"Do you need anything?" Jinx asked.

"Water."

"I will get some. Hold tight." She took off and flew toward the cave.

Shadow moaned as he lifted himself up, clutching his temple to fight the throbbing. "What ... happened?"

Blade didn't respond. He lay there, looking toward where Jinx flew.

"The assassin!" Shadow cried, the memory flashing back to him. "He is escaping!" He scrambled to his feet, and caught sight of Blade and Demon lying side by side, blood pooling around them.

"Gods!" Shadow cried. *No! Do not be dead! Not because I fell unconscious! Please, gods be merciful!*

He ran to them and knelt. Relief flooded through him as he saw them both breathing and Blade's eyes open.

His soul froze as he saw the monstrous scab. *Oh, no!* "Are you well, Blade?"

"He ... he caught me off guard. I will be fine. Just superficial. A light cut," Blade muttered, staring at the sky the entire time.

"That's good," Shadow said, trying to hide the tremors of rage in his voice. "I will be back. I have a superficial cut of my own to inflict." Without glancing back, he followed the assassin's tracks.

Drops of blood mingled with the blades of grass, and the tracks betrayed Cearon's unsteady footsteps.

He is weakened. Shadow looked up at rolling hills and clenched his jaw. *But his magic is still strong.* His throbbing head was proof of that. *It won't be if I cut his throat in his sleep.*

Shadow followed the trail into the grassland, moving along at a quick pace. The trail was easy to follow. He ran through the grass, his leathery wings folded behind him and his face snarling.

A cut for a cut—it is only fair. And perhaps a few dozen cuts after that. I am sure he has well earned them. He followed the trail northeast, away from those he loved and those he knew. He forsook the Guard, forsook his friends, and forsook his king for the burning call of vengeance.

Chapter Eight

King Leon sat upon his lavish throne, his chin resting on his palm and his brow furrowed, as he brooded in silence. The guards in the room looked uneasy, fidgeting nervously in the deafening silence.

They know as well as I that they do not stand a chance against the assassin. He sighed angrily. *They will run if he shows. I cannot trust any of them, no more than Father should have trusted that traitor adviser of his ...*

The large doors leading into the throne room creaked open. Leon's eyes darted to them. *Is it an assassin?*

His eyes narrowed in annoyance as Marcus entered the room.

"Be gone, Marcus. I am in no mood for you."

"Of course not, my lord," Marcus said with that arrogant smirk of his. "I simply thought it would be poor manners to take my leave unannounced. Recent events have made this castle seem less ..." he paused as he glanced at the human guards standing around King Leon, "secure."

"What do you mean?" *I cannot trust him. I should have him imprisoned.*

"I have decided I am no longer as safe here as I should like." *Where is safer than my castle?* "I shall be leaving immediately."

"Where do you go?"

"I have a small military unit loyal to my cause—and loyal to me. I shall be staying with them."

"Military unit? What military unit? Are you attempting a rebellion?" *I will have him imprisoned for this! Yes, imprisoned and killed!*

"No. You judge me wrongly, my lord. Did I not fight loyally for your father when the elves tried to seize Elfwatch? Did I not warn him of the traitors in his midst? I am your man, sire."

He was true to my father ... "What sort of military unit is this? Mages?"

"Some. Others are sell-swords from the north."

"Elves? You bring elves into my lands after my father fought to keep them out?"

"Your father fought a single battle, my lord, and even then, it was mercenaries from the east who did most of the work. Regardless, one battalion of elves south of the forts will not be the end of the Kingdom of Shale. King Darien fought off four elfin armies that made it as far south as Syienna and Lokthea. I am sure you could do the same, my king."

"Do not mock me, Marcus! We both know I am not King Darien the Savior. The peasants call me King Leon the Meek, and elfin lords snicker my name into their goblets. Bringing them armed into my lands smarts of betrayal, Marcus." *Would he still smirk hanging from a gibbet?*

"I do not betray you, my lord. If you wish agents to attend me, by all means send them. I have nothing to hide; if I had, I would have snuck from the castle in a more clandestine manner, as others close to you have."

That smirk is unbearable when he knows something! "Who else has left?" *If you play me false, old man, you will regret it.*

Marcus looked about the hall casually. "The castle does seem short on hybrids, does it not, nephew?"

Is he mocking my choice to send them to Aetha? "I sent them; they did not sneak away. And don't pretend to be family, you're nothing more than the product of my grandfather's infidelities."

"It was not those hybrids I was referring to, my lord," Marcus said with a curt bow. "And I will remember what you said, Your Grace,"

I should have his lips cut off. His grin would not be so superior then! "What do you mean?"

"I would suggest you call for the unicorn, or the phoenix. Perhaps I am wrong, though; perhaps they have found a way to turn as invisible as the gremlin you keep. Now, without further scandal, I do hope I might take my leave, your grace."

"I am sending a spy to watch you. One false step, Marcus, just one, and my lancers will ride you down. You're a powerful magician, but you're not the match of my kingdom just yet." *That should keep him in line.*

"No, I am not," Marcus agreed cavalierly. "But my lord, as I said, you have nothing to fear from me. I am not the treacherous one in your midst. I side with you, and I fight for the cause of humanity, as you do. I have no ulterior motives stirring in my blood. Besides, had I wanted to kill you, I could have done it already." He spun nimbly on his heel and walked out of the throne room with utter insolence, and yet King Leon could only think of one thing.

There is a traitor in my midst! But who?

"Are you ready?" Silver asked urgently. "We must be out of the city before night." He stood with the four other Guard members, all of whom were wearing traveling cloaks that covered their faces, for what little it did to hide their identity. Only Howl truly looked human. Pyre's wings were the most obvious hybrid feature there, though Crash and Crunch's height and girth gave them a close second. Even Silver's hair and eyes made him stand out against the crowd.

We'll be lucky to make it halfway there, Howl thought.

"We've all been ready long before this," Crash said. He eyed the throngs of people moving through the city streets warily.

Howl knew why: *Any one of them could be a spy.*

"Let's move," Silver said. "The Trade Road should be nearly empty with the siege at Bel. If any riders come, we hide immediately." With that, they left, all of them following Silver as they headed for the west road and toward Bel.

"If any riders come upon us," Howl said, "they would obviously be the king's men, but unless they come in battalion strength I doubt they will succeed in coercing us to come home."

"Even so," Pyre grumbled uncomfortably as all the passing peasants and lords stared at his wings, "I don't relish the thought of being executed for treason."

"We hybrids have nothing to fear of execution," Howl said with a grin. "We're too rare."

Crunch chuckled. "No, we'll not be killed for this, just beaten within an inch of death. There's a big difference in that little inch, you know."

Silver shrugged as he spoke sarcastically: "Well, come now, it's not like that inch is a matter of life or death now, is it?"

Crash rolled his eyes. "That's almost sarcastic enough to be something Sting would say."

Howl looked about at the multitude of buildings surrounding them. They all paled in comparison to the grandeur of Castle Shale; their stone was roughly hewn and required mortar to hold together. The stones of Castle Shale fit so closely together that they appeared to be one solid piece, and there was no mortar between them the Howl could see.

He cast a glance down at the cobblestone street beneath

his feet. The stones were worn from centuries of footwear from the city's populace and the trading caravans. About him, water still pooled in the streets from the storm the night the assassin had come. Horse manure was left to rot in piles by the many horses carrying riders and pulling carts through the streets. He watched as a woman hurled a bucketful of refuse and sewage into the gutter of the street—not twenty feet from where a baker called out his wares of pastries and breads.

Howl curled his lip in disgust. How could they live like this? The houses all around were caked in squalor, and most of the commoners going here and there seemed bathed in dirt and grime. He found himself wishing for Castle Shale, or at least somewhere with less of a reek. The city's stench was near overpowering.

He glanced back to the castle; its outer walls still loomed above even the tallest of the city's buildings, and the top of the keep, along with its tall spires, towered above, mocking the city's quaintness. *Whoever built that was much greater than those responsible for this city.*

"Who was it, do you think, who built Castle Shale?" Howl asked, breaking into the conversation.

"Hmm," Silver mused as he glanced back at the castle. "I can't imagine it was humans. They haven't built much else that compares to that."

"Maybe it was the warlocks," Crash jested with grin. Howl cast him an annoyed look.

"Maybe the humans were once better at building things," Pyre said seriously. "I mean, if the humans of old made the Relic Sword, why couldn't they construct something like Castle Shale?"

"Did they make the Relic Sword?" Howl asked.

"I assume so. Was anyone else around back then?" Pyre responded.

Howl mused for a moment. "I guess not. Maybe elves? But why would they build Castle Shale for humanity?"

"I wonder what it would be like battling with whoever made the Relic Sword," Silver thought out loud. "Whoever they were, they would be more than capable of putting that smug little assassin in his place." The unicorn-man smiled at whatever vision he had conjured up in his head.

Crash chuckled. "Maybe it was the gods for all I know. History is for Shadow."

Crunch laughed, too. "Yeah, or maybe it was fairies, or perhaps a necromancer, or dragons, or any of those other myths. If the gods were real, where did they go? Something that powerful does not just vanish of its own accord."

"Well, whoever built that castle, it's impressive," Howl said, giving the immense structure another look.

How much of this world do we know nothing of? Crash is right: for all I know, the gods from those old myths made everything here. Howl smiled at the thought.

"I hear that Krone is even more imposing," Pyre said. "A human in the Castle told me it was carved out of a mountain, and that many strange spells are interwoven with the stonework. He told me that the walls themselves will shrug away any siege ladder raised against them, and the metal gates will bend and fold to a battering ram as easy as silk, but they repair themselves the moment the ram is pulled away."

"That's just soldier talk," Crash grunted. "No magic can do that."

What does he know of magic? Howl thought, mildly irritated. "I have heard many strange things about Krone, also. Apparently, it was one of the only fortresses that never fell to the elves during the Third Elfin War. It was besieged by an entire army, yet it held. There must be something special about it if it can do that."

"The ever gullible Howl believes yet more mere rumor," Silver said with a smile.

Howl cast him an angry glare. *There is a difference between rumor and history, idiot.*

"I've heard that whoever goes into the dungeons of Krone never comes out the same," Pyre pressed on, ignoring the tension. "There is supposed to be some kind of dark madness that lurks down in the pits below."

"Humans bend and stretch the truth as they repeat it," Crash said dismissively. "I'm sure it is dark, but some human decided his story would be more interesting if it became so dark that whoever went down there went mad."

Howl shrugged. "Say what you will. All I know is that there must be something very strange about Krone."

Pyre added: "It predates any written records the kingdom has. I'm sure there's much about it we still know nothing of."

As the conversation moved on to this and that, the buildings passed by until the five warriors had traveled over the bridge spanning the Snowmelt River. Soon they were walking through vast expanses of grassland and fertile farmland that stretched across the countryside. Normally, the road would be strewn with trading caravans bound from the coastal cities to Syienna—especially from Lokthea, the aquatic gem of the Kingdom of Shale—but the siege had waylaid all travelers bound to or from the coast.

As Syienna disappeared into the distance behind them, they pulled their hoods down and breathed a sigh of relief. They had passed out of the city without being stopped by any of the guards who patrolled the border and watched the bridge. Now their only worry was whether a company of horsemen would come charging down the road with the king's banner waving above their heads.

"I wish we could have brought our armor ..." Crunch said mournfully as he looked down at the thin layer of cloth he was wearing.

"Who, besides perhaps Shadow, would wish otherwise?"

Silver asked. "But there's no way we could have slipped away with it on."

"We might have packed it out," Pyre said.

"Have you forgotten the size of it?" Howl asked. "Or how it groans at the slightest movement? It would have been far too conspicuous for us to try to haul it all out. Besides, we can get armor from the army if we truly are in dire need of it." *And this means I am free from that clunky, uncomfortable metal suit.*

He felt free to move, dash, and dodge now. *The assassin would not have bested me if I had not been encumbered by that suit.*

Pyre frowned. "It won't be the same." He, like most of the Guard, loved the security and intimidation that the armor provided.

"Howl's right," Silver said. "We don't need it. We can slay just as many Rogues without it."

"Yeah, well," Pyre grumbled, "you don't have to fight naked then, do you?"

I hadn't thought of that. The moment Pyre ignites, his clothes will burn off.

"Well, just don't ignite, and you can keep your clothes," Silver said with a wave of his hand.

"Will you also be telling Howl not to transform? That's how I fight."

"Stop griping," Crash said sternly. "We'll get you some armor from the soldiers."

"Will we?" Pyre asked skeptically. "And what soldier will I borrow armor from that has wing slits cut into it?"

"I don't know," Crash mumbled. "Maybe one who was on the wrong side of a battle-ax ..."

"...or two," Crunch added.

"Don't worry, Pyre," Howl said. "You'll still be feared by any human out there. Even not aflame, you are unlike anything these people have fought before."

"Still," Pyre said with better humor than before, "it's more fun to fight when I'm burning."

"Eh," Crunch said with a wave of his hand. "You'll have plenty of fun. After all, this is going to be the first full-scale battle with hybrids in it. This will make history."

"Maybe even have a tapestry made of it," Crash said with a hopeful smile.

"How long do you think it will be before our disappearance is noticed?" Pyre wondered.

Not long enough, Howl thought.

"I don't know. I'm just keeping an eye on the road," Silver said, glancing back down the road toward Syienna. There was still no sign of pursuers.

"Do not worry," Howl said. "I can hear hoofbeats from a very long way off. I can smell horses from farther, if the wind is right." *I can still smell the stench of the city on the breeze, too.* He wrinkled his nose.

"We won't be missed for quite some time," Crash said.

"Castle Shale is immense," Silver agreed. "They will try to search it for us first, which will take a very long time by itself. Then they'll search the city, which will take even longer. We'll be long gone before the king even considers that we've headed for Bel."

Unless one of the people walking the streets of Syienna told the wrong person about seeing your hair, Crash's height, or Pyre's wings, Howl thought uncomfortably.

The breeze shifted, and fresh air from the hills and valleys of Syienna County blew across the road. Howl breathed deeply.

This is how air should smell! The others didn't seem to notice, but he allowed himself a broad grin while he filled his lungs again and again with the clean air.

"Why is our wolf all smiles?" Silver asked.

"The air," Howl explained. "It's fresher. It smells ... free. Wild." He took another deep breath.

Crash laughed. "Truly, a castle is no place for the untamed spirit of the wolf."

"Nor a sasquatch, either." Howl grinned back.

"Certainly not a unicorn," Silver added.

"What about a troll?" Crunch asked.

"Well, perhaps if the castle had a proper bridge for you to sit under." Silver laughed.

"I prefer scary dungeons, personally," Crunch said with a good-natured grin.

"How about the dungeons of Krone?" Crash asked.

"I am already mad," Crunch agreed. "It might be the perfect place for me."

Howl took a deep sniff of the air as the others continued to banter. The green countryside was overpowering after so long in the city. It smelled alive, as if the land itself were a living, breathing object. He wanted nothing more than to dive into it, to run free across the landscape.

"How do you think the others are doing at Aetha?" Pyre asked.

"I think there is a dead assassin to match a dead city by now," Crash said.

"One can only hope," Silver said. "Do you think they may have found the Relic Sword?"

Pyre shrugged. "Maybe. If so, we can only hope they're on their way now with it to behead Marcus."

The wind shifted once more, sending the stench of refuse swirling around Howl.

So foul! He noticed that the scent was weaker. *I suppose our distance has lessened its potency.* A thought entered his head.

"So when do you think they will give me the Sword?" Silver asked.

"Wasn't just the map at Aetha?" Crash asked.

"Well, then, they should give me the map. The gods know I'm the only one smart enough to read it."

"How about you race Shadow's mind for it? I do love watching you fail." Crash laughed at his own wit.

"I think I'll scout ahead," Howl said as he transformed into his wolfish form.

"Scout what?" Crash asked. "How much dirt the road has?"

"There is nothing up there," Silver said. "If we're going to be attacked, it will be from Syienna."

"Perhaps," Howl answered, "but one never truly knows 'til one's scouted ahead." With that, he dropped to all fours and tore away, speeding down the road as fast as he could.

This is what I am meant to be doing: running free. He felt the wind rush by his face, its scent growing cleaner every moment. He gripped the still-moist earth of the path with his claws, scattering the dirt behind him as he passed far beyond the sight of his friends.

Roads are for men. I am wolf. He turned abruptly and ran through the countryside, rising over hills, and descending down into the valleys as easily as a breeze. He darted through fields of crops, sending flocks of crows squawking indignantly into the sky. He passed through a farmer's corral as horses stamped and whinnied and pigs squealed in fear of him. He passed the animals as a young girl stepped out of the chicken coop with an armful of eggs. She screamed with fright, sending the eggs raining down about her feet as he bolted by her. *They all know to fear me, man and beast alike.*

He hurtled over the last fence of the farm, landing amid the wild grasses of the field. He ran on, feeling the tall grass sliding against his short fur and smelling the wildflowers that grew along the hills. Farther and farther he ran, the reek of the city long gone, lost in the aroma of the fields.

His muscles were warm, and his breath came in strong pulls when he slowed his pace.

I should have done this long ago. He strode to the top of a nearby hill and rose to his hind legs, looking out across the massive landscape. *The freedom that this place offers! How can I ever go back to that castle?*

But as much freedom as he now had, he still desired more. He wanted a forest to dart through, running between trees, hunting in sunlit clearings, and rising to the tops of large hills to howl his glory to the moon.

He breathed deep. *The smell of this place!*

The air had clarity to it that the city could never compete with. He took another smell and caught a strange scent. He sniffed again. It smelled like some kind of animal—sheep, maybe. He took another whiff and caught a small hint of horse and man. Perhaps there were some shepherds nearby.

Howl lay down in the grass, supporting himself on his forearms as he imagined a wolf would. He wondered if he looked as noble as he felt. He felt like the lord of the wild, looking out over the kingdom that he ruled with dignity and might. He sighed contentedly. If only he were lord of the wild. How much he loved it here. *If only I never had to set foot in a city again.*

He heard the sound of hundreds of footsteps passing nearby. He rose above the grass and saw a veritable army of sheep marching through the valley below him, with shepherds riding atop their horses, their slings by their sides and their eyes watching the flock carefully. Shepherd dogs ran about, snapping at the heels of sheep and barking now and again to keep the sheep moving together.

He heard the patter of small feet as a dog came running up the hill toward him. It was a small creature with shaggy, black-and-white fur. It halted several paces away from Howl and growled menacingly, baring its teeth.

You dare growl at me, the lord of the wild? Howl thought, amused. He growled back, baring his teeth at the dog. It barked; Howl roared. Instantly, it turned with a terrified whimper and ran with its tail between its legs. *It would seem I am victorious.*

"Werewolf! Werewolf on the hill!" a shepherd cried out as he pointed toward Howl. Another shepherd whistled to the dogs, which ran up the hill toward Howl with selfless loyalty. The shepherds spurred their horses up the hill, fitting stones to their slings as they rode.

"Protect the sheep!" another shepherd cried out.

Fools, Howl thought as the dogs approached, barking fiercely. The first one sprang at him, and he swatted it aside with a clawed hand. Another vaulted at him, and he grabbed it by the throat and threw it bodily back toward the other dogs. He roared fiercely, snarling and preparing his claws for more combat.

The dogs, brave though they were, would not attack this strange creature that fought with the ferocity of a werewolf and the intelligence of a man. They circled around him, barking and whining but making no move to attack.

The shepherds rode up the hill, spinning their slings above their heads. They loosed their stones at Howl with remarkable accuracy. Howl grinned to himself as he easily deflected the stones away from him.

"The werewolf wields magic!" a shepherd cried out with dismay.

"It's an abomination! It wears clothes like a man!" another shouted.

"I am no abomination," Howl growled wolfishly at them.

"It speaks!" another shepherd cried out in terror. "He is the lord of the werewolves! Slay him!"

Though Howl was enjoying his feeling of power, he had no desire to kill these shepherds, annoyed as he was at their determination to kill him just for who he was. His scimitar remained at his belt, concealed beneath his cloak.

The shepherds urged their horses onward; swinging their slings as if they were mace-and-flails, they charged Howl. Howl was loathe to retreat, but he would not slay the shepherds. He dropped to all fours and ran back toward the road.

The shepherds galloped after him, leaving their dogs behind; only the horses had a chance of keeping pace with Howl. Several shepherds loosed stones as they rode, and Howl, with his back turned to them, did not see. A stone struck his back leg. He yelped in pain as he tripped and tumbled across the grass.

The shepherds bore down on him, and Howl rolled aside to dodge a rock swung at him like a flail. He growled in anger. *Why won't these shepherds leave me be? I am trying to escape without ending their wretched lives!*

The shepherds formed a circle around Howl. One spurred his horse forward, charging at Howl. Howl roared, baring his teeth and flattening his ears at the horse. The horse spooked, shying away from the predator its master was urging it toward. The shepherd cursed his mount as it stomped wildly at the ground. Howl rushed toward it with a snarl, and it bolted in fear.

Howl sprinted away, fleeing through the gap the spooked horse had made in the circle of shepherds. Stones fell around him, but Howl watched this time, deflecting or dodging any stones that would strike him.

The shepherds gave chase and soon were running just behind Howl.

Howl growled in frustration. He was doing everything he could to avoid them, but they persisted in trying to kill him. *If it is their wish to fight, so be it!*

With a howl, he slowed suddenly so that he ran next to a horse and its rider. He leaped, pounced upon the rider, and knocked him from the saddle of the horse. The rider cried out in fear and the horse whinnied in terror as Howl and the rider descended to the ground.

Howl and the shepherd struck the ground, moving so fast that the two tumbled together before they came to a rest. Howl jumped on top of the man, his clawed hand raised above his head, ready to slash.

The shepherd stared in terror at the wolf man who held him pinned to the ground. Howl glanced up at the man's horse, which ran fast in the opposite direction. He looked at the other shepherds, who were turning to come to the aid of their comrade. Howl looked down at the shepherd again. *His life isn't worth taking.*

He ran forward again, charging the other shepherds riding swiftly at him. He leaped up at one of them, rising above the head of the horse. The rider swung his sling like a club at Howl, but Howl deflected it aside with magic before he pulled the shepherd from the saddle. Howl landed on top of the shepherd and instantly broke into a run, speeding away from the others. The shepherds stayed to help their fallen friends while Howl made his escape.

He ran back toward the road, fuming.

These humans, these creatures I am trying to protect, seem to be the creatures most determined to kill me! He growled in anger as he felt the bruise on his leg forming. *Perhaps I should have used the scimitar on them.*

He made it back to the road, passing through several fenced farms to do so. Following his nose, he quickly found the others, who had grown silent after the long miles they had trudged through.

"Hello, Howl," Pyre said as Howl skidded to a halt in front of them. He transformed back into a human as he rose to his hind legs.

"Hello," Howl said darkly as he fell into step with the others.

"What's gotten you into such an awful spirit?" Silver asked. "You were grinning like a fool when you left."

"I'd rather not talk about it," Howl said. "Let's just get to Bel."

"Well, we have some news that should cheer you up," Crunch said happily.

"Oh?"

"We've decided to name you the leader of this expedition," Crash said.

"Only because they knew I wanted the title," Silver glowered.

"You'll be leader next time," Pyre assured him.

"I did all the planning," Silver said, not placated in the least.

"And next time, Howl will do all the planning, and you'll get to lead," Crash promised.

"Why me?" Howl asked.

Silver spoke bitterly. "Because they knew I wanted it, and they're sadistic beasts."

"It's good for you," Crash said. "You can't have everything you want all the time. You'll get spoiled."

"I have no problems with being spoiled."

"I do." Crunch laughed. "You unicorns have it easy enough as it is."

"Hmph." Silver made no other response.

Crash and Crunch continued to talk avidly, with Howl and Pyre chiming in occasionally. Silver, however, held a stony silence for the rest of the day.

"The sun is beginning to set," Crash said, noting the red horizon they now marched toward. "We should make camp soon."

"My feet hurt," Crunch said, casting a glance down at the blistering appendages.

Silver sneered. "Someone got soft in the castle."

"I think I did," Crunch said as he gingerly bent down and rubbed a blister on the back of his foot.

"Don't you wish you had Rocky's skin sometimes?" Pyre asked. "It must be nice to have stone skin."

"It must be nice to be able to engulf yourself in flame," Silver said as he walked off the road. "I suppose a small valley will serve as an excellent campsite."

"Act like it all you want; you're still not the leader," Crash teased.

"Well, who's following whom?" Silver asked grumpily.

This is stupid. "Just let him have it," Howl said impatiently as he walked after Silver.

"Fine. Pyre, you're leader," Crash said. Pyre rolled his eyes as he left the road.

"What do you say, Pyre? Want to get a fire going?" Crunch asked as they crested a hill and descended into a valley veiled from the road.

"No fires," Howl said. "By now, the king should have agents combing the roads for us. Let them search without us giving off a beacon." *Does the idiot want to be captured?*

"And that, Silver, is why Howl should be leader," Crunch said.

"I'll keep that in mind."

"Who takes first watch?" Pyre asked.

No one said anything. No one wanted to stay up while the others slept.

"I'll take it," Silver said. "I'm not tired. I suppose unicorns have more endurance than other, weaker species."

"We'll see who's weaker than whom when we get to the battle, little horsey," Crash said as he patted his battle-ax.

"We will," Silver answered. "When you get perhaps two kills to my fifty, I'll try not to gloat too much."

"You may be the one who's staying awake, Silver, but you're dreaming," Crunch said with a laugh.

And with that, they had a quick, if somewhat cold, meal of dried meats and fruits before settling down for the night. One by one, they dropped out of conversation and into sleep while Silver watched over the makeshift camp. A fog settled in as the moon rose, casting its pale light over the countryside. It was a full moon.

Chapter Nine

Cearon walked through a forest of large trees as he staggered onward, up into the Grey Mountains. All around him were towering evergreens that reached up toward the heavens from the rocky, dry terrain. Beneath the trees, small glimpses of winter could still be seen fighting stubbornly against the warmth of spring. Patches of snow lingered here and there, clinging to life in the shade of the trees by hiding from the sun's rays that cascaded down from the blue sky. Streams of dappled sunlight poured through the treetops, lighting the particles of dust in the air into a golden mist.

A limp was evident in Cearon's step, and he gripped his shoulder while he ambled doggedly forward. The blood on his tunic had turned brown, and his ribs ached with every breath, but he forced himself on. *Keep going. You fought three hybrids and survived. You'll not let pain be your downfall.*

He had been ambling on for three days without any real form of rest.

I am so tired, but I have it. He grinned triumphantly despite his fatigue. Tucked into a hidden pocket was the map. It was the key to everything he fought for. The first, most important step of his quest, he had taken, and his footing had not slipped.

All this pain will be nothing but an unpleasant memory when I am done. After I see this through, I will be glad to have paid this price. I will be glad to have paid ten times this price.

Once I am done, I will have a home, I will have a family, and I will be free.

He paused and closed his eyes as he focused his mind and searched the land before him. His senses had weakened with his wounds, but he knew the camp was nearby somewhere.

What I do not know is if my companion was trustworthy. He hoped he had not been abandoned, but he knew it was unlikely that Harold had stayed. *Why wouldn't he run? What loyalty does Harold have for me?*

But to his surprise, he sensed the camp, and he sensed Harold there as well.

He waited all this time for me … but why? What did he see in me that inspired him to stay? Why not run when he had the chance? What inspired him to follow me to begin with?

Cearon opened his eyes again. *I will find out soon enough.*

He half walked, half staggered through the ferns and brush until he reached the camp. It was set in a small clearing between the trees with a single shaft of sunlight settling on it. A campfire burned smokelessly, and over it cooked two young rabbits. Their charred flesh made Cearon's stomach roil as thoughts of the burned men of Aetha flashed through his mind.

Around the fire were numerous potion-making implements ranging from a simple mortar and pestle to fragile glass flasks. Herbs, roots, leaves, and other ingredients of the trade were piled in an orderly fashion on stone slates around the fire.

Cearon walked into the camp, stepping between two makeshift beds—only one of which was filled.

The man lying in the bed dozed lightly. He had brown hair that he had grown out long that was pulled back into a neat topknot. He wore green mage robes, and he had stubble forming around his chin from his long exposure to the wild. He had a curved nose and would perhaps have had a nearly rugged appearance, had he not clearly been so pampered his entire life. His skin was pale, and his hair was well kept, combed, and washed—even out here. His fingernails were just beginning to grow out again after years of being well manicured, and his hands bore no calluses whatsoever from any physical labor, be it with plow or sword. His skin was pulled taut over his bones; he was remarkably skinny, looking almost as if he were starving.

"Miss me, Harold?" Cearon grunted with a nudge of his foot to the sleeping magician.

Harold sat up with a jolt and pulled a knife from his sleeve, his eyes large with fear until they rested on Cearon. He sighed in relief and sheathed the knife.

"Thank you," Cearon said. "I have had enough steel for now." Harold quickly threw his blankets off.

"Cearon! You are back! I was beginning to fear the worst." The man was no older than twenty-two, though he often acted wiser than his years. Harold looked over Cearon's wounds. "And it seems my fears may have been well founded."

"The Royal Guard. Marcus must have told them where the map was. I didn't expect them there so soon. The winged ones held the city when I came. They almost got the map, too. The gremlin was holding it when I came to the room."

"How many did you kill?" His tone brooked no doubt that Cearon had killed.

"None," Cearon answered honestly, sitting wearily on the other bedroll. "Well, maybe one. I stabbed the griffin ... because, I ... I was desperate. They forced me. Know that I don't want to kill anyone, Harold—especially not hybrids. Them, at least, I can respect."

"You will have to kill before the end of this," Harold reminded him.

"Maybe. Well, definitely. That doesn't mean I must now, or that I must try to." He paused for a moment, looking down at his wounded shin. "You will hardly believe the help I got. In the city, ghosts appeared—real ghosts." Harold's face revealed his skepticism. "They said they knew of my blood and wanted to atone for their pasts by helping me. They attacked the Guard for me until I took the map. Then they mobbed me, filling my mind with ... visions. Like some dreams I've had, but from the other perspective—visions of being burned instead of burning. Somehow, the gremlin made them kneel before him—"

"Maybe they were his illusions. I have never heard of ghosts in anything but legend. I heard the gremlin dabbles in strange magics."

"Maybe ... but then why did they help me?"

Harold shrugged. "I was not there. I could not say."

"After that, three of the Guard trapped me. I barely survived. I kept this, though." He tossed the map at Harold's feet triumphantly.

"This is it!" Harold scooped it up excitedly. "The locations of the Relic Sword! Lokthea, Trake, and ... Krone." He said the last name uneasily. He looked at Cearon. "Krone? That's suicide. There's no place better defended in the whole of the kingdom."

"I know," Cearon said wearily. "Perhaps we will figure something out. Perhaps we will die then and there. As of now, I am too tired to think so far ahead. We shall simply have to deal with that as we come to it."

"Do you think it would be best to start moving?" Harold asked. "It's more than possible that my father may be tracking me. I've been uneasy for the past few days. I won't go back, Cearon."

"I need sleep. I cannot go much farther without some rest and some healing. Give me three hours, and I'll go," Cearon said as he lay on the bed gingerly. The ground was hard, and he still hurt ... a lot.

Sleep will help with that.

"All right," Harold said, somewhat disappointed. "But

we need to leave quickly. Marcus has many resources at his disposal, more than you know. I don't want to be here when they come."

"I know," Cearon said. "I do not underestimate him, but I haven't a choice. I need rest"—he pulled the blanket up over him—"and healing." *Take the hint.*

"I know. You cannot be too sleep deprived to fight," Harold said nervously. "But all the same—"

Cearon cut him off gruffly. "Heal me, or let me sleep."

"Right!" Harold said, and his face turned a shade of red. "You need healing." Cearon nodded where he lay. "Well, what happened to that potion I gave you?"

"Shattered in the fight. I used as much as I could get from my stained tunic, but that was barely enough to even scab my shoulder. Have any more?" *The stuff burns like dragon fire, but it's better than these hurts.*

"Only a little. I didn't think to make any more. You had enough with you to heal you ten times over. I gave you a whole vial."

"Well, the little I actually used worked well enough. I'll take whatever you have."

"All right. It will take me a while to cook up some more, though—hours. That's if I can gather all the ingredients. Some of them are rare. I have this, though." He handed Cearon a small vial. Cearon drank it down without question.

Hopefully I can sleep through the burning. He already felt the warm liquid spreading from his stomach to his wounds. It hurt, but he knew it was a good pain.

"Fine," Cearon said as he rolled over. "We will deal with the rest of my wounds later. I need sleep more than anything. I'm strong enough to live through this."

"You're fortunate," Harold said. "I wish I could fight and be as strong as you. I wish I could be a hero. My body is weak."

"My strength comes with a curse," Cearon said grimly.

"Would you be willing to bear it? To never be able to show anyone your eyes for fear that they will try to kill you?" *Now be quiet, and let me sleep.*

"Do you wish that your blood were not blessed?" Harold asked.

"Blessed? I hardly feel blessed. My life has been tragedy after tragedy because of this ..." He paused. *You will never know what I have endured. How could you? You hate your father, but you did not see him cut down before your eyes.* "Yes, sometimes I want to be normal. Sometimes, I want to walk up and speak to someone without them staring at me in fear. Sometimes, I want to walk up to some woman and her children and show them my eyes without them running in terror. Sometimes, I want a woman to love me for longer than it takes her to look upon my face. Yes, sometimes I wish my blood was not cursed ... but what does it matter? I am what I am, and nothing shall change that."

"There is not a day that goes by that I would not trade you without hesitation," Harold said. "And the things that you do! Any man would be willing to part with his dearest treasure to be able to do half what you can."

You are a fool, then—and so are the rest of these men you speak of! "Good to know," Cearon mumbled as he rolled over and pulled the blankets tighter around himself.

My wounds do hurt too much for sleep, he thought grimly.

"And I would be willing to give even more," Harold muttered to himself as he moved to his potions equipment.

Is that charred flesh? The smell sent the images from Aetha through Cearon's head again.

"Your rabbits are burning," Cearon grunted.

"Oh, no!" Harold exclaimed as he rushed to the fire and pulled the spit from the flames. "Well, lunch is ruined." He tossed the rabbits into the surrounding brush.

"You'll survive," Cearon said, his voice just barely rising

from his prone figure. "Put the rabbits in the fire. They could attract bears."

"Oh, right," Harold said as he went to collect them.

He knows nothing of survival. He treats this place like a castle garden. Cearon sighed. *He'll learn, I suppose, and he survived this long. He'll make it another few hours ... I hope.*

Shadow stood behind a tree, listening carefully to the conversation. The one called Harold grew silent as well as Cearon.

Cearon? Shadow pondered the name. He knew the elfin language well, and he knew what Cearon meant. *Cursed one. Why is he cursed? What is different about his blood from Harold's?* Shadow frowned. *I don't like knowing so little about my enemy.* Whoever this Cearon was, he clearly was no ordinary man. *Ordinary man or not, he'll still die when a blade pierces his heart*—or at least Shadow hoped.

He heard Harold moving around the fire, rummaging among his possessions. Slowly and with the utmost caution, Shadow peered out from behind the tree. He had coated his face with dirt and grime and put twigs and brush through his hair. He was nearly invisible against the background of the forest, and the spells he had cast over himself only augmented the effect. Just as long as he made no sudden movements, he was all but invisible.

He looked over the camp. *Two beds in a small clearing with a fire between them. Easy enough.* He saw Cearon lying, most likely asleep, and Harold stood with his back to Shadow. He looked familiar, even from behind. *Where have I seen this man before?*

It doesn't matter. He is sided with Cearon, therefore he is an enemy. Shadow ran a thumb along the blowgun in his belt. *One poisoned dart, and he will crumple to the earth, dead in a moment.* He furrowed his brow. *But the poison is not powerful enough—no poison is. He would have time to cry out and wake Cearon, and even in Cearon's wounded state, I doubt I could defeat him. He is too powerful a magician, and his blankets and hood will protect him from a dart. That leaves the traditional knife work, I suppose.*

Shadow drew his dirk silently. Slowly, ever so slowly, he crept from behind the tree, pulling himself low to the ground as he cast another spell of hiding over himself. He crawled closer, stopping only when Harold turned his way. Harold probably wouldn't have noticed Shadow anyway as he busily mixed plants and herbs together. *Focus on your task, mage, and it will be over soon.*

Shadow felt his nerves rising on edge as he grew nearer the camp.

This is it. I can end all this madness now if I just keep patient, and fortune doesn't conspire against me.

"A little dragon's fern ... crush with heart fruit ... mix with just a drop of unicorn blood ..." Harold muttered to himself as he worked deftly with his potions. He clearly knew what he was doing; his fingers moved with the deliberate speed of an expert.

Shadow came to the edge of the clearing. His dirk was ready; the point seemed to beg for Harold's neck.

"All right," Harold muttered. "Let that stew for a little while." He wiped his brow as he breathed a deep sigh. "What I really require," he mused as he stroked his chin, "is salamander leaf. I saw some ... did I? Down by the stream, I think." He answered himself as he looked over toward Shadow. Shadow held perfectly still. His heart raced as his grip tightened on his dirk handle.

Don't you dare see me!

"Yes. Yes, I think that's where it was," Harold said, stepping toward Shadow tentatively.

Shadow felt his whole body tense. If this gaunt man saw

him, it would all be over. He prepared himself to spring. If he could move quickly enough, he may be able to dispatch the mage before he could scream.

"Or was it by the funny-shaped rock?" Harold muttered to himself, stopping in his tracks. He turned west and took a step away from Shadow. Shadow relaxed. If Harold left, Shadow could slip a knife between Cearon's ribs and leave before Harold came back.

Spares me the spilling of innocent blood, Shadow thought gratefully.

Harold took several steps away, looking into the forest as if it would answer his questions.

"No, it was by the stream," he said conclusively and took three quick steps, accidentally bumping Shadow with his foot.

Shadow rose up and grabbed Harold with an iron grip, spinning him around so that his back was to Shadow.

"By the gods!" Harold exclaimed in terror. "Cearon! Intruder!"

Shadow held the dirk close to Harold's neck and gave a nervous sigh as Cearon threw the blankets violently from himself and drew his sword, rising to meet the attacker.

"Release him!" Cearon said with authority on his voice.

"How the tables do turn. Now it is you who demands me to release a mage," Shadow said, buying time as he looked for an escape.

"You would be wise to do it."

"I would be a fool," Shadow said. "He is my leverage—for now. Drop your sword, or I'll slit his throat."

"Slit his, and I slit yours. He's my leverage, too. As long as he's alive, so are you, but should you kill him, you kill yourself."

He knows this game, or else he is unnaturally quick while sleep deprived.

"I'll not hesitate to kill him," Shadow said. "Drop your sword."

"You are a fool if you think for a moment I will fall for that."

"So we have a standoff. As long as he lives, I live, but if I kill him, you will cut my head from my shoulders. Quite the impasse."

"Quite," Cearon agreed humorlessly.

"So, while we are here, we might as well get to know one another. I am Shadow."

"A gremlin by any other name is still a gremlin."

Shadow just smiled in response. "And you are Cearon, and this is Harold. Good afternoon to you."

"How did—" Harold began.

"He's been listening to us, Harold."

"Harold," Shadow murmured. "It's a weak name to go with a weak person. But where have I seen you before?"

"You seem angry." Cearon spoke mockingly. "It couldn't be from my second stunning victory against three of your Royal Guard, would it? Or should I count it five of you to fail this time? That's how many of you I counted in whole."

"Is that bloodstain on your tunic the victory you speak of?"

"Do not worry about that, I will survive … but will your griffin friend?"

The memory of Blade lying in his own blood flashed. *Don't you dare jest about that!*

"You will suffer greatly for him," Shadow promised.

"So he did die, then. So now there are thirteen of you. Before the end, every one of your Guard will be lying in their blood—and Marcus, too."

"Well, you missed your chance. He was at Castle Shale when you broke in."

"I am saving him for later," Cearon answered.

Liar. Your body language betrays your surprise. "Or is it closer to the mark that you are simply afraid of him?"

"I fear no man, but you fear me, don't you? Why else would you hide behind my friends?"

"You are not so powerful as you believe," Shadow answered. "The Royal Guard will stop you. You barely escaped with your life against three of us; imagine all fourteen."

"Thirteen," Cearon corrected.

"Your fight is nothing more than a delusion," Shadow informed him. *For all I know, he is right: it might be thirteen.*

"So is your hope. You will not leave here alive." Cearon took a step forward.

"Stay. Even your mastery of magic could not stop me before the poisoned tip of my dirk pricked your friend's neck. It is tragic, Harold. This blade was meant for Cearon, but it will take you without complaint. Besides, there will be poison enough to kill him as well."

"Stand there as long as you wish, gremlin. Your guard will drop, and I will be ready." Cearon unexpectedly sat down as he spoke.

"Well, then, I'll just have to kill him now, won't I?"

"Another empty threat? Let me show you how to make a threat. Should my friend die, no more will I fight nonlethally against your friends. You have seen me fight. Every time I slash the face, I could have stabbed the neck. Every time I slash through armor, I could have dug the blade deep enough to kill or maim. Every time I stab, I could kill right then and there. Should he die, I guarantee you that your friends will weep because of your stupidity."

Shadow was silent. *That is not an idle threat. He could have killed me in the courtyard.*

"Nothing to say? No attempt at a witty remark? My words must have cut deeply. You heard those words; now hear these. We are not enemies. Our enemy lies to the north, past Krone and Queenstown. Our enemy marshals beneath the king's very nose, in the king's very castle, and yet the king sees nothing. Release my friend, and I swear by whatever honor I have that you will leave here unharmed to defend the king you swore to guard."

"Can I trust the word of an assassin? You have no honor."

"I am no assassin," Cearon said angrily. "Who have I assassinated? No one! I am not an assassin; I am a freedom fighter."

"I don't care what you call yourself. I do not trust you."

"How long must we stand here?" Harold asked.

"However long it takes ..." Shadow began, absentmindedly pulling the tip of the dirk away from Harold's neck. Harold popped his foot back and kicked his heel into Shadow's groin. Shadow gave a small gasp of pain and slightly loosened his grip. Harold pulled away, but Shadow grabbed him again and was about to pull him back when Cearon struck like a thunderbolt. A powerful wave of magic blasted both of them, knocking the two apart. Shadow struggled to his feet and brought his defense up in time to see Cearon's sword smack the dirk from his hand.

Shadow struck out with his other hand, but Cearon blocked it and attacked with another wave of telekinesis. Shadow felt the breath knocked from his lungs as the magic crashed him into the ground.

"Run!" Cearon screamed to Harold.

Shadow rolled over and spread his wings wide, trying to fly away.

I must escape! He will kill me. Cearon leaped after him with fantastic strength. He easily jumped fifteen feet and tackled Shadow back to the ground. *How did he do that?*

Shadow elbowed Cearon hard in the ribs as they fell to the ground. Cearon grunted with pain and grabbed Shadow in an embrace that trapped Shadow's arms to his side. He rolled them to their feet and hurled Shadow bodily into a nearby tree.

Shadow fell to the ground. He tried to rise, but Cearon posted his foot on Shadow's back, shoving him back to the ground. Shadow rolled over, twisting from under the boot. He threw himself at Cearon with his wings. Before he was halfway up, Cearon kicked him in the chest, throwing him back into the ground.

Shadow's head snapped back on impact, and his world erupted into a world of bright lights and stars as the back of his head smacked into the tree. His knees gave out, and he crumpled to the ground.

Cearon grabbed him by his hair, punching and elbowing his face mercilessly.

I will be unconscious soon, and it won't hurt anymore. Shadow felt his senses begin to fail as the punches and elbows rained down upon him.

Is this where I die? He thought of Jinx and all the things he wished he could have said to her; he thought of Sinister and all the things he wished he could have yelled at him. *I don't want to die.*

Each blow seemed to grow fainter and fainter, as if his mind were being pulled away from his body. It was like watching himself being beaten from a distance.

Suddenly, a guttural, animalistic roar filled the air, followed shortly by another. Shadow was only half aware of it in his beaten state, and he saw through blurred vision the silhouette of a great beast flying through the air.

Is it a dragon? Do they really exist? Is it like the old myths? Has it come to save me with a god sitting on its back?

"Drake!" Shadow heard Cearon cry urgently. "Run north, Harold!"

Shadow's vision began to clear, and he saw not just one drake, but five flying circles overhead. They had strange lumps on their backs—no! They had riders on their backs!

The riders were smaller than the average man, and they had bows drawn to full length. They were loosing arrows at Cearon with surprising accuracy for how fast they were moving. Cearon diverted the arrows with magic, sending them spinning through the air away from him.

Cearon roared as he magically threw a rider off of his mount. The rider fell to the earth with a sickening crunch and lay still.

"Kchatal!" one of the riders called. Gold and red cloth ribbons streamed from his shoulders and from his helmet. His great drake swooped down toward the earth, its wings opening low to the ground as it swept toward Cearon, talons and teeth ready. The drake beat its wings as it hurtled toward Cearon, guiding it and its rider through a narrow passageway through the trees.

Cearon charged the drake, his feet kicking up pine needles and dust as he drew his blade. The drake now flew just a few feet from the ground; its mighty wings creating a small hurricane of foliage and pine needles behind it as it raised its great talons to grab Cearon.

Still Cearon charged, his shimmering sword flashing as his arms pumped through the air.

He is mad! Shadow thought groggily. *This beast could devour him whole!*

The drake reached out with its talons, groping for the lone man. At the last moment, Cearon threw himself down and slid beneath the drake's talons. The shimmering sword flashed as it streaked through the air, carving through the talons and the gut of the creature alike.

The drake roared in pain, twisted awkwardly in the air, and crashed into the ground. It rolled over its rider several times before coming to a halt among a fog of dust and the hail of pine needles that had been tossed into the air.

Cearon ran back toward the fallen drake with speed unlike any Shadow had seen in a man. Miraculously, the rider had survived and pulled himself out of the saddle in a daze. He saw Cearon charging; he raised his bow, notched an arrow, and let fly. The other riders followed suit, but Cearon threw the arrows away with ease. He vaulted through the air—easily fifteen feet again—and ran his sword through the rider.

The other riders cried out in dismay and loosed arrows with a new vigor. Still Cearon blocked the arrows as he picked up the fallen rider's bow. He loosed an arrow, and it homed into one of the drakes. The beast gave a roar of pain, but kept flying. Cearon sent another arrow forth, and it struck the same drake—this time, right under the wing, penetrating into the chest and through the heart. The drake tried clumsily to keep flying, but it fell to the earth with a great thud, killing its rider with it.

The two other riders both cried out, "Gama! Gama!" and flew up toward the clouds. Cearon loosed a last arrow, and Shadow heard another drake roar in pain, though it kept flying.

Cearon watched them fly away for moment and then tossed the bow aside. He grunted in pain and mumbled something Shadow did not catch as he looked down at his leg. An arrow was sticking out of Cearon's calf, and blood dripped on the ground.

"Cursed elves!" he yelled as he snapped the shaft, leaving the arrowhead in his calf.

He looked at Shadow with rage in his eyes. He stormed toward the gremlin

"Did you bring them? Have you allied yourself with those scum?" Shadow tried to get to his feet, but a strong wave of magic shoved him back down with a painful thud. "Where is their camp? How far away are they?" Cearon screamed. "How many riders are there? Talk!"

"I don't know! I've never seen them before!" *He really has gone mad!*

"Liar!" Cearon screamed. "They serve your true master, don't they? Where is their camp?"

"I don't know," Shadow said honestly.

"Elves don't care who they kill; they'll take me or you. Perhaps I should leave you tied to a tree. They like easy kills, and I could use something to delay them ..." Cearon's voice trailed off. "Where are they?" he asked more calmly, but no less malevolently.

"I have never seen them before. The king never mentioned elves, and he certainly never mentioned drakes. By the gods, they haven't been in the Kingdom of Shale in force since King Darien's wars!"

Cearon looked at him, his eyes unbelieving. "You lie. You led them to me; you are working with ... with those murderers! You're no better than they are to me!" he said as he raised his already bloody sword up to strike. He stared down at Shadow, hatred in his in eyes beneath the black hood, but his hand did not move. There was a long pause, and Cearon remained motionless.

"Haltera! Haltera esh chens joalt!" Shadow heard a shrill voice cry out. He looked past Cearon and saw dozens of elves marching forward. They were all just over four feet tall and had the elves' pointed ears protruding from their helmets. They wore dark armor edged with some golden metal, and behind them waved red and gold banners depicting a snarling dog with drake wings flanking it on either side.

They marched toward Cearon in rank and file. The front row had large block shields that covered most of their bodies and short, stabbing swords. The second and third row had smaller shields and long spears that reached past the front row, making a wall of spear points. The final row was a row of archers, who were already notching arrows to their bows.

"Saved by your allies," Cearon said. He magically threw a small log toward the masses of elves and sprinted toward them.

"He's suicidal," Shadow said to himself as he went to pick up his dirk.

However, it seemed Cearon knew what he was doing. The log knocked a hole in the first few rows of elves, opening a way through the spears and shields. Cearon charged in headlong, dodging spears, deflecting swords, and cleaving through armor as he roared with battle rage. With a blast of magic, several elves went spinning through the air. A second blast scattered others like sand beneath a wave. Suddenly, Cearon sent fire roaring from his mouth into a group of elves, consuming them in flame as the elves broke apart and fled in terror.

What magic sends fire from the mouth?

More drakes flew in overhead, bellowing savagely. Their riders loosed arrows down toward Cearon regardless of the elves around him. Cearon blocked the arrows heading toward him as he let loose another torrent of flame onto the last elves fighting around him. They could take no more, and they routed in terror, dropping their weapons and holding their shields over their backs as protection from Cearon's flames.

A drake landed in front of Shadow, and the elfin rider motioned him to follow. He took to the sky with Shadow close behind. Shadow glanced back and saw Cearon running north, blocking arrows, and firing some arrows of his own from a bow he had taken from a fallen drake. It wasn't long before even the drake riders pulled their monstrous mounts away and flew after the remnants of the scattered and defeated soldiers. Shadow could see well over twenty dead elves lying among the trees below, as well as four drakes.

Who is Cearon, and what man can defeat an entire formation of elves alone?

Shadow followed the drake and its elf rider up into the clouds, his mind pouring over what he had just seen. He had witnessed mages conjure up fire before—Silver did it often— but he had never seen it done like that. All the mages he knew called forth fire from their palm, where every offensive spell Shadow knew came from.

But Cearon spewed fire from his mouth. What kind of magic is that? Who is this Cearon? Why does he fight so fiercely against the Kingdom of Shale, and what is the mystery of his blood? Shadow was certain that Cearon's blood held all the answers to his questions.

But today, I allow Cearon to flee. I must discover who has led these elves so far from their northern homelands.

Chapter Ten

Howl found himself in a dream. A thick layer of mist hung all around him; it was so thick that he could barely see a foot in front of him—though, somehow, he knew that behind the fog was nothing but endless, unchanging landscape.

He heard a long howl off in the distance and turned to face it. There it was again, and again … no, that one was different. Howling came from all around him. Louder and louder rose the din, until it seemed as if Howl's entire existence was nothing more than the howling of wolves.

There is pain in their calls, he realized.

Through the thick mist, Howl began to see shapes moving in the fog—dozens of black creatures darting in and out of sight. Howling came from everywhere. More creatures, more howling.

Without warning, it stopped. Howl looked around, waiting. He knew they would come to him.

I am their lord. He looked down. He, too, was werewolf.

Out of the mist, a lone werewolf walked toward him, its feet patting the ground silently as the mist swirled about it. Mist billowed from its nostrils with each breath, and its black eyes stared fiercely at him. Howl felt no danger.

I am his lord. He knows it. He stood patiently and waited for the creature to approach.

Howl could smell the werewolf; it was a familiar smell. The werewolf paused, smelling the air for Howl's scent. It circled Howl, sizing him up with smell and sight. It made one full revolution before it stopped and sat down in front of Howl. It let out a long howl that seemed to split the sky. The fog rolled back as more werewolves appeared from the mist. Walking toward him from all directions, the creatures were silent, intent, and hopeful. The moonlight fell softly on their dark eyes as the mist dispersed, revealing ever more werewolves. The familiar smell filled the air.

This is my pack. These are my people. The werewolves pressed in around him, sitting as close to him as their numbers allowed. They looked bemusedly at the sword strapped to his side and the clothes on his back. It was as if he could hear their thoughts.

Why do you wear man-cloth? Why do you wield man-steel?

As the werewolves sat and stared, the fog vanished completely. The moon appeared in the starry sky, and miles upon miles of land lay before Howl. The wolves sitting around him were as uncountable as the stars, filling the land with their presence. Howl stood upon his hind legs. They remained seated, watching him, like peasants before a king.

Howl unstrapped his sword and dropped it to the ground. He ripped and tore at the cloth man had fitted him with, shredding it to tatters as it fell from his body. As he did, a sense of the wild flooded through him.

Here I belong. The human thoughts of logic and calculation left to be replaced by the savage thoughts of the pack; he reveled in them.

Suddenly, he heard a yelp, and another, and another. He saw a werewolf fall amid the group with a cry of pain. Another werewolf beside him stood up with a pitiful whine and an arrow in the back. His eyes stared mournfully at Howl before he fell with a heavy thud.

The savage wild within Howl's mind filled him with utter rage. Snarling fiercely, he searched for something to maul.

More yelps and whines filled the air, along with the whistling torrent of arrows. Arrows seemed to fall from everywhere.

Howl noticed a large cliff rising behind him that seemed to have appeared from nowhere. Atop the cliff, dark figures were etched against the starry night—dark figures with bows!

With a roar of rage, he turned to the werewolves, expecting them to leap up and charge the intruders, but they didn't. They sat where they were, a sad look in their dark eyes as arrows rained down on them.

Human logic and calculation came back to Howl.

I must stop this slaughter, or I will lose my pack. His clawed hand grabbed his scimitar, and he charged the cliffs with a roar.

He climbed up the rocks with speed he had not known himself capable of. The hard stone cut and bruised his hands, but he did not stop. He had no room in his head for pain—only the pack.

He vaulted over the top of the cliff, his scimitar ready. The dark figures saw him, but did not react. They continued firing arrows at his brethren.

Howl fell upon them savagely; he attacked with sword, claws, and teeth. Dozens died before him, but their numbers were beyond count. Every one he killed left hundreds more untouched. The dark figures gave no cry of pain as he ripped through them; they only collapsed to the ground.

Howl continued to carve through them with werewolf ferocity, but so many remained. At last, one of the dark figures notched an arrow to his bow and took aim at Howl. Howl saw him and ran toward him with sword raised high. The arrow struck Howl in the chest with a thud. Howl felt it, but the pain seemed distant, clouded. He struck down the dark archer, but another one turned and aimed for him.

The second arrow thudded into his stomach, and a third went deep into his back ... and then a fourth, and a fifth, and a sixth. He fell to the ground and watched as his blood pooled around him. The dark figures gathered around him and stared down at him where he lay dying, their merciless human eyes dark in the moonlight.

Howl let out a low growl as they stood watching him bleed.

I would kill you all if I could!

From the ground, he struck at them, but they stood too far away for claws or sword to reach. He heard the twanging of bow strings as more arrows were launched at the pack.

Howl felt the life leaving him, and the sky grew darker and darker. In a last act of frustration and desperation, he howled. He felt the noise start in his lungs and rise from his throat. The piercing howl seemed to explode from him and blanket the entire land with its call.

"What the—?" Silver cried out in alarm as Howl suddenly leaped up in his werewolf form; the air rang with his wolfish call.

Crash grabbed his ax and rose, ready to fight. Pyre drew his sword as he cried out in surprise, pushing himself up with his wings. Crunch rolled onto his feet and, still dazed from sleep, mistook a lone tree for an enemy. His club thundered into the trunk as bark, leaves, and seeds flew.

Howl drew his scimitar with a roar. Pyre, Silver, and Crash formed up back to back to back, waiting for enemies to charge from over the hill. Crunch, recognizing his club was embedded in a now badly wounded tree, yanked it out and stood with his back to it; it tilted with a groan and fell on his head. He brushed it off with his great strength and an angry grunt.

All that could be heard was heavy breathing and a low growl emitting from Howl. Minutes passed by like hours.

Pyre, Silver, Crash, and Crunch looked around at each other in confusion.

What is the danger? Silver wondered.

"What is wrong, Howl?" Silver asked. Howl didn't make a response. He looked toward the breeze, still growling. He sniffed the air, and his lip pulled into a snarl. Slowly, he transformed back to human, though his face still snarled.

"Howl, what's going on?" Pyre asked.

Something is terribly wrong here, Silver thought. *What is going on?*

Without any sign of acknowledgment to his comrades, Howl sprinted through the grass, scaling a hill swiftly and effortlessly. The others tried to keep up with him, but none of them could match his speed, even in his human form. Pyre took to the air, and the others followed the direction he flew. They crashed through the brush and shrubbery blindly.

This is not good. What has happened? Silver glanced up at the full moon. *Oh, gods, don't let him have gone feral!*

Silver, Crash, and Crunch came to the crest of a tall hill and saw Howl below. Before him, two men with bows stood over a creature lying on the ground with five arrows piercing it; one of the hunters fired a sixth into its prone form. Howl stood unnaturally still about ten feet away from them, staring down at the stricken creature lying in the grass.

"What happened here?" Silver called out to the men as he descended the hill. Pyre landed next to Howl. The men cried out in alarm.

"Who are you?" one of them asked.

"Speak. Now," Pyre said coldly.

"We … we shot this werewolf," one of the men said, giving an apprehensive glance to Howl, whose shoulders rose and fell in rage. "We caught him lurking outside our barn, and we tracked him out here. Stuck him full of arrows while he was stalking a deer. He's a good-sized one, too."

Don't do anything stupid, Howl! Silver thought as he approached.

"His head will certainly look fine over the fireplace, that's for sure," the other man said. "We heard another werewolf howl not far from here, and while we were riding this afternoon, a group of us saw the werewolf lord! He spoke and used magic! There's a bounty out for him. You fellows want to help us? We'll split the bounty half and half."

"My pack ..." Howl said under his breath.

"What?" the first man asked.

"You search for the werewolf king?" Howl asked abruptly.

No! Silver thought.

"Yes. Would you like to join the hunt?" the other man asked.

"Search no further." Howl's eyes darted from the fallen werewolf to the two men standing over its carcass. Small hairs grew over Howl's body, and his jaws jutted out like a werewolf's.

"Stop him!" Silver cried out. He sent a wave of magic at Howl, and to his shock, Howl blocked it. Pyre reached toward Howl when Silver's telekinesis knocked him from his feet.

"The lord! The lord is here!" the two men cried out as Howl bore down on them.

No! "Stop him!" Silver shouted to no one in particular.

Howl ran the first man through with his scimitar. He pulled the blade free and spun around at the same time with a spinning slash at the second man, beheading him.

Howl stood, breathing deeply with rage, his whole body quivering.

"What have you done?" Silver asked almost disbelievingly.

Howl didn't look at them. He stared out at the night. The wind blew softly through his short, gray hairs, and the moon shone bright above his head. He looked slowly down at the dead werewolf. It had long, dark black hair, and its snout was longer than Howl's. It had the same clawed hands and half paws, half feet that Howl had, and the same black eyes as Howl, though they were glazed over in death. The werewolf's blood pooled alongside it in the grass, mingling with the human blood still spreading.

"What's happened to you, Howl?" Pyre asked as he rose from the grass.

Howl turned and looked at them. His eyes looked mournful as he slowly returned to his human form. He stood there and looked down at his bloody sword, at the bodies of the two men he had killed, and finally at the dead werewolf.

"I'd do it again," he said solemnly as he walked back toward the camp.

The four others looked at him in disbelief as he walked by. They didn't say a word—just watched Howl go into the grasslands.

What happened while he was scouting? Silver wondered. *Is this even the same Howl?*

Howl disappeared over the hill, but his comrades still stood in shock. Finally, Crash spoke.

"I'm going to make sure he is well—and that he doesn't do anything like that again." He jogged back toward the camp.

Howl walked slowly toward the camp. He took a side trip to wipe the blood off of his blade on the grass. He sat down for a moment, thinking about mankind with distaste. He heard the others running past him toward the camp. Undoubtedly, they were trying to find him.

I didn't do anything wrong. Those men deserved it.

He would understand if the men had killed the werewolf because it had attacked them, but they had killed it simply because it existed: much like the humans in his dream and the shepherds he met in the fields.

The others will think the wild took my senses, but it hasn't. I knew what I was doing. I know justice when I see it.

That werewolf had been purposely avoiding the humans. It had hunted the livestock in the barn and fled as soon as it had seen humans. If it had been hunting humans, it would have attacked the men; instead, it had left to hunt deer. Not all werewolves were man-eaters; they were just all treated as if they were.

Man is more vicious than most werewolves—more murderous, anyway. If anything, werewolves should kill man on sight for their own protection, not the other way around. He sighed and walked back toward the camp as he sheathed his sword with a halfhearted spin.

When he returned, only Crash sat in the valley, awaiting him. Crash watched Howl closely as he sat down and lay back on the ground, as if he intended to sleep.

"What happened to you?" Crash asked in his usual blunt way.

"I was defending my species," Howl muttered.

"By killing the other half of your blood? Both creatures in that field were your species," Crash said.

He was ready for that answer.

"Where are the others?" Howl asked, avoiding the subject.

"They're looking for you. Where do you think? We don't want you to murder another—" Crash began.

"It wasn't murder," Howl interrupted.

"Then what was it? You killed those men in cold blood, and why? Because they had killed a werewolf that had been hunting in their village! Is that a crime to you?"

"It was justice! That wolf wasn't hunting humans! Had it been, it would have attacked and killed both of those curs! It was hunting cattle, and they killed it! It wanted to survive, but I suppose humans have grown so important that it is their decision whether a beast is allowed to live or not. If the wolf had been aggressive, I would have let them live, but it wasn't, and they killed it anyway! They got what they deserved."

"Justice? Gods, Howl, can you hear yourself?"

"Yes," Howl growled and then paused for a second. "Crash, what would you have done if you saw a sasquatch dead on the ground in front of you, and the humans responsible were gloating in front of you about their kill—about how they intended to make a trophy of its head?"

Crash looked at Howl for a long time. Finally, he spoke. "I ... I don't know."

Silver walked over the crest of the hill. "He's back?"

"And back to his senses," Crash said.

"I never left my senses," Howl corrected angrily.

"Your clear senses told you to murder, then, did they?" Silver asked skeptically. "They sound like poor senses to me."

"They told me to kill. That wolf hadn't been hunting humans, but they still killed it. I treated them the same way I'd treat any murderer. It was justice."

"You murder and then dare call it justice???" Silver asked furiously. "What you did was murder," he shouted, pointing an accusing finger at Howl. "What they did was self-defense!"

Howl sat up, his face flushing with rage. "If it had been a unicorn lying in the grass with arrows riddling it, would it have been murder then?"

"Yes, it would have been murder! What do you think? I'm no executioner, and neither are you! You don't have the right to cast sentence, much less carry it out! Life is not something you can take away on a whim, Howl! Think of their families! Think of everything they will never get to do! And if you are so offended by their treatment of werewolves, why do you justify their fears with your actions? You want them to treat werewolves kindly, yet you kill them as a werewolf? You are a fool, Howl."

Howl paused. He looked at the ground with his arms crossed.

I hate it when he makes sense. "Let's just get some sleep," he said as he lay back down on the ground.

Chapter Eleven

Cearon and Harold walked north, following the Silent Road, though they remained far from it; they avoided walking along roads unless absolutely necessary. The roads were far too exposed to the sky and far too predictable a route to travel, as Freeze had thoroughly proven to Cearon in their last confrontation. And now, more than ever, they were trying to avoid any kind of fighting. With Cearon's growing list of wounds, they were by no means prepared for even a short skirmish.

Harold looked worriedly at Cearon as the other man limped quickly, stepping over branches and stones even still with a warrior's grace.

"All right. We've put enough distance between them and us. Let's make camp, and I'll begin working on the healing potion."

"No," Cearon grunted. "A bit farther ... just a bit." He looked over at Harold's concerned face. "They'll scour the land for us, Harold. We can't be here when they do."

"How much longer can you walk on that foot?"

"As far as I need to," Cearon said stubbornly. He cast a quick glance over toward Harold. Cearon quickly looked away as he saw Harold still watching him. "I'll survive; I've lived through worse."

"But why push your luck?"

"Because I have to!" Cearon snapped angrily. Harold jumped with fear, and Cearon regretted his words. "I know you're trying to guard my health, but we must escape before we can worry about healing."

And hopefully it was only something you carried that they tracked us by, not you yourself. But why would you run from the elves if you were the one who betrayed me to them?

They walked along in silence, with Harold moving at an easy pace and Cearon struggling forward with his many wounds. His shoulder had reopened and was spilling blood down his tunic's arm once more, his ribs hurt worse than ever, and his calf made him wince with each step.

"Who were they?" Harold asked, suddenly breaking the silence.

"Elves. I don't know whose, but I'd wager Marcus's. This isn't the first time he's used them; he captured me with them." Cearon's jaw clenched with anger. "They killed my parents and my sister." *If you are a traitor, you will already know this.*

"So that is why you hate them so." Harold spoke in genuine wonder. *Or perhaps he is well trained.*

"It is an old vendetta I have—one I shall probably carry with me to my grave."

"What do you think they are doing here?" Harold asked.

"Maybe looking for the map," Cearon said. "Probably looking for me. I don't know. What I really want to know is who led them down here. I've not heard of elves delving this far south since the Third Elf War. I wish I knew how many of them there were and how they tracked me."

"At least it seemed as if you dispatched a great group of them with relative ease," Harold said, his voice filled with admiration. "And you conjured up fire like no mage I've ever seen before."

Did they tell you nothing about me? Maybe you didn't betray me. But the timing was too convenient! I would have been sleeping were it not for that gremlin.

"It's a gift I was reborn with," Cearon said. "A useful one, but not an invincible one. I can't burn through their shields or armor. If they had formed a shield wall, I'd have been in trouble. Luckily, most of their number seemed new to battle."

"How much farther before you rest?" Harold pressed again.

Why are you so intent on stopping?

Cearon paused and took a deep breath. He looked up at the sky; he sensed and saw no drakes. He closed his eyes beneath his hood and focused. He paused for a long moment before he spoke again.

"There is a cave to the east. It should hide us well enough. It's between those two large pine trees. See them in the distance?"

Harold looked through the forest, but there were many large pine trees in these mountains. "Not ... specifically," Harold admitted.

"Those two." Cearon pointed to two pines set on top of a large mound of rocks. Most were small rocks, but they all seemed to be set around one, massive rock that rose triumphantly above the rubble at the top of the mound. Sure enough, just where the large rock rose was a small entrance to a cave.

"I see."

"Go to it. Get it ready as best you can; I will follow at my own pace. No fires," Cearon added.

Harold stopped running as abruptly as he had started. "I need a fire to make the potion," he protested.

Or to make a signal? "Can you make it smokeless?" Cearon asked.

"Easily. There's plenty of dry wood around," Harold said, glancing about him at the piles of sticks strewn about.

"I still don't like it, but if you must, then you must. But if it smokes, I'll kill you." There was no humor in Cearon's voice. "Now go."

Harold looked at him cautiously and then ran ahead toward the cave.

Cearon still limped along. He looked down at the wound in his calf and sighed angrily. He felt stupid for not seeing that arrow. There were only a few archers, but that arrow somehow had eluded his senses. He looked down and saw blood running down his boot into the dirt.

Great! I am even leaving a trail of blood to follow. Harold doesn't need to be a spy for them to find me. His circumstances seemed to grow worse and worse. He looked down at the rest of his body. *My tunic sure isn't like it used to be, but combat does have a funny way of ruining clothes.*

He continued to limp on, ignoring all pain. He had been trained to ignore pain—trained by the very people he so hated now. To be fair, he had hated them before, but not nearly as much as he did now. As soon as he found out it had been his trainers who had allied themselves with elves—even the elves who had murdered his family—his hate for them had simmered with an intensity that would have made the Fire God proud.

Elf.

The very word seemed to burn within his mind as his thoughts strayed to his younger days. The elves had seemed so large then; they had stood a couple feet over his head.

He remembered his father fighting, his mother screaming, and his sister crying.

Or was that me crying? He couldn't remember—probably both—but he did remember the sound of a child wailing. His father had nothing but a scythe from his field, and the elves had full armor, spears, and swords. Some had fought his father while others looted. His father had stood between the elves and his family. Cearon smiled proudly. His father had been a lowly farmer, but he had been brave. He had died a hero defending his family.

Father. Cearon thought about the word. All he really

knew of his father was that his father had been strong. Four elves were dead at his feet before their numbers had brought his father down. He remembered seeing the first elfin spear pierce his father's side, followed by another, and another, and soon his father lay in a pool of blood as the elves stepped over his body.

They struck down his mother first, and then his sister. One was poised to slay him when a voice had called for them to stop, calling to them in coarse elfish. He remembered cruel elf hands gripping his arm tightly; they had thrown him into a wagon with several other children, each of them wide-eyed with terror. An impossibly tall man in dark armor had stood next to the wagon, inspecting the children. Every child flinched under the man's cruel eyes, and he had laughed at their fear.

Cearon could only watch helplessly from the back of the wagon as the elves looted and burned the only home he had ever known.

"Cearon?" Harold called from the mouth of the cave as Cearon approached the mound of loose stone. Cearon snapped back to reality.

"Huh? What?"

"Are you all right?" Harold asked with concern.

"I'm ... fine ... I just need some rest." *And to be sure of your loyalty.*

Harold looked at him for a while, trying to figure out what Cearon wasn't telling him. "Are you sure?"

Cearon brushed off his concern. "How's the cave?"

Harold paused a moment longer before responding. "It's good—big enough for us both, and it even has a hole at the top to give us sunlight and a chimney. I think it might be an old bandit hideout."

"Perfect," Cearon said as he scaled the mound. The loose rock was difficult to climb, and Cearon was tired, but his will was set like iron. He didn't stop once until he was at the mouth of the cave, panting from exhaustion and pain.

"What do you think?" Harold asked. Cearon looked into the cave. It was rather large—about nine feet across in both dimensions and five feet high at its tallest point. A beam of sunlight poured down in the corner, lighting the cave well—and, as Harold had said, providing a perfect chimney. As long as Harold didn't make any smoke, they would be invisible from the air.

"It's perfect," Cearon repeated, looking around at the rocky walls and floors. He saw a patch of moss in the corner to lie down on. It was actually rather comfortable—more comfortable, even, than most beds he had made for himself in the wilderness. He laid his head on an especially springy patch and closed his eyes slowly.

"I'll start working on the potion. You sit tight and try not to get into a fight with any—" Harold began, but he saw that Cearon was already asleep. Quietly, he exited the cave.

Shadow followed the elf rider on his mount for ten minutes of rapid flying. He watched the vast forest passing by underneath him; the foothills of the mountains flattened as he re-entered the grassland that stood between the Grey Mountains and the Colossus Desert. He saw gazelle grazing here and there, leaping gracefully about the tall grasses.

In the distance, he spotted dozens of tents and could just make out the shapes of drakes, both flying and tethered to the ground. Small groves of trees stood here and there, but the majority of the landscape was taken up by large grasslands, with the Grey Mountains looming over them like a titan of rock. In five minutes' time both he and the elf rider had landed among the tents. Hundreds of elves ran around doing various jobs: some cutting down what little wood was available, others cooking over strange pots, and others sharpening and tempering the many weapons in the camp. The rider motioned Shadow to wait and entered the largest of the tents.

He soon emerged with an incredibly tall man in black armor. On his hip was a large mace and flail, which was also black, but for a bone white handle. His armor groaned as the stride of his mammoth limbs carried him high above the well-trampled grass. His helmet covered his face with a black mask that snarled evilly. His black cape billowed behind him as he moved, and so great was his weight that Shadow could feel his feet thudding into the ground with each step.

As he approached, Shadow was surprised to see that this man dwarfed him by more than two feet; he was even bigger than Crash by nearly half a foot. The man had to look down at Shadow from the demonic mask with the sun glaring behind him as it moved into the western sky.

The man's deep, harsh voice boomed out from beneath his armor. "Who are you?"

"I am, uh, Shadow," Shadow said nervously. "A member of the ... um, Royal Guard. I was ... was fighting with the assassin ... uh, Cearon ... before ... the elves flew in."

"You were fighting him alone?" the man asked, his voice sounding almost amused. "Well, you have courage, at least, despite your timid speech. I am Gourn, but most simply call me the Emissary." Shadow was about to ask why, but the dark figure cut him off. "Don't ask."

Both became silent. Shadow felt more awkward than usual.

"There's food in there if you want it," the Emissary said, pointing at a tent.

Is he trying to get rid of me?

"Sounds ... nice," Shadow said as he turned to walk toward the tent.

"Yes. I must speak with my allies. I shall call upon you soon," the Emissary said, almost as if it were a warning.

"Sounds … nice," Shadow repeated. *And just who are these allies? And who are these elves, and what are they doing so deep into the Kingdom of Shale?* Shadow didn't like their presence here or their tall leader in the least. Armed elves had not been past Queenstown since the rule of King Darien the Savior.

He walked toward the mess-line and glanced over his shoulder. The Emissary turned back and re-entered his tent. Shadow quickly ducked behind a tent and pressed himself flat on the ground, casting a spell over himself that made him nearly invisible. He glanced around to see if anyone had seen him.

No one.

The elves were much too busy doing their jobs to notice much of the world around them; they didn't even greet one another as they passed each other on their way to this job or that.

Shadow crawled forward, slowly approaching the tent that the Emissary had retreated to. It wasn't long before he pulled himself next to the large tent, and with one more glance about him to ensure his secrecy, he gingerly lifted the side of the tent and put his ear next to it.

"He seems trusting enough," the Emissary said to someone inside the tent.

"Which one did he say he was?" said a woman unknown to Shadow.

"He called himself Shadow. Apparently, he was working alone."

"A member of the Guard working alone? That can't be … unless … did he look like a gremlin?" the voice asked.

How much do they know about the Royal Guard? Shadow thought in surprise.

"I don't know. What does a gremlin look like?" the Emissary asked, his annoyance clear.

"You're useless," the woman's voice said scornfully. "It's a dark creature with leathery wings. Looks almost like a gargoyle. Did they teach you nothing in the west?"

"Be mindful of whom you are speaking to, Bloodmane," the Emissary said vehemently.

"I don't fear you, Gourn. Besides, the master favors us more than he favors you. You're expendable; we are not. You be mindful of whom you speak to. Now, where is this Shadow now?"

"He went to the mess tent," the Emissary answered. "Should I have him poisoned?"

"No, don't be rash. He might prove useful to us. I'm sure he knows much that we could use."

"Like what?" the Emissary asked.

"I don't know, but the master told me not to have any Guard members killed unless he ordered it directly. Keep him in the camp until the master arrives; detain him if necessary."

"All right," the Emissary said. "That's easy enough. There could be one problem, though."

"What?"

"What if he's not alone? There's something about his story I don't trust. He claimed he alone was doing battle with the traitor. The Guard would not be stupid enough to send only one man to battle with him; I would be hesitant to fight him alone, let alone this little man with a dirk. There must be others with him. Detaining him could be throwing a rock at a hornet's nest."

"You, Gourn? Facing the traitor alone? Don't make me laugh. But if the Guard rat is only armed with a dirk, it must be the gremlin. It makes sense that he is alone; he is the Guard's assassin. They probably hoped he would kill Cearon while he slept. Why the Royal Guard waste time with that stupid gremlin, I'll never know."

"Your speculation doesn't solve my problem," the Emissary angrily.

"You have a full battalion of elves at your back," Bloodmane said. "The guard can't fight all of your seven hundred swords."

"I still don't want to die. They may have enough power to kill me if they all attacked. I'd probably bring down about half of them ... but still, even I'm not invincible."

Bloodmane laughed mockingly at him. "Just put all the riders in the air, and if anyone does attack, use them to hold the attackers off while the rest of the army surrounds the Guard. I doubt anyone's with him, though."

"I'd rather not find out the hard way," the Emissary grumbled. "I'll inform you when he's detained."

It's clear he does not enjoy speaking with her. Well, whoever these people are, at least there is division amongst them.

"See that you do," Bloodmane said icily.

Shadow heard the Emissary's heavy footsteps walk out of the tent. Shadow lifted the tent a bit more and peeked under the fabric. The room was poorly lit, with only one torch by the door. There was a table with a small crystal on it, a bed, and several bookcases. Other than that, the room was empty, but for one elf standing at attention by the door. One poisoned dart later, and the elf fell in a crumpled heap.

Shadow pulled the tent flap up and rolled into the tent silently. He cast one of his spells on the door; it would tell him if anyone were approaching. He walked up to the table and inspected the crystal. It was a small, jagged crystal of milky white, no bigger than the size of his fist. He knew what it was: a speaking crystal. They were designed for communicating over long distances with another who had a crystal.

So whoever this Bloodmane is, she is a long way away. That is good to know.

He pocketed the crystal, and turned his attention to the papers scattered on the table. Most were maps, and were marked with positions of different military units. He saw that the Royal Guard was listed specifically on its own among the garrison of Castle Shale. The rest were lists—some of items, others of soldiers—and sets of orders marked with a strange seal. The seal was a long sword wreathed in flame. He would have to find out who it represented back at the castle.

Shadow smiled at how easy this was; this Gourn must be a fool to have his command tent so poorly guarded. He folded up the papers and stuffed them in a pocket. Then he grabbed a blank piece of paper and a feather pen. He went to the bookcase and took down names of books he thought important. He wanted to know what these people were studying.

The Magic of Unicorns, Various Mythical Creatures, Potions and Pastes, Siege Tactics, and *Spells of Destruction* had all been added to Shadow's list when a cold sensation went down his spine. Someone was approaching the door. He pulled up the tent wall and rolled out just before he heard the Emissary's heavy footsteps enter the tent. He heard a roar of rage, and the ground vibrated as the Emissary stormed back out of the tent.

He must have discovered my theft. Shadow smiled pleasantly to himself. *Now I just have to make sure he doesn't catch me.*

Shadow looked to the sky and saw dozens of drakes gliding through the air, scanning the surroundings as they circled the camp.

Can I outrun these drakes? Perhaps in a sprint, but their enormous wings would make them nearly impossible to outdistance. He had a better idea.

He waited patiently for a drake to swoop down low, being ever mindful of the Emissary scouring the camp for him. He could hear the giant man's heavy footsteps stomping about the camp and heard him roaring in elfish, ordering soldiers to aid him in his search. Shadow looked behind him. He could see an elf soldier looking through tents, dangerously close to Shadow's position. The soldier moved from tent to tent, getting closer and closer to Shadow; it was only a matter of time before he would stumble across the Guard assassin. Shadow looked up at the drakes; they were still too high. He looked back at the soldier and slowly got his blowgun out.

He put a poisoned dart in it and placed it to his lips. Just as the soldier opened another tent flap, Shadow let the dart fly; it found its mark in the unfortunate elf's neck. The elf gave a small gasp of surprise before his eyes rolled up and he fell in the tent. Only his feet were visible, jutting out from under the tent flap.

Shadow gave a sigh of relief before his adrenaline spiked again. He saw the Emissary himself moving down the same row of tents the elf had moved down, coming ever closer to Shadow and to the elf's dead body. Shadow knew neither dart nor throwing knife would be able to pierce his dark armor.

The Emissary threw open tent flap after tent flap as he zigzagged down the row of tents, often checking the spaces between tents. Shadow pulled his dirk out in preparation; he would have to end this quickly. He knew exactly what it would take: a sudden leap and a fierce knife-thrust to the opening at the Emissary's neck, hopefully finishing the fight before it began. However, Shadow knew the moment the Emissary fell that every elf in the camp would come charging after him. He took a deep breath and readied himself as the Emissary drew yet closer.

Shadow gave one last glance skyward; his heart leaped. A drake swooped down, coming in just a bit lower than it should have. Shadow smiled at his fortune.

He flew into the air, and before the rider had a chance to react to him, Shadow had buried the tip of his poisoned dirk in the elf's neck. The Emissary roared with rage.

He sees me. Shadow swooped the drake down and hurled the elf's body down toward the massive man. It landed dead on the mark, striking the Emissary on the chest with enough momentum to knock the massive man to the ground.

An elf guard following the Emissary with a bow pulled an arrow from his quiver and began to notch it to his bow; Shadow hurled a throwing knife as fast as he could. The darkened blade embedded itself in the elf's shoulder—luckily for the elf, as Shadow had aimed for his neck. The elf cried out in pain and dropped his bow.

Shadow dug his heel into the drake's side. It gave a small grunt and flapped its mighty wings faster, lifting it and Shadow high into the air as Shadow tugged at the reins, turning the large creature north. The air whipped by as Shadow sped toward Castle Shale with his drake mount. He glanced back and saw that the Emissary had thrown the elf's body off with ease and was now trying to get the attention of the elf riders high above. However, they were busy scanning the horizon; they flew so high that few heard the Emissary's roars, and none cared about a lone drake flying away, for there were many scouts among their number. Shadow sighed in relief. This certainly hadn't been his most seamless escape, but it would do.

Chapter Twelve

Silver, Crash, Crunch, Howl, and Pyre walked in stony silence on their way to Bel. Still they were surrounded by uncounted miles of rolling hillsides covered with farms, vineyards, and rolling pastures. However, it was clear that they were not far from Bel; smoke rose ominously over the horizon, and the land here was oddly silent. Birds did not sing; no travelers wandered the roads; and shepherds and their flocks were nowhere to be seen. Farmers did not stir from their homes, and their stables were empty. The air held a threat, as if the war goddess herself had settled down among the hills and valleys.

To make matters worse, Howl had taken to suddenly departing from his friends, transforming into a werewolf, and running into the countryside without so much as a good-bye. The others were uneasy at this, remembering all too well the events of the previous night. Out of fear of another murder, Pyre took also to following Howl from high in the air. Howl quickly noticed. In response, he sprinted across the landscape, seeking to lose his pursuer; though Howl's feet were quick, he could not outrun Pyre's wings, even in the open landscape.

And so Howl was contained and guarded, much to his irritation, for his heart did not desire blood, but rather to sit quietly alone atop a hill and think deeply about his recent deeds. His mind was a tumultuous sea of doubt; though his anger for humans still burned, Silver's words had touched him.

While Pyre chased Howl across the land, the others kept their march toward Bel. As they drew closer, the sounds of battle could be heard echoing through the hills. The sound of steel clanging against steel; cries of victory and agony; and occasionally a strange rumble rolled over the hills that seemed to shake the earth to its very foundations.

Though the hybrids were confident in their abilities, their anxieties grew as they moved ever closer to the din of battle. Silver gripped his sword nervously, and even stalwart Crash shrugged his ax tensely from shoulder to shoulder. Though none were strangers to combat, this was the largest battle they had ever even been near. Silver's mind flashed back to what Halifin had once told him during training: No one was invincible. All it took was one lapse of attention or one stray arrow, and even the mightiest of warriors could fall.

Every now and again, Howl and Pyre would return, both out of breath from trying to outpace the other, and walk silently along with the group. However, Howl would always soon transform again, and with an irritated groan from Pyre, the two would again begin their battle of speed over the grassy hills.

It was in this fashion that the group marched the rest of the way to Bel, arriving just as the sun descended into its sleep below the horizon. The sound of fighting had long ceased when they approached the outskirts of the army's camp. Howl and Pyre were still roaming about the countryside, and so Crash, Crunch, and Silver were the first stopped by the night watch.

"Halt!" a guard demanded from atop a dark hill that rose next to the road. A large circle of torches surrounded the camp, lighting a ring around it where the hidden sentries could keep watch for any spies seeking to gain entrance to the camp. Through the light of the torches, the hybrids could see tents innumerable standing upon the hills surrounding Bel, lit by the odd torch, cooking fire, and a few tents from within by a forge that even in the night hours was sharpening and making new weapons. The camp was for the most part quiet, but for the hammers in the late-working forges.

"We come in peace," Silver said, hearing the noise of a bow pulled taut.

"Who are you, and why are you here? Have you not heard the king's decree that these roads are off-limits to travelers?" the guard called out from the darkness. Not only did the torches light the land around the camp, but their light also made the surrounding darkness seem yet more dark, concealing the sentries within it.

"Do we look like mere travelers?" Crash challenged, pulling his battle-ax from his back and stepping farther into the light, showing his sasquatch features.

"Not sure that's helping, Crash," Silver muttered.

"Who are you?" the guard asked aggressively.

"I am Crash, a hybrid of the Royal Guard. With me are Crunch and Silver, also hybrids of Castle Shale. We are sent by King Leon to help in the siege of Bel. Who are you?"

A long pause ensued as the guards considered this with hushed whispers. "Why have our leaders not informed us of your assignment?" the guard challenged.

"We were sent in secret," Silver said, also stepping into the light, allowing his shining hair to reflect the red light of the torches. "The king did not wish it to be common knowledge that his Royal Guard was weakened." Crunch, too, followed into the torchlight as Silver spoke.

"Now, who is it we are speaking with?" Crash demanded.

"The questions are mine to ask," the guard responded.

"Give us some light, Silver," Crash muttered.

"Gladly," Silver murmured back. He raised his hand, and a brilliant white flame burst to life in his palm. The sentries on the hill cried out in surprise as the nearly blinding light fell upon them, showing the hybrids four men with long bows arrayed in black cloaks. Two had arrows drawn, pointed already at Silver and Crash. In their surprise, they released the arrows, but before their missiles had made it halfway, Silver sent the darts spinning away with a wave of magic.

"You dare shoot at the King's Guard?" Crash shouted to the sentries.

"Put out the light!" they cried out. The commotion set the camp to stirring, and a drumbeat sent a garrison stationed in a nearby tent charging out, their weapons drawn.

"We do not come to fight you!" Silver shouted as the garrison charged upon them. They did not heed him and kept charging. He raised his palm and, with a powerful wave, sent them tumbling head over heels away from him.

"Enough of this!" Crash roared, his deep voice booming out into the night sky. "We are not your enemies!"

"What is the meaning of this?" a man with a billowing red cape and four of his own personal guards cried out angrily as he approached. The torchlight betrayed cold, pragmatic eyes set in a stern face strewn with scars. His shoulder-length, golden hair was pulled into a short ponytail, a long sword hung at his hip, and beneath his arm he carried a great helm with two steel horns rising from its brow.

"These men attacked us!" one of the sentries proclaimed.

"We lit a light," Crash growled at them. "It was you who loosed your arrows."

"Who are you? Speak quickly, or I shall have you slain here and now," the caped officer said as his guards helped their comrades back to their feet.

"We are hybrids—members of the Royal Guard," Silver explained calmly. "We have been sent in secret with the blessing of the king to aid your fight here in Bel, though it would seem your men are more interested in attacking us."

"Hybrids?" the officer asked, his tone astonished. He looked at the twenty or so men just now pulling themselves off the grass. "And one of you is a magician?" he asked hopefully.

"We all are, though Silver here is a master at the art," Crash said, patting Silver's shoulder with a heavy hand.

"Thank the gods!" the officer cried out. "I am called Francis. I apologize for your treatment, but many spies have tried to enter the camp. Two of them were caught just this night, thanks to the vigilance of these sentries, so do not judge them too harshly."

"It is good to find a man of reason, Francis. I am called Silver, and this is Crash and Crunch."

"All of you are aptly named," Francis said, looking from one to the other. "Tell me: how strong in magic are you, Silver?"

"I am among the best magicians in the land," Silver said proudly, and he raised his hand, letting another fireball form in his palm to illustrate his point. "Are you in need of one?"

"To put it as an understatement, yes! Perhaps you heard the rumbling during your journey? A powerful mage is with the Rogues. He hurls boulders at our soldiers, stops our arrows dead in the sky, and sends lightning at us. Three times the city would have fallen, but for him."

"What about your battle mages?" Crunch asked. "Could they not stop him?"

"They can turn his boulders from our men and stop a lightning bolt or two, but they are by no means great at their art. He makes fools of them more often than not," Francis admitted bitterly. "I myself have been sent rolling down the hill by a wave of his magic."

We shall put a stop to that easily enough. Silver smiled grimly. "He has not dealt with hybrids before. This city will fall."

Francis grinned broadly in the torchlight. "Come—I shall take you to General Nathan. He will be pleased to hear of your coming ... hopefully."

"The general is sleeping now, sir," a guard said to Francis.

"We shall wake him, then. He needs to hear of this."

The guard replied with a skeptical snort.

"Two of our companions are still out in the hills," Silver said. "One often travels in werewolf form, and the other has the wings of a phoenix."

"They do not travel with you?"

"The wolf has a love of the open country," Crash said. "He has taken many unexpected detours—to our annoyance."

"He is a werewolf. Is he ... safe?"

"More or less," Crunch answered honestly.

"That answer is not exactly comforting."

Silver vouched for Howl. "He is wild, but he knows his friends from his enemies. His ferocity will be saved for the Rogues. Trust us, you will be glad to have him." *He had better not make me a liar.*

Francis looked far from convinced. "Perhaps ..." he began, "... it would be better simply to ... well, keep him separated from the rest of the men."

"That will not go well with him," Crash said warningly.

"And a werewolf among the camp will not go well with the soldiers. Their kind are wild, dangerous, and untrustworthy; one must not take risks where unnecessary."

"He is good at heart," Silver insisted. "His humanity has control, not the wolf in him; he is no risk."

"Even so, most of these men were raised in werewolf country. They know the dangers and the potential disaster werewolves can bring; they will not be happy to let him into the camp, and even less to fight alongside him. The bloodlust of werewolves is legendary. Will he be able to tell friend from foe under its influence?" Francis asked.

"You judge him wrongly," Crunch said, scrunching his trollish features into a frown.

"Perhaps. Perhaps his valor overcomes his wolfish nature,

which earns him that much more respect from me. But for now, we go to the general. It is his decision whether your wolf stays or goes. I warn you, though: he has no love for werewolves. His father was slain by one of the creatures."

"Let him meet with Howl before he casts his judgment," Crunch said. "Howl is perhaps the most civil of us all."

Crash snorted in disagreement, but otherwise kept silent.

"I think he will be unwilling, but perhaps you may convince him," Francis said, before he paused momentarily. "But he is the most civil? I thought you warned me he was wild?"

"We all are," Silver said with a savage grin.

Francis nodded slowly. "Then may the gods help the Rogues. They shall need all the help they can get against your kind. Come, we have wasted enough time. Henry, Jeremy"—Francis pointed to two of his guards—"Go to the sentries, and tell them not to loose at any werewolves or winged men."

"Yes, my lord," the two said in unison. They instantly split, one heading one way along the circle of torches and the second heading the other way.

"Now let us wake the general. He is famous for his moods and his laziness, so expect him to be ill-tempered when he awakens," Francis said, choosing his words wisely.

Silver heard a guard mutter "Napping Nathan" into his glove. Those around him snickered.

"We've dealt with the king; I am certain we can handle him," Crash said. Francis just laughed and led them through the camp.

"The men are of poor spirits," Francis explained as they marched through the camp. Men sat about campfires with melancholy faces, many sporting wounds from the recent battles. They all looked with awe as the hybrids walked by—most staring at Crash's great height, to Silver's annoyance.

I could defeat a dozen Crashes, yet they fawn over his massive size.

"We have done what we may," Francis continued, "but that cursed magician has proven too much for us to overcome. I'm glad you're here. Not only are you a new weapon to wield, but you raise the men's spirits, too."

"How many Rogues are in Bel?" Silver asked as he looked about the tightly packed tents.

There must be thousands of soldiers here! All the men sat idle, recovering from their recent loss, but for the few who still had the heart to sharpen their blades in preparation for the next battle.

Francis stopped in his tracks. He turned back toward the hybrids, his confusion evident. "You were not told? We have been sending many reports back to Castle Shale."

"We left in a hurry," Crash said quickly.

Francis was no fool; he looked at them warily. "Is that so? Then I should have expected you would have arrived much sooner. It is a week since this siege began."

"We were hindered on the road," Silver said. "Bandits attempted to ambush us."

"And this made you many days late?" Francis asked as he began to lead once more through the grim camp, still speaking to them over his shoulder.

"One of us was wounded," Silver said quickly.

"By poorly trained bandits?" Francis questioned skeptically. "Perhaps the Rogues need not fear you."

"A lucky arrow," Silver said, his thoughts once more roaming to Halifin's words.

"And who was wounded?" Francis asked.

"I was," Crash said quickly.

"May I see the wound?"

"It was healed," Silver said. "That is what delayed us."

"Is that so?" Francis said, sounding quite unconvinced. "Your story sounds well conceived." He laughed. "But I do not care why or how you came here, as long as I may count on fighting alongside you. And if Nathan asks you why you came late, I would suggest simply saying King Leon withheld you until the situation grew dire."

"You are a clever one indeed," Silver said darkly. *I should have taken more time on the road to plan a story.* "It is a wonder you're not the general here."

"I have been blessed with a quick mind," Francis admitted. "But I prefer to lead as a captain, fighting alongside my men. To be a general is to lead from behind. Seems cowardly to me."

"This human I like," Crash said with a smile.

"I am honored, hybrid, both by your praise and your presence. I cannot stress how needed you are. Three times we have charged up that hill, and three times those black-haired warriors have sent us retreating in humiliation and disgrace.

"I swear," Francis continued, "were King Leon the Conqueror alive today, he would curl his lip in disgust at what his army has become. We are led by spoiled nobles seeking a name for themselves and foggy old men who've seen more winters than you could count. Napping Nathan isn't even the worst general. I doubt even Queen Christina the Great could have won her wars with the army like it is."

"Surely there must be some competence," Silver said.

"There is some here and there. General Roderick and General Erick know the battlefield, and I have heard good things of the Philliships. I suppose old King Phillip's ships haven't lost their edge yet."

Crash laughed. "You know your history better than I do."

Francis shrugged. "Much can be learned from the mistakes of the past; Derek the Cruel is proof enough of that."

"And what did he do?" Crash asked, clearly mildly bored.

"He brought on the Scourge, whatever exactly that was. According to legend, 'Derek's Folly' almost destroyed all of mankind," Francis said as he stepped before a massive tent at the center of the camp. Two guards with poleaxes stood before the entrance at rigid attention. As Francis approached, they barred the entrance.

"General Nathan is asleep," one guard said. "Come back in the morning."

"Jacob, I would not come if I did not have important news. Let me in," Francis said in a hard voice.

"The general has given strict orders," Jacob said. "None may enter. You know the rules as well as I do."

"Perhaps it would be best if we came back in the morning," Silver said, looking with irritation at the obstinate guard. *If only Jinx were with us ...*

"It would," Jacob agreed.

"No, it wouldn't," Francis said sternly. "These are hybrids sent by King Leon himself. We need to make a plan around them. Their presence changes everything."

"But the general—" Jacob began.

"—is not the king," Francis said, cutting him off. "This is of more importance than Nathan's sleeping time."

Jacob was silent for a long moment. He looked to the other guard, who appeared equally caught between a rock and a hard place. Jacob glanced back at the entrance to the tent.

"Well?" Francis demanded.

"You ..." Jacob began, his face still bewildered. He paused again as he thought. "... may enter." He pulled his poleax away from the door, and the other guard did likewise.

"My thanks," Francis said briskly as he threw the tent flap aside and entered.

"I very much like this human." Crash smiled as he followed.

"General Nathan, I have news," Francis said loudly as he approached the general's bed. It was enormous—fit for a king, like the rest of the objects in the tent. A massive oak table in the center was covered with maps of Bel, as well as all sorts of other tactical papers and a speaking crystal. Massive bookshelves lined the corners of the tent, though few of the books were of strategic importance; most were poetry books. The bed itself was made from a very dark wood and covered with cushions, sheets, and thick blankets. Beside the bed was a bath, which was filled with water that still steamed in the cool night air. Silver wondered how much all these unnecessary luxuries weighed, and who was unfortunate enough to have to bear them on the long marches.

"Is it morning already?" Nathan grumbled as he rolled over, pulling more blankets over him. Francis shook his head irritably.

"No, sir. It is still early evening."

"Francis!" the general said angrily as he sat up in his bed. "How dare you wake me!"

"We are in need of you, sir," Francis said. "You have often scolded me for working without you; will you scold me also for including you?"

"Is the matter so grave it cannot wait until morning?" Nathan asked irritably as he rubbed sleep from his eyes.

"Not grave, sir," Francis said. "We have received a great gift."

"This could not wait for the morning?" the general asked angrily as he reluctantly pulled himself from his bed, wearing silk pajamas. He pushed his feet into rabbit-skin slippers and stood up out of bed. He was a fat man, though he was young. His brown hair was cut short, and his blue eyes were lined with fatigue. His pale, soft skin suggested a life of ease, as did the many jewels he decorated himself with.

Silver had to hide a smirk. *He is noble born if I've ever seen a noble before ...*

"It is a matter that could change our tide in this battle. Do you not wish to incorporate it into our designs?"

"We can incorporate it in the morning," Nathan said as he sat back down in his bed with a stretch and a yawn.

"Do you wish to even hear what it is?" Francis asked, just a tinge of his anger touching his voice.

"In the morning," Nathan said sleepily as he lay himself back down in his bed. He did not even pay heed to the three strange men standing behind Francis.

"As you wish, sir," Francis said. He spun on his heel furiously, his cape billowing behind him. He walked forcefully from the tent, snatching a map from the table as he went, and motioning the hybrids to follow.

"Well, he is certainly an interesting man," Silver said after they left the tent. "I wonder how he got the name Napping Nathan, though?"

"How such incompetence and slothfulness is allowed in such a high position in our military, I shall never understand!" Francis fumed. "If his father weren't a lord in Syienna, he would be just another fool among men! Perhaps he could be head kitchen scullion without his father's coats to cling to!" He went to another tent with a single guard before the door. The guard saluted him as he passed inside, but Francis ignored him. "That's the curse of nobility: competence comes second to class." He stopped at the entrance to the tent. "Come inside; I will brief you without him."

The others entered, looking about Francis's tent. Its decor was as much the opposite of General Nathan's as possible. A small table sat in the center of the room, and a few rolled-up blankets lay on the earth for his bed. A single lamp lit the room, hanging from the highest point of the tent. He laid the map down on the table, which did not even have chairs about it.

"This is Bel," he said, pointing to a spot on the map with buildings drawn on it. "The street layout is on this map, but it's hard to see in this light."

"I see it fine," Crunch said.

"Well, good, then. The city is surrounded by cliffs on these three sides. The city was built as a refuge against bandits long ago during the reign of Jeremiah the Builder."

"Well, if Jeremiah the Builder built it, that tells me everything I need to know," Crash scoffed.

"An education is a valuable thing. Never mock it," Francis retorted. "Now, the only passable way up to the city is on the northern slope, which has a palisade wall built across it. We've long ago battered the gate down, but they've stopped it up with rubble. The wall has been breached here, here, and here by our siege weaponry, but once more, that mage of theirs has moved rubble to seal it. The city itself is near ruin. We've been lobbing stones and spears into it for a week now, and even that mage of theirs can't stop our weaponry forever."

"How many hold the city?" Crash asked.

"Difficult to tell," Francis admitted. "We've seen as many as a hundred and fifty hold the walls against us, but arrows still come from the city to pepper our positions. I would estimate their strength at two hundred—maybe two hundred and fifty strong. They've borne losses at our hands, but only slight ones. We, on the other hand, have lost many. Just earlier today, we left nearly a hundred men strewn about that hill."

"I take it they are organized, then?" Silver asked.

"Very. They move about in small units, and they fight to the death. We've taken none of their number prisoner; even when we surrounded a group of them, they each fought to the death. It is hard to fight such men."

"What is your current strategy?" Silver asked.

"Barrage the city as best we may, then charge up the hill," Francis said. "We try to knock as many holes in the wall as we can before we charge, and it weakens their mage to have him ward stones this way and that before we fight."

"Ever thought of having some soldiers climb up the back?" Silver asked.

"Of course," Francis said. "But it would be a suicide mission.

The moment such soldiers were discovered, the Rogues in the city would descend upon them with a vengeance. They may be able to distract the archers for a short while, but the price to pay for it would be terrible, and it still leaves us on the hill to deal with that magician."

"What if they had a hybrid or two escorting them?" Crash asked.

"Well, that … that may be more doable. Have you much climbing experience?" Francis asked.

"No," Silver admitted. "Crash and Crunch are too heavy; I'm not sure they should go climbing."

"You doubt us?" Crunch asked indignantly.

"No, I doubt the strength of the stone here."

"He is right," Francis said. "The stone is weak. It is little better than shale. An armed human would be pushing its weight capacity."

"Perhaps Pyre could fly up the back?" Silver asked.

"And Howl," Crash suggested. "He is light and fast. He could scale it."

"I am reluctant to let the werewolf fight," Francis said. "Though Nathan is incompetent, I am still bound by his orders. I doubt he will look favorably on your wolf."

"Pyre, then," Silver said. "He wouldn't even have to climb; he could just fly to the top."

"I would not want to be in your shoes when you tell Howl he cannot fight," Crash said. "He didn't come all this way to sit back and do nothing."

"Well, then, I'll let one of you tell him," Francis said. "Or perhaps the good general can. Regardless, I would not count on him being in your number. The general, as I am sure you noticed, can be most adamant on these kinds of issues."

"We noticed," Silver said.

"Francis, the werewolf is here," a voice called from outside the tent. "Do we admit him?"

Francis leaned against the table. He gave a heavy sigh. "Is he being reasonable?"

"He threatened to chop me in half if I didn't stand aside," the guard said from outside the tent.

Francis looked at Silver, and then to Crash, and then to Crunch. He stood straight and crossed his arms.

"He stays outside," he said finally. "Let him sleep out in the field. I am sure the wolf in him will enjoy that better anyway."

"And the phoenix?" the sentry asked. "He is here, too."

"He may pass."

"This will not go over well," Crash said. "I will go with the sentry, just to make sure."

Silver nodded. *This could end badly.*

"I will have a tent raised for your kind," Francis said. "In the morning, we will find if any armor here fits you suitably." He looked doubtfully at Crash's height and Crunch's solid frame.

"Thank you," Silver said. "Hopefully, nothing bad will happen this night." Francis just nodded grimly.

Howl paced angrily back and forth, his scimitar drawn and his eyes always on the sentries who thought themselves hidden in the darkness. Though Howl's eyesight was no better than a human's, his wolf eyes could see in the dark nearly as well as he could in the daylight.

"Stay calm, Howl," Pyre said warningly. He had his broadsword drawn and stood between Howl and the sentries.

Howl growled menacingly, making the sentries more uneasy. They held their bows with an arrow notched, ready to be drawn and loosed at a moment's notice. Howl wasn't the least bit intimidated; he could toss the arrows aside with ease.

"Howl, this is no time for your anger," Pyre said.

"This is a perfect time for my anger! I am judged simply for my blood!"

"Stay reasonable, and they won't be able to claim their judgment just!" Pyre retorted.

"Reason? I once thought that was a trait of man, and now here I stand, exiled for no other reason than how I was made!" Howl shouted. "For how I howl!" And with that, he tilted his head back and gave a blood-chilling howl that rolled over the hills. From the distance, a howl answered him.

"Do you wish to make yourself seem feral?" Pyre shouted.

"I am rejected by the very race I protect," Howl growled. "There are few things that sting one's pride worse."

"Then be the better of the two, Howl! Bear the sting, and they will see they are wrong."

"Those hunters I slew ... they had chased me the day before. I did everything to avoid them, but they hunted me relentlessly. They only stopped after I had unhorsed two of them, and even then, they came for me that night! These humans are relentless, Pyre. They will follow their hate to their graves!"

"And what are you doing right now, Howl? You are strong, but you cannot defeat an army! Keep acting like a wild animal, and you'll follow your hate to your grave."

Howl growled with frustration and kept pacing along the border of the camp with the sentries watching in fear as the silhouette of a werewolf paced against the darkness of the hills. The scimitar clutched in his clawed hands shone red in the torchlight.

"They will let you in, Howl, but only if you stay calm," Pyre assured him. Howl slowed his pacing, but his breathing still sounded infuriated.

"Howl? Pyre?" Crash called out as he approached with the sentry.

"We are here," Pyre called back, not taking his eyes from Howl.

"Francis has ordered—" the sentry began.

Crash cut him off. "You can't come in, Howl. They don't trust you."

Howl roared in fury. "These humans are fools!"

"Howl, can you blame them? You threatened to cut their sentry in half!" Crash said, stepping into the ring of torchlight next to Pyre with his ax held at his side.

"Only because he was a fool!" Howl shouted, his voice distorted through his wolfish throat.

"Where is he to sleep, then?" Pyre asked indignantly.

"Francis said he may sleep out in the wild," Crash said, "where his heart would prefer to sleep anyway."

"This is not right, Crash," Pyre said. "Howl is as much a part of the Guard as the rest of us, and he should be treated with the same honor. He has guarded the king more dutifully than most the rest of us have."

"Given his recent acts, can we really trust him around humans?" Crash asked.

"You told them?" Pyre asked disbelievingly. "That was an isolated occurrence!"

"Howl, your choices have brought you here. You must see that—" Crash began, but found he was talking to an empty land. Howl was racing away into the night.

Pyre shook his head with disdain. "And so we alienate one of our dearest friends. How can he feel like one of us when he is forced to sleep out in the fields like an animal?"

"If he did not act like an animal, he would not be in this position."

"It is humanity who makes him act like this, Crash! How would you feel to be seen as a mindless beast by the very people you are sworn to protect?" Pyre shook his head again.

"I would not go berserk like him," Crash said, turning to go. "Now, come—Francis has prepared a tent for us."

"Oh, so I'm allowed in just because I am a phoenix?" Pyre asked angrily.

"And because you have yet to murder anyone."

Pyre didn't move. "If Howl is rejected, than so am I. What is decreed for one of the Guard is decreed for all of us. I sleep in the fields." With a whoosh of air, he leaped into the sky and flew away.

Pyre's eyes, though they were superb at seeing in daylight, were not designed to pierce the darkness, so he could not find Howl among the many dark hills. Even so, he refused to lay his head down in the camp that had treated his friend so dishonorably, and so alone he lay down in a field and slept.

Two Rogues sat upon the remains of the palisade wall: one calmly sharpening a long, curved blade, and the other sitting and gazing out at the camp stretched across the hills before the city. The Rogue with the sword wore bronze chain mail and a helm with a red plume of horsehair. The other wore nothing but comfortably fitting robes and held a staff with a blue crystal set on the top, which glowed softly.

"What do you think?" the armored Rogue asked between slides of the whetstone. He had a sharp nose on an angled face. His long, black hair was pulled into a ponytail behind his head, and his olive skin gleamed with oil and grime in the moonlight.

"I think whoever made that light is a very powerful mage," the robed man said, gripping his staff nervously. He too had olive skin, but his face was round, his features soft. His hair was cut short, and his skin well washed. "And the howl … well, that I can't figure anything from. Perhaps a werewolf wandered near their camp."

"How powerful a mage, Richard?" the man with the sword asked, as if it were nothing of great importance.

"I told you. Very powerful."

"More powerful?" the armored man asked, pausing in his work with a glance up toward Richard as he spoke.

"There's only one way to truly find out, Anthony."

"Will you be able to defend us from the soldiers and him?"

"I don't know, Anthony!" Richard exploded suddenly. "If I showed you a soldier standing somewhere, would you be able to tell if you could defeat him?"

Anthony sighed deeply. "Well, we knew we couldn't hold them forever. We knew the moment they trapped us in here that it was a doomed fight."

"Maybe we can still hold," Richard said. "Maybe Frederick will find a way to rescue us still."

Anthony paused long as he looked out over the many lights of the Kingdom of Shale's army. He sighed despairingly.

"Maybe," he said. "Regardless, we'll fight them with everything we have. We'll make them remember in sorrow the day they defeated us."

✴ * ✴ * ✴

Jinx landed awkwardly before the main gate of Castle Shale. Her wings ached terribly from a pulled muscle, and her armor was gone, cast aside far behind on the Silent Road to lessen her weight. Her feathered hair was in sweaty tangles, and she stank of hard travel.

"Who ... who are you?" a guard standing by the castle gate asked nervously, as he brought his halberd to the ready. He and his companion were set to guard the main gate, even though the drawbridge had been raised since nightfall. King Leon took no risks anymore.

"Mer? Where is Mer?" Jinx panted from exhaustion.

"Who are you?" the guard pressed again.

"I'm Jinx, of the Royal Guard. Where is the Guard? Bring them here!" she half gasped, half shouted.

"I shall bring them," he said with a look at her wings. He slipped through a postern gate alongside the main gate. He soon returned with Sinister beside him. *Of all the Guard, he finds the one I hate most.*

"Jinx?" Sinister asked as he approached.

"Sinister, where is the Guard?" she asked breathlessly.

"They're on duty. Come in—what's happened?" he asked with concern.

"Blade. He's wounded, badly," she said as she stepped inside the great hall of Castle Shale. "We need Mer. And where's Pyre? He can fly a potion to them."

"He's gone," Sinister said. "He abandoned his post."

"What?" Jinx asked in disbelief. "Well, where's Howl? He can run out to them. Blade may not last long."

"He's gone, too," Sinister said as they approached the stairway of the indoor balcony. "Abandoned his post same time as Pyre. So did Silver, Crash, and Crunch."

"What?" Jinx couldn't believe her ears. "So it's just you, Rocky, Sting, and Mer?"

"It is," Sinister said.

Jinx gave an angry cry of frustration. "Well, where in the name of the gods did they go?"

"I suspect to Bel. Apparently, there's a battle with the Rogues there. The king is quite angry."

"I know they often talked about leaving … but to actually do it?"

"They did, and now the rest of us have to bear the wrath of King Leon for their stupidity," Sinister said sourly. "But where are the rest of you? Are they with Blade?"

"Only I could fly. Freeze is wounded, Shadow is missing, and Demon is using what little strength he has left to try to heal Blade. He doesn't have what it takes, though. We need Mer."

Sinister nodded. "I'll look for him. You go to the king and convince him to get a carriage to ride out to them."

"All right. Be quick. I don't know how much time Blade has left. He was too weak to even stand when I left." *Is Sinister actually being helpful for once?*

"I will," Sinister promised. They both took off through the massive hallways of Castle Shale, with Sinister heading for where he had last seen Mer and Jinx running doggedly for the king's chamber.

Every moment counts.

Up the stairs Jinx climbed until finally she reached the top of the keep, where the king's throne room was. She ran across the hallway, with all guards allowing her to pass; they had seen the winged woman many times and knew she was allowed admittance. She burst through the doors to the throne room.

King Leon jumped nervously where he sat on his throne. Before him was one of the generals of the Kingdom of Shale's army, though she didn't know his name.

"What is the meaning of this?" King Leon asked irritably before the realization dawned on him. "Jinx? Your group has returned! Thank the gods—I am secure once more!" he cried out happily. "But, why are you so … disheveled?"

"Something terrible has happened, my king," Jinx said. "Blade has been severely wounded. He lies on the Silent Road, close to death. We must send Mer to heal him."

"What?" the king cried out in dismay. "Have you lost to the assassin once more?"

"We wounded him gravely, and Shadow hunts him as we speak, but before he ran, he wounded me, Freeze, and most of all, Blade," Jinx said, showing her cut shins.

"Where are they now?" King Leon asked urgently.

"They are on the Silent Road, miles away from the Trade Road," Jinx answered. "We must send Mer by horseback."

"Your number prove less and less valuable with each battle," the general said bitterly.

"Quiet, Erick. Do you believe your soldiers could handle this assassin any better?" King Leon chided his general before turning back to Jinx. "I shall send him by the fastest horses in the stables. And Erick …"—he turned back to the general—"… send twenty of your finest lancers to escort him there. They can follow Jinx from the ground."

"My wing is wounded, my lord," Jinx said. "I was barely able to fly here. I will not be able to fly back, but if your men ride down the Silent Road, they will not miss them."

Mer suddenly came through the door, with Sinister and Sting following closely behind them.

"Blade is wounded?" Mer asked urgently.

"He was stabbed by the assassin," Jinx explained. "It has become infected."

"I will send you in my carriage," King Leon said to Mer. "Can you heal while you travel? I want everyone back to the castle as soon as possible."

"I can," Mer said confidently. "Just get me to him."

"Erick, prepare your men and the carriage," King Leon said.

"Yes, my king," General Erick said with a quick bow before he turned and left the throne room.

"Sting," the king commanded, "I want you to accompany them, just to ensure their safety."

"Yes, Your Grace," Sting said happily, giving a curt bow before he ran after General Erick.

"Mer, gather up whatever healing objects you may need and send Rocky to me if you find him. Then join the others in the stables," King Leon said with authority. Jinx smiled to herself.

King Leon the Meek is almost sounding like a leader.

"Jinx, go to the infirmary. Get whatever healing they may have to offer. I want you back to full health as soon as possible."

"Yes, my lord," Jinx said. She turned and did as she had been bidden. She lay down in one of the infirmary beds as mages gathered around her. She was so tired that despite her fears, she was soon asleep.

Chapter Thirteen

"Hold your sword correctly, boy!" a cold voice said. Cearon could feel the tears running down his young face as an imposing figure stood over him, holding a willow stick with bits of cloth and blood stuck to it. "Do you want another beating? Then hold your sword correctly!"

All around the dark, stone underground room, a dozen children stood in a rigid stance, holding their swords as perfectly as they could while their young muscles shook from the exertion.

Cearon complied with the drive that only pain could provide.

"And for the gods' sake, stop crying, you weakling!" the cruel man spat at Cearon venomously. Cearon's small arms trembled as he tried to support the heavy sword. He felt his muscles burn, but he kept holding. This pain was better than the pain of the willow branch.

"Hold your stance!" the cold voice called, and Cearon heard the cry of another young boy as the willow stick descended on him. "Next stance—move!"

Every child transitioned to their next stance with unnatural precision.

For the past year, it had been like this: hours of practice every day, along with the beatings. Cearon had more scars than most adults, and it was a true rarity for his skin not to have at least a few bruises. The only thing that kept him going was the fear of pain and a deep-rooted hatred for those who had done this to him—a hatred that passed far beyond his few years.

After over an hour of stance work, the children were forced to fight each other with wooden swords, spears, and any other weapon that their trainers wanted them to grow accustomed to. Then they exercised for two hours and then repeated the process, screamed at all the time by merciless instructors and receiving new welts to cover old welts.

"I'm breaking out of here," Tiger-Eye said. "Will you come with me, Eagle-Claw?"

Cearon turned in his sleep; he knew this dream well. He had had it many times since the reality had occurred.

"No!" Cearon whispered urgently, fear tightening his voice. "You remember what the master said—he only needs five of us, and there are twenty-two people here! He will kill us if he catches us!"

"They cannot stop us; they've trained us too well," Tiger-Eye said. "We can make it, Eagle-Claw. Besides, I can't take another moment of this place. I'd rather die than stay!"

"Don't go. They'll kill you!" Cearon whispered after Tiger-Eye as the other boy threw off the one sheet that protected him from the cold and started toward the lone window of the dormitory. All the other boys in the dormitory watched him go through the room, fear in their eyes, but they did nothing to stop him.

"If I stay here, I'll be dead anyway," Tiger-Eye said, pausing to look back at Cearon. "I'm not strong like you; I can't compete here. I will not be one of the five to make it, and you know it. At least this way I have a chance to survive." He turned away and disappeared into the darkness.

That was the last time Cearon had spoken to his best friend—and the second-to-last time he had seen him. The next morning, the children were awakened earlier than usual and marched to the great hall. There, Tiger-Eye was held suspended from the ceiling by his thumbs. When all the children had entered the room, the master began to beat Tiger-Eye harder than any child there had been beaten before. It wasn't long until Tiger-Eye hung from the ceiling, dead.

"No!" Cearon roared as he sat up swiftly, nearly bumping his head against the low cave ceiling. He breathed heavily, his fists clenched. He thought back to his time in the Academy. He remembered that two days after that, he had gone to the master and requested that his name be changed from Eagle-Claw to Cearon—elfish for "cursed one."

"What?" Harold asked as he was adding the final ingredients to his potion. The fire below the cooking pot was smokeless, just as he had promised.

"Nothing," Cearon said. "It was just a dream." He leaned back in the moss as his voice calmed. *Well, he didn't kill me in my sleep. Maybe he's not a traitor.*

"The potion's almost ready. I found the ingredients more easily than I thought. Give it another few minutes to stew."

"Fine," Cearon said apathetically. He did not care how long the potion took, as long as he was healed before the end of the day. He looked down at his tunic. It was tattered, soaked with blood, and far too easily recognizable. *I will need a new one, and soon.*

He took out his sword to pass the time and stared into the unnatural shine of the metal. Even in the dark cave, it still cast a strong reflection. He smiled proudly. He had made it himself at the Academy. It had taken him nearly two years to get the enchantments right, not to mention the time it had taken to get the steel correct. As a result, even after all the fights he had taken it through, not a nick could be seen on the blade, nor had he had to sharpen it since its creation. He ran his finger carefully along the keen edge.

How many times will this blade take life before the end of this journey? Likely no small number, but sacrifices must be made for the greater good. At least that was what he forced himself to believe.

"There, all done," Harold said as he gingerly lifted the pot off of the fire. "There should be more than enough potion to completely heal you."

Could he be giving me poison? Cearon thought nervously. *I suppose I must trust him. Who else will heal me? And I will surely die if I fight again in this state.*

Cearon limped over to the pot and dabbed the potion to his various wounds. He cringed as the burning liquid began to grow his skin back.

Certainly seems like the real thing. He raised the pot to his lips and drank deeply of the foul-tasting liquid. It burned as it passed down his throat, and he felt the heat in his belly. Gradually, it passed through his body, slowly stitching torn muscle and mending broken bone in a manner that was actually more painful than the wounds themselves.

This must be healing potion; it hurts too bad to be poison. He gritted his teeth and sat down, preparing his mind for the pain.

"So if you don't mind me asking, why didn't they teach you to use healing magic where you were trained?" Harold asked.

"Different people were taught different skills, depending on their ability. I showed prowess in attack spells, so they mainly taught me how to attack. I could make fire appear when I left," Cearon said through his winces as the potion moved into his blood. His whole body felt as if it were on fire.

"Why did you leave?" Harold asked. "Do you mind if I talk?"

"No—it takes my mind off pain," Cearon grunted. "They killed my family, and they killed my best friend—both of them before my eyes. I hated them. I escaped a short while ago, but before I did, I slew the man I had once been forced to call master. I barricaded the body in his room and left through the chimney. No one even knew about the murder until weeks afterward, I'd imagine; the monster always was a reclusive man. I suppose people just thought he was sulking in his room all that time ... probably up until it started to smell."

They sat in the cave in silence as minute after minute rolled by: Harold lost in thought, and Cearon gritting his teeth.

"Ever been to Trake before?" Harold asked.

"No. It had been my first time in Syienna when I broke into Castle Shale. The only place I've been is Lokthea."

"Ah, fair Lokthea. A beautiful city."

He sounds well traveled.

"Didn't get to see much of the beauty," Cearon replied. "The only time I set foot in it was when we went on raids."

"That was your group who was behind those raids? So that's why the garrison couldn't stop the attacks."

"Yeah, it was us. It was supposed to train us in infiltration, but many took to killing unnecessarily. I was lucky enough to have a mind matured past the others'. I was never fooled by Marcus's attempts at indoctrinating us." *I forgot just how badly this potion can hurt ... or maybe it is poison.* "I knew the truth. I knew the monstrous nature of the orders we were given."

"Lucky you did. I've heard of terrible stories about those raids—how the bandits would mutilate bodies and leave all valuables untouched."

"Most of that came from Death-Talon. He is a sadist." Cearon grimaced as the pain from the potion came in a new wave. *If it's poison, he's crueler than his father.*

"I don't know who that is," Harold admitted. "But he sounds like a terror."

"Eh." Cearon shrugged. "He is strong, but not by any means the strongest. Bloodmane, now she was dangerous. So was Firespawn. The two of them were a force to be reckoned with."

"More so than you?"

Cearon laughed. "I was … special," he admitted. "My curse also gives me great power—power that the others had a very difficult time contending with. I was rarely, if ever, defeated by any of them."

"So your blood made you more powerful than them? I take it that's why you seem capable of handling the Royal Guard?"

"Yes. They are strong—stronger than I expected, to be honest," Cearon said. "If the four of my old comrades fought with them, I don't think they would be able to overcome the Guard."

"So Marcus is not yet able to overthrow the kingdom?" Harold asked hopefully.

"Not yet. Not without the Relic Sword, especially since Halifin created the Royal Guard. I couldn't imagine what those hybrids would do to regular infantry. They would be devastating to face on the open battlefield. Marcus must know this, so he bides his time, waiting for the Sword."

"But we have the map," Harold said proudly.

"Yes, at the moment we actually have an advantage. We know where the relics are hidden, and he does not."

"What about Krone? I remember Father talking once about a great power held there. He may know that's where the pommel stone is."

"That one is safe for now, even from us. We studied all the fortresses of the Kingdom of Shale in the Academy, and none filled us with fear like Krone did. That fortress is invincible, and many of the king's most elite soldiers and mages reside there. It's as unconquerable as a fortress can get; the Third Elf War proved that well enough. Marcus would need a lot more power before he tried to take those walls."

"Well, at least we are safe for the moment. Father does not

know where the other pieces lay. We can get two pieces of the Sword before we have to face him again."

"That's if his spies don't find us first," Cearon said. *Or if they don't follow you to me ... or perhaps it was something you carried that led them to us. That staff you left behind had strange magic about it. Maybe that was it. Maybe you're not a traitor.*

The pain began to ebb. Only dull throbs filled his body, and he was nearly healed. The potion healed more quickly than magic did, but it left the person healed feeling drained and tired, while magic left the person being healed feeling energized at the cost of the healer's energy.

"I think I'm about healed," he said as he probed the old hurts of his body.

"Anything still hurt?"

Cearon shook his head.

Harold grinned. "Well, then, shall we go? Trake is not too far from here—just a day's journey or so."

"I'm ready when you are." Cearon was tired still, but he could march on. *Probably farther still than Harold,* he thought proudly.

"Let's be off, then," Harold said. "We can't hide out in this cave for too long. Besides, I didn't see a single drake in the air while I searched for ingredients. It looks like we made a clean escape."

"Really? Not a single one?" Cearon asked worriedly. *That's a bad sign.*

"I figured that would be a good thing," Harold said.

"It means either we have the fortune of an incompetent leader among our enemies, or they're sending something stronger."

"Stronger? Like what?" Harold's fear was clear.

"Like my old comrades," Cearon answered as he stepped outside the cave. He slid nimbly down the loose rock.

Ah, it does feel good to have my strength and speed back.

He waited at the bottom while Harold scrambled clumsily down after, often losing his footing in the shifting slope. *He certainly is clumsy, and loud, too.*

"Let's try not to talk too much," Cearon said. "We'll have to walk near the road to get through the Razor Pass, and there are some with exceptional hearing." Harold just nodded. He already looked tired from his scramble down the hill.

They walked in silence, both keeping a keen eye on the sky and behind them. Only their footfalls broke the quiet, along with the odd woodpecker or birdsong—or, rarely, the noise of a stream of melt water rushing down out of the Grey Mountains, likely to join to the Snowmelt River.

I must have slept more than I realized, Cearon thought as the sun descended into the horizon, bathing the land in a soft orange glow. Whenever the trees parted and the horizon was visible, he could see the clouds about the sun glowing in the sun's light. *One can say much against the Kingdom of Shale, but all have to admit it's beautiful.*

They made slower progress than Cearon had anticipated, much to his frustration. As they came higher into the mountains, the air grew thinner. Cearon handled the thinned air easily, but Harold less so. His breathing became labored, and on several occasions, his face grew pale as he hyperventilated. Cearon always helped him sit down and patiently awaited his recovery.

"Haven't you traveled these roads before?" Cearon asked as Harold stood up, nearly recovered.

"Always in carriage," he gasped.

Cearon nodded. *Truly, his life has been a soft one.*

They made about half the distance, stopping just below the pass into the Trake Valley before they made camp in the dead of night.

Cearon was clearly dissatisfied with their progress but did not vocalize his thoughts. He permitted Harold to make a fire, for they had left much of their extra clothing and bedding at their old camp when the elves had attacked. Cearon kept away from the fire.

If they are still tracking him somehow, I don't want to be sitting next to that fire when they come. Besides, I never get cold anyways. As the frigid breezes and the chill night air pressed in against Harold, Cearon did not give even a single shiver.

When dawn broke, Cearon raised Harold from his uneasy sleep, and they began their journey once more. This time, however, their progress was even slower. Harold's limbs were sore from the constant trekking of the previous day and could not keep pace with Cearon's nearly unending endurance.

Perhaps I should just leave him! A child could travel faster. But still, whenever Harold needed a rest, Cearon waited patiently, not even bothering to sit, as Harold summoned the strength to rise again.

As the two men went on, they were forced to move in closer and closer proximity to the Trade Road; the Razor Pass was nearly as narrow as the name implied. If the books Cearon had read from were correct, it was less than a hundred feet across. Cearon grew more and more on edge as they moved closer to the pass.

If they are planning on ambushing me, this will be the place. If it weren't for Harold, he would have chosen to pass over the tall mountaintops and hike the unexpected road, but he doubted whether Harold could survive the journey. The biting cold and the merciless sun beating on the tops of the Grey Mountains had claimed many of the hardiest of adventurers; Harold would fare no better.

Closer and closer they came to the Trade Road as the steep mountain cliffs hemmed them toward the Razor Pass, until every now and again, Cearon could see it through the trees. He both saw and sensed traveling merchants hurriedly rushing back down the road, all still bearing the goods they had carried all the way from Syienna. *That can only mean trouble ahead.*

A new noise broke the silence: voices, barely audible, coming from far ahead on the road. They could hear the sound of crying, and of shouting.

"What is that?" Harold asked worriedly.

"I don't know. Highway men, if we're lucky," Cearon muttered, and kept walking.

"Shouldn't we wait? Maybe they'll leave before we pass."

"It could be an ambush, and an ambush won't leave. It will wait as long as it needs to."

"It sounds like the people may be in trouble. Should we hurry, then?"

"As much as I like to save people, I don't like dying in vain trying to save people. Now, quiet—I don't want them hearing us."

They moved forward. Outwardly, Cearon knew he was the picture of calm, but inwardly, his veins seeped adrenaline. His eyes glanced back and forth, soaking in every detail of the road he could glean. His ears picked up the slightest of noises. His sense of smell grew acute, aware of the scent of the dirt and the trees. His mind swept through the forest, sensing deer, rabbits, and bugs, but no assassins.

There are ways to hide from mental sight, he warned himself.

Regardless, he pressed on until they reached the Razor Pass. The road ran through two cliff faces set not a hundred feet apart, and between the cliffs, no trees or any other kind of substantial cover grew. Cearon saw immediately why it was called the Razor Pass: the cliffs rose straight and sheer as the walls of Castle Shale for thousands of feet, rising all the way up to the snowcap of the mountain. It was as if someone had used a massive razor to cut the pass from the rock.

He glanced at the road and saw several wagons stopped, one tipped over, and another with smoke billowing from it.

Cearon paused a moment and sighed. He ran his mind over the scene and quickly sensed what he had hoped he would not find.

"Wait here and hide," he said to Harold before heading toward the commotion. Harold needed no second bidding.

Twelve highway men were rummaging through the wagons, looting them, while four more held two families at swordpoint. The families were clearly very well off by the clothes they were wearing—most likely of noble birth, which only made the highway men hate them more. Several of the men in the families were bleeding, and one was dead in the middle of the road. The children cried as the women tried to comfort them through their own tears.

Still, Cearon did not change his pace. He kept walking forward with confident strides as if he were passing a family picnic. *Act unnatural, and they will not know what to do with me.*

"Who's this there?" One of the highway men holding the families hostage cried out as he turned toward Cearon. Cearon did not answer. He only walked onward.

"You want to die?" another highway man called out after Cearon's silence lasted a few seconds. Still, Cearon said nothing. "He wants to die," the highway man concluded.

As Cearon began to walk by, a man stepped in his way.

"There's a toll for this road," he said menacingly. Cearon stopped in front of him, resting his hand on the hilt of his sword.

"If I see the king, I'll pay it," Cearon said casually.

"Ha," the highway man said humorlessly. "We got a funny one here." They formed a circle around Cearon. "Well, you can pay the king what you like, but you're going to pay me that pretty little sword of yours, or I'll kill you just like I killed that fellow." He motioned toward the dead body.

"I've killed more men than you've known. Don't try to scare me with your petty tales of murder."

"And it seems you've come out on the worse end of it," the highway man said, motioning toward the bloodstains on Cearon's tunic.

Cearon glanced around. The highway men had all stopped looting and were circling him.

"All right," Cearon said to no one in particular. "Enough of the show. I know you're here, Dragonsfire." The highway men looked about uneasily, some even drawing their blades. "You insult us both with this petty attempt at deception," Cearon called out again. "Show yourself, Dragonsfire."

A harsh laugh came from inside a wagon, and a man with heavy armor stepped outside with a broad, nearly maniacal grin. His hair was gray, but not from age, and cut short to his head. His face was young, though it was covered in scars, and a large chunk of his right ear was missing. He was missing one of his front teeth, and in his hand he held a massive claymore. His eyes seemed to smile maliciously along with his lips. His arms were muscular, with veins bulging from beneath the skin as he held the massive sword against his shoulder; it was nearly the same height as him. He carried an air of confidence about him as he swaggered toward Cearon, his grin never leaving his scarred face.

"You always were a hard one to trap, Cearon," Dragonsfire said through his grin. "But I don't think you'll be escaping this time regardless."

"We shall see. I've defeated you enough times before. I can do it again." Cearon pulled his sword from its sheath.

"Your arrogance will be the death of you, Cearon," Dragonsfire said jovially.

"How many times have you beaten me, Dragonsfire?" Dragonsfire decided not to answer, but his grin never faded. *That's right: one time out of hundreds.*

"I'm taking you back to Marcus, Cearon. He wants to have words with you."

"He can wait." *I'll find him in due time.*

Dragonsfire grew menacing. "Marcus waits for no man."

"He will suffer to wait for me. What have you here? Sixteen men? You cannot take me with sixteen men. I think Marcus has no choice but to wait."

Dragonsfire let out a shrill whistle that echoed from the cliffs. On cue, the noble born, even the women and children, drew swords and daggers. They moved to surround Cearon.

"I should have known," Cearon said with a shake of his head. "They're even using children in battle now? That's monstrous, even for Marcus."

"They're hopefuls, like me and you so long ago," Dragonsfire said. "If they even wound you, they are guaranteed a spot in their top five."

"So you're still telling lies like you used to, are you, Dragonsfire? These children aren't like us. You know neither they, nor you, have a hope of defeating me."

"Don't mistake me for a fool, Cearon. I've grown far more powerful since you ran. You don't stand a chance."

"Ever fought off an entire battalion of elves?" Cearon asked the armed crowd gathered around him. "I have." The people looked nervously at one another. *So they have heard stories about me already. I can use that.*

"Not with me fighting with them, you haven't," Dragonsfire said. His words gave them confidence.

If I show them how frightened he is of me, they will lose heart.

"Then you'll have to die first." With this, a ball of fire flashed in Cearon's hand. Dragonsfire took an involuntary step back. "You never were much skilled at magic, were you, Dragonsfire? You always relied on me or Bloodmane to protect you from spells. What will you do now that you have me trying to kill you?" The crowd grew uneasy and edged slowly away from Cearon.

Dragonsfire looked uncertain. His eyes went nervously

back and forth between Cearon, the flame, and his faltering soldiers.

"Your blood is strong, Cearon, but not as strong as you think." Dragonsfire's words were more confident than his voice.

"You already know about my blood; I suppose I don't need this," Cearon said as he pulled his hood down, revealing his face to the crowd around him. His raven hair hung down to his eyebrows and just below his ears. His skin was pale—almost unnaturally so. His nose angled down sharply as it moved away from his skull, giving him a falcon look, and his jaw was narrow but well defined. However, it was his eyes that caused the crowd to recoil from his gaze. They seemed to burn with intensity and stood out against his pale skin with their bright orange color and slitted pupils.

"Kill him!" Dragonsfire cried out urgently to his soldiers as they backed away from Cearon. No one moved; no one wanted to be the first to face Cearon's wrath. "Well?" Dragonsfire asked angrily. "What are you all waiting for?"

Finally, a brave soul stepped forward and swung at Cearon. Cearon knocked the man's blade aside and ran him through before he could blink.

"Who's next?" Cearon asked calmly as he jerked his blade out of the man.

"Charge him!" Dragonsfire shouted, and his soldiers reluctantly complied.

They all surged toward Cearon, closing the circle. Cearon raised his hand, and telekinetically knocked down four of his attackers, and leaped for the hole in the wall of oncoming soldiers. He landed, swiped an incoming sword away from him, and threw a ball of fire on the attacker. The man cried out in terror as he rolled, trying to extinguish the ethereal flames.

Again the mob of people tried to rush him to use their greater numbers to fell him. Cearon inhaled deeply, and as he exhaled, fire rushed out of his mouth and ignited the first few attackers. They screamed in terror as the flames consumed them. The others looked in horror as their comrades fell burning to the ground.

The crowd stared at Cearon for a few moments with fear in their eyes. Not one dared move.

"Kill him!" Dragonsfire screamed. Their fear of Dragonsfire and who he worked for drove the people to charge once more.

This time, Cearon charged them as well. He dodged a sword and ran the man through, spun around, magically blocked a sword, and lopped off the owner's head. A child with a dirk swung at his shins, but Cearon kicked the boy to the ground before the dirk made contact. A man stabbed as another man slashed; Cearon knocked both of their swords away from him with one sweep, spun, and cut one of the men clean in two. A woman stabbed at him as a man tried to tackle him. He blocked the woman's sword as he sent the man tumbling with a wave of magic.

With a final charge, those still alive rushed toward Cearon with their weapons held ready.

"Argh!" Cearon grunted as a wave of magic exploded from him in all directions, sweeping those around him away and sending all but the heaviest of them flying through the air.

The people lost heart. The broken unit fled from him in terror as he sent small balls of telekinesis to strike them like stones. One or two who were fleeing near where Harold was hiding he slew with telekinetic spikes. The spikes were easy to block mentally, but these people obviously knew nothing about magic; they scattered before it like leaves in the wind. He cut down a few more people with invisible spikes as they fled until only Dragonsfire remained.

Cearon turned to face him, his breathing barely elevated from the combat. "For old times' sake alone do I let you leave,

Dragonsfire. Go, and tell Marcus that one day soon I shall come for him."

"I'm not going anywhere," Dragonsfire said. "I have beaten you before, and I can do it again." He brought his claymore to bear.

Cearon laughed softly. "You only beat me the week I had the stomach flu. I will not extend this offer again. Run."

Dragonsfire stared angrily at Cearon, but relented.

He is competitive, but also a realist. He knows that alone he can't defeat me. He will leave.

Dragonsfire leaned his claymore against his shoulder and began to walk down the road, giving Cearon a glare as he passed.

"And Dragon, next time, don't insult me with such inexperienced soldiers. I thought we knew each other well enough to know these people aren't good enough to kill us."

"We do. I have angered Marcus greatly—though not nearly as greatly as you have. He sent me here to die and hopefully kill you in the process. I have no loyalty to him anymore. I only stayed around as long as I did for formality, just in case one of the soldiers glanced back as he fled. I don't have any desire, both from self-preservation and from fond memories, to fight you. You were one of the few in the Academy I actually respected. Good luck, Cearon. May you kill Marcus—and soon," Dragonsfire said before he continued on his way.

"Dragonsfire, wait."

The large man stopped, and turned around to face Cearon.

"Yes?"

"Your speaking stone. Give it to me."

A look of fury crossed Dragonsfire's face, but he said nothing as he pulled a jagged stone from his pocket and tossed it in the dirt before leaving.

Cearon ran the point of his blade through the stone,

shattering it into a thousand pieces as Harold emerged from hiding.

"That was intense," Harold said as Cearon sheathed his blade once more.

"Hmm," was all Cearon responded with. *Why was that such a weak ambush? Were they surprised I was coming here? Was this the best they could put together?*

"He seemed to sympathize with your cause," Harold said. "Why didn't you ask him to join us?"

"Because I know him. He wanted me to invite him along so that he could kill me in my sleep. Marcus didn't send him out here to die; our kind are too valuable to that corrupt old magician. Maybe they saw your fire last night, and this was the only ambush they could put together in such little time." *If so, that means they aren't tracking us anymore. Surprise is ours again.*

"Does that mean Marcus doesn't have much strength here in Trake?"

"We can only hope," Cearon said. "Let's try not to find out, though. For now, let's get through this pass. We can go into hiding once we reach the other side." He looked up at the cliffs before him. They were frightfully unnatural looking. On both sides of the path, a sheer cliff towered up thousands of feet over them. *Who, or what, could have done this?*

There was no one to answer; whoever it had been was long gone now. He looked through the straight-cut pass and stepped between the cliffs.

Chapter Fourteen

A thin mist hung gently in the air, wafting over the rolling hills around Bel. Smoke rose from cooking fires, both in the besieged city and in the camp surrounding it. An uneasy tension filled the air. Both sides knew that today would be a day to remember, if one lived to remember it.

The word "hybrid" swept through the camp of the King's Army like wildfire. Silver, Crash, and Crunch could not step far outside of their tent without being met with roars of cheers. The morale of the soldiers had been raised just by the knowledge that these inhumanly strong warriors were here to fight alongside them.

It wasn't long before Francis and a very well-rested General Nathan walked into the tent. Francis wore his usual cape along with a steel breastplate, greaves, and holding his horned helm. The general wore a fabulously ornate breastplate molded in the shape of a remarkably muscular chest that curved around his actual girth. He wore chain mail beneath that and had a helmet tucked beneath his arm with many colored feathers set atop it.

"Francis, I don't know why you didn't tell me that we had hybrids from Castle Shale itself!" General Nathan said as he walked into the tent.

Don't you try to pass the blame, Silver thought.

"It was you, sir, who did not wish to hear what I had to say," Francis replied calmly.

"Yes, but you still should have told me of this. You're far from excused," Nathan said in a jovial manner, trying to distance himself further from fault in as good-natured a manner as possible.

"You have often made it clear—" Francis began.

"Oh, enough of this," Nathan said. "Let's just begin planning."

"We already have—last night, while you dreamed," Silver said as he rose to greet the two. Crunch was washing his face in a basin, and Crash gave General Nathan a stony glare as he stretched on the floor in preparation for battle.

"Oh, without me? Well, you've definitely stepped over your bounds this time, Francis!"

"I apologize, sir. I simply felt it was needed to acquaint our new allies with the battlefield," Francis begrudgingly explained.

"It's a simple plan," Silver said. "Our flier will accompany the best climbers you may gather up the back while we draw attention to the front of the city. We'll hit their defenses from both sides."

"Oh, well, I don't think that will work," General Nathan said.

"Why not?" Crash asked, rising from where he was sitting. He needed to crouch to keep his head from brushing the roof of the tent.

"It's too risky."

"We are prepared to take the risk, and I'm sure you will find many soldiers willing to risk it as well," Silver said. "Besides, it will be safe enough with Pyre accompanying them. His skill with a broadsword will be legendary soon."

"Yes, the soldiers may be willing to risk it, but not I," General Nathan said. "It's not good because—"

"It's not your idea?" Silver cut him off.

"Because it weakens the attack on the main wall," General Nathan said angrily. "And you may be a hybrid, but I am still general of these men, and I will be treated with the respect that this office earns me."

"I apologize; I spoke out of line."

"Quite," Nathan agreed.

"Sir, we can spare men from the main wall," Francis said in his calm voice. "There's only about five hundred feet of wall and ten thousand men to seize it with. It would be impossible to bring all the men to the base of the wall at once, and if we could get even fifty soldiers and the hybrid up the back, we could do serious damage."

"I'll not risk it."

"Risk what?" Crash growled angrily. Nathan looked up at him, clearly intimidated by his size.

"The ... um. The lives of the men," General Nathan sputtered.

"There will be a hybrid—" Silver began.

"Or the life of the hybrid, for that matter," Nathan interrupted. "This is not a time for heroics, but for tactics and clear thinking."

"What, then, are our tactics, sir?" Francis asked with his same calm demeanor. Clearly he was quite used to this sort of behavior.

"Um ..." Nathan began. "Uh, what ... what is it that each of you do again?"

"Spell-sword," Silver answered impatiently.

"I hack things," Crash said.

"I crush them," Crunch added as he showed his club.

"Well——" the general started.

Enough of this nonsense. He may control Francis, but he doesn't control us. "I'll bring down the mage that's been causing all these problems," Silver said, cutting off General Nathan. "Crash, you take the right flank; Crunch, you take the left flank. Howl will come with me down the middle, and Pyre can assail them from the sky."

"Now, hold on," General Nathan protested. "I'm in charge here!"

"No, you're not," Silver said flatly. "You may be in charge of these men, but we hybrids do not come and go at your command. We'll be fighting up on that hill today, General, and if you want to bring your soldiers up there with us, well, that would be fine by us. Now if you'll excuse us, General, we need to prepare for the battle."

Nathan glowered at Silver. "You presume your blood buys you more authority than it does."

"Speak with the king about it," Silver responded before he turned away. The general left in a fury, and Francis followed after him with a broad grin.

Pyre awoke in the early morning with dew matted to his hair and clothing. He grumbled to himself with irritation as he shook the unwelcome droplets from his hair and brushed them from cloth and skin. He didn't feel particularly cold, however; it took a lot to get Pyre to feel cold. He always felt a burning heat within him—a heat that completely enveloped him when he lit himself aflame. He imagined all creatures of fire probably possessed it.

He sat up and gave a small jump of surprise to see Howl sitting near him, looking intensely at the city of Bel.

"Howl? When did you get here?"

"Last night," Howl said dispassionately. "Your scent was not hard to follow."

"Ah."

"Thank you," Howl said, turning to look at him. "For not sleeping in the camp. It means a lot to me."

"You're welcome." Pyre paused, trying to think of what to say. "It just didn't seem right to leave you out here all alone."

"I found a werewolf last night," Howl said suddenly. Pyre was lost for words; he looked at Howl nervously.

Did he kill?

"Don't worry," Howl assured him as he glanced at Pyre's worried expression. "I'm not going wild. I just ran with it for a while. It seemed to enjoy the company."

"There's a fine line between the civilized world and the wild, Howl. Make sure you never lose civilization."

"The wild's not so bad, Pyre. It's just. You are judged for your actions, not simply for who you are."

"Really? Do you think that werewolf would have run with me?"

Howl didn't respond to this. He sat, looking at the city before him.

Pyre groaned as he stood up. "I could use a bite to eat."

"I already got one," Howl said with a grin. "Deer tastes better raw, if you want to know."

"To some, perhaps." Pyre stretched his wings.

"You think they'll let me fight?"

Pyre looked at the ground thoughtfully for a moment. "I doubt it," he answered honestly.

"I know friend from foe, Pyre. It's not right," Howl growled angrily.

"I know you do. But you know how humans can be. Do you mind if I go find the mess tent? I didn't have any deer."

"Go ahead. I need to think anyway."

Pyre nodded and soared into the air.

Howl watched Pyre grow smaller as he sped toward the camp on his red and orange wings.

Must be nice to fly. Howl frowned. *Must also be nice to be treated fairly, too.*

He pulled out his scimitar and looked at it. He ran his

finger along the ancient letters he had chiseled into the blade so long ago. He still remembered the agonizingly long process of enchanting the blade. It had taken him almost a year to finish embedding the metal with the spells of resilience and sharpness he had put on it.

I didn't spend all that time making this sword perfect to sit idly by while battle rages. He looked up at the city. The cliffs along the side reminded him of the cliff he had climbed in his dream. *Perhaps the dream was a sign.*

He grinned wolfishly. *There is only one way to find out.*

He felt his skin crawl and his skeleton morph as he released the wolf within him. He ran a claw through the intricate lettering along the scimitar, and he felt the strength of the wild flow into his hands as he gripped his sword. He looked at the lettering.

I named the sword well, he thought as he read its name. *Agras Dol.* He smiled. *Wild Heart.*

He stood up and looked to the city. He spun his sword in his wolf hands and sheathed it. Dropping to all fours, he ran down the hill toward the cliffs. *I will fight whether the humans want me to or not.*

Anthony stood above the ruined gate of the palisade wall, overlooking the camp with Richard. Rogues behind them ran here and there, moving rubble from the city to try to further barricade the breaches in the wall. None of them spoke, and their anxiety was high. They had all seen or heard of the great light that had burned out in the fields the night before, and word of a magician—a magician who was great, powerful, and set against them—had the soldiers in poor spirits. None spoke of it, but the thought of the day as a last stand was present in everyone's mind.

Anthony sighed nervously. "They'll be charging up that hill soon."

"Same as they have before," Richard responded bitterly.

"Not like before. This time, they hold all the advantages but this city."

Richard said nothing, but nodded solemnly in agreement.

"Anthony, should we set a watch on the cliffs?" a Rogue soldier down below asked.

"No, Brandon, no," Anthony replied. "They haven't attacked that way before now. Why should they start today?"

"As you say," Brandon said with a respectful bow.

"Why are you having them move rubble to the walls?" Richard asked Anthony as Brandon returned to his duties.

"I'll do all I can to hold the wall. Once they're past, we'll be swept away, sure as the tides."

"You should have them sharpen their swords, polish their armor, and wash their faces. Let them die in glory, not in squalor."

Anthony looked to Richard and then to the camp spread out before them. "We might just hold. We might just be able to repel them."

"No. I can't explain it. It's something some magicians have—a sense of when something powerful is nearby. There is something down there, Anthony ... something terrible. I have a feeling what we saw last night was but a taste of that power. We cannot hold. Let them go to the Halls of the Sky in honor."

Anthony looked once more at the men rushing back and forth from the city to the meager walls. Much of the walls were blackened from the fire that the king's siege engines had flung upon them, and some sections were but charred skeletons of the wood, ready to crumble at the slightest push. Anthony sighed. The wall was a lost cause indeed.

He turned to face his men and raised his blade above his head as he put on his helm.

"Hear me, my brothers. We stand now before a great and terrible foe. Doubtless you know of the light last night, and doubtless you know that a magician has been brought, perhaps from the desecrated halls of Castle Shale itself, to bring upon us our ruin. But remember the promise made to our kind, long-ago friends. Our spirits are not destined to walk aimlessly in search of a home. We have a place waiting for us—a place of glory!" He was greeted by a few scattered cheers from the men.

"Today," he continued, "we go to those halls to meet with the only ally we have for our faithfulness, and to meet all who left for the halls before us. Today, we shall show ourselves to be men of valor and might!" More cheers rose.

"Worry not for the wives and children you leave here in this world. They shall follow after you soon enough to share with you eternity! Think of all the great heroes of our past! Think of yourselves standing among their number, crowned in glory and honor, revered by our kin for your courage and faith in the face of certain destruction!" Roars of cheers greeted him.

"We shall leave this land of blood and suffering with one final battle—a struggle against the dark powers that hold sway over this land and ours! Fear not death or pain! Fear not their magician or their power! We have an ally stronger than all of them, and today, we go to meet him! Now, forget these stones, for they shall fade away to dust before your spirit fails. Go now, and prepare yourselves for your last battle! Prepare for your glorious entrance into eternity." With thunderous applause, the Rogues turned back toward the city to prepare for their doom. Glory in death would be theirs.

"What was that?" Silver asked as he heard the sound of cheering coming down from the city. The hybrids stood at the mess tent, receiving a breakfast of oatmeal and eggs. All eyes of the soldiers were fixed on them, and all faces reflected awe. Crash did his best to ignore the attention, as did Crunch, but Silver reveled in it.

"It's the Rogues up in the city," a cook said as he plopped oatmeal into Silver's bowl. "They often cheer the morning of a battle."

"How do they know there's a battle today?" Silver asked.

The cook simply shrugged as he plopped oatmeal into Crash's upheld bowl. "Maybe spies. More likely, they saw that light you made last night. They probably know we have a magician now. Usually they don't start cheering until our soldiers begin to move into formation."

"I take it they're not afraid to die, then," Crash said as another wave of raised voiced rolled over the hills.

"Certainly doesn't sound like it," Silver said as he walked to the opening of the tent, forgoing his eggs to get a quick look at the city. He could just see the top of the cliffs sticking up over a tent in front of him. He couldn't see any Rogues, either along the cliff face or along the wall.

Suddenly, he caught the sheen of bronze in the sunlight and saw the tiniest speck of a red crest of horsehair over the gate. *Looks like a leader. I'll have to watch for him in the battle.*

"What do you see?" Crunch asked as he got his oatmeal.

"Looks like their leader is on the wall. Probably giving a pep talk," Silver mused as he went back inside. *Let him talk. They'll lose all the same.*

"Stranger things have happened." Crash shrugged.

"You nervous at all, Silver?" Crunch asked suddenly.

"Nervous? Why should I be nervous?" Silver asked quizzically. *If he brings up the assassin, I'll kill him.*

"Well, this is clearly a powerful mage you're going to be grappling with. I mean, after all that with the assassin ..."

"He caught me off guard—nothing more. I won't underestimate another human. I'll be using my full strength against this one; he will crumble."

"Come on, Crunch," Crash said with a grin. "You've seen what our magician can do. Rogues will be sent flying through the air before his mental strength and before our strength of arms. This battle is already won. All we need to do is walk up to that city and take the victory."

"Well said, Crash," Silver agreed.

The tent flaps suddenly blew open as if by a great wind, and through the partial opening, they saw Pyre land softly. He gave his wings a good stretch before he folded them behind him and stepped into the tent. The little amounts of chatter in the tent went completely silent as all focus went to Pyre and his wings.

Everyone always focuses on those ugly wings, Silver thought with a tinge of jealousy.

"How was sleeping in the field?" Crash asked.

"Not bad. I've slept in worse places. How was sleeping in the tent?" he asked as he walked up to the cook. The soldiers waiting in line did not in the least mind letting him cut ahead of them.

"Comfy," Silver said. "They gave us sleeping mats and blankets."

"I've never needed blankets. I have a fire in my heart that keeps me warm, and the sky is a better roof than some dusty tent."

"Whatever you say." Crash laughed.

"So, since you refused society last night, you missed the planning," Silver said as Pyre took a bite of oatmeal.

"Let me guess," Pyre said around a mouthful of food. "I fly at them?"

"Well ... all right, more or less," Silver conceded.

"I figured," Pyre said with a smile. "After all, who else is going to do that?"

The sound of a war drum began to beat, its thrum reverberating through the air. The soldiers immediately stood up from their meals and made their way outside the tent.

"What is that?" Crash asked.

"Call to arms," a soldier said as he passed.

"The battle is soon to begin," another said as he passed.

"Excellent," Silver said with a grin. *But what if I'm not more powerful than this magician?*

Howl clawed his way up the cliff. It was far more difficult than his dream had made it seem; he had almost fallen twice now from the loose rock, and his arms burned from the exertion. However, for his efforts, he was well over halfway up the cliff face. It wouldn't be long now before he was among his enemies. He grinned eagerly and continued.

"Anthony! Our enemies form up! They prepare to charge!" a sentinel on the ruined wall called back toward the city. Anthony breathed deeply and rinsed his face one final time with water from the well.

"To the walls, men! Make them pay for every inch of the city they seize! Make them remember every second of battle with fear! Let us bring a host of enemies into the afterlife with us."

Silver watched with admiration as thousands of soldiers streamed out from the camp to answer the still-beating call of the war drums. They were armed and dressed for battle, carrying long spears with large block shields as well as short swords on their sides. The blue banners of the King's Army with the golden crown set in the center streamed above the heads of the soldiers as they formed into massive block formations; their spears reminded him of a forest, so great were their number. *So that's what ten thousand looks like.*

Crossbowmen with kite shields on their backs came from the camp. They moved up the hill and into range of the walls, turning their protected backs whenever a salvo of arrows flew at them. The crossbowmen then peppered the walls and the city with their bolts, only doing minimal damage, as the magician within the city sent most of their darts spinning away harmlessly through the air.

Silver breathed a nervous sigh.

He is powerful indeed. Again and again, the mage sent the bolts from the crossbows away with a powerful wave of magic. *But everything he's doing, I can do too, and I am a hybrid. But how much does that really count for?*

"Here comes the moment of truth," Crash said as he stepped out from the line of tents, holding his battle-ax against his shoulder. "You ready for a proper battle?"

"I've been ready for years," Silver said, flexing his fingers in preparation for the magic that would soon flow through them.

"I feel the same," Crash said as he ran a finger along one of the blades of his battle-ax. "After this thing tastes battle, it will need a name. What do you think I should name it?"

"Your ax?" Silver asked. Crash nodded. "I don't know ... how about Choppy?"

"Choppy?" Crash asked with no small measure of disdain.

"I don't see anything wrong with Choppy," Silver said with a grin.

He watched as oxen hauled lumbering siege weaponry in

range of the walls. Engineers hurried back and forth between the camp and a long trench that had been dug for the siege equipment at the base of the hill. They carried ammunition to the trench for the massive weapons. Most of the siege machines were ballistae, with their enormous spears, but several were catapults designed to launch heavy stones and large pots and barrels filled with burning tar.

"I don't see what's right with Choppy," Crash muttered.

"Where're Pyre and Crunch?" Silver asked.

He watched the siege weaponry set up. The engineers twisted wheels; bound cords of sinew rope on the weapons were pulled taut. Spears were loaded into ballistae, and stones into the catapults. A man in a blue cape screamed out an order, and with a terrible creak of wood and the twang of sinew rope, the machines unleashed their destruction on the city. In midair, the missiles suddenly swerved away from the wall and fell harmlessly into already broken buildings behind the wall. *All the stones at once! That is impressive—far better than the average human, anyway.*

"Pyre, I think, is talking with Francis, and Crunch, well, he's doing whatever it is trolls do before battle."

"In all seriousness, Crash, are you worried at all?" Silver asked as he watched the siege machines reload.

"About the battle?"

Silver hummed an affirmative reply.

"Yeah, I'm on edge. I just keep in mind all the advantages stacked in my favor, though. Then I worry less."

"What if those advantages were lies? What if they deceived us when they said we were so much more powerful? What if that's why we were never allowed to leave Castle Shale—because our only weapon was a lie?"

With another cry from the commander, the siege machines fired again, and again their missiles were guided away from the wall. Again, the siege machines were reloaded.

"You think too much." Crash placed a heavy hand on

Silver's shoulder. "You saw their faces when you lit up the countryside with your magic. You were a better magician than Halifin, and he's considered great among humans. This Rogue doesn't stand a chance."

"Right … not a chance." *That's what we thought about an assassin, too.*

"All of our confidences were shaken by that assassin, but don't worry: we still have the edge over these humans. Ah! That's what I'll name it! The Edge!" Crash said suddenly while he looked proudly at his ax.

"Edge?" Silver laughed.

"What's wrong with Edge?"

"What's right with Edge?"

Crash gave a sarcastic laugh in response.

Pyre landed next to them with a whoosh of air.

"Hello, gentlemen," Pyre said as he adjusted his broadsword. He glanced over as the siege machines attacked the wall again unsuccessfully.

"Hello, Pyre. Did you talk with Francis?" Silver asked.

"I did," Pyre said. "He said he'll speak with the engineers. He said they will likely work with you if you can give them any success."

"Those stones will strike the wall. I'd bet his ax on it." Silver nodded toward Crash.

Crash laughed. "I'm glad you're willing to risk something so dear to your heart."

General Nathan rode out from the camp on a white horse, dressed in his ceremonial battle raiment. The brightly colored feathers streamed behind his helmet as his guard of ten lancers, each bearing a standard of his family crest of a red rooster on a green background, rode behind him. He stopped in front of the ranks upon ranks of soldiers, who stood at attention before him with spears and banners held high.

General Nathan drew his sword and raised it above his head in a heroic manner. With well-disciplined unison, the soldiers struck their spears against their shields and cried out as if in one voice, "Shale!" It was an intimidating sight and sound to behold as the shouts of ten thousand soldiers rang out together again and again.

Nathan then lowered his sword, and the entire land fell into a hushed silence. The general gave a speech to his men, though Silver paid attention to little of it.

"He rides out there as if it is by his hand that the city will fall," Crash said disdainfully.

"Or even by his plans," Silver added. He looked over at the siege weaponry and saw Francis wearing his horned great-helm, speaking with one of the engineers. He pointed over at Silver as he spoke, and the engineer nodded. "Looks like the catapults are mine to control."

Crash glanced over. "Good. The less wall that stands before us, the better."

"Pyre, where's Howl?" Silver asked.

Pyre shrugged. "Last I saw, he was out in the hills. Why, are you worried about him?"

Silver nodded. "I don't think he'll be sitting idly by. I'm just worried that he'll do something foolish and get himself killed."

"He can take care of himself. I'm not chasing him halfway across the country again. We must have gone a hundred times the distance you three traveled." Pyre sighed at the irritating memory.

"Fine, then. Would you scout the city over? See if you can spot any Rogues, and just make sure he's not sneaking around the ruined streets, would you?"

"I'll look for the Rogues, but I am not Howl's caretaker. If he decides to sneak around the city, I won't stop him," Pyre said and leaped into the air without another word.

Howl was in the city in his werewolf form. He skulked through the vacant streets, the scent of human all around him. But this was not the human scent he had grown accustomed to living in Syienna or Castle Shale. This scent carried a different tone to it—a tone he had not come across before. He put it in the back of his mind as he moved onward.

The streets here were probably at one time beautiful, but war had left them marred and hideous. Rubble from damaged and broken buildings lay strewn across the dirt streets. Gardens among the buildings were now unkempt and overgrown—and, in some cases, blackened and burned by the flames of the siege weapons. A strange, muted silence pervaded the whole scene. Signs above shops and inns swung gently in the breeze, creaking quietly as the muffled noise from the army arrayed against the city came through the streets with an ethereal quality. It seemed almost as if Howl were a ghost in a dead city.

If not a dead city, then certainly a dying one, he thought as he noted the destruction the king's siege weapons had unleashed here.

As slowly as a predator stalking its prey, Howl moved. The streets were laid out around a central main street that connected with the Trade Road from Syienna. Around the main street there was little more than back alleyways bordered by small houses, inns, shops, and several large granaries.

Many of the buildings along the alleyways were made of wood and were badly burned from the siege weaponry. Most of those houses were little more than piles of charred wood, sometimes topped with the burned skeletal remains of walls. The buildings along the main street were primarily built of stone and so had suffered little more than a blackening from the smoke of the flames. However, the stones launched over the wall by the catapults had knocked holes through the roofs and damaged some of the closer buildings enough to scatter their stony components across the street as if they'd been disemboweled.

He was amazed at how vacant the city was. *The Rogues didn't seem to be expecting anyone to scale the cliffs; there wasn't even a single guard at the rear of the city. They must have their entire strength at the wall in preparation for the assault of the king's men.* Howl smiled grimly to himself. He moved down the street toward the wall, where shouts and the crash of spears against shields suddenly came clearly to his ears. *I will bring a most unwelcome surprise to the Rogues.*

He gripped the bone handle of his scimitar as he looked down the main street. He could see the Rogues gathered about the ruined gatehouse. One especially, he noticed: a man with a bronze helmet with a plume of red horsehair running down it, ordering the men around him about with authority.

He paused where he stood. There was something strange about these men; even from a distance, he could see it. Their skin was not pale or pink like that of the other humans he had seen. It was darker, as was their hair. From beneath their helmets, long, black hair flowed down against their olive skin. Howl's brow furrowed.

What on earth could this mean? Are these people in fact men, or are they something different entirely? He moved forward again, but with a new plan: he would watch, he would wait, and he would study this enemy before he engaged them. *I will not allow myself to be taken off guard—not now, not ever.*

Silver walked along the edge of the trench, watching the engineers calibrate their weapons with the experience only years of service could provide. So far, despite their repeated volleys and the efforts of the crossbowmen—who still fought before the wall of the city, firing at will—very little damage had actually been done. Several new ballista spears were embedded in the wall, but all the stones of the catapults had been diverted. All told, the wall had barely any new damage inflicted upon it, and not a single new breach had been made in it. *I will change that.*

"Aim for the main gate," Silver said calmly to the engineer with the blue cape. "Try to clump the stones as close together as possible. Fire the ballistae spears wherever you may; I have no intention of guiding them." The engineer was a grizzled old war veteran with a long gray beard and shoulders hunched from years of carrying heavy siege components and ammunition.

"But, sir, the magician tosses our stones aside in midair more easily when they are together. It is best to spread them out and make him have to deal with them one at a time."

"Leave him to me," Silver said with a smile. "Your stones will land where I wish them to."

The engineer smiled broadly at Silver's confidence. "If anyone can do it, it's you, hybrid."

Silver just nodded and said, "Prepare to loose on my mark." *Let's see if I actually am as strong as I thought.*

Anthony and Richard stood together next to the gate of the palisade wall. That was where Richard preferred to be, for it was as close to the center of the wall as he could get; from there, he could best protect the men from the siege weaponry and the crossbowmen of the King's Army. They watched anxiously as the siege weapons so far away were slowly repositioned under the guidance of a man with shimmering hair.

"Do you think that is your opponent?" Anthony asked,

pointing to the strange man with shining hair walking along the trench.

"Could be. I've never seen a man with hair like his before," Richard mused.

"What are you thinking?" Anthony inquired.

"What if ... what if he is a hybrid? One of the Guard of Castle Shale?"

Anthony was silent for a long moment. "If he is, we do not stand a chance."

"Catapults! Loose!" a voice called out, only dimly reaching the two from so far away.

"I suppose now we find out," Richard said, his voice tight with anxiety as he raised his staff. The catapults lurched forward with a violent creak as the hook restraining their taut lines was pulled, and the stones sailed high into the air.

"May the god be with you. Perhaps the staff will be enough to give you victory."

Richard didn't reply. He raised his staff, ignoring the ballistae bolts and focusing all his energy on the stones, which were all heading toward the remains of the gatehouse. He knew his opponent would be doing likewise. He sent a wave of telekinesis against the stones. The stones scattered apart, but quickly turned again toward the gatehouse. A second and third wave from Richard's staff were met with similar results. With a last, final wave using everything at Richard's disposal, two of the seven stones were turned from their mark at the last moment, while the others crashed into the remains of the gatehouse with unnatural precision. Wood snapped and cracked before the stones as the already weakened gatehouse was torn asunder and crashed down in an avalanche of broken wood. The king's men gathering in the fields below cheered as the gatehouse crumbled to tinder.

Anthony looked at the wreckage. He had hoped against this, but nonetheless expected it. He gave a deep sigh. "Their siege weaponry will be more potent than ever."

Richard was sweating from the exertion of turning just the two stones. "He is strong. He is very strong indeed."

Anthony didn't respond. He stood with his arms crossed as he watched the engineers reload their weaponry. The stones had struck a devastating blow against the gatehouse, and the ballistae, now unhindered by Richard, had struck all along the wall, shaking the foundation of the already heavily battered and burned woodwork.

Crossbow bolts fell about the wall with terrible hisses as the pointed ends cut through the air, also now free of Richard's influence. The Rogues were only lightly armored and had nothing but small, round shields to defend them from the rain of death falling upon their heads. They fired arrows in response to the crossbow bolts, but they could impose little effect against the large, metal kite shields fielded by the king's crossbowmen.

Again the catapults fired, this time with their salvo aimed at a section of wall. Far below, the king's silver haired magician stood with his hand raised, his mind enveloping the stones, guiding them on their terrible trajectory.

This time, Richard tried a different tactic: he, too, enveloped the stones with his mind and sought to turn them away from the wall. He struggled, pulling and tugging the stones this way and that, but his opponent's mind was as strong as steel. For all of Richard's efforts, the stones only zigzagged in the air before they smashed into their intended targets. A massive hole was ripped through the wall as the stone shattered the charred timber before it like matchsticks.

Again and again, the stones rose into the air, and again and again Richard strove against the power of the king's magician to guide them, and again and again, the majority of the stones struck the wall with devastating precision and force. Wood yielded, breaking before the stone in a spray of splinters, and the Rogues were forced to dive away from the wall and make a perilous leap to the ground below as the wall crumbled beneath their feet.

The crossbowmen launched their last bolts with a final volley against the wall. Their efforts were not ruinous to the Rogues, but neither was their effort unrewarded. Many more Rogues than Anthony liked had been pierced by the crossbows, and more still had been crushed between the stones and the wall. Still ever and always did the ballistae launch their spears against the wall, weakening it yet further. The crossbowmen returned to the camp to gather more bolts before they would return to the battle to assail the walls with renewed vigor.

"If this keeps up, we won't have even a foot of wall to stand on, nor a man to stand upon it," Anthony said as another section crumbled before the magician's power.

"I am doing what I may," Richard said. Indeed, he was. Sweat clung to his robes and his hair from the mental exertion. His normally sharp-looking eyes carried a dull expression, and his jaw hung loose as he panted for air.

"What do you think of him?" Anthony asked, pointing with his falchion blade to the silver-headed man causing such destruction.

"He is strong—too strong for me. And his thoughts are strange. I have never met a mind like his. It is almost ... inhuman," Richard said as he gathered what stamina he could while the siege operators reloaded.

"You think he's a hybrid?" Anthony asked as he caught a crossbow bolt with his shield.

"If he is not, I would be extremely surprised," Richard said as the machines once again launched the stones. He focused hard and sent a wave of magic against them, stirring one from its path, but the rest demolished another section of wall. By now, the gaps in the wall were larger than the expanses that remained intact.

"We can't hold out here much longer," Anthony said. "If this keeps up, we'll have to fall back to the city."

"No. You may fall back with the men, but here I stay. I'll vie with this magician until my last breath."

Anthony nodded, but he did not move. He could not give a reason for it, but the thought of re-entering the city filled him with dread, as if a silent terror waited within.

Howl was not impressed with what he had seen; the magician was completely overshadowed by Silver's abilities. The walls lay ruined before the combined might of Silver and the siege machines.

Truly, these dark-skinned people are nothing special compared to the humans I have already encountered. Even so, several hundred of them remained along and around the wall. *As good as I am with my scimitar, I don't want to press my luck.*

Howl sat down on a chair in a nearly ruined house at the end of the main street, still in his wolf form. He ran his claw through the engraved letters in Agras Dol while he watched the battle through a shattered window, biding his time.

When the king's men attack, so will I.

Silver received much applause, pats on the back, bows, and anything else the soldiers could do to show their praise. Sweat ran down his brow and matted his silver hair, but all in all, he was still in fighting shape after the struggle. The Rogue's magician had proven powerful indeed; there had been several moments where he had nearly wrenched the stones from Silver's mind, but always Silver had been able to hold on, even if just barely. *I am as strong as I thought.* He grinned. *When*

the time comes for me to attack this magician directly, it will be me who emerges victorious.

"My lord, we have run out of stones to hurl," the grizzled engineer in the blue cape told Silver with the utmost reverence in his voice. They had taken to treating Silver almost like a king.

"What else have you to hurl?" Silver asked calmly, keeping his eyes ever on the ruined walls.

"Firepots, my lord."

Silver grinned. "Load them, but first send for Francis. I can control them easily enough. The men should charge as the firepots fall."

"Yes, my lord. It will be done ... but wouldn't you rather speak with General Nathan?"

"No," Silver said bluntly. "Francis is the man who should be leading these men, not Napping Nathan. Now send for Francis."

"Yes, sir."

❈ * ❈ * ❈

Pyre, Crash, and Crunch stood at ease by the tents, looking over the destruction Silver was causing.

"Think we'll be charging anytime soon?" Crash asked as he looked up at the sun. It was already beginning to move past noon.

"No way to tell, really," Pyre said as he pulled his broadsword to practice and distract himself from boredom.

"They'll wait 'til after the siege machines have done as much damage as they can," Crunch said. He moved into the shade of one of the pavilion tents and sat down. He had never enjoyed the sun much.

"Did you see Howl anywhere in the city, Pyre?" Crash asked as Pyre danced with his blade.

"I saw something," he said absentmindedly as his expert hands swung the heavy sword.

"What does that mean?"

Crunch laughed. "It means he's not paying much attention to you."

"It means that I saw something," Pyre said with a grin. "I saw something dart quickly across the street. Other than that, I saw nothing but Rogues gathering at the wall."

"Well, who do you think that creature could be but Howl?" Crash asked.

Pyre just shrugged as he transitioned between stances. "I don't know if I even really saw anything. Just looked like a gray dot dashing across a gray background. Like I said, could've been anything. Could've even been a trick of the eye."

"Not likely—not with those eyes of yours," Crash said. "You can spot a mouse in an acre of grass."

Pyre shrugged again.

"Hope he's all right," Crunch said. "I hope he doesn't do anything foolish like ... well, you know."

Crash nodded. "I had thought I knew Howl before that, but now? Now he seems as unpredictable as a rabid wolf."

"He'll be fine," Pyre said. "Even from my bird's-eye view, I barely caught a glimpse of him. I think if he can catch the Rogues by surprise, he could do a lot more damage than we would have expected."

"Let's hope," Crunch muttered. The war drum began to beat again.

"What's going on now?" Pyre asked as he looked out over the sea of soldiers. They were beginning to form up into phalanxes as the war drum beat. Francis stood before them, his horned helmet atop his head and his cape billowing behind his large shield and drawn long sword.

"Charge now, men, in the name of the king!" Francis cried out as the catapults sent a volley of flaming barrels flying over his head. They smashed into the walls with bursts of flame as the tar spilled out onto wall and Rogue alike. With a roar, the soldiers charged up the hill.

"About time!" Crash said happily as he loped on his long legs toward the wall with Crunch following close behind him.

"I'll see you two in the battle," Pyre called after them as he flew into the air.

⁂ ⁂ ⁂

"Here they come," Anthony said calmly after the catapults had slammed burning tar into the remnant walls. His men were already beginning to scatter before the onslaught of the artillery; he couldn't blame them. The king's magician had made a terrible weapon truly horrifying in its destructive abilities.

"This ends now," Richard said, his jaw set with anger. "Too long now, this magician and I have fought through the artillery. It's time we crossed face-to-face." He focused; mentally, he wound a path through the air until finally he connected it with the magician far below. The magician felt the energy and raised his defenses just as a lightning bolt shot through Richard's palm at him.

⁂ ⁂ ⁂

"So you seek to hasten your death, do you, Rogue?" Silver said as the energy from the bolt of lightning dissipated into the air around him. "Cease fire with the catapults," he barked at the engineers. "It's time I put my focus elsewhere."

They obeyed his word as if it were law. Silver focused, and a flame appeared in his hand. He launched it at the magician, but with the great distance between the two, the Rogue had enough time to easily block it. Silver frowned and moved up the hill. He wouldn't be hindered by range for long.

254

Anthony breathed a sigh of relief as he saw that the engineers had stopped loading the catapults. He would be able to fight them here for the ruined wall after all. He looked out over the hordes of men surging up the hill to take it from them as four of his most trusted men gathered about him to act as his guard. This would be their last stand, and he would ensure his enemies paid dearly for it. He took a deep breath, standing on one of the last spots of intact wall as the might of his enemies descended upon him.

"Archers! Crossfire!" he shouted.

The Rogue archers were well trained and knew how to handle enemies with large shields. Rather than firing directly at their enemy, they turned their arrows, firing across the battlefield instead of straight into it. The arrows struck the charging soldiers from an angle, oftentimes slipping past the shield. With a twang, the bows launched their arrows across the battlefield.

Many of the king's soldiers fell before the volley of arrows, but still they charged, stepping over their dead irreverently in their thrust forward. They had been encouraged by the destruction of the wall and by the two enormous hybrids who strode among their numbers—one wielding a mace, and the other a battle-ax. Again the archers fired, and again many of the king's men fell, but the charge was not broken.

"This is it," Anthony said as the horde of men drew nigh. "Draw swords!"

The archers tossed down their bows and pulled curved blades from their scabbards.

The wall suddenly shook violently, and Richard was almost sent flying by a powerful wave of magic from the king's magician, who advanced with the men and now stood not a hundred feet from the wall. Richard sent a wave of his own, which, though the magician blocked it easily, sent many soldiers around him tumbling back down the hill.

Magic poured forth, crashing between the two. Their waves of magic collided, sending resounding booms through the air like two great walls smashing together. Lightning arced from Richard's staff, and fire flew from the silver-haired magician's palms as the two dueled, seeking to destroy the other, but neither able to find a weakness to exploit in his opponent.

Soldiers from both sides were knocked from their feet by surges of telekinesis that flowed between the two, and the wall and grass around the two magicians burned brightly from their respective forms of magic. So great was the battle between them that the charge broke. Rogue and Shale soldiers alike stared in awe at the two great magicians wielding the elements like a sword, and they backed away from the dueling wizards to avoid the deadly magic. None wanted to be caught in the crossfire.

Howl heard the men charging, and he saw the archers along the wall firing volleys of arrows.

Now is the time to move.

He had kept a keen eye on his target, the man with the plumed helmet, but once more his plans had changed. He had watched their magician's battle with Silver intently. He knew Silver was strong, but he couldn't tell whether Silver was getting the best of him, and he didn't like how long the duel was lasting. Normally, Silver crushed human magicians like an afterthought, but not this one.

Could this magician in fact be stronger than Silver? Howl couldn't imagine he was, but he noticed that unlike Silver, this magician did his magic through a staff. *Perhaps the staff is like the Relic Sword in that it augments one's power?*

Whatever the case was, Howl's mind was made up: this magician would die, and die soon.

He stood up from the chair, and sheathed his sword. He would be going on all fours for this one. He dropped down, his claws scratching into the wooden floor of the house, before he burst forth from the door. He sprinted down the street, dirt flying from beneath his feet as he ran.

He watched as Pyre dived down at the magician but was chased off by a wave of magic. *Pyre never was much good at magic, and unlike me, he won't have the element of surprise.*

He sprinted to a section of ruined wall near the magician. He vaulted on top of the rubble and then jumped up onto the wall. He landed lightly on the top of the wall, and with a snarl, he leaped for the magician.

"Richard! Look out!" Anthony shouted as a werewolf seemed to appear from nowhere. It pounced, jaws wide and claws outstretched, for Richard. Richard turned, the terror evident on his face as in his panic he sent a wave of telekinesis at the wolf. To Anthony's shock, the wolf blocked the wave as it traveled through the air, falling upon Richard with claws and teeth.

"No!" Anthony cried out in dismay as the wolf ripped into Richard. Its claws were devastating, and its teeth tore into Richard's neck. Richard didn't even get a cry of surprise out; he just stared in awe as the wolf stood up and looked down at his quarry pitilessly. Richard gave one last look to Anthony and mouthed the word "run" before he died.

The wolf looked up at Anthony, blood still dripping from his claws and mouth, and drew a gleaming scimitar. Anthony's four guards stood between the wolf and their master.

"Look upon me with fear, humans," the wolf growled as it stepped forward. The guards did just that, their eyes wide with terror at the creature approaching them, but they did not run.

"I do not fear you, creature of death," Anthony said as he held his blade ready.

"Why then do you stand behind your guards, human?" The wolf laughed. "Perhaps you think they shall save you?"

With this, it sprang forward, its blade but a silver streak in the air as it cleaved and hacked through the four guards viciously. In what seemed like a moment, all four were dead. "You do not know what it is that you fight."

"I do not fear death," Anthony said as the wolf stood victorious over the bodies of the men protecting him. "And what have you to wield against me but death?"

The wolf gave a contemptuous snort. "You do not fear death? Then I shall help you embrace it!"

The wolf swung the scimitar at Anthony, but he ducked beneath it just in time. With a roar, he stabbed at the wolf, who stepped aside with inhuman reflexes and swatted Anthony with a clawed hand, knocking him back and carving thin scratches into his bronze helmet. The wolf swung down at Anthony, who blocked the blade as he struggled to his feet. The wolf's strike was strong, knocking Anthony's sword aside and leaving him open to a kick. The wolf's powerful leg thudded Anthony against the wooden battlement of the wall. With a snarl, the wolf swung again with both hands, just barely missing Anthony's head as he once more ducked down. The scimitar cut through the plume of horsehair and deep into the wooden battlements as Anthony staggered to his feet, backing away from the wolf.

The wolf smiled grimly as he tugged the blade free of the wood. Anthony stepped forward and chopped down at the wolf's neck. The scimitar once more streaked through the air, batting Anthony's sword aside as the wolf stepped in close and sank his teeth into Anthony's shoulder.

Anthony screamed in agony and beat at the wolf's face

with his free hand. The wolf growled, lifted Anthony by his shoulder, and shook him like a doll before tossing him back onto the wood.

Anthony groaned as he looked at his ruined sword arm, but he would not yield. With his left hand, he hefted his sword while he struggled once more to his feet. The wolf laughed and looked around.

"See how men fear me?" he said through his dripping jaws as he motioned toward the soldiers on either side of the wall. The king's men charged, and the Rogues defended, but all kept a healthy distance away from the werewolf who fought like a man. "And they shall fear me all the more once I cast you down to your ruin."

"They may fear you, but not I," Anthony struggled to say without betraying his pain over the sound of battle. "Never shall I fear you."

"Then you are a fool," the wolf said. "I am the lord of the wild, king of nature. Beasts bow before me, and so shall you."

"My body will only bow to you when I lie in a pool of my own blood, but still my spirit will not bow. You shall never be king of me, foul creature. I answer to only one."

"So be it," the wolf growled. "Then bow to me as you wish it!"

He lunged forward, and before Anthony could react, the wolf sliced his left hand from his arm. The wolf howled in victory as he lifted Anthony above his head with a clawed hand.

"Behold! I, Agras Dol, am lord of the wild!" the wolf called out to the men streaming up the hill. "I am king of all beasts, and what is man but a clever beast?" He pointed his scimitar at the Rogues, who watched in horror as their leader kicked and struggled pathetically against the creature. "You shall bow before me, one way or another."

He ran his blade through Anthony with a final, victorious

howl. He lowered Anthony, who immediately fell to his knees as his life and strength ebbed from him.

"And so, with your spirit still in your body, you bow to me, human," the wolf said as his lips pulled up into a smile.

Anthony looked up, his face turning pale as his blood drained from his body, but his eyes were as fierce as ever.

"Perhaps in body, wolf, but not in spirit. Never in spirit." With the last ounce of strength he possessed, he rose to his feet and cast himself from the wall. He would not die with even his body bowing to the tyrant of the wild.

The werewolf grunted contemptuously as he watched his opponent fall to his death, his body ruined upon the ground below—ruined, but in its own right victorious.

The king's men cheered loudly as Anthony's body fell, and they assaulted with new vigor as the Rogues fell back from the wall.

Rogues flew through the air as Crash and Crunch's weapons scattered them with terrifying force, cleaving and crushing swords and shields alike. Silver burned enemies with magical flame and tossed them through the air with powerful waves of telekinesis. Pyre burned brightly as he fell from the sky upon the Rogues, cleaving them with his broadsword and searing those who tried to fight him with the flames wreathing his body.

The effect of the hybrids on the Rogues was terrible; the Rogues fell before their might as the sea of soldiers charging beneath the king's banner swept away the few Rogues who could avoid the wrath of the hybrids. It was not long before the king's banner waved victoriously from the city. Bel once more belonged to the king, and all those who had taken it from him lay dead.

No surrender had been asked for, and none had been

offered. Even against the dreadful might of the hybrids and the insurmountable numbers of the king's soldiers, the Rogues had fought to the end, fear and terror in their eyes, but courage always in their hearts.

With a final, mighty swing, Crash slew the last of the Rogues. It would not be long until the stories of the power of hybrids were told across the land, and Crash told Silver that he hoped to hear his own name spoken with reverence along with the heroes of old.

After the victory, the hybrids turned for home, praises being sung in their name and apologies given to Howl—who, though he said nothing, clearly rejected them with the stony look upon his face. No apologies would sway his mind now. Now he saw that the world was not as it had been painted for him. Now he saw that man was neither his ally, nor he theirs. The question burned within Howl's mind: *If they are not my ally, then who is?*

In this fashion, they started their journey home: with Howl brooding quietly to himself, his mind turning over the recent events, growing stronger and stronger in its resentment.

Chapter Fifteen

lade awoke to the sound of birds chirping outside his window. His body felt sore, but not nearly as painful as it had before Mer had worked his magic. He looked at the scar on his stomach and ran his fingers over the damaged skin. It was pink and tender, but other than that, it was healed. He threw back his blankets and stepped out of bed. He stretched and winced slightly as he tried to work out knots and stretch sore tendons.

I can't believe how close I was to death. Just a few days ago, he had been feverish, his wound oozing pus and his body so weak he couldn't even sit up. *If it weren't for Mer, that assassin would have killed me.* The thought made him angry.

He barely remembered the last few days. He remembered a desperate scramble along the Silent Road, his feet weak and clumsy beneath him. He remembered Jinx flying away for help and Demon trying unsuccessfully again and again to heal him. By the time Sting and Mer had apparently arrived in the king's carriage, he must have been unconscious, for he didn't remember a bit of it. *All because of that assassin.*

He looked out of his room's window at the early morning courtyard. He breathed deeply and felt his stomach stir.

Perhaps the kitchens have something prepared. He stepped out from his room, not even bothering to put on a shirt. He made his way toward the mess hall, capturing the stares of all humans as he walked by—most looking at either his wings or his scar. Both seemed to impress them, though the wings seemed held in higher regard. He smiled to himself. *How easy it is to impress a human.*

He opened the door to the mess hall, stepping lightly over the cold stone floor; the mess hall was one of the few places in the expensively arrayed Castle Shale that had no carpet to speak of. Blade went to the kitchens and peeked inside to see the cooks flipping pancakes on slabs of stone over the fires. His stomach growled at the smell. *It's not often that something appetizing comes out of these kitchens. It really is my lucky day.*

The head cook saw the half-naked man looking through the door and rushed toward him, muttering things about nosy soldiers. He was a plump, short man with a look of utmost seriousness, and he strode with an air of authority within his small kitchen kingdom.

"Kitchen's private! Get out of here, soldier, before I—" the cook began, until Blade opened the door to show his bronze-colored wings. He extended them as far as they would go, giving them a few light flaps for good measure. The cook's jaw dropped. "... but I suppose we could get you an early breakfast, um, hybrid."

"I appreciate it," Blade said as he folded his wings and stepped inside. The cook scurried away. The chastened man grabbed a plate and loaded up several hot pancakes straight from the cooking slabs, even pouring honey over them. He handed the food to Blade wordlessly and then rushed off to return to his business. The other cooks all glanced up from their work at the hybrid standing before them as he folded the first pancake and devoured it. He nodded at them appreciatively as he licked his fingers and stepped out.

His feet grew cold against the chilly floor. He sat down at one of the many vacant tables and held his feet up on the opposite bench while he finished off another pancake. He looked out the stained-glass windows as light streamed in from the early morning sun. He stretched comfortably. *Today will be a good day.*

He finished his last pancake as the first soldiers streamed in for their breakfast. He didn't bother to clean up his plate; someone would get it, but not him. He had been on the precipice of death a day before in the name of the king; he had earned a bit of leniency.

He walked down the hall, smiling at any he passed, but receiving only wary glances in return. The hybrids may be well respected, but it was a respect born of fear.

Blade wandered aimlessly about Castle Shale, giving the rich architecture much appreciation and pausing to look at the many pictures and tapestries that hung from the walls. He even spent time in the great hall, looking over the countless pieces of art depicting the heroic past of the Kingdom of Shale, including the mythical scenes of the gods painted on the high-arching ceilings.

He looked up at a portrait of the Fire God painted into the ceiling, who stared down mercilessly out of the picture, his hair made of flames and his eyes glowing like coals. In his right hand was a sword wreathed in flame, and in his left, he held the Gems of the Gods. The stones supposedly anchored a god in the mortal world; the Fire God had captured the stones and used them to rule the other gods as a tyrant. Only the Sky God had always remained free of the Fire God, and it was supposedly by the Sky God that the Fire God had been banished. After weeks of battle, the Sky God had with one final slice cut the Fire God's gem-encrusted hand from him.

Behind the Fire God stood his burning hordes—warriors made of flame and molten stone. They looked like a force to be reckoned with. Blade was certainly glad they were nothing more than myth. *It'd be like fighting an army of Pyres.*

He continued wandering the castle, nodding to Sting as they passed each other in the hallways. Sting was on guard duty; regardless, he stopped to talk.

"Glad to see you're feeling better," Sting said earnestly.

"So am I. I really thought that might have been the end."

"Ah, it'd take more than a little nick in the side to bring you down," Sting said with a dismissive wave. "Besides, you had to stay alive so you could pay the assassin back in kind."

Blade ran his fingers over the wound. "Yes, that certainly was a source of inspiration. How's Mer doing?"

"Tired," Sting answered truthfully. "How do you think he'd be? He completely fixed you up in a single sitting. That man has healing magic pure down to his soul. I've never heard of anyone able to heal like he can."

"Lucky for me," Blade said, glancing down at his scar.

"Didn't feel like dressing today?" Sting asked as he cast an eye at Blade's exposed chest. "Or did you just feel like showing off the old war wounds?"

Blade grinned. "Ever try to get a shirt on with wings sticking out of your back? It's not fun."

Sting laughed. "Try putting on trousers with a tail, but you don't see me walking around in the buff."

"Fair enough, but I was on the verge of death just hours ago. I think I deserve a little break here and there."

"In that case, I should stab myself. I want to be treated like a prince, too."

"If you really want, I'll do the honors for you." Blade half drew his sword.

"No, no, it's all right. I appreciate your concern for me, though. Really, I do." Sting laughed as Blade returned his sword to its scabbard.

"Where is Pyre?" Blade asked. "I haven't seen him since I left. I'm surprised he didn't fly out to meet us on the road."

Sting suddenly became solemn. "Pyre ... left."

"Left? When? Where to?"

"A few days ago. He went with Silver, Crash, Crunch, and Howl."

"Where'd the king send them?" *Strange—the king had*

been so concerned over losing just my group, much less four more...

"Nowhere. They left on their own. We think they went to Bel. Apparently there's a siege there."

"Are they coming back?"

"Your guess is as good as mine." Sting shrugged. "I hope so. That way, next time they leave, they can take me, too."

"Aren't you two abominations supposed to be on guard?" a human elite guard asked as he passed by, still dressed in his golden armor.

"Watch your tongue, human," Sting warned.

"Your days of special privilege are numbered, hybrid. With each defeat, you grow less valuable in the king's eyes."

"And yet we'll still always be above your kind," Sting retorted.

"Filthy mutt," the soldier said as he continued. Once he was gone, Sting moved to resume his patrol.

"Sorry," Sting said, "but he'll probably send for an overseer, or even complain to the king directly. The human guards have become more and more unfriendly of late. We'll have to talk some other time."

Blade just nodded. Sting moved away with a wave and soon disappeared among the winding corridors.

So Pyre is gone, along with four other Guard members. Will they ever return? Something inside him doubted it, but he hoped they would. *If they do run away, would I be part of it? It would certainly be better than being stuck in this castle my whole life.*

He continued to wander the halls, working his way to the battlements of the keep. He walked along the flat, stone roof, looking up at the massive tower rising from it, with its numerous smaller towers branching off it like the spikes of a trident. They were beautiful, yet foreboding, and they appeared to be of an impossible build.

They look as if they should crumble and fall at any moment, and yet they stand strong and have done so for hundreds of years. Perhaps there is magic in the stonework?

He walked to the edge of the roof and looked down at the extensive gardens below him, bordered by the massive wall keeping out the city.

A walk in the gardens would be nice. He stepped on the battlements, tucked his wings in, and leaped into the air. He extended his wings and glided gently down to a small river that swept through the gardens. He landed lightly and took a deep breath of the cool morning air.

He splashed his face in the water, shrugged away his thoughts, and dunked his head up to his shoulders. He pulled his head from the water and shook the drops out of his short hair. He looked at the dust and grime that still covered him. *I could do with a bath.*

Despite being half dressed, he fully immersed himself into the water. It felt good to finally clean himself. He felt the cold water wash through his feathers and wings. He cleaned the dirt off, as well as the sweat in his hair, and stepped out of the water. Dripping, he shook the water from his wings and hair before beginning his walk through the gardens. He stopped every now and again to admire a flower or tree. He picked an orange from one of the trees, but it wasn't yet ripe. *Pity—I love oranges.*

He looked up at the towers from his lower vantage point; he had to crane his neck to see the tops of the spiked tower. *How could anyone possibly have built something so strong as to stand so tall and support all the towers that jut out from it?* It was undoubtedly a miracle of architecture. *It must be magic. Even Aetha didn't have anything to compare to this, except maybe that old temple.*

As he stared up at the stonework, his sharp eyes caught sight of wings flapping high above. Some dragonlike creature soared toward the castle, and Blade just barely made out a rider upon its back.

The rider descended lower and lower toward the castle. The archers on the wall saw it and notched arrows, took aim, and prepared to loose. However, no arrow soared.

"Is it friend or foe?" Blade heard an archer ask.

"I don't know. How can you tell with all these blasted hybrids flying around?"

Lower and lower the rider came until he was circling a hundred feet above the roof of the castle keep. The rider's face was obscured by the large drake, but Blade could see a gray cloak trailing behind him.

"Whatever it is, just shoot it!" an archer cried out. Arrows sped from the wall toward the beast. The rider raised his hand, and the arrows spun wildly away from him and his mount as he guided it onto the top of the keep. The creature landed, and Blade just barely heard the sound of its claws scraping on stone.

Blade had seen enough.

Fate would make me fight on a day like this. The alarm bell started ringing as he drew his sword with a flash and flew into the air. The archers cheered as they saw the hybrid streaking to intercept the intruder. *Now they like having hybrids around …*

The rider dropped down from his mount just as Blade landed lightly on the battlements with his sword at the ready.

"Stand and face me!" Blade shouted. He still couldn't see the face of the intruder. The rider's cloak was gray, thoroughly drab, and indistinct in every manner, yet somehow vaguely familiar.

The rider turned around slowly, his face concealed by the gray hood.

"It's, uh … it's me. Shadow." He lowered the hood, revealing his face. He waved his hand over himself, and suddenly his features became much more distinct.

Must be another of his strange magics.

"Shadow!" Blade said happily as he dropped down from the battlements, sheathing his sword. He walked up to Shadow and slapped him lightly on the shoulder. Shadow winced, and Blade saw the many bruises and cuts on his face. "You're injured."

"Uh ... yes, he ... he um, caught me. I was saved once ... uh, once more. By elves ... um, sort of." He trailed off, his face reddening slightly.

"There's no shame. He fought three of us at once and nearly killed me, too. You did considerably well if that's all he managed to do to just you." Blade looked over the bruises. "These aren't too bad, anyway. You could get worse in a tavern fight."

"Yes, I ... uh, I suppose," Shadow said timidly. He reached into his cloak and pulled out some odd papers. "Take this, um, to ... to the king. I ... um, well, I stole them from the elves ... they, uh, they tried to, well, um, detain me. Have you ever heard of a man ... called, the Emissary?"

"No, I haven't, but I'll take these to the king. You get to the infirmary and get those wounds looked at." Blade looked at the numerous documents. Some were written in a strange language, and the others were strange lists of military units across the Kingdom of Shale.

Are these some sort of invasion plans? "Hmm. Perhaps Marcus would know something about this—" Blade said as the door flew open behind them.

Soldiers, as well as Sting, Rocky, Jinx, and Demon, ran out onto the rooftop. Demon lowered his bow as he saw the two hybrids looking somewhat startled by the sudden intrusion.

"Shadow!" Jinx said excitedly. She ran forward and embraced him tightly. He gave a small gasp of pain but said nothing. She released him, and a worried expression came over her as she saw his face. "What happened?"

"I ... um, I got ... caught," he said somewhat reluctantly. "He ... he almost, uh, almost got me, but elves ... they, well ..."—he swallowed hard—"... saved me. I, well, I'm sorry I ... uh, well ... I ... abandoned you." He turned his face away from her.

"Don't worry," she reassured him with a soft pat on the shoulder. "We're just glad you are alive. We feared the worst."

Demon looked less forgiving, but kept silent. Rocky and Sting both patted Shadow welcomingly on the shoulder as the human soldiers returned to their posts.

"What took you so long?" Blade asked the other hybrids. "I figured you would have been up here in seconds after the bell."

"It's somewhat difficult to respond to something before you hear about it," Rocky said with a snide tone.

"We all thought the attack was on the wall," Demon said, as serious as ever. "It took a while to realize it was here."

"So Shadow is back," Sting said happily. "That only leaves the other five to return."

"The other five?" Shadow asked. "Where are they ... and, um ... who are ... they?"

"I don't think it matters much to you, deserter," Sinister said. The others turned and saw him leaning against the door to the lower levels, his red eyes locked on Shadow—and on Jinx's hand, which still rested on Shadow's shoulder.

"He did his duty for the king," Rocky said. "And aren't you supposed to be in the throne room?"

"The king sent me to investigate after he locked himself in his secret chamber," Sinister said venomously. He turned his gaze back to Shadow. "So why did he abandon the others, nearly costing Blade his life?"

"To hunt the assassin on his own—something you would never have the courage for," Sting responded for Shadow. Sinister's eyes flitted menacingly toward him.

"I suppose this means you don't have to guard the king

anymore, Sinister," Blade said, thinking Sinister would be cheered by the idea.

"Yeah, I suppose—if King Leon still trusts this wayward assassin, that is." Sinister's voice was cold iron. "Shadow, come with me. The king will want to see you." Shadow nodded and followed him down the stairs reluctantly, taking the papers from Blade.

"I, uh ... guess I can, well, show him myself," he mumbled as he followed.

"He won't even let him go to the infirmary first, the cruel tyrant," Jinx said as she watched the two go. "Sinister looks for every way to make Shadow miserable."

"If we ever do leave, we'll make sure to leave him," Sting said as he turned back toward the stairs.

Sinister led as Shadow followed, though Shadow knew the way well. Neither of them spoke—not that Shadow ever spoke much to anyone other than Jinx. Shadow noticed that Sinister cast glances back at him whenever he thought Shadow wasn't looking. *Maybe he is still angry from our last encounter? I don't care. He attacked Jinx, and I defended her. I would do it again a thousand times.*

"So ... you met with the assassin? I take it things didn't go well?" Shadow noticed the mocking tone on Sinister's voice.

"He, well ... his friend, um, almost, stepped on me." Shadow felt his face flush with anger. *He enjoys hearing about my failures.*

"Hmm," Sinister said with clear apathy. "Well, I suppose he was more than a match for you, then? Pity."

"Indeed." Shadow's tone frosted over.

"Touchy subject, I see. Well, perhaps you will have victory next time. I wouldn't count on it, though." They approached the entrance to the throne room. Sinister knocked loudly;

no one answered. "I forgot. He's in hiding." He opened the heavy door.

Shadow stepped through behind him as silently as possible.

I'll make a fool out of you. Sinister turned, and Shadow stepped around his back smoothly, keeping out of his vision. He stepped silently through the throne room, heading toward the king's secret chamber.

Sinister looked in confusion at the vacant doorway behind him and poked his head through the door to see if Shadow was still there. Shadow came to a small door behind the throne that led to the king's hidden room. He tried the door, but it was locked.

Of course. He cast a spell on the lock, and the tumblers lifted. The door slid open, and Shadow entered to find the king hunched in the corner of the room, his eyes filled with terror.

"I'm ... um ... back, my lord." Shadow dropped to one knee.

The king's relief was palpable. "Shadow!" he exclaimed. "I haven't been able to have a good night's sleep since you left! Was it you the archers shot at?"

"Yes."

"How'd you ... how'd you do that?" Sinister approached, his confusion plastered on his face.

"Er, do what?" Shadow asked, allowing himself a coy grin.

Sinister's face locked into a deep-set frown. "Nothing."

"Never mind whatever he did!" the king exclaimed happily. "I have my assassin again! I may sleep peacefully once more!"

"I have these ... um, my lord." Shadow handed him the papers he had stolen.

The king took them without even casting a glance at them. "I'll have someone look them over."

"They suggest invasion, Your Grace."

"Preposterous!" Sinister sneered. "Who would invade? The elves? Every war they try against the Kingdom of Shale loses them more land."

"Invasion?" The king looked down at the papers and saw the lists and tactical information. "This can't be a major force. They only have marked enough food for a battalion. Most likely sell-swords for some—" His words stopped abruptly. A frown formed on his face. "Marcus."

"Sir ... um, I ... I don't, uh, I don't think I should ... stay ... long." Shadow felt the weight of the others' stares.

"What are you talking about? Of course you'll stay here! You're needed here!"

"You can't leave! You just got here!" Sinister said angrily.

"But ... the assassin. He ... he's got the map. I ... I need to ... to ... to head ... him off," Shadow said, his face turning red at the angry stares both were giving him.

"I don't think this Relic blade even exists!" The king threw his hands in the air in frustration. "It's just a lie my enemies conjured up to weaken my Guard."

Sinister added, "Our king is right, you—"

"No one asked you!" Shadow said angrily. *You would counter anything I said, even if you agreed with it!*

"He has a right to speak," the king warned.

"If ... if it's not ... not real, why, uh, are there ghosts protecting ... protecting Aetha?"

"Ghosts? Ha!" Sinister mocked. "I doubt there were any ghosts anywhere. You just drank a little too much mead on your break from the castle."

"Did you see us carry any mead?" Shadow's voice was venom.

"Ghosts or not, that's not enough evidence to prove the Sword's existence. You will stay here and make sure I am safe."

Shadow fumed. *How I hate this obstinate, cowardly, selfish man I'm forced to call king. He is willing to sacrifice the kingdom to his delusions of assassins in his closets!* Shadow hid his rage behind an impassive face.

"May I, uh, have some time to rest?"

The king looked at him warily. "I suppose, but make it quick." Shadow nodded and walked out. "Follow him," Shadow heard the king say to Sinister. "Make sure he stays put."

"Yes, my king," Sinister said as he walked after Shadow.

It took Shadow but a moment to leave Sinister poking about in the hallway and glancing behind tapestries in a futile attempt to find him. Shadow went straight to his room, figuring he had at least a few minutes before Sinister came checking. He unlatched the door and collapsed on his bed, exhausted. Drakes were much less comfortable to fly than he had thought, and the whole ordeal he had endured since he left the castle left him feeling drained. However, he knew he couldn't rest—not just yet. He had one more thing to do while he still had solitude.

He reached within a hidden pocket and pulled forth the crystal. He sighed as he focused on it, activating it. *Let's see what, exactly, I can learn from whoever answers.*

"You certainly took your time reporting back to me, Gourn!" the woman's voice said suddenly, angrily. Shadow kept quiet.

Sometimes, silence can get people talking better than any words.

"Marcus will be furious with you! He's been asking me for hours if you captured the gremlin or not!" Still, Shadow said nothing.

So those were Marcus's elves, and it seems the king knows, too.

"Well? Have you?" Her voice was sharp.

A long silence passed as she waited for a response. He

could hear her angry breathing and wished he could see her face.

Oh, well—at least this means she can't see mine, either.

"This isn't Gourn, is it?" Her voice tried to hide her dread.

"No," Shadow said calmly.

"Have you killed him?" she asked.

Shadow laughed in response.

"You think yourself clever, gremlin?"

"The elves, what were they doing so far south?"

It was the woman's turn to laugh. "I'll tell you nothing, Guardsman. You'll have to make do with the little you've learned."

"The king won't be happy about a battalion of elves in his land, be they Marcus's or not. He'll send lancers out for you and your master. They'll find you and hang you for this treason."

The woman laughed again. "Let them try, gremlin."

"Tell Marcus that his list of allies grows short."

"He only needs one," the woman countered. Shadow suddenly felt a chill run down his spine as someone approached his door. *Sinister must be coming. He always has had the worst timing.*

"'Til next time ... what was it you were called? Bloodmane?"

"'Til next time, gremlin. I hope for your sake we never meet face-to-face." The crystal went dark. Shadow pocketed it, curled up on his bed, and closed his eyes as Sinister came busting through the door.

"Leave," Shadow said without opening his eyes.

"The king told me to make sure you don't disappear, and if that means I have to watch you sleep, so be it," Sinister said angrily.

He's mad because I left him in the halls. Well, perhaps if I ignore him, he will leave. He turned his back to Sinister, folded up his wings, and began to think deeply of what he had learned. *Let Sinister think I'm asleep.*

Sinister found a stool in front of a desk and sat down upon it. He glanced about the room. Papers were scattered all over the desk—some written in Arignese, some in elfish, and some others in languages Sinister had never even seen before. Behind the papers were massive volumes, and most of the titles on the large books were foreign. On the walls were numerous sketches of people, places, battles, and gremlins with their dark bodies and leathery wings. They were done fairly well from charcoal pencils—and, judging from the charcoal pencils scattered around the room, Shadow had drawn them himself.

Other than that, the drab stone room seemed to have nothing in it but the bed and Shadow.

How does he spend so much time in here? Hardly anything stimulating could be found in the room besides the small particles of floating dust, which only stimulated one to sneeze.

Sinister grew bored; he drummed his fingers on the desk as he leaned his chin heavily on his other hand.

I really only sat here to annoy Shadow, but Shadow looks far from annoyed. He simply looked asleep, his shoulders rising and falling slowly with steady breathing. In Sinister's boredom, he looked around the room for something to do. Soon, his attention settled on the desk, which was covered with papers. *Shadow will get angry if I read through all his personal writings ... but really, why would that stop me?*

Sinister rummaged through the many different papers, taking care not to make too much noise. He glanced over at Shadow several times to see if Shadow noticed; but for a slight twitch in his wing, Shadow didn't make a move. Sinister skimmed over the papers in Arignese, an ancient language he had learned long ago. It was the language in most spell tomes. Some of Shadow's papers were historical documents about past battles, events, myths, and other things that thoroughly bored Sinister. Some were hard-to-read spells that aided in stealth, along with some other, stranger spells he could not make heads or tails of, all in Shadow's own handwriting.

Sinister looked the papers over thoroughly, but they all seemed to be too complex for him to understand—or too boring for him to care about. Finally, he found some that piqued his interest. They described the patterns and behaviors of different mythical animals. He noticed all the beasts on the paper were animals used in the Guard: a gremlin, a phoenix, a werewolf, a golem, and even a basilisk. Sinister noticed certain sentences underlined in the description of the basilisk: *secluded, solitary. Has no love of life. The snakes are known for their willingness to attack and kill animals with no provocation and no desire for food. They are known as the murderers of the animal kingdom, and are a natural enemy of gremlins. The snakes have been known to go to great lengths to kill entire families of gremlins.*

Sinister glared at Shadow.

So this is what Shadow sees when he looks at me? A mindless, murdering snake? He probably thinks I bother him just because he's a gremlin, too. Sinister's cheeks flushed with anger. His eyes blazed, and he massaged his fangs with his tongue. *I never much liked Shadow—and less so now that he clearly believes me a monster.* Sinister stood up and took a small step toward the sleeping gremlin before him. *What would happen if Shadow turned up dead?* He smiled. *I could always say he tried to run ...*

Shadow listened to Sinister rustling through the desks on his paper. *Let him look; there's nothing important there, anyway. All my secret things are hidden.* Papers shuffled audibly, and Shadow wondered what Sinister was reading. He heard Sinister stand up.

Maybe he's leaving. After a long pause, he heard Sinister's footsteps moving toward him nearly silently. *What is he doing?* He put his hand on his dirk. *I'll give him a little surprise if he gets too close ...*

A knock on the door came suddenly. Shadow turned over and saw Sinister standing a few paces away, his eyes wild. Shadow stared at Sinister suspiciously, and Sinister looked away. Shadow looked at the papers on his desk and saw they were clearly out of order. *He didn't even try to hide his snooping.*

"Get out," Shadow said sternly. His wings extended behind him to intimidate Sinister. *He always was a coward.*

"Shall you try to make me?"

Shadow took a step forward, and Sinister instinctively grabbed the hilt of his sword. Shadow stopped and glanced at the sword. Someone knocked at the door again. *I may be able to slip my dirk in his neck before he draws the blade ... but why take the chance?*

"Come in," Shadow said calmly. The door opened to Jinx. She looked at Shadow and then at Sinister. He had forgotten to take his hand off his sword.

"What's going on in here?" she asked suspiciously, eying Sinister guardedly.

"Nothing," Sinister said as he loosed his grip from his sword.

"I heard Shadow ask you to leave. Why are you still here?"

"I have orders from the king himself," Sinister sneered.

"Leave, now!" Jinx ordered. Shadow could sense the magic of her bewitchment working.

"Make me," Sinister said as he turned to face her.

I'm surprised he could resist. He must be stronger willed than I thought.

Jinx spoke again, furiously this time: "You pathetic worm, leave!"

"I can be here, and you can't make me leave!" he retorted.

"Pathetic little man." she muttered darkly.

I've had enough. Shadow walked up behind Sinister and tilted his sheath up; Sinister's sword slipped out and fell to the floor with a clatter. He quickly bent to pick it up, and Shadow shoved him hard on the rump with his foot, sending Sinister rolling out of his room, head over heels. Shadow tossed the sword out after him.

Sinister stood up, his whole face red with rage. He glared at both of them as he stooped down to pick up his sword. He stood up again—without sheathing it. His eyes had murder in them.

Shadow looked at Jinx. She had left her spear, and even her armor, somewhere else. Shadow was armed only with his dirk, which was not designed to cross blades with a long sword.

If he does do something, one of us might very well get hurt.

Sinister took a step forward and held the sword over his head, a look of blind rage on his face. Sinister paused. Shadow could see that Jinx's whole body was tensed, and he felt that his was, too.

Sinister seemed to be fighting with two conflicting forces in his head: his loyalty to the Guard and his hate for Shadow. *Unfortunately for us, the force wanting to kill me seems to be winning.*

Sinister took a deep breath and stepped forward, his arms poised for a swing. Shadow rushed in close. He grabbed Sinister's sword arm at the shoulder and elbow, and pushed him up against the wall. Sinister hissed with rage and kneed

Shadow in the gut. Shadow grunted with pain, let go of Sinister's shoulder, and elbowed Sinister across the jaw. Blood trickled from Sinister's mouth.

Sinister struck Shadow with his free hand, hooking him in the ribs over and over. Shadow brought his knee up and pinned Sinister's free arm to his chest, then head-butted Sinister in the temple. Sinister looked dazed, and Shadow seized the opportunity. He grabbed Sinister's sword hand at the wrist and elbow, torquing it like a chicken wing, locking Sinister's shoulder. He kneed Sinister in the stomach—and, in a final strike, kneed Sinister in the face as hard as he could. Shadow's hardened leather knee guard snapped Sinister's nose with a cracking sound. Shadow twisted the locked arm more until it was about to pop out of place and threw Sinister to the ground while still holding his arm. He jerked the arm, causing Sinister to cry out in pain and drop the sword.

Jinx grabbed the sword and held it at Sinister's neck. Sinister gave a small whimper of pain as his face bled, and his shoulder was on the verge of ruin. Shadow saw that Jinx had the sword and released Sinister's arm to get up.

And that's that, it seems.

Sinister turned with snakelike speed, grabbed Shadow by the throat, and forced him to stare into his eyes. Shadow saw the bright red irises and felt his strength sap as he struggled against Sinister's grip. His vision started to fade. He saw Sinister's hand reaching for his dirk as he began to fall backward.

The last thing Shadow saw was the hilt of Sinister's sword crashing into the back of Sinister's head and an enraged Jinx stomping on Sinister's hand until he dropped the dirk. He heard scuffling and the sound of strikes. Then: nothing.

❋ * ❋ * ❋

"Shadow? Shadow, wake up! Shadow!" He heard Jinx's

voice first, felt her shaking him second, and saw her worried face third.

"Where is he?" he asked as he sat up. His head swirled, and he felt as if he were going to vomit.

I am going to kill him, if Jinx didn't already. He saw blood where Sinister had been, and his sword lay next to Jinx with blood on the pommel.

"He ran when I started to beat on him," Jinx said as she helped support Shadow to his feet. "I would have followed after him, but I didn't want to leave you lying in the corridor. Here—I got this back for you." She handed him his dirk.

"He attacked us again," Shadow said darkly. He stood a little too quickly, and spots filled his vision, but he ignored them. "Halifin should have known better than to trust a half human, half basilisk. Those snakes are ..." he searched for the proper word, "evil." *That doesn't seem to do it justice. They're more than just evil.*

"Don't worry," Jinx said vehemently. "We'll repay him properly the next time we see him." She picked up Sinister's sword and tossed it outside a window. "May he never find it."

Shadow looked at her. *She's even beautiful when she's angry, but why would she ever love me?* He thought about how she had come to visit him; no other Guard member had. *Maybe she does? No! Why would she? I'm shy, I stutter, and I'm not even big and strong! She should love someone like Blade, or Howl, or Pyre, or ... not me.*

She looked over at him, and despite the circumstances, her face pulled into a smile. "You're probably hungry after looking into those eyes. Come—you should eat something." She pulled lightly on Shadow's wrist. He willingly followed her. *Does she? No! Now think of something else.*

"Maybe we'll, uh, find Sinister ... on the way."

"We can only hope." Jinx laughed. "I wonder what Silver

and Howl will promise to do to him when they hear? They weren't pleased last time Sinister attacked us."

"Thanks for … for saving me."

"Anytime, my good gremlin," she said, nudging his shoulder lightly with hers. "Besides, now we are only even."

Does she? he wondered as they moved through the halls.

The day passed uneventfully. Shadow and Jinx were unable to find Sinister. Coincidentally, the king hadn't called for Shadow to guard him, either. Shadow assumed the king must be giving Sinister sanctuary in the throne room in return for lies Sinister would tell about Shadow.

Finally, at the end of the day, everyone in the castle was cheered by the return of Crash, Crunch, Howl, Silver, and Pyre as they called out the victory of the King's Army over the Rogues. The king was less happy with their news and far more furious at their absence. He berated them lividly, cursing them, their mothers, their mothers' brothers, their mother's brothers' sisters, and anyone else he could think of who was even of slight relation to them. They endured his curses and threats in silence until finally he had run out of breath. He then resorted to simply asking what they had to say for themselves.

Silver was the only one to respond: "It's good to see you, too, Your Majesty."

Silver was whipped and given three weeks of guard duty with breaks only to sleep. He claimed it was worth it.

Chapter Sixteen

Cearon and Harold walked through dense forest toward Trake—at least according to Cearon. Harold clearly had no idea what direction they were heading. He sweated profusely, breathing deeply from the exertion of the hike with his eyes locked on the dirt his legs slowly carried him over.

Now that they were over the pass, Cearon had relaxed some. Harold's sluggish pace didn't even bother him.

As long as we stay away from the road, I doubt we'll see anything of our enemies until we're in the city. The thought put Cearon in a fine mood. He hummed one of the few tunes he knew as he marched along, stepping lightly through shrubs and over logs.

"Must you hum that insufferable tune?" Harold asked breathlessly.

"I suppose I don't have to, but I want to," Cearon said good-naturedly.

"So what puts you in such a good mood?" Harold grumbled.

"Where I trained, we didn't get outside often," Cearon said. "I've spent most of my life in a subterranean temple. As you could imagine, it's nice to be able to walk through a forest."

"You've seen other forests before. What's so special about this one?"

Cearon shrugged. "I don't know. I think mostly it was

seeing the look on Dragon's face, really. It reminded me of what I escaped. That will make any man thankful to think about."

He paused as they came to an opening in the trees on a steep hill, and before them, nestled into the enormous valley between the mountains, lay the entire County of Trake. The bowl carved into the rock stretched nearly as far as Cearon could see, only rising again to the snowy heights of the mountaintops so far away that the rising land was partially obscured by a dull haze, even in the clear day. At the center of the valley were the white cliffs surrounding Trake, which looked more akin to walls than cliffs. The tall, imposing rocks rose to entirely circle the city, but for small gaps on the east and west side, where a river cut through the cliff face and formed the opening for the gates of Trake, which stood on drawbridges over the river itself. *Those cliffs must have been formed by magic. No natural stone stands so straight and sheer—or creates a perfect circle around a city!*

Though the cliff walls were towering, standing at least two hundred feet high, the two could still see clearly into Trake itself from their high vantage point. The city was filled with white buildings, a bowl-shaped arena on the northern edge of the city, the high ziggurat Temple of Light on the southern edge, and the architectural giant that was the mayor's mansion rising from the center of the city, straddling the mighty Snowmelt River and displaying many brightly colored flags and banners. *It truly is an impressive city—grander than Lokthea, even.*

"First time seeing Trake?" Harold muttered after the long silence. Cearon nodded. "It is a special city. They say every artist can hear the call of Trake in their hearts. I think they just see the hundreds of white buildings as free canvas, personally."

Cearon laughed. "Is it so obvious I'm new here?"

Harold shrugged. "Fairly. How much do you know of the city?"

"Next to nothing. We mainly studied castles and forts in geography."

"Well, there's not too much to know. Just keep an eye about you for cutpurses and pickpockets, and avoid the Blood Valley crowds. They're known for violence and rioting if the arena fights were bad or a favorite fighter died. I've heard of some vampire worship, too, but not much since the days of Nath the Slayer. I've also heard of warlock hunters, so, considering your eyes ..."

"That won't be a problem," Cearon said quickly. "I can hide them easily enough." *And if anyone is fool enough to stick their hand near my pockets, they'll lose a hand.*

"True. Shall we continue onward?"

Cearon could not help but chuckle as he marched on. "You are hurrying me along? Now I've seen everything."

"You are hilarious," Harold said dryly as he watched the city appear and disappear behind the trees. "The city is amazing, though. Did you know no one knows the origin of the city? It's like Castle Shale, Krone, the docks of Lokthea, and the foundations of Aetha; no one has the slightest hint as to who the original builders were. King Leon the Conqueror took them much as they are now."

"Who do you think built them?"

"I haven't a clue. Maybe it has something to do with the Scourge?"

Cearon just laughed. *He really has no idea ... but then again, my own memories don't go much beyond then, either. I don't know who built the city, at any rate.* "No, it wasn't the Scourge."

"Well, you certainly are in a laughing mood today. Father better hope you're in such a fine mood when you two meet."

"Trust me, I won't be," Cearon said a bit darkly.

"Good—then you'll likely kill him. Have you ever seen him before?"

"He toured the Academy on occasion. I remember his face clearly. I don't really forget things—especially not things about Marcus."

"So what do you know about him?"

"I know he's the illegitimate son of some noblewoman. I know he grew up in an orphanage and was taken into the mages' ranks when his prowess with magic was discovered. I know he quickly rose through the ranks until he became head mage. I know he is widely considered to be the best magician alive—a gross overstatement. I know he has no training with sword or unarmed combat. I know he is considered to be somewhat of a military genius, proving himself in the Battle of Elfin Folly. I also know he is known for being ruthless and brutal with his enemies. His hands are soaked in the blood of many innocent people—people like my family," Cearon added, feeling his good mood die. "I know he is the one who has cursed my life. He has created the monster that I am, and I know I will destroy him."

"That's a lot of knowledge."

"I've been studying a long while, and certain people are willing to reveal much about Marcus."

"Like who?"

"Frederick, the Rogue leader. He knew much of Marcus. The two fought together at one time. Frederick led the battle mages from the Eastlands during the Battle of Elfin Folly."

"Where did you meet Frederick?" Harold asked in disbelief.

"I swore I would not reveal his whereabouts to anyone, even those I call ally."

"Well, how'd you know where to look, then?"

"I captured a Rogue on one of our training raids. He told me," Cearon lied.

"I've been wondering, Cearon, you keep talking about these raids; did you kill anyone on them?"

Cearon was silent for a while. "The blood on Marcus's hands dripped onto mine. I didn't want to, but the punishment for mercy was pain. Pain is a powerful persuader."

"It's not––" Harold began.

"I suggest we refrain from talking," Cearon cut in. "We're getting close to the road again, and I don't want unfriendly ears to hear us."

"The road? I thought we were avoiding it. Doesn't it go––"

"We're too close." Cearon turned on Harold and ended the debate with a final look.

Harold swallowed nervously and nodded.

They traveled on in relative silence, punctuated only with Harold's struggled breathing, and the odd question he had now and again: which was occasionally given a curt answer, but mostly just a glare.

After over an hour of this, they arrived at the gates of Trake.

Trake is a truly massive city, Cearon thought. The natural wall around it was even more formidable than the walls of Castle Shale. The cliffs were made of smooth marble that dove into the ground at as straight an angle as any man-made wall. The top of the cliffs were completely flat, but for a small ridge about half the height of a man that ran along the edge. *Like the battlements of a wall. This must be made by magic, but who ever had the power to do this?*

The two entrances to the city followed the Snowmelt River as it flowed from the mountains, through Trake, and then underground to Syienna County. The western gate stood before them, standing over the river behind a drawbridge, built into the very rock of the wall. Workers scurried around the badly damaged gates on scaffolding. The forest grew up to about a hundred yards of the gates.

Before the gates of Trake stood a large company of the king's soldiers, arrayed in chain mail and wearing the cheap, blue tunics of the king's sentinels. They were little better than mercenaries who were given a contract by the king to assail enemies of the Kingdom of Shale. Though they were often of questionable moral standing, these sentinels made highly effective units as they roamed about the kingdom at will, engaging enemies of the kingdom wherever rumor of such enemies existed. They were often the first units to respond to Rogue assaults, being quite similar to the Rogues in tactics themselves. It was clear why they were here: they camped as a guard unit while the battered gate of Trake was being rebuilt. Signs of a small battle remained all over. Arrows stuck in the ground were scattered about, along with dried bloodstains that dotted the road and the grass, as well as a few broken swords, shields, and spears. *Who could have raided this city? Has Frederick truly grown so bold?*

The blue-clad soldiers huddled around cook fires as cool night air slowly filled the valley. Their small, but cleverly designed tents were propped up all along the riverbank next to numerous fishing rods stuck into the ground with thin lines trailing into the swiftly running water.

"What happened here?" Harold asked.

"I don't know," Cearon answered, "and frankly, I don't care. I just need a way to get past these men. Do you think my description is known well enough for them to recognize me?"

"It's more than possible. Speaking crystals can send reports from Syienna to even the farthest corners of the kingdom in an instant. Regardless, your clothes aren't exactly inconspicuous." He cast an eye over the tattered and bloodstained tunic that hung like rags from Cearon's frame.

"Well, I certainly can't walk in there naked but for a cloak, can I?"

"Well, you certainly can't walk in there as you look now—especially with that sword strapped to your side."

Cearon looked down at the short sword on his hip. "I'm not leaving it here." *It means too much to risk over something this stupid.*

"It would be best. Are you expecting a fight in there?"

"I'm always expecting a fight."

"Well, you'll get one if you enter the city dressed as you are and wielding a sword. If they don't recognize you for who you are, they'll think you're a bandit."

"Well, what else can I do?" Cearon asked with frustration.

"Especially with your eyes. They're too close to red, like a warlock's. I hear a group of them are constantly attacking Trake and harassing traders on the roads. They will hang you if they even suspect you're a warlock, Cearon."

"So I must be dressed differently, but still so that people may not see my eyes." He looked down at his clothing once more.

"Maybe I should go in first? No one will stop a simple mage."

Cearon didn't respond; he was too busy thinking and planning. After a few minutes of contemplation, his lips pulled back into a smile.

"Ever wanted to travel with a warrior monk before?" he asked.

"What are you talking about?"

Cearon ripped a particularly clean strip of cloth from his tunic—or at least it looked clean, for it was from the black section of the garment. He tied it tightly around his eyes and ripped the rest of the tunic at the shoulders. He then tore the shirt of his tunic into strips so that it fell about his legs, almost like a kilt.

"And suddenly, I am the Blind Wanderer," Cearon said with a proud grin.

"Blind Wanderer?" Harold asked skeptically. "Can you even see anything from beneath that blindfold?"

"I don't need to," Cearon said. "I see with other eyes."

"Right. Do you think they'll let you pass?" Harold motioned at the king's sentinels as he spoke.

"Why wouldn't they? I'm the fabled Blind Wanderer, a warrior monk who has blinded himself ... for some reason ... and who wishes to test his mettle at the fabled Blood Valley Amphitheater, to prove himself once and for all the mightiest of warriors."

"Did you come up with all that just now?"

"I've always been creative."

"Do you think it will work?"

"Why shouldn't it? Who doesn't want to see a blind man fight?"

"What about me? Who am I in this fictitious world of yours?"

"Why, clearly you are Ebenezer Trentfoot the Third, esquire and noble companion of the Blind Wanderer."

"Clearly. How could I have missed something so obvious?" Harold said sarcastically.

"You're forgiven. Are you ready?"

"We're doing this now?"

"If not now, when?" Cearon said with a step toward the city.

"Wait, who am I again?"

"Ebenezer Trentfoot the Third, esquire and noble companion of the Blind Wanderer," Cearon said impatiently.

"Trentfoot? What kind of name is that?"

"Your name. Let's go." And with that, Cearon strode boldly down the road, his feet stepping over stones, sticks, and any other obstacles on the road as easily as anyone with sight. Harold ran forward to catch up with Cearon's quick strides, tripping clumsily over a shattered spear as he went. He nearly planted his face in the dirt before his legs caught him.

Two sentinels sitting by the road stood up and barred the path as Cearon approached, and Harold just caught up. Cearon stopped before the two of them and smiled.

"Excuse me, good sirs, but you bar my entrance to the city," Cearon said quite good-naturedly.

"That's the point, nitwit," the sentinel to the right said. He had short, black stubble on his face, along with pockmarks and a wicked-looking scar that ran a jagged path up his cheek to his ear. His thick, dark hair was matted with grease and grime, and his teeth seemed to have more growth on them than moldy bread. He held his hand on a dirk tucked into his belt as his eyes strayed warily to Cearon's sword.

"I suppose politeness is wasted on your kind," Cearon said, almost with disappointment.

"It is," the other sentinel said. Despite his efforts, he looked nowhere nearly as rugged as his counterpart. He was a man cursed with a thin beard of light brown hair that, though he had done a marvelous job at keeping it unkempt, looked more comical than fierce. His eyebrows were angled into a look of constant surprise, and his feet fidgeted nervously, as if the slightest provocation would send him running.

"Well, then, let us get down to business. Why are you barring me from the city?"

"Got to question every traveler. It's Grindle's orders," the unintimidating man said with a nervous grin, casting a glance to his compatriot as if to make sure that this answer was acceptable.

"Fine. Question away. Mustn't ignore Grindle's orders, after all."

"You've got a lot of lip for a blind man," the other sentinel said darkly.

"I am not just a blind man, my dear sentinel—" Cearon began.

"How'd you know I'm a sentinel if you're blind?" the gruff one asked.

"I can see, just not with my eyes."

"Sounds like warlock tricks to me," the sentinel responded.

"Warlocks? No. I am the Blind Wanderer. I blinded myself many years ago, trusting that the truth of the world would make itself known to my sacrificed eyes."

"Did it?" the unintimidating sentinel asked.

"Sure as your beard's wispy, it did."

"How could you know that if you're blind? You're just a liar!" the scarred one accused. "You had your servant describe us before you walked down here."

"Perhaps, or perhaps not," Cearon said with an apathetic shrug.

"What sort of answer is that?"

"It is the best answer you shall be getting. Now may I pass?"

"Well, who's he?" The light-haired sentinel motioned toward Harold.

Harold gave a sigh, almost as if he were reluctant to play this little game. "I am Ebenezer Trentfoot the Third."

"What business have you in Trake?" the dark-haired sentinel growled.

"I am esquire to the Blind Wanderer."

"Noble esquire," Cearon said with a smile.

"Yes ... noble," Harold agreed unenthusiastically.

"What business have you got in the city?" the dark-haired sentinel asked Cearon.

"Why, I am here to test my mettle at the famous Blood Valley." Cearon said as if it were simply the most obvious thing in the world.

The two sentinels looked at each other with more than a hint of disbelief.

"What? You are going to fight in Blood Valley?" the more rugged of the two asked through suppressed laughter.

"This sword isn't just for show," Cearon explained.

Both of the sentinels burst into laughter, drawing looks from the soldiers camped all around.

"Something is particularly funny to you?" Cearon asked coldly.

"Well, if you want to shed your blood in the sands, that's your business, I suppose," the dark-haired Sentinel said through his gales of mirth.

"And if you want to bet against me, that will be your money lost, I suppose," Cearon retorted.

"We shall see, blind man, but my money's going on Ripper, same as always."

"May I pass into the city, then?" Cearon asked, just a hint of impatience apparent in his voice.

The meeker of the two sentinels looked toward his more rugged counterpart, who in turn shrugged and stepped aside. "I suppose I don't see any harm in it. The city always has room for another blind beggar."

"Good to know I have something to fall back on," Cearon said as he stepped past the two sentinels.

"No, you don't," the sentinel said as he began to step aside for Cearon. "There's no falling back from Blood Valley. If you fall, you fall into sand stained with your own blood, and nothing else."

"I shall simply have to make a point not to fall, then."

"Sure thing," the dark-haired Sentinel said as he stuck his foot out to trip Cearon. Cearon popped his foot up over the man's before stepping down upon his instep with enough force to make the scarred man wince with pain. *Cruel idiot.*

"Oh, I'm sorry, sir. I did not see your foot there. How careless of me," Cearon said as he walked away toward the city, Harold following closely behind him with both sentinels glaring after them—one massaging a very sore foot.

They walked over the massive drawbridge and through the battered metal gate, which was surrounded by scaffolding. Craftsmen climbed here and there, working to repair the destruction.

"Your gate has seen better days, I can tell," Cearon said to a worker on a low scaffold who was trying to undo a hinge so that the door might be removed from the wall and given the proper attention it needed to rework the warped metal.

"It certainly has," the worker conceded without a look back.

"What happened to it?" Cearon paused on the road, running his mind over the ruined metal. At one time, it clearly had been covered by engravings that mimicked a forest glade, but now the metal had been bent and twisted, so that the trees had become a twisted and flattened bramble.

"It is the work of the Rogues," the worker said, still without looking back. "Some say Frederick himself led the attack. They had a powerful magician against us. He gave their ram the strength to destroy the gate." He glanced back and saw Cearon with his blindfold. A look of confusion crossed his face, and he looked about, trying to spot who had spoken. His eyes settled on Harold, and he seemed content.

"Well, my blind friend, let us leave this man to his work," Harold said as he lightly pushed Cearon through the gate.

"I wish you good fortune in repairing the gate," Cearon said with a smile to the worker as he allowed himself to be swept away. The worker stared after the two with bewilderment.

"You're enjoying this a little too much," Harold warned as he followed Cearon into the city.

They entered a large plaza covered in a mosaic pattern that mimicked the river that ran beneath it. In the center was a large fountain, which spewed water into the air from the mouth of a great stone fish that seemed to be rising from the mosaic river. Throngs of people milled about, moving between the shops that lined the plaza and stepping onto numerous, white paved streets that branched out from the plaza to go deeper into the city.

"Perhaps," Cearon admitted. "But how often can one be called the Blind Wanderer? I want to enjoy it while I can."

"Be careful about telling too many people you'll be fighting at Blood Valley. They may come to expect it, and that's attention we can·do without."

"You worry too much," Cearon muttered. He knew Harold was right, though.

Cearon swept his mind across the city. The streets and houses were all built from the most common rock around: marble, which was quarried in the eastern hills and traded for food and exotic items from distant Syienna and Lokthea.

The streets seemed to glow white with the sun, but for the many mosaic plazas that colorfully displayed scenes from Trake's history and myths. The houses also were made from white marble, and he saw that the structures were often used as canvas by the artists within the city. *Trake must be the most colorful city in the Kingdom of Shale.*

The amphitheater, he knew, was called Blood Valley; it stood on the northern side of the city. Even now, the sound of thunderous applause could be heard as spectators watched the warriors fight.

The mayor's mansion stood in the center of the city, surrounded by numerous opulent houses that nonetheless paled in comparison to the mansion's grandeur. The mansion rose many stories above the land, looking almost like a castle with its high walls, but for its many balconies and hanging gardens. Water from the river was siphoned up and used to water the massive quantities of plants, hedges, and even a small copse of trees that hung out over the buildings below from the enormous, pale walls of the mansion, held in place by chains that looked as if they could leash the sea.

The roof of the enormous house rose like a pyramid, forming a point at the center that almost reached the height of the cliffs surrounding the city. At the top of the roof was a statue cast in silver, the features of which were mostly lost in the bright of day to the gleaming reflections cast by his shining clothes, cape, sword, and skin. In his right hand, the statue held a curved sword loosely at his side, and his left hand rose up, beckoning people to come and stand beneath his protection. His cape was cast as if it were billowing behind him, and his face was kindly, looking down on the city with mercy and compassion. Running up the four corners of the mansion's roof were many statues of marble, made of past heroes and leaders, each of them holding a brightly colored flag depicting the most memorable deeds they had performed in their lives.

The house itself was built like a massive bridge that arched over the river, allowing the water to flow beneath it and be diverted into chutes that carried water to the hanging gardens and gave the mansion an endless supply of cool, running water.

At the southern end of the city stood the enormous Temple to the Light, which also rose nearly to the height of the walls in a ziggurat, with its many plateau-like layers built of the purest marble. Torches and lamps always burned brightly around the temple, casting their golden light onto the pale stone, making it appear to glow itself like an heir to the sun, even in the dead of night.

"I know my father, and I know his spy network is massive and often in unexpected places, Cearon," Harold insisted. "We can do with as little attention as we can get."

"I know," Cearon conceded, but said nothing further.

"So what do we do first?" Harold asked, looking at the mammoth stone fish spewing water into the air as they walked by it.

"First we consult the map, but not here. We need a private place in plain sight, where no one will look for us. There must be a noisy tavern around here." Cearon's mind roamed about the plaza to find what he sought. There was nothing suitable here—only fashionable cafés filled with wealthy people and their servants, all of whom quietly listened to music while they dined.

"If there is, it probably won't be around here. This plaza is too grand for the kind of place you want," Harold said as he, too, scanned the plaza—albeit with his eyes.

"Well, where would it be, then?" Cearon asked. "I haven't much experience navigating cities."

"Probably toward the inner parts of the city. That's where the shabbier buildings usually are," Harold said. "Follow me."

Cearon obliged and put his hand on Harold's shoulder as he tilted his head down, mimicking a blind man as best as he could, nonverbally submitting to Harold's demand for more clandestine movements.

He's right: we need as little attention now as we can get. They avoided the public eye as they headed toward the center of the city.

Harold constantly kept an eye out for any kind of cheap tavern, but he had been wrong. The deeper they went into the city, the grander the buildings became as they neared the mayor's mansion. The white houses shimmered as the sun beat down on them wherever the marble walls were not covered by beautifully painted murals. Rich reds, blues, greens, and yellows met Harold's eyes as they walked through the art-lined streets, avoiding carriages and mail deliverers on horseback as they went.

Truly, Trake is a city for the arts, Cearon thought with a glance beneath his blindfold as they passed over mosaics ranging from brilliant sunsets to epic battles.

They traveled to the east end of the city, where the poor had been stuffed into small, ramshackle homes that seemed to scar the face of the city. Here the poor stayed, paying high rent to the wealthy landlords and working in the quarries in the eastern foothills—or perhaps trying to pan for gold in the fast-flowing river. Few people wandered through these streets, as most—even the children—were quarrying the rich marble out of the mountainside. It was here that the two men found a tavern that Cearon thought suitable to their needs, and they entered it.

They were both somewhat disappointed by the quiet nature of the room, but encouraged by the private booths set away from the bar, along with the straw-covered floor clearly meant for dancing.

The bartender gave them a suspicious look as he stepped out onto a staircase leading to the second floor, where the barkeep resided. His disposition toward the two travelers changed little as they opened a tab, asked for a room for the night, and ordered a pint of ale before retiring to a private booth without showing even the slightest glint of gold.

"All right, get the map out," Harold said after the surly barkeep brought them their drinks and went back to the bar, where he made a show of wiping the coarse wood down with a damp cloth while he watched them carefully, ensuring they would bring no trouble.

Cearon pulled out the map and set it on the table. He looked it over carefully from beneath the blindfold, while Harold looked at it upside down.

"Well, it looks like an older version of the city, but this little drawing on the side here is definitely a map of Trake." Cearon pointed to a small sketching of the city. Other than a few lines representing streets, a couple buildings were shown, including the mayor's mansion in the center and a ziggurat-style building on the edge with a star over it.

"Obviously," Harold mused, "this little star here represents where the piece has been hidden, so it's in the temple. But the question is, where in the temple?"

"The temple in Aetha was enormous. If I hadn't had a guide, I could have spent an entire day searching in there and found nothing. I don't see any kind of writing or drawing explaining where the relic is within the temple itself. I suppose the mapmakers figured whoever actually found the map would know where in the temples they were to be hidden. But that doesn't really make sense. Why bother with a map, then?"

"Right," Harold agreed. "If the searcher knew it was in a temple, he would hardly need the map. There can't be more than a half dozen temples all throughout the land."

Cearon looked at where the other stars were located on the map. "Any temple in Lokthea?"

"You should know. You did raids in that area, didn't you?"

"We didn't exactly memorize the buildings. We just broke into them and stole things—sometimes people, if you want to know" Cearon said harshly.

"There is," Harold said, quickly changing the subject, "the Temple of the Water."

"And then we have the star over Krone," Cearon said, looking at the star over the dark walls drawn near the northern lands. "All of them enormous structures. It could be hidden anywhere inside them, and it could take me a week just to visit every room."

I doubt the priests will be too happy with me poking about in their secret rooms, either.

"Indeed. Looks like we only get a vague outline of where the Sword is."

"Perhaps I will be able to sense it once I'm near it. It's the best idea I can think of," Cearon said, ignoring the bartender staring openly at the blind man who was looking at a map.

"You're not much at keeping a low profile, are you?" Harold muttered as he drew the map away from Cearon and laid it out before himself, pointing as if he were describing it to Cearon.

"I can at times, but generally, no, it's not my specialty," Cearon admitted with a smile.

"Fascinating. Now, how are we going to search the temple? The one in Aetha was deserted ... well, mostly deserted. But this one will be teeming with religious men who won't take kindly to you peeking in at their holy sites. And if I remember right, there are only a few religious rites open to the public each year, and I would be very surprised if any of them happened to be anytime soon."

"That's easy enough to take care of. I just need to pay the right night guards and stuff the pocket of a priest here and there, and I should be able to sneak into the temple."

"That leads us to the problem of where you are going to get the money to pay off said night guards. Are you going to rob people?"

"No, of course not—I'm no common thief. But you seem to forget one of the major attractions of this city. There's an amphitheater here, and I just happen to be a fairly accomplished warrior."

"You'll draw attention to yourself," Harold warned. "Either you'll have to show them your eyes, or you'll have to pretend to be a blind man fighting. Neither bode well for subtlety."

"Don't you see, though? That's how we'll have a small fortune. Everyone will bet against the blind man on the lists——everyone but you. We'll put everything we have on me, and when I crush the competition, we'll earn a handsome sum."

"Which brings us back to the fact that we don't have anything to bet with. We're broke. That's what our problem was originally ... well, that and the temple."

"Don't worry yourself, Harold." Cearon grinned deviously. "Money is easy enough to separate from people's purses. Plenty of people in this city have more money than they need. All we need to do is part them from it. It shouldn't prove too difficult."

"Who will we rob, then? There seem to be plenty of wealthy people in this city."

"Rob? I never said that. Why put ourselves in needless danger? No, we're going to get their money another way. All we need are three shells and a box."

"Wait—the monks in the Temple to the Light have taken a vow of poverty. How, then, do you expect to buy any of them off?"

Cearon's grin didn't leave his face. "Trust me, Harold, there's always someone who can be bought. Always. And besides, some extra money to help finance our adventures will be worth the risk."

"Admit it, you just want to fight in the arena."

Cearon shrugged. "I wouldn't say I'm opposed to the idea."

Harold wasn't satisfied. "Do you really think it's worth the risk?"

"Yes, and so do you."

"Well, I'm glad I see it your way now," Harold said mockingly.

Cearon smiled. "I thought you might. Don't worry. No ill will come of it. A blind man fighting in the arena isn't going to cause much of a stir, and even if it does we'll be out of this city before we can get caught up in it."

"I hope your right," Harold said, still sounding less then convinced. Cearon left it at that.

Chapter Seventeen

Silver sat in the mess hall alone. He was supposed to be on guard, but he had decided to take an unscheduled break.

Besides, the mess hall needs protecting, too. He knew if the king caught him, he would be punished severely, but he didn't really care. He was already being punished severely. He could still feel the stings of the whip on his back. *What more can the king really do, short of revoking my right to breathe? Though, I suppose he could have me whipped again ...* He decided not to think about that.

He breathed an irritated sigh.

King Leon grows ever more ridiculous. The king had drastically increased the amount of time they all were to patrol the castle, not just the ones being punished. The Royal Guard hardly ever had any breaks anymore, let alone time to go enjoy Syienna.

He's probably afraid that if we set foot in the city, he'll never see us again. He certainly wouldn't see me again. But that wasn't even the most irritating part. The king had recently locked himself into his throne room, refusing to see anybody but Sinister, who sat by the king like a pet bird and chirped paranoid delusions into his ear. *Next time I see Sinister will be the last time anybody sees him.*

The king and Sinister had developed a symbiotic relationship: Sinister was too terrified to come out, because he knew Shadow would absolutely destroy him on sight—that was, if Jinx, Crash, Silver, or Howl didn't do it first; and the king enjoyed having Sinister around, because the latter fed his ever-growing paranoia.

Silver continued to ponder the recent events in the castle among the noise of the chaotic mess hall as Freeze walked in. All her wounds had been healed by either Mer or the castle mages, and she stepped with a new vigor. She walked by the dozens of human soldiers, who all turned to look at her and her strange wings. She sat down next to Silver.

"Just about all patrolled out, too, are we?" she asked.

"Indeed." Silver snorted. "To say the least."

"Somewhat less exciting than Bel was?"

"A tad," Silver said with a smile. "But this has its own perks. After all, who could ever tire of looking at these beautiful black walls? And there's always the stuffy castle air to invigorate one's senses. Now that alone is hard to beat, but not as hard as the abject boredom is."

Freeze laughed. "Well, it sounds as if it went better for your group than it did for mine. I don't think there was a time when we weren't miserable, bored, or being chased by ghosts."

"So the city actually is haunted," Silver mused. "I always thought it was just a myth."

"Either it is haunted, or all five of us went mad at the same moment."

"Entirely possible. You always were a rather strange bunch ..."

"Oh, this coming from you, of all people?" Freeze smiled. "I don't think you exactly have the high ground on strange."

"Strange is nothing but normality to a different point of view."

Freeze laughed. "I can't really argue with that."

"That's because I'm always right."

Freeze rolled her eyes. "I seem to remember some times you were wrong in training."

Silver shrugged. "To the slow-witted eye, perhaps."

"So when you challenged Howl and Blade to a swords-only duel—both of them at once—you felt that was a good idea?"

"It had its merits."

"I seem to remember Mer getting a lot of healing training that day and none of it from Howl or Blade."

Silver laughed sarcastically. "You caught me. I'm not perfect. Congratulations. You should be a magistrate."

Freeze seemed pleased with herself nonetheless. "Why, thank you."

During the brief lull in conversation, they both sat and watched the humans eat.

Humans are a strange bunch. Silver thought. They ate remarkably sloppily, shoving one another playfully as they chewed—and spilling porridge, soup, and mead all about the tables. They also seemed to enjoy making as much noise as possible, laughing boorishly loud and shouting out jokes and insults above one another. Silver couldn't help but find their behavior impossibly annoying. *I can see why Howl has taken such a strong dislike to them.*

"So the king has been acting strange, hasn't he?" Freeze asked, breaking the silence.

"Anything else new?" Silver asked miserably.

"I suppose not," she said with a small smile. "But nevertheless, he's been acting strange—even for him."

"True. He's been even more reclusive than normal. I doubt he's leaving the throne room even for the toilet anymore."

"And he's in there with that traitor, Sinister. I'd like to get my hands around his slimy throat," Freeze said darkly.

"What is it about Jinx that sets him off like that?"

"Haven't you seen the way he looks at Jinx? And the way Jinx looks at Shadow?"

Suddenly, Shadow walked in. "Well, look at that—there's

Shadow in the flesh," Silver muttered. *He looks tired and hungry.*

Shadow glanced at the food being served in the mess, and his lip curled slightly. It was stale bread and some sort of soup that gave off a curious odor. He took it anyway and turned to see where to sit down.

"Shadow," Silver said, waving his hand over the crowd. Shadow walked over and sat across from Freeze and Silver.

"How are things, Shadow?" Freeze asked.

"Not good. The king, uh, he's um ... he's afraid of me. Keeps sending me to, uh ..." He sighed deeply. "... do pointless jobs."

"He's afraid you'll turn on him, isn't he?" Freeze asked angrily. "That paranoid little ..." She struggled to find the right words to express her frustration. "Argh, no one cares whether or not he lives or dies!"

"Maybe we would be doing the kingdom a favor to turn on him," Silver grumbled. "His leadership isn't exactly bringing this land into a golden age."

"Careful how you speak," Freeze muttered with a glance at the boisterous human guards. "You don't want to give fuel to the king's paranoia." The human guards, however, were being far too loud to hear anything the hybrids were saying.

"I ... I ... uh, I want to ... leave. I think we ... we all should."

"A gremlin after my own heart," Silver said.

"What? The king would have us all executed for sure," Freeze said.

"Not if um ... all ... uh, all of us, went. But ... it's probably not a ... uh, good idea."

"I like it," Silver said. "We need to do something. We need to stop the assassin from getting that sword, and we need to break the backs of the Rogues, and we're wasting time sitting here in this castle, rotting. We're the only ones who can save the kingdom, and we're forced to guard this pitiful excuse of a king. If King Leon the Conqueror were alive, he wouldn't keep his right hand tied at his back; he would send us out to bring down his wrath on his enemies."

"You know I agree," Freeze said, "but think for a moment. The kingdom is enormous. It took us two days just to *fly* to Aetha. Where would we start? We have no idea where the assassin will be—or where the Rogues are."

"That's uh, not exactly true," Shadow said. "I ... I um, I know ... uh, where ... he'll be ... probably."

"What? How?" Freeze asked.

"I saw the map."

"You did?" Silver asked. "Why didn't you say so? Where is he going to be?"

Shadow cast a few glances about him to ensure no one was listening in. He didn't seem to like the amount of people sitting around.

"Not here ... we should go to my room. Marcus's listeners aren't there," Shadow said. He quietly got up and walked out of the mess hall in a way so nondescript that only those looking directly at him noticed him move.

"Listeners?" Freeze asked before she got up and followed, with Silver close behind.

On the way to Shadow's room, they encountered Howl standing alone, spinning his scimitar deftly in his human hands and glaring fiercely at any humans who walked by. None of the humans matched his gaze; they stared at the floor and hurried past.

He's becoming a bully, Silver thought.

"Follow us," Freeze said to him. Howl gave his sword one more spin and returned it to its sheath as he walked after them, casting one last venomous look at a passing human.

They all crammed themselves into Shadow's small room, and Shadow cast one of his strange spells on the door.

"So what's all this about?" Howl asked.

"Shadow might know where the assassin has gone," Silver answered.

"Really?" Howl asked intently.

"I saw … uh, the map," Shadow said. "Briefly."

"Why haven't you spoken about it before?" Howl asked.

"Nobody asked him," Freeze said with a smile.

"And I don't trust the king," Shadow said.

"He didn't stumble with his words," Howl said. "It must be important."

Shadow just smiled and nodded.

Howl smiled as well. "So, enough chitchat. Where's the assassin?"

"I only glanced at the map, but I saw where the marks were. There was one on Lokthea, another over Trake, and the last one over Krone."

"So where do you think the assassin is?" Freeze asked.

"I think it's obvious, don't you?" Silver said bluntly. "He's at Trake. He can't fly, and everyone in the kingdom wants his blood. He's going to head for the nearest piece. From Aetha, that's Trake."

"That does make sense," Howl said.

"So how do we get there?" Freeze asked.

"I think we should send some fliers to Lokthea, just in case he's headed there," Shadow said. "Perhaps Freeze, Demon, and Blade could go to Lokthea, and the rest of us could take horses to Trake and search for the assassin."

"The king was already furious about five of the Royal Guard leaving," Freeze said. "He'll be out for blood if we all leave."

"That's true," Shadow said, "but we won't be leaving him alone. We'll make sure to exclude Sinister from our plans. I've never thought him to be much of a fighter anyway."

"I don't care who we leave, as long as we leave soon," Silver said.

"We'll go as soon as we can," Howl said eagerly. "The

assassin won't be there long." Though the wolf man's logic was sound, Silver doubted that it was logic that fed his desire to leave so quickly.

"So we're agreed—" Silver began.

"Someone's coming," Shadow warned. Everyone went quiet.

The door creaked open, and Sinister poked his head inside. "Oh, Shadow! Where are y—" he began with malevolent glee. He stopped dead as he saw the three other hybrids watching him.

I should kill him now, Silver thought.

"I, um ..." Sinister began. He lost courage and took off running, slamming the door behind him.

Howl threw the door open and leaped after him, transforming as he went. He tore down the hallway after Sinister, who screamed in panic as Howl pounced upon his back, pinning him to the ground before he could take more than a dozen steps. Sinister twisted and tried to stare Howl in the eyes, but Howl pinned his face against the ground with a clawed hand. The hackles on Howl's back stood up as he let out a vicious growl.

"Don't hurt me! I come on the king's demand!" Sinister simultaneously whimpered and shouted indignantly.

"You attacked Shadow and Jinx ... again!" Howl roared through his wolfish mouth as he dug his claws in deeper.

He seems to have things under control, Silver thought happily.

"So," Freeze asked, "what exactly was this 'king's demand' that brought you out of hiding?"

"You may let him up if you wish, Howl," Silver said. "He'll not get anywhere."

Howl looked to Silver and then to some human guards who were forming a small crowd in the hallway to watch the hybrids fight. He let Sinister up. Howl faced the humans and roared at them. The less stout-hearted humans turned and ran, while the rest recoiled with surprise.

"What are you looking at?" he snarled at the remaining human guards as he transformed back. The other humans scattered, going back to their business.

"So, my dear Sinister, why were you here again?" Silver asked.

Sinister pulled himself up off the ground and rubbed the indentations that Howl's claws had pressed into his skin. He looked at Silver, began to open his mouth, and turned running down the hallway.

You're as foolish as you are cowardly.

Silver raised his hand, and magic poured forth from his palm, knocking Sinister to the floor. Then he grabbed Sinister by the ankles with his mind and raised Sinister in the air, suspending him upside down.

"You could have kept your comfort and your dignity," Silver said, "but now I'm afraid you've forced my hand. Now: what were you here for?"

"Go roast in the dungeons of the Fire God!" Sinister shouted through tears of anger.

"That was a bad thing to say," Silver said. He let Sinister drop, and Sinister crashed into the ground with a clatter of armor. The basilisk-man barely had time to moan before Silver picked him up again. "Perhaps you will be more civil now?"

Sinister stuck out his hand, attempting to counter Silver's magic. Silver brushed the counter aside with a lazy wave and let Sinister drop again before he picked him up a third time.

"You're wasting your time, and worse, you're wasting mine," Silver said calmly. "Now tell me why the king sent you, or next time, I'll throw you out a window." He jerked Sinister toward a stained-glass window to illustrate the point.

"He sent me to tell Shadow to report to the dungeons. That's it, I swear to it!"

"Why would he want me to go to the dungeons?" Shadow asked.

Freeze drew her katana. "What have you told the king, you worm?"

"I've said nothing!" Sinister pleaded.

"Liar!" Freeze shouted. She stuck her hand out and blasted Sinister with a wave of magic, knocking him loose of Silver's grip and slamming him into a wall. "What have you done?" she yelled at him as she walked up, her katana ready. "You couldn't kill Shadow yourself, so you decided to get the king to aid you? Coward!"

"Freeze," Shadow said calmly. She stopped in her tracks. "Let the serpent go. If you kill him, the king will lock you up also."

Freeze and every other hybrid in the room looked at Shadow.

He has been betrayed by Sinister for a third time, and he speaks of mercy?

"I'll go to the prison," Shadow said. "Tell the rest of the Guard what we talked about."

"He also wanted me to take your dirk," Sinister said.

Shadow grew angry. "I think you've said enough here, Sinister. I will give my dirk only to fellow members of the Guard, not the king's snake."

Sinister turned red. "So I'm not part of the Guard now, am I?"

"No, you're not," Howl said menacingly. "And if I see you in the halls again, I think you might just have an unfortunate accident while I'm training with my sword. I can't control it if you step in front of my blade while it's moving, and I have been feeling rather clumsy lately." Howl drew his scimitar.

Sinister's eyes grew large as he contemplated crossing blades with one of the best swordsmen in the Guard. He at once ran away down the hallway,

"Coward," Silver said. He let him go, though. The Guard

couldn't do too much to Sinister without getting in trouble with the king.

Well, more trouble, anyway.

"Are you really going to the prison?" Freeze asked Shadow.

"No, I think I'll disappear on the way there. They can't imprison me if they can't find me," Shadow said humorlessly. "Gather the others. I'll see you around the castle, but you won't see me." He melded into the shadows with a quick spell.

Silver stared at the spot where Shadow had been just a second before.

I'll have to get him to teach me that someday.

Chapter Eighteen

Cearon had been right: it hadn't taken any time at all to get a few gold coins' worth of silver and copper out of people with his back-alley game. It was easy enough to con people with the three-shell game, but with magic, it was almost as if they were lining up just to give him their money. Sometimes Cearon had let a few people win small prizes, just to persuade others watching to try their luck and give him yet more coin.

"That was definitely a much better plan than robbing someone," Harold admitted after Cearon told the increasingly angering crowd that the game was done.

"I told you: I am no common thief," Cearon said with a smile as he looked through their plunder. *It will be more than enough for what we need.*

"No ..." Harold grinned. "Just a con man."

"That's harder to argue," Cearon admitted as they returned to the tavern.

This time around, the atmosphere was quite different. The workers had returned from the quarries, and the room was now thronged with people: many gathering around the bar for drinks and others herding onto the straw-laden floor to dance to a tune played by several musicians on various instruments. The ale flowed, jokes flew through the air, and laughter erupted from all parts of the room. The room was filled with the noise of people in the midst of merrymaking and singing barroom ditties, and many of the private booths were occupied by groups of friends and their drinks. A smile formed on Cearon's lips as he surveyed the commotion.

This is a place where we may hide in plain sight.

"Here," he said to Harold, "pay for the room. Make sure it's private. I'm going to enter myself in the arena. Buy me a drink for when I get back."

"Try not to make yourself known to everyone in the world," Harold said dryly as he took several of the silver coins.

"I make no promises," Cearon said with a smile as he stepped outside, while Harold approached the ever distrusting innkeeper, whose attitude toward the odd pair completely changed at the appearance of actual money.

Cearon was in a good mood as he walked through the poor district of the city toward the immense amphitheater that rose above the surrounding buildings while the sun set into the western mountains.

I am so close to retrieving the first piece of the Relic Sword— the key to all of my plans.

He felt the air growing ever cooler and the light dimming; he would have to walk quickly to get there in time to register.

He strode briskly through the streets, brushing gracefully past people as he went—much to their surprise, when they saw he was blind. The streets of Trake were well made and easy to navigate; it didn't take him long at all to get to Blood Valley.

Cearon walked up to the massive building, its pale oval walls covered with equally pale statues of past combatants, and entered through a towering archway that led to a massive hallway. The hallway encircled the arena sands beneath the soaring bleachers, which rose up as the ceiling for the hallway. This was where gamblers would place their bets and pay their debts, and this was where the fighters would go to risk their lives for the sake of profit. People from all across the Kingdom of Shale—and a few from beyond—milled about, having traveled vast distances to enjoy the sights, sounds, and adrenaline of the blood sports offered here.

A small group of fighters stood together and talked as the crowds slowly streamed out of Blood Valley. Cearon approached the fighters, and with the most amiable smile he could muster, he asked, "Excuse me, but where can I sign up for the fights?"

The fighters stopped their conversation and looked Cearon up and down.

"You're blind?" one of them asked. He was a thick man covered with hardened leather. He wore iron gauntlets with spikes protruding from the knuckles and carried a saber tucked into his belt. His face was littered with scars, but his eyes were somehow kind regardless.

"Yes," Cearon admitted in a dismissive tone.

"How can you fight if you're blind?" another fighter asked. He was a tall, gaunt man whose cheeks seemed too small for his jaw. It was immediately clear he was not a very successful fighter; he had scars all over his body, which was clothed in cheap animal skins for protection. At his side hung a battered and dented iron mace, which was beginning to rust over with age, or perhaps poor care. "I think what you really want is the betting stations. Here, I'll show you where they—"

"No, I know the difference between betting on a fight and fighting in a fight. I meant what I said. Where do I sign on?"

"Look, you can't fight if you're blind," the first fighter who had spoken protested.

"Have you ever seen a blind man fight?"

"No," the thick man admitted with a smile at the ridiculousness.

"Then you have no idea how well we fight. Now where do I sign up?" Cearon asked. The fighters looked at each other. Finally, the thin one relented.

"It's you're life; waste it as you will. Here, follow me." He took Cearon's hand and put it on his shoulder before leading

Cearon to where quite a few young men stood in line, each eagerly imagining the glory they would have out in the sands. "When you get to the front of this line, give them your name, and you'll have to pay a silver coin. Entrance fee." With that, the fighter returned to his friends.

All of the men in line looked at Cearon strangely. Some muttered about the blind man; others laughed at him; and others simply ignored him, minding their own business. *As long as they don't bother me, there won't be any problems.*

"What are you doing here, blind man?" one of the laughers asked.

"Same as you: I'm entering the fight," Cearon said casually. *There may be problems.*

"I've never killed a blind man before. This should be interesting," another man said. He had a sadistic look in his eye and was clearly something of a bully. The other young men around him seemed to nervously follow his lead, even as they knew deep down that badgering a blind man was the lowest of dishonorable behaviors. The laughing young man didn't seem to mind, however.

Cearon was surprised to note that he appeared very young indeed—Cearon wouldn't have guessed a day over eighteen—and yet many of the older people around seemed shackled by his will. The sadistic young man did have the advantage of clearly being of a wealthy family, however. He wore fashionable robes with a large collar, along with a hat with several feathers pinned to the side. He had several gold rings with jewels embedded in them, and at his side was an incredibly expensive long sword, with embedded gold leaf making swirling patterns along the hilt and probably down the blade. In the pommel was a ruby the size of Cearon's knuckle.

I do not like this spoiled brat already.

"I've killed plenty of men with sight," Cearon said with a shrug. "This will be nothing new for me."

"You? You have killed people before?" the rich young man asked with skeptical, mocking laughter.

"I have killed when I needed to. People always forget that there are more ways of seeing than by sight alone."

"Can you see this?" the man asked as he threw a punch at Cearon. Cearon ducked out of the way and kneed him hard in the stomach, knocking the wind out of the boy. Before the rich young man had a chance to do anything else, Cearon elbowed him hard across the jaw, knocking him both to the ground and out of consciousness.

"Actually ... I could," Cearon said as he stepped lightly over the body. The other men in the line instantly stopped all laughing and conversation as they stared at Cearon in awe, some fearfully taking a step away from him as he came forward.

Already, I have their fear. This will be an easy job.

"How ... how did you do that?" one of the men asked.

Cearon smiled and said, "With secrets only known to the blind."

The rest of his time in the line was uneventful. He paid the entry fee, signed on for the most advanced as well as dangerous circuit, and told them his name was The Blind Wanderer. On his way back to the tavern, he visited a tailor and bought a gray cloak, a shirt, and tough traveling pants.

Cearon then returned to the tavern, noting the presence of several of the fighters, all of whom seemed intent on relaxing and forgetting the dangers of their next matches. Cearon had a single drink with Harold and then retired for the night. He slept soundly, without a single nervous thought of the fights yet to come.

The next day came quickly in Cearon's mind, even though he slept late into the morning. He ate a light breakfast, jogged a mile through the streets, and washed himself in the river. He spent the rest of the day focusing mentally, preparing himself as best he could to use magic.

It's not likely I'll need it, but it's good to be prepared.

Before long, it was just past noon, and time for Cearon to go to the sands of Blood Valley. Cearon gave the remainder of his money to Harold and told him to bet it on the Blind Wanderer.

They both left for the arena, with Cearon wearing his new, but already scruffy-looking clothing. He still wore his bandanna from his old clothes, which somehow seemed to meld well with the rest of the clothes. He looked for all the world like a well-traveled blind man.

When they came to the arena, Cearon and Harold parted paths, with Cearon heading for the fighters' pit and Harold leaving for the spectator stands after he bet every coin the two men had on the Blind Wanderer. He noticed happily that no one else seemed to wish to bet their coin on a blind fighter they had never heard of.

That just means more money for us.

Cearon found the fighters' pit easily enough. It was the only door at the end of a staircase descending below the arena stage, and the words "Fighters' Pit" were written on it in a red that somewhat reminded Cearon of blood.

Is that intentional? If so, it fails to intimidate me. He casually stepped through the door.

The room was dark, but that was no hindrance to Cearon's mind. The room was dank as well, and had the smell of old and new sweat. In the center was a basin filled with filthy water intended for fighters to clean themselves with between matches. Benches and chairs littered the room haphazardly, having been carried around here and there by fighters and never returned. Many chairs and benches were already occupied, but it was clear this room had been designed to accommodate more than the men standing here. Cearon figured their numbers were few because few dared enter the arena with this elite class of fighters.

Or perhaps they simply kill one another faster than they can be replaced.

A total of thirty-two fighters had entered the competition, so the winning fighter would have to fight his way through four rounds. Cearon wasn't worried; he had knocked out one of the fighters with ease just yesterday, and though that man had barely been more than a boy, Cearon was better with a blade than he was at hand-to-hand combat, and he had magic. He smiled to himself as he found a seat in the corner of the room.

I will make this a show to remember.

Everyone inside the room stared openly at Cearon. They had all seen the Blind Wanderer on the roster, but they still couldn't believe a blind man was actually entering the ring with them, the most elite of the warriors in Blood Valley. It was men like them who had given inspiration for the statues that crowded the wall space of Blood Valley. However, most seemed to respect him, at least—some even fearing him superstitiously. They had all heard about how he had knocked out a young warrior just the day before—a young warrior who was standing in that very room.

"You—blind beggar," the young man said, now dressed in shimmering chain mail, a shining steel breastplate, and a steel helmet with a plumed crest atop it. He was also now sporting a bruise that ran from the back of his jaw to his nose. It looked almost like a stripe of blue war paint.

Cearon sighed with irritation. "What do you want, boy?"

"I don't think you're blind at all," he accused, with several other fighters gathering around. It was an unspoken rule that no fights ever broke out in the pit, and the other fighters would not allow these two newcomers to break that rule.

"Indeed? Well, that's good to know," Cearon said with a

bored countenance. "Whatever you need to tell yourself to nurse that injured pride of yours, I suppose."

"You caught me by surprise!" the boy said defensively as he gripped his wonderfully made sword hilt. The other fighters took a step forward, with one even laying a hand warningly on the boy's shoulder. "I could take you in a fair fight," the boy continued, as if the intimidating men around him weren't there.

"Fine," Cearon said calmly. "See if you can't beat me on the sands, but I warn you: I'm better with a blade than I am with my hands."

"Each fighter is allowed two kills in a month," the boy said maliciously. "I think you shall be my first. And when you're lying before me, beaten, I think I shall rip that blindfold off and make you as blind as you say you are with the point of Starlight here." He patted his sword proudly as he spoke.

"Starlight is the name of your sword?" Cearon laughed. "Sounds like a fairy name."

The boy frowned, seeing that Cearon was obviously not going to be intimidated. "We shall see who's laughing at the end of the day," he said as he turned to go.

"And we shall see your regal blood spilling into the sands," Cearon called after him.

The boy just laughed. "Do that, and you'll never fight here again."

As the tension died, the fighters went back about their business; only one stayed near Cearon. It was the large, but kind-looking fighter Cearon had met briefly in the main hallway of Blood Valley the previous night.

"You certainly pick enemies poorly, blind one. That is Lord Darren the Third, the son of Lord Darren the Second—the man who runs this arena."

"Is this supposed to mean something to me?" Cearon asked.

"Well, if you want to live through the day, I would suggest going easy on him, no matter how much of a brat he is."

"He's not defeating me," Cearon said flatly.

"It would be wise to let him. This is his first time here, and his father has warned us that any who defeat him will face dire consequences."

"Like what? I don't get to fight here again? That doesn't concern me. This is the first and last time I participate in the sport."

"Lord Darren the Second is a good man, but his love for his son overcomes his common sense. He is not above killing another man for publicly humiliating his son."

"Let him try."

"How many of you are new to this arena?" a man asked as he walked through a small door in a shadowy corner that made the opening nearly impossible to see to everyone but Cearon. To most, it seemed as if this man had appeared out of nowhere.

The man was tall and rather muscular. He had dark black hair and a furrowed brow. The scars on his face and his arms made it clear that he was no stranger to combat. His hair was pulled into a ponytail and braided as it went down to the small of his back.

Cearon raised his hand in response.

"All right: listen well, blind man, because I don't repeat myself. This is not a fight to the death. If every fight went to the death, we wouldn't have much business. You are to fight to submission. Either disarm your opponent or show that you could have killed him. That, of course, doesn't mean the odd death doesn't happen. If the crowd calls for you to kill, or you just slip up a little, there will be no grudge held against you. However, kill more than two fighters in one month, and you will never work here again. Understood?" He paused, but Cearon said nothing. The other man seemed to take that as a yes. "I assume you have your own weapons, because we don't supply them to you. That's your job. Now, the first fight will be Head Banger against the Blind Wanderer. Good luck, blind man—you'll need it."

"Don't you know who you are speaking to?" Cearon asked.

"Enlighten me," the fight chief responded casually.

"I am the winner of this tournament. I am the Blind Wanderer, the greatest warrior ever to walk the paths of this earth."

"We shall see," the fight chief said with a skeptical grin. "The fight will start in five minutes. Get yourselves ready."

"Already am," Head Banger said. He had a large mallet and was admittedly an immense man. He stood more than six feet tall, and his arms were as big as most men's legs. He wore a full suit of armor, and a horsehair mane adorned his helmet. "I'm going against a blind man," he said with a grin as he looked toward Cearon. "I could win without a weapon."

"The bigger the pride, the more satisfying it is to watch the fall," Cearon said with a smile. He got up and walked to the large wooden doors that led out to the arena grounds.

"Keep your guard up," Cearon said as Head Banger came and stood next to him.

"Thanks. Try to keep your head from caving in," Head Banger responded.

"I usually do."

"Hope you win, blind beggar," Lord Darren the Third said. "I want the pleasure of killing you myself."

"Don't count on it," Head Banger said.

The doors opened, and light cascaded into the dark room. Head Banger held his hand over his eyes until his vision became accustomed to the brightness, but beneath the blindfold, Cearon's eyes were comfortable.

"Here come our first fighters!" the fight chief shouted to the crowd. He had slipped out his nearly invisible door and was standing at the center of the arena stage. A roar of cheers swept through the stadium, and the crowd greeted the fighters with thunderous applause. Cearon couldn't believe how many people were in the stands; there had to be thousands. He noted that many were chanting Head Banger's name.

The applause died down as the fight chief motioned the audience to silence. "In his signature armor, we have a frequenter of the arena: the strong, the mighty, the ruthless Head Banger!" the fight chief shouted, working the crowd. Once again, applause thundered throughout the stadium.

"In the drab cloak, we have a newcomer: the mysterious, the unknown, and the proud Blind Wanderer!" Only scatterings of applause rippled through the stands as people stared at Cearon in disbelief.

"They all know you are going to die," Head Banger whispered to Cearon.

"They're just stunned you were willing to fight me," Cearon muttered back. "It's pretty much suicide."

Head Banger laughed. "I have to admire your courage in the face of death, blind one."

"I was about to say the same to you."

"Fighters, to your marks!" the fight chief shouted. Once again, he was greeted by the roar of cheers from the audience.

The arena was, in essence, a giant oval of sand surrounded by seats. The seats were elevated almost twenty feet above the fighting ring, giving the stage—and indeed the whole building—its name: Blood Valley.

"Fighters! Are you ready?" the fight chief shouted.

Head Banger answered with a war cry.

"Only if he is," Cearon said with a smile. He hadn't even drawn his sword yet.

"Then let the fight begin!" the fight chief roared as he stuck his fists in the air—the signal to begin. He withdrew to the edge of the sand.

"Aren't you going to draw your sword, blind man?" Head Banger jeered. "At least pretend to fight back!"

"Give me a reason to draw it, and I will." *I will humiliate this man.*

Head Banger charged with his mallet held high over his head; Cearon didn't move. Head Banger quickly crossed the distance between them and swung down at Cearon. Cearon stepped out of the way at the last moment; the mallet thudded into the sand, burying its head.

Cearon punched Head Banger in his stomach and blasted him with magic at the same time. Head Banger flew head over heels from the magical blast, leaving his mallet embedded in the sand as he tumbled awkwardly in his heavy armor.

Cearon walked casually toward Head Banger, who lay prone on the ground, staring in terror at the blind man strolling toward him.

"Who are you?" he gasped.

"Someone far more powerful than you," Cearon said as he drew his sword. "Why don't you go get your mallet, so you can pretend to fight back?" Cearon stepped aside, motioning him toward his lost weapon.

Head Banger looked at Cearon cautiously and then ran to retrieve his weapon. He tugged it out of the ground and circled Cearon, this time guardedly. Cearon stood still, turning with his sword held at ready in front of him to face Head Banger wherever he went.

Head Banger charged again, this time swinging horizontally. Cearon stepped back, allowing the mallet to get within inches of him before he leaped behind it. Head Banger spun around and swung again. Cearon slid underneath the mallet, regained his footing as it passed overhead, and knocked Head Banger's feet out from under him with the flat of his blade while he rose to his feet.

Head Banger spun in midair as his feet were knocked from beneath him, and he thudded into the ground, releasing his mallet as he fell hard onto the sand. He was weaponless. He tried to rise to his feet, but Cearon kicked him back into the sand and rested his blade against Head Banger's neck.

"We have a winner! The Blind Wanderer!" the fight chief shouted, his voice failing to conceal his surprise. The crowd remained deathly silent, scarcely believing what they saw. Head Banger was one of the best fighters in the arena, and this new, blind warrior had just defeated him with ease.

Finally, one of the crowd shouted, "All hail the Blind Warrior!" His call was answered with roaring applause; spectators rose from their seats, chanting Cearon's name.

Cearon pointed his sword to the sky in acknowledgment and then sheathed it. He bowed to his opponent, who was struggling to get up.

"I told you it was suicide." Then Cearon turned and walked back to the fighters' pit.

When Cearon entered, all of the fighters looked at him with nervous apprehension. They hadn't been able to watch the fight, but they all wondered how the blind man had come back into the waiting room and Head Banger had not.

"Where is Head Banger?" one of them asked.

"Gone," Cearon said as he sat himself down in his dark corner. All the fighters looked at each other nervously and then back at the strange man in the corner.

Cearon remained in his corner until he was up to fight again; he had to wait seven rounds of boredom. Half of the fighters had been eliminated, and one had been killed. All the other fighters had bruises and minor cuts. Cearon was the only one who was completely untouched.

As he did before each match, the fight chief walked in and announced the next fight: "The Blind Warrior against Dragon Eye."

"I'm called the Blind Wanderer."

"The crowd remembers you as warrior," the fight chief said.

"Will I still be able to claim my winnings at the end if my name changes?"

The fight chief laughed. "I don't think anyone's going to forget you."

Cearon went to the door. Dragon Eye stood next to him. Dragon Eye, who carried a broadsword and a shield, was arrayed in chain mail and a red cape. He was called Dragon Eye because he had a crazy look in his eyes, and his face was long and angular, almost looking like a dragon's.

"You should see some real dragon eyes sometime," Cearon muttered beneath his breath.

"What?" Dragon Eye asked nervously.

"Nothing ... nothing important, anyway. Good luck out there."

"Oh, uh, thank you," Dragon Eye said brusquely.

"Do you want to wish me good luck as well?" Cearon asked. The doors opened, and brilliant light flooded in.

"No. I'm going to kill you," Dragon Eye said, giving Cearon a cruel grin before he stepped out into the arena.

"Well, that's not very nice," Cearon murmured to himself. The crowd gave deafening cheers as they saw the Blind Warrior enter the arena again. This time, many chanted his name.

"Please welcome back to the arena the quick, the terrifying, the deadly Dragon Eye!" the fight chief shouted. The crowd applauded. "And also returning is the crowd-pleasing, the powerful, the sightless Blind Warrior!" The crowd went wild with applause at Cearon's name.

"Fighters, on your marks!" Both fighters went to their marks. "Are both fighters ready?"

"Prepare to die!" Dragon Eye shouted.

"Only if he is," Cearon said.

"Let the fight begin!" the fight chief said as he raised his fists in the air and receded to allow the opponents their battle.

Dragon Eye exploded off his mark, charging straight toward Cearon.

This is a reckless bunch of fighters here.

Cearon stood with his sword drawn and didn't make a move. Dragon Eye slashed at Cearon, and Cearon blocked it easily. Dragon Eye then swung like a madman, striking with both sword and shield. Cearon blocked and dodged it all. *Dragon Eye is quick, but I am far quicker.*

Then Cearon swung out at the same time Dragon Eye slashed with his sword, aiming his strike at Dragon Eye's blade. Cearon batted it aside and spun around, elbowing Dragon Eye's nose as he did. Dragon Eye's head jerked back from the impact, stunning him. Cearon finished the turn and slammed the hilt of his sword into Dragon Eye's chest, blasting him with magic along with it. Dragon Eye flew violently back and slid to a halt in the arena sand.

He groaned and slowly pulled himself back to his feet. He looked at Cearon walking calmly toward him. Dragon Eye licked at blood coming out of his nose, and his lip curled in rage. He stood up, his face contorted and his shoulders hunched with anger.

He ran forward with a war cry, screaming, "Die!" with all of his breath.

He lunged forward, stabbing at Cearon. Cearon brushed the blade aside and then ran his blade along Dragon Eye's stomach, cutting just beyond the chain mail. Cearon stepped past Dragon Eye, and as Cearon's sword slid by his opponent, he spun it in his hands so that he held it backward, and stabbed it back, stopping it just short Dragon Eye's spine.

Dragon Eye looked in disbelief at the blood spilling from his stomach. He fell to the ground, trying to keep blood from escaping the gash. Cearon wiped off his sword on Dragon Eye's cape and sheathed it.

"And we have a winner: once more, the great Blind Warrior!" the fight chief called out to the crowds. The crowds exploded in cheers once more as Cearon waved to them and walked back to the fighters' pit. All of the fighters looked miserable to see Cearon enter. *No one wants to fight me—and especially lose to me. Even that Darren brat seems displeased to see me.*

"How hard was Dragon Eye to beat?" the thick man Cearon had spoken with before asked as Cearon walked once again to his corner. Cearon stopped and answered without turning to face the man.

"No more difficult than the average person." When Cearon sat down, he saw the fighters were yet more disheartened and frightened.

Cearon sat in his corner and waited for his next fight. All the other fighters slowly migrated to the opposite side of the room, trying to keep away from this blind warrior. Rumors were beginning to spread quickly of Cearon's powers being derived by some sinister force. The word "warlock" was reaching Cearon's keen ears more often than he would have liked.

The wait for his next fight was much shorter this time. There were now only four fighters left: Cearon; Lord Darren; the man Cearon had spoken with, who was nicknamed Saber; and a gaunt, insane-looking man called Ripper. Everyone else was eliminated or dead. As usual, the fight chief walked in through his nearly invisible door.

"Next fight: the Blind Warrior against the Ripper." With that, the chief walked back out into the arena.

"You won't get past me, blind one!" the Ripper said with a maniacal laugh.

"Perhaps," was all Cearon said.

The Ripper looked thoroughly mad. He had a nervous twitch and was freakishly skinny. His skin was taut and shone with weeks worth of oil. His eyes were actually black and always bore a demented expression. His hair was a raven-colored, greasy mess as oily as his skin that fell in tangled heaps down to his shoulders. He wore only a hardened leather chest piece and a tattered and bloodstained pair of trousers. He brandished a broadsword with runes running along the blade and nothing more. Cearon had heard rumors that it had a spell on it granting the user great power, but at the cost of his sanity.

They both stood in front of the door. Ripper didn't look at the door, but rather stared at Cearon.

"I may be blind, but I can still tell when I'm being watched," Cearon said. Ripper responded only with a demented smile.

The door lurched open, and bright sunlight streamed in once again. Both fighters walked out, greeted by the cheers of thousands.

"You know and love him: the mysterious, incredible Blind Warrior!" the fight chief shouted to the crowd. The stands exploded with cheers. "Another well-known fighter: the demented, the cruel, the insane Ripper!" Cheers stormed from the stands for the insane man. Ripper jumped in the air, waving his hands around wildly at their cheers. He did a backflip, landed it, and jumped straight from it into a front flip.

Clearly, he is athletic.

"Are you ready to die?" Ripper said through his crazy laughter, still leaping around wildly.

"We'll see," Cearon said.

"Fighters, to your marks!" the fight chief shouted. Both fighters went to their designated positions, with Ripper doing flips and spins the entire way there. "Are both fighters ready?"

Ripper answered by giving a high-pitched shriek as he stared at Cearon through his crazy eyes. *This is truly an odd man.*

"Only if he is," Cearon said.

"Let the fight begin!" the fight chief shouted as he raised his fists into the air.

Ripper gave a maniacal laugh as he circled Cearon. Cearon drew his blade; it glimmered in the sun with its unnatural shine.

"Your move, madman," Cearon said.

"Your death, blind man!" He cackled wildly.

Ripper charged in. He jumped in the air and did a front flip, slashing out with his sword as he rolled through the air. Cearon stepped out of the way, causing Ripper to strike only air.

Ripper landed on his feet and slashed at Cearon with incredible agility. Cearon turned Ripper's blade aside with his and then smacked Ripper's leg with the flat of his sword. Ripper stumbled as one of his legs was knocked out from under him, but he recovered quickly and stabbed at Cearon. Cearon swept the blade aside and stepped toward Ripper, ramming his shoulder into Ripper's face. Ripper was knocked to the ground, but rolled away before Cearon struck the killing blow.

It hadn't seemed to have even entered Ripper's mind that he was losing the fight, just narrowly avoiding death. He seemed to have room for one thing in that skull of his: *kill*.

He pulled himself to his feet and leaped at Cearon, spinning in the air and swinging his sword horizontally. Cearon stopped the sword with his own and shoved his shoulder into Ripper's legs, spinning him wildly over Cearon's head.

Ripper flipped in the air and landed in the arena sand with a thud. Cearon turned, getting into a runner's start position before he had even stopped sliding, and charged toward the prone Ripper.

Ripper swung his blade at Cearon as the psychotic man tried to rise, but Cearon blocked it and stomped on Ripper's shoulder, pinning him back to the ground. Ripper tried to raise his sword again, but Cearon cleaved his hand off at the wrist and then stabbed downward, stopping the point of his sword just an inch from Ripper's neck.

Ripper's whole body clenched as he anticipated his death at the blade. He slowly opened his eyes and saw the sword just above his neck. So much adrenaline was going through the madman that he had yet to even realize his right hand had been cut off.

"We have a winner!" the fight chief shouted to the crowd. The crowd cheered wildly. *Blood is always a popular sight.* "The Blind Warrior has made it to the final round!"

Cearon walked back to the fighter's pit without even acknowledging the crowd this time. He stepped inside the room, and the two fighters left did not look happy to see him.

"How do you do it, blind man?" Saber asked.

"It's possible to see with more than your eyes," Cearon said. "Your mind can read the world much more clearly. Your eyes see lies and truth as the same, but your mind is never fooled." He wasn't lying; he did look at the world through his mind as much as he did through his eyes. He had been taught long ago that one's mind had the clearest view of the world around it; one just had to learn to look through it.

He sat in his corner, waiting for his last fight, as the other two, Saber and Lord Darren, walked out into the bright sunshine. Cearon sat in solitude, waiting for the two fighters to finish their fight. It lasted a long time. After many minutes, a fighter returned, and Cearon was not surprised to see that it was Lord Darren.

The young boy sat down and panted as he rested his head in his hands. "I'll be ready soon. Just give me a few minutes," he said through his heavy breathing. Cearon could see the fear in his eyes. The other fighters had let him win because of his father, but he knew Cearon would not extend him the same courtesy.

"Take your time. There's no rush." *Your humiliation will come eventually.*

The young man rested for about ten minutes and then put his crested helm on and stepped up to the door; Cearon followed suit. They stood next to each other, Lord Darren eying Cearon fearfully.

"So what does the world look like through your mind?"

"That would be like you describing to me what blue looked like."

Darren swallowed nervously. The door flew open, and the two of them walked out into the bright sunlight.

"I give you the championship fight!" the fight chief roared as the fighters walked out. As usual, the crowd thundered. "This is the final match! The Dark Lord faces the Blind Warrior! Who will prevail? Fighters, to your marks!" The crowd roared as the fighters went to their positions. "Fighters, you had better be ready by now! Let the fight begin!"

Lord Darren drew his long sword and walked cautiously toward Cearon.

So he is not as reckless as the others. He will fall just the same. Cearon noticed the left forearm of his opponent had spikes covering it. He raised an eyebrow. *How did I miss that before?*

Lord Darren came closer and closer to Cearon until finally he was within striking range. The crowd erupted as the two warriors crossed blades.

Lord Darren was strong—and, surprisingly to Cearon, actually was skilled with a blade. He swung, crashing his blade into Cearon's, and then lashed out at Cearon with his spiked and armored forearm.

Cearon was much faster, though; he stayed one step ahead of the spoiled lord. Lord Darren slashed his sword into Cearon's, lunged forward, and then grabbed Cearon with his gauntleted hand, trying to pull him off balance. Cearon stepped back, pulled his knuckle blade from where it was hidden in his belt, and slammed the blade in a space between Darren's metal gauntlet. Darren cried out in pain as he released Cearon.

Cearon had no interest in letting this fight go on for long. He batted Darren's sword aside and slashed at the boy's head. Darren saw the danger and ducked as quickly as he could, dropping to his knees. Cearon's blade cut the feathers from the top of Darren's helm. Following his momentum forward, Cearon kneed Darren in the head, knocking him back into the sand.

Darren slashed out at Cearon as he tried to rise, but Cearon blocked the slash. Then Darren followed with the spiked gauntlet, forcing Cearon to step back as Darren stumbled to his feet. Cearon charged, and Darren slashed at him. Cearon blocked the blow and slammed the knuckle blade into Darren's shoulder, failing to pierce the well-made armor but knocking Darren back.

Darren swept his blade out horizontally as he stumbled back with a grunt of pain, but Cearon blocked it, following Darren back and kicking him in the leg. Darren fell to a knee as his leg buckled from Cearon's kick. He brought his sword around, and struck again at Cearon while he moved still closer. Cearon hit the blade aside and palmed Darren in the face with his off hand, blasting Darren to the ground with magic. Darren slammed into the sand, instantly knocked out from the impact. Cearon rested his blade point against Darren's neck.

"We have a victor!" the fight chief shouted. The audience went fanatic. "The Blind Warrior is the winner of the tournament! Those of you who have bet on him may go collect your winnings, and those of you who doubted him may go pay your debts."

"Not just yet," someone said suddenly. A man stood up from his seat in a noble's private booth built into the very wall of the arena stage. He was dressed in a rich man's finery.

He wore dark blue clothes, and his hands and neck were adorned with the most expensive of jewelry. He had a regal beard, and in his hand he carried a gold cane that looked more like a king's scepter than anything else. The crowd went silent at his voice. "This Blind Warrior has fought well and defeated the best of our combatants with ease." *This man must be Lord Darren the Second.* "I present our champion with a great honor. We have recently captured Strind, the leader of the warlocks. We will allow this Blind Warrior to perform Strind's execution ... by combat, of course."

The crowd booed and hissed as Lord Darren the Third was carried from the arena and a man was brought forth bound in chains and with several mages following him closely, containing him with their minds as he kicked and struggled.

"Come now!" Lord Darren called out to the crowds, calming them as best he could. "Who else has earned the honor of slaying Trake's greatest foe?" Still the crowd booed. Mages came and stood guard around the arena, ready to recapture Strind after he slew this Blind Warrior.

Strind's chains were released, and the guards carrying him tossed a sword by his side before they retreated from the arena. Strind looked joyfully down at the sword and then to Cearon, his red warlock eyes glinting in the sun. He had a matted, dark beard and wild hair. His clothes were in tatters, and his body was covered with self-inflicted scars shaped into runes and words of terror. He grinned, and his yellow, crooked teeth greeted Cearon.

"You are more animal than man," Cearon said. "I feel no remorse in slaying you."

"I never feel remorse in slaying," the wild man cackled, "and you have no idea what it takes to fight me!" He raised his hand and sent a magical spear at Cearon. Cearon blocked it with an easy wave of his hand.

"A spear? Is that the best you are capable of, warlock?

You have much to learn. It appears, perhaps, that discoloring your eyes and carving your skin is not the best way to learn magic."

"You're stronger than I thought, human. It is no matter—you cannot match the power of a warlock!" He reached out with both hands. Dust flew in all directions as a powerful wave of magic flew out from his hands.

Cearon stuck out his hands and threw the wave aside, and then, with a roar, Cearon pressed his hands forward. Magic poured from him, ripping through dirt and sand with ease. Sand blasted everywhere as the invisible wave moved across the arena; it was powerful enough to dig a trench through the sands as the magic tore toward the warlock. The magic wall slammed into Strind, who, despite how hard he tried, was quickly overcome by the magic. He flew back and slammed against the wall so hard the stone cracked.

Cearon raised his hand, which glowed as he concentrated on fire. A bolt of flame flew out from his palm, striking Strind. Flames erupted toward the sky as an unnatural fire covered the warlock. He screamed in terror as he rolled in the sands, trying to extinguish the ethereal flames.

Cearon then stuck out his hand toward the warlock. The warlock was lifted up off the ground and carried toward Cearon, still smoking and whimpering.

"It seems that I was beyond you, warlock," Cearon said as Strind dangled in the grip of his magic.

"Who are you?" Strind gasped.

"I am the cursed one," Cearon said. "Now go to the abyss you profess to serve." Cearon ran his blade through Strind, pulling the blade out as the warlock fell dead into the sands of Blood Valley.

The crowd and even Lord Darren the Second were stunned into silence. Cearon wiped his blade on Strind's body and walked out of the arena. The sounds of thunderous applause greeted his ears as he left. He smiled to himself.

This will be a day never forgotten.

"How much did we get?" Cearon asked as he approached Harold, who was standing next to a handcart laden with a large bag.

"We have a small fortune, Cearon!" Harold said excitedly. "I don't think we'll have any problems with money again. Over two hundred gold coins!"

"Good," Cearon said. "That should keep us moving financially for a while. We need to go to the bank—come."

"The bank? They charge you ten percent to store your gold!"

"What do you suggest? That we carry this everywhere we go? I'm stronger than I look, but I'm not that strong, Harold, and we will still have enough for what we need."

Cearon grabbed the handcart and began hauling it through the city, with many people chanting "Blind Warrior!" as he passed. The bank was nearly a mile away, but they covered the distance quickly.

"By the way," Harold said, "you looked good fighting in those clothes. Very mysterious. I think you should keep that look."

"It'll have to do for now, but I liked the tunic better."

"I can't believe how aware you are just using your mind," Harold said somewhat enviously. "I've never heard of a mage who could actually see better with his eyes shut."

"I learned it from necessity. I needed to be able to watch people without looking at them. It saved your life at Castle Shale, too. That gremlin would have stabbed us for sure if I hadn't been able to see him mentally."

Harold laughed. "As I recall, he was trying to stab you, not me ..."

A man wearing the black armor of the city's prefects walked into the prefect headquarters near the mayor's mansion. The headquarters was a large marble structure with massive steps leading up to a large metal door. Two prefects stood on guard at either side of the door; the man nodded to them as he walked through.

"Sir!" they both said as they stood at attention. He walked through the main room, which was filled with cells—most occupied by warlocks captured from the surrounding hills. Many of the warlocks were being beaten by prefects as he walked through; he had the authority to stop them, but he didn't mind—in fact, it was he who had told the prefects to beat the warlocks whenever they were captured. It kept the warlocks on their toes. They didn't want to be captured if they knew a beating was in store for them, and it was better than executing them like the mayor wanted. This way, he could sneak some of them out from time to time and return them to their work.

He walked into his private quarters and pulled the blinds over the windows. The room became dark, lit only by a small oil lamp on his desk—which, besides a small chest hidden behind the desk, was the lone furniture in the room. He walked to the chest, which was bolted to the floor and had a large lock keeping it shut. He pulled a key from around his neck and unlocked it. He opened the chest and took out a small crystal the size of a child's fist. He placed it on a table and held his hand over it, concentrating.

"Why have you bothered me, George?" a voice said from the crystal.

"My lord, I believe I have spotted the traitor you spoke of," George said. "He just slew the warlock leader, Strind, in single combat."

"What? Why didn't you stop him?" the voice asked angrily. George cried out as his head ached with an unnatural pain.

"I am sorry, lord!" George said pleadingly as he clutched his temples. "I thought for certain that Strind would slay the man and escape as planned, but this warrior … he slew him! He was so strong! He must be the one you are looking for."

After a long pause, George's pain left him. "Are you sure he is the traitor? Describe him."

"I didn't see much of him. I was standing ready to let Strind out of the arena, but he wore a blindfold. He called himself the Blind Warrior. He was stronger than any I've seen before. He dispatched all the combatants with ease; he could launch fire from his hands, and he was terribly fast."

"Blind Warrior? Why would Cearon name himself that? Ahhh," the voice said knowingly. "He was afraid to show his eyes. Clever Cearon … clever, but foolish all the same. What kind of weapon did this Blind Warrior carry?"

"A sword—not impressive in size, but it had an unnatural shine to the metal. It looked as if it were made of a mirror."

"So, Cearon, you have come to Trake. But why fight warlocks?"

"He entered Blood Valley. The warlock was slain in the arena," George explained.

"Arena? That was very foolish of you, Cearon. Why would you enter the arena? What are you planning to do with that money? How will that help you get the relic? I suppose it is of no importance. I shall be there soon, George, and I will be bringing a battalion of elves. Prepare the city; I want that gate open. I do not feel like storming the cliffs of Trake."

"Yes, Lord Marcus," George said. With that, he put away the small crystal and went back to his duties as leader of the prefects. With the gate in its damaged state, George would not need to do much sabotaging to ensure Marcus's unhindered entrance. He was thankful for that at least.

Chapter Nineteen

"Ready to go?" Howl asked as he burst into Silver's room.

Silver pulled his head up from his pillow and looked at Howl through drooping eyelids. He glanced about his small room, which was filled with fine pillows, tapestries, and incense he had bought from the town with his gambling winnings.

What in the world is this about?

"Is this some cruel joke?" he asked as he looked out the window and saw the midnight sky.

"No. If we're leaving, we need to leave now," Howl said as he gathered some of Silver's things together.

"What's the difference between now and later?" Silver grumbled as he reluctantly pulled the sheets off himself. *I hate the cold air!*

"Now is now, and later is too late. I've already disabled the night watch at the gates and—" Howl began.

"What?" Silver exclaimed through his grogginess.

"They're just unconscious … probably. Now gather your things," Howl said. He glanced over at Silver and saw him sitting on the side of his bed, staring at Howl in shock. "Get up," Howl said with irritation as he pulled Silver off the bed.

"Oh, that's cold!" Silver said as his bare feet fell on the stone floor. He quickly relocated to a nearby pillow.

"Get into some proper clothes. Finish gathering your things; I need to wake the others."

"You might have run this plan by us before you just barged in," Silver said as he donned his armor.

"I couldn't risk any spies hearing about it. It had to be unexpected. Now move. I'm not staying in this castle another minute longer than I have to. When the king betrayed Shadow, he betrayed us all." Howl left the room.

I doubt he'll be coming back to Castle Shale, Silver thought as he continued to gather his belongings.

Howl went from room to room, gathering all of the Guard he deemed necessary to the mission, which turned out to be every one of them but Sinister. It wasn't long before the Guard were gathered in the stables—even Shadow, who had rematerialized once Howl had dispatched the night guards at the gate.

"This doesn't seem like the Howl I always remembered," Silver whispered to Jinx.

"You can only push a wolf so far before he bites," Howl replied, his sharp ears picking up Silver's words. "We've been ruled by a pathetic excuse for a king for far too long now. How much could we have already accomplished if he hadn't been holding us back? I say it's time we let this king stew in his paranoia while we actually do something. The assassin is a danger to the entire Kingdom of Shale, and, indeed, to all of the world. I think it is high time he was stopped."

Pyre spoke up next. "What do you have in mind, and more importantly, how do you plan to escape the king's wrath?"

"We go to Trake. If that's where the assassin is heading, that's where we're needed. As for the king, you saw how much favor we gained with the humans after Bel. We'll leave Castle Shale forever and begin defending the kingdom from the Rogues directly. If the king tries to capture us, we will hide wherever we need to. There's a lot of wilderness to disappear in, and many commoners who will be willing to hide us."

"How are we getting to Trake?" Rocky asked.

"We borrow some horses—" Howl began.

"Steal horses," Blade corrected. "Call it what it is."

"Steal horses," Howl admitted, "and meet up with the fliers at Trake."

"Go to the temple," Shadow said. "That's where the relic will be if it's anywhere. I'd bet my knife on it."

"Now let's move," Howl said. "We must escape before the guard changes."

Crash ruffled the hair on Howl's head. "I always knew this pup would come in handy."

Howl snarled, brushing away Crash's hand with irritation. *You dare pet the lord of the wild?*

"A feisty pup," Crash said as he pulled his hand away.

"Enough talk." Howl pulled a horse from its stall and threw a saddle over it. The other walkers did the same.

"We'll meet you there," Blade said. With a gust of wind, he took to the air with the other fliers following close at his heels.

Howl dug his heels into the side of his horse. It took off, galloping through the courtyard, through the now unguarded gates, and through the streets.

Gods willing, I'll never have to see that castle again, Howl thought hopefully.

Jinx, Shadow, Pyre, Blade, Freeze, and Demon flew as fast as their wings could take them, each eager for another chance to slay the assassin. Blade remembered the oath he had made back in the ruins of Aetha, and imagined his sword protruding from the assassin's chest.

They flew high above Syienna, heading for the Grey

Mountains, following the Trade Road far below them. They crossed the wide fields and plains of Syienna County and entered the forested foothills of the mountains. They flew higher and higher as the land rose up below them. The air grew thinner, and their lungs burned as their wings fought with the thin atmosphere for lift. Still higher they flew until they were above the peaks of the Grey Mountains themselves, and they began to descend into Trake Valley.

They flew down into the city of Trake, and quickly spotted the ziggurat Temple to the Light, which still glowed against the surrounding darkness with the gold light of the many torches that reflected off its walls. They landed in front of the main entrance.

Blade recovered his breath before speaking. "Demon, Freeze, you two fly above, and try to spot the assassin on the streets. He may not be in the temple." Freeze frowned, and Demon nodded. "The rest of us will check the temple. All right?"

"He won't escape this time," Pyre said as he gripped the hilt of his broadsword.

"Stay cautious. He may have the relic," Shadow reminded them.

"Let's kill him," Jinx said.

Freeze and Demon flew into the air, and Blade pounded on the door of the temple. The door opened, and a young priest in ceremonial blue robes came out, his eyes growing wide as he saw the hybrids standing before him.

"What are you doing here?" he asked.

"Have you seen a man in a bloody tunic?" Pyre asked.

"No. Should I have? What has this to do with the temple?" the priest asked nervously.

Jinx looked down and saw a small bag of coins hanging from his belt. "What's that? I thought priests were meant to live in poverty."

"I … I was going to donate it to the temple. How else shall we feed the poor?" the priest asked defensively.

"Why do you have that gold?" she asked, focusing on the priest's mind. His eyes glazed.

"A man gave them to me," he said in a monotone. "He wanted priest robes."

"What was he wearing?" she asked.

"Brown, rough clothes and a gray cloak. He had a sword. He stood in the shadows. He frightened me."

"Is he still inside?" Jinx demanded.

"Yes …" was all the man could say before Blade shoved him aside and wrenched open the large door of the temple.

"Be careful. We won't be able to tell him from the other priests," Shadow said. "He'll blend with the crowd the second he realizes we're here. Let me go in first; I'll find him."

"How will we know when to enter? Or if you're in trouble?" Blade asked, halfway through the door.

Shadow paused for a moment and looked at Jinx. "She'll tell you." They looked at him quizzically—especially Jinx. "I know a spell to make us share thoughts … but … I do not know the counter."

"Do it," she said. He sighed nervously and put his hand on the side of her face. He closed his eyes.

Jinx felt a cool rush run through his hand and into her. Suddenly, she could sense his thoughts like a low murmur in the back of her mind. She could picture what he pictured and feel what he felt. She felt his nervousness, she saw his plans unfolding in his head, and she could sense his feelings for her. She smiled.

"Are you all right?" Pyre asked.

"I can see his thoughts," Jinx said.

"It's a spell I made a while ago," Shadow said. "It … seemed useful … at the time. It seems I was right. You will hear from me soon." He turned, and quietly walked through the door.

Shadow stepped into the temple. It was well lit, with torches along the white walls providing the same golden light that graced the building's exterior. He cast a spell to conceal himself as best he could in the relatively bright light and looked around. He was in a large hallway, and fortunately, it was empty. He crept forward, using magic to extinguish the torches as he went.

He pressed on until he reached an immense room near the center of the building. Torches were mounted on the walls, and candles hung from massive crystal chandeliers that swung on chains from the ceiling. At the center of the room was a large stone altar, and before the altar were nearly a hundred priests, all kneeling in prayer while their leader stood in his gold robes and sang incantations over the altar. Shadow knew that the assassin was in here; he could feel him. There was something of great power in the room.

But then again, that could be something else ...

Cearon knelt in blue robes amid the multitude of priests. They all had their heads bowed and eyes closed, but Cearon stared intently at the altar.

It must be in there. His sightless vision told him there was something very powerful in that altar. He couldn't see any way of gaining access to it, however. The altar seemed more of a tomb for the relic than anything else.

I wondered if it is the Sword's power these priests feel when they pray over it. He imagined it must be.

He closed his eyes and let his mind sweep through the room. His eyes opened with alarm as he sensed another person that he hadn't sensed in a long while—*not since that elf raid.*

He cast a glance over his shoulder, but he saw nothing. He closed his eyes again. There the newcomer was, sitting in the shadows; Cearon saw him clear as ever. The gremlin was here with his hand on his dirk. But there was something strange about him. *Is that a line of magic moving from his head? What strange spell could that be?*

Cearon looked deeply into it with his mind and heard one thing: "I've found him."

Cearon's eyes shot open, and his hand instinctively went to the sword hidden beneath his robes. He remained still and closed his eyes once again to focus his mind. *The Guard is here; I just need to find out where.*

❋ * ❋ * ❋

"He's found him!" Jinx said as Shadow's thoughts came into her own. She saw a picture flash of a large group of priests, with one of them casting a wary glance over his shoulder while clutching at something hidden beneath his robes. She knew exactly who it was.

"Lead the way!" Pyre said as he ignited. Flames surged up through his armor as they charged into the building.

❋ * ❋ * ❋

Cearon kept his eyes closed as he searched the temple with his mind.

There they are.

He saw three other Guard members running through the hallways toward him. He saw that the magic streaming from the gremlin's head went to the head of the harpy. Cearon grimaced.

I need to stall them—and quick.

An idea formed in his head. He thrust his mind into the

magical stream and mentally cried out, *Stop!* The harpy held her hand out and stopped the others.

I bought a bit of time, but it won't count for anything if I sit here and do nothing. I need to get that Relic, and I need to get it now.

He stood up, and the priests cast irritated glances at him for disrupting the ceremony.

"I can see you, assassin," Cearon said as he drew his sword. A dart flew out of the darkness, but it stopped in midair and fell to the ground, halted by Cearon's mind.

The gremlin sighed, stood up, and stepped out from the shadows. The priests gave frightened gasps as he materialized, and they recoiled at the sight of his wings.

"Give up, Cearon," the gremlin said. *He called himself Shadow, if I remember right.* "We have more people coming."

"I know—three in the hallway. I've beaten three before."

"I seem to remember you nearly dying from it."

"I don't have time for talk." Cearon charged Shadow. Shadow had been inching his hand toward his throwing knives as they had spoken, and as Cearon launched himself at Shadow, Shadow hurled the blade.

Out of reflex, Cearon reached his hand up to blast the knife away with magic, but the knife struck first, embedding itself in his hand. Cearon growled in pain and launched a wave of magic at Shadow, which also threw the knife out of his palm.

There's the first wound of the day.

Shadow drew his dirk as he brushed the magical attack aside, staggering from its strength. Cearon closed in and slashed at Shadow, but Shadow stepped back, letting the blade pass by before he lunged in with the point of his dirk aimed for Cearon's neck.

Cearon reacted with the speed of blind instinct. With his free hand, he pushed Shadow's wrist away from him, causing the dirk to go astray, and then Cearon stepped past Shadow's right shoulder, slashing as he went, cutting Shadow's leg. Shadow grunted as his leg gave out from under him and he fell to his knee. Cearon concentrated and struck with magic. The magic smashed like a fist into the back of Shadow's head, slamming Shadow into the ground and knocking him out cold.

The priests ran in terror, scattering all around. Cearon wiped Shadow's blood off and sheathed his sword. He ran to the altar, shoving priests roughly aside as he went. Soon the crowd was gone; the priests had run from the main room in fear of their lives. Only the high priest stayed, standing resolutely by the altar in his gold robes.

Cearon threw the hood down, revealing his orange, slitted eyes as he approached the head priest. "Where is the Relic?"

"I will tell you nothing, warlock," the priest said.

Cearon spoke forcefully. "I'm no warlock! Now how do I get the Relic? Speak—before I lose patience!"

"Don't try to fool me, warlock. I see your wickedness in your eyes, and I don't even know what relics you are talking about. You waste your time."

"Part of the Relic Sword is in that altar!" Cearon said irritated as he gestured toward the altar.

"There is nothing but altar in that altar," the priest insisted.

"I'm no fool, priest. I can see it in there." He searched with his mind, and sure enough, he saw once more something of power inside the altar. He looked into the hallway and sensed that the three Guard members were charging again; they were almost upon him. In desperation, he raised his hand and blasted the altar with magic.

"What are you doing? That is a holy altar!" the priest exclaimed.

Cearon didn't care. *I need that relic, if for nothing more than to hide it myself.*

Again he blasted it, and the stones lurched, dust flying from the cracks as the mortar crumbled. Summing up all of his strength, Cearon sent the most powerful wave he could at the altar. The stones seemed to burst as they were wrenched apart; dust, mortar, and bricks flew in every direction.

And then Cearon saw it: lying among the ruined temple altar was the hilt of the Sword. It was nothing as he had imagined it would be.

I always thought something called the Relic Sword would be an old, decrepit weapon. Lying before him was a beautifully crafted hilt that sparkled even in the light of the dust-choked torches. The cross guard was angled down to protect the swordsman's knuckles on the lower end, and to catch sliding weapons between the blade and cross guard on the upper end. The actual handle of the weapon was bound in leather that bore ornate designs of some metal with a bluish hue that reminded Cearon of the sky on a clear day. There was a slot at the top of the hilt where the blade had once been, and there was a hole at the bottom where the pommel stone had been set.

The priest didn't see the Relic as he coughed and sputtered in the dust that still lay thick in the air. Cearon stepped forward slowly, gazing with awe at the glorious hilt before him.

"I've risked so much for this day," Cearon said to himself as he bent down and gently picked up the hilt, as if it could shatter as easily as his dreams. "No one will understand why I have to do this. No one will understand that this is a quest for freedom. No one but my kind." He gently brushed his finger along the ancient patterns set into the grip of the handle.

"Hello, Cearon," a voice said.

Cearon leaped to a combat stance with his blade before him and the Relic held defensively in his off hand. His eyes darted wildly around, trying to find the source of the voice as his mind swept the room for anything suspicious. He found nothing except the members of the Guard, who fast closed in on him. The first of them charged into the main hall: a flaming warrior whose armor was beginning to glow with the heat of his flames. All thoughts of the voice left Cearon's mind as he stood, ready for a fight. *Hopefully, I won't bleed too much after this.*

"Assassin," the harpy said. "We meet again."

"It won't work," Cearon said as he felt her trying to bewitch him.

"I had to try," she said with a smile.

"You insult us both," Cearon said with a frown as he searched for a path around the Guard. There were several windows high up that he could reach by climbing tapestries and curtains, but the winged Guard members would skewer him before he made it halfway to the window. He sighed as he prepared for a fight; he was so close to escaping with the hilt.

All that stands in my way are these hybrids. If they must die, so be it.

"So quick to kill," he heard a voice say. He glanced around, but there was no one near him. Even the gold priest had fled.

"Shadow!" the harpy cried out as she saw Shadow lying unconscious on the floor. "I didn't see that you cut his leg!"

"Let me go, and no more damage need be done," Cearon said. He sensed many humans running down the long corridor. *The city guard must be on their way. I must get out—I can't fight the city and them at once!*

"You will die here—tonight. That is the only damage that will be done," the phoenix said as flames licked his armor with their burning tongues. The image of the phoenix engraved in the chest of his armor glowed from the heat.

"The phoenix ... this will be new," Cearon said with reluctant acceptance.

"The last time we met, I swore I would end your life,

assassin!" The griffin spat his venomous words with a snarl as he drew his sword. "I don't make idle threats."

"And the griffin. I remember you as a skilled swordsman. This will be a difficult fight indeed."

"No, an impossible one!" the phoenix shouted as he charged with his flames streaking behind him. Cearon launched him hurtling back with a wave of magic.

Cearon rushed forward, chasing the receding figure of the phoenix.

I have to end the fight with him quickly; he's the most likely to burn me to death. Before Cearon completed two steps, he was forced to veer to the side to avoid the harpy's spear as the griffin took to the air, circling above Cearon's head.

The harpy stabbed again, and Cearon parried her spear, sliding in along the haft for the kill, when his mind's eye told him that the griffin was striking from above. Cearon braced a foot on the harpy's hip. He kicked off, diving away and sending the harpy sprawling as the griffin slashed after Cearon.

Cearon spun in the air and landed awkwardly on his side before he rolled onto his feet, standing just as the phoenix attacked again, swinging his heavy broadsword with fierce strength. Cearon barely blocked the blow, but the force of the impact made him stagger back. The phoenix swung his blade around and chopped down at Cearon's shoulder. Cearon sidestepped the attempt and trapped the phoenix's sword with his. He blasted the phoenix telekinetically, hurling the burning warrior to the ground.

Cearon took a step toward the phoenix. The griffin seemingly appeared out of nowhere with his sword whistling through the air.

He caught me!

Cearon jumped aside, but the griffin cut him in the left shoulder and across the chest, just above the pectorals. *He almost cut me in two!*

With a cry of pain, Cearon crossed blades with the griffin, grabbed his sword hand and stepped toward him, taking advantage of the gap in his guard. Cearon pinned the griffin's arm next to his hip and elbowed him in the face while sweeping a foot behind his. The griffin tumbled to the ground, giving a cry of surprise that barely was heard over the clatter of armor. Cearon spun his sword in his hand so that he held it backward and raised it above his head to stab down.

"No!" the harpy cried out. Cearon saw a spear hurtling toward his chest. He stumbled back as he jutted out his hand, sending the spear spinning away from him only inches from his chest. He felt heat behind him and turned around slashing at the oncoming phoenix, who just barely raised his sword in time to block.

They're everywhere!

Twenty prefects rounded the corner in their black capes and looked on in amazement as three hybrids fought with a sword-wielding monk—a monk whose hood had fallen down, and a monk whose eyes gleamed orange in the flames of the temple's torches.

"Warlock!" their leader cried.

"Kill the warlock!" the mob shouted as they charged forward.

Cearon blocked another blow from the phoenix and then kicked him in the hip, causing his legs to shoot out behind him. Cearon jumped away from the burning warrior, his boot smoking from the kick, and turned toward the group of charging men. He raised his hand, and fire poured forth from his palm and fingers, forming a wall of flame that surged forth with searing heat, hungrily devouring the charging prefects. Cearon looked at his hand in surprise.

The best I've ever been able to cast before was a stone-sized ball of fire. He glanced at the hilt he clutched in his hand. *It's the only explanation.*

The harpy, the phoenix, and the griffin stared in awe as

heat waves hung over the burning bodies. The heat from the blast had been so intense that the men had died before they could even scream.

"So much death ... nothing has changed," a voice said bitterly inside of Cearon's head. He jumped with surprise and looked around.

Where is that coming from?

The phoenix came at him again, and this time, the burning warrior had the harpy behind him, stabbing over his flaming shoulder. The griffin flew above, waiting for Cearon to put his guard down.

They're too much for me when they fight together. I'm bleeding, and they barely have a bruise between the lot of them. I need to separate them somehow!

Cearon snarled with anger as he struck aside the phoenix's sword and then stepped back to keep from being impaled on the harpy's spear. He stuck his hand out and sent a wave of magic flying forward, but the phoenix and the harpy's combined mental strength was enough to withstand his blast—if just barely.

Even if I could get past their blades, the griffin would cut me to pieces before I could put a nick on any of them!

Cearon felt his mind growing tired from the constant magic use, and his body was beginning to move slower from the effort of fighting. He stood, glancing between the phoenix, the harpy, and the griffin, who circled overhead.

I must do something unexpected ... He looked about the room with his mind. *The gremlin! Of course!*

With a grunt of effort, he reached for Shadow with his mind and lifted the body off the ground. The phoenix looked where Cearon was pointing his hand just as Shadow's unconscious body slammed into the harpy, knocking her from her feet.

The phoenix flinched back just as Cearon stepped in, crossing swords with him. With a shove, Cearon wrenched the phoenix's blade down and stepped one foot past his opponent's, opening his guard.

I have a straight cut at his neck! This ends now!

The phoenix realized that Cearon had passed his guard and tried to step back and duck aside, but his bulky armor slowed him. Cearon's sword streaked through the air, glimmering red in the phoenix's flames as it slashed deep into his throat.

Cearon knew he had struck a killer blow. He stepped past the phoenix, whose flames extinguished as he fell. Cearon ran to where the harpy was rolling Shadow off her. She rose to a crouch, and with a cry of rage, she hurled her spear at Cearon; he deflected it magically aside. She reached for Shadow's dirk, but not quickly enough. As Cearon rushed by, he kneed her head hard where her jaw met her skull. Her helmet flew from her head as she was knocked unconscious.

Only the griffin now! Cearon whipped around, turning to face the griffin. He lowered his sword as he took in the sight of the griffin with tears in his eyes, cradling the phoenix's head. The griffin-man let out a cry of sorrow as the phoenix's blood spilled out onto the floor, hissing as it boiled on the phoenix's glowing armor. The phoenix tried to mouth something, but no words came through his bleeding neck. His eyes slowly shut as his face paled.

"No!" the griffin screamed as he pressed his forehead against the phoenix's. He let out another wail, this one unintelligible, as his tears fell on the phoenix's face, making it appear as if the phoenix himself were weeping.

"He was like a brother to him," the voice in Cearon's head said. This time, Cearon did not try to find the voice; he just let it speak as he watched the scene before him. "They grew up together. Always they relied on each other through hardships similar to your own, and now you have killed him. The blood flowing from those veins is on your hands. Look." Cearon looked at his hands. The phoenix's blood dripped to the floor from his fingers. "You may think that your quest is worth your blood, but have you ever considered if it is worth the blood of others?"

Sacrifices must be made sometimes, Cearon thought, trying to rationalize the feeling of guilt away. *It was not my choice to kill him. He chose to fight. He killed himself on my blade.*

"Avert the blame all you will, Cearon, but the fact that you feel guilty shows that you have never truly empathized with those at the end of your blade before now. It shows that you have no idea of the pain you inflict upon the world with each thrust of your sword. How can you be so careless?" Despite its accusation, the voice sounded smooth, and pleasant, as if it were coming from an old friend, though the voice was also stern, like a veteran warrior who knew the horrors of the world better than most.

"I have a right to defend myself," Cearon said audibly.

"But you do not have the right to kill wantonly at your discretion. All the people on this world have a right to live. You should know that better than most."

"Who are you?" Cearon demanded.

"I am the previous owner of this sword," the voice said. "I am something entirely beyond you."

"What sort of answer is that?" Cearon was angry. He was angry at the guilt he felt, angry because his mind was tired, because his body was sore, and because he had no idea who he was talking to. *Have I gone mad?*

"I didn't answer at all!" the griffin cried out from behind him. "That's what kind of answer it is, murderer!"

Cearon turned again to face the griffin, and he saw him standing with his sword in hand. The griffin breathed deeply; his face was set in a deep scowl, and in his eyes burned a hate that could only be forged by the death of a brother.

From outside came the sudden clang of alarm bells ringing.

Soon, the whole town will be descending on me, Cearon thought unhappily.

"We don't need to continue this fight," Cearon said. "Let me go, and tend to your wounded. I am sorry for your friend, truly I am, but you would have done the same were you me. For what it's worth, I too have lost a brother."

"You are sorry for his death? No, you are not as sorry as you should be! He was a great man! He is a great man! He was worth ten of you! I will kill you for what you've done!" Spittle formed around the griffin's mouth as he spoke; his wings twitched from rage; and his hair was wild and sweaty from the fight.

"So be it. But I cannot die—not when I am this close to success. I am sorry."

"Don't say sorry ... not until you know the true meaning of the word ... not until I teach you!"

The griffin took a step forward, when the phoenix's body burst into flames so bright and hot that both warriors shielded their eyes from his body. The flames seared the air as they roared up from beneath the phoenix's armor. The inferno burned for just a few moments before it died down to a mere flicker and then went out.

A pile of ashes and melted steel lay where the phoenix's body had been. A tiny hand reached up from the ashes.

Kill one phoenix, and you only give birth to another, Cearon thought as a baby with crimson wings pulled itself from the phoenix's ashes.

"What ... is it ... is it Pyre?" Blade asked in confusion.

"No, it is his son," Cearon said. The griffin remained silent. "Do you still wish to fight me? Or do you wish to save the son of your fallen friend from a life of servitude and violence?"

"What do you mean?" the griffin growled.

"Everyone wants a hybrid to fight for them. *Everyone.* If word gets out that there's an infant phoenix for the taking, you can imagine what lengths people will go to in order to seize him. King Leon will want him. The mayor of Trake will want him. Marcus will want him. The elves will want him. Everyone will want him. But no one knows of his existence, and if you spirit the child away, no one will ever know. They will assume that the phoenix died like a human and did not reproduce. The child will be safe."

The griffin stared at Cearon, hatred burning in his eyes and his sword held naked in his hand. His wings were extended, and the muscles around them were tense, ready to spring. The feathers ruffled as they moved with the griffin's breath, and the talons on his off hand clacked together as he thought.

"You face a choice." Cearon spoke slowly and calmly. "You can eke out the vengeance you desire on me, or you can put your hate aside and give your friend's son a chance to avoid the curse we bear."

The griffin closed his eyes a few moments and took a deep breath. When he opened his eyes, he sheathed his sword.

"Do not think this means our fight is finished," the griffin said as he scooped up the naked baby. "When he is self-sufficient, I will find you, and I will slay you."

Cearon said nothing; he just watched as the warrior turned around, holding the squirming babe against his shoulder, and walked out of the temple. Cearon could not help but admire the discipline of his enemy.

He was able to put all his thoughts of vengeance and retribution aside for his friend. Cearon wondered what it must be like to have friends willing to do that for him.

Cearon looked at the Relic hilt in his hand. He thought briefly about the voice in his head.

What exactly is the source of this sword's power? He knew a magician must have enhanced it, but that fire wall he had cast was well beyond any enhancement any magician he knew of was capable of giving a weapon. *And this is but a third of the total weapon! There must be some sort of mystical power about this sword.*

"You're clever, I see," the mysterious voice said. "Not many people wonder about the nature of the Sword's power. It is good that you are cautious of magical items. They can be treacherous."

"So are you treacherous?"

"No, but that is also what I would say if I were treacherous; you must judge my character yourself. It is time you left. There are many people looking for you, and the streets are filled with fighting."

"Right." Cearon said, looking for an exit.

"Climb a tapestry that leads to a window. You can kick through it. Leave your monk robes here; they will be searching for those."

"Escaped many times before, have we?" Cearon asked as he pulled the monk robes off.

"No. Well ... once, but that wasn't the same. I've never had need to escape like this before, but I am naturally talented at things."

Cearon began to climb up a tapestry. "So, my talented friend, do you have a name?"

"Call me Sky, for now."

"Sky?" Cearon asked quizzically.

"Save your strength."

He certainly is demanding, Cearon thought.

"I apologize if I seem rude, but right now you do not have time for debate."

How did ...? "I can hear your mind. Now keep moving; things will not be pleasant if you do not escape."

Cearon pulled himself up the tapestry and crawled through a small, square window that was used to cast sunlight on the altar. He kicked through a rusty, decrepit iron grid barring the window. He dropped down outside the temple, landing lightly on his feet.

"Head toward the east gate," Sky said. "There are too many at the west gate."

"What's going on?" Cearon asked. He heard shouts, steel clashing, and other sounds of battle ringing through the streets. In the distance, fire burned, making the still-darkened sky glow with a red tinge. He swept his mind through the city and saw people with swords battling tooth and claw throughout the streets.

"The town is under siege. There are elves in the city." No sooner had Sky said this than a drake with an elf rider soared over Cearon's head; the drake roared, and the rider loosed an arrow.

Elves! I should kill them all!

"There is no time for you to fight; there are people searching for you."

"How do you know all this?" Cearon asked. *I can see without eyes, but Sky seems to see everything.* Whoever this Sky was, he seemed more and more powerful by the moment; he was beginning to frighten Cearon.

"I have perceptions beyond yours—that's the most explanation we have time for. Now run." Sky's explanation was far from satisfactory, but Cearon heeded his advice.

Freeze and Demon flew low above the streets of Trake. Demon's eyes were capable of piercing the darkness, but Freeze's were not. But for the odd torch burning within the city and the brightly glowing Temple to the Light, the whole city was little more than different shades of gray and ghostly outlines of the white buildings to her.

Why was I sent to patrol? Freeze thought angrily. *This sort of duty would suit Shadow more. He can see in the dark much better than I can, and I can fight twice as well as he.*

They had been flying over the city for almost fifteen minutes now, staying mostly by the rear entrance of the temple, yet they had caught sight of no one but the odd drunkard and homeless man. With each passing minute, Freeze became more frustrated.

Finally, with a call to get Demon's attention, she landed on top of one of the white stone buildings overlooking the rear entrance of the temple.

"What are you doing?" Demon asked as he landed next to her.

"Don't you realize how ridiculous this is? We're doing nothing up here. We should be assaulting through the rear door."

"But what if the assassin is not in there? We're the only thing watching for him."

She rolled her eyes. "He's in there. Do you think the others would have delayed this long if he weren't? This whole plan was rushed and sloppy. I don't like it. It's sloppy planning that allows this cur to escape us time and again."

"You're right about that," Demon relented. "How can we form a better plan now, though? Everyone is inside already."

"Listen, the way I see it, either the assassin is in the temple, or he is not. If he is, then the others could use our help; if he isn't, then we can get everyone together and form a better plan. We might even be able to wait for the walkers to catch up with us."

Demon sighed apprehensively. "I don't like the idea of leaving the door unguarded. I can watch it easily enough from here while you rendezvous with the others. If he comes this way, I can stick an arrow in him, or at least get you some warning."

She nodded. "Alright. If I'm not out in ten minutes, you can assume that he's in—"

An alarm bell rang in the still air of the city. Freeze and Demon both turned toward the sound. It was coming from the western gate of the city.

"What is that? Is the assassin escaping???" Freeze asked urgently.

"That's not the assassin," Demon responded, his eyes locked on the sky. "There are drakes flying over the wall."

"What?" She looked up, and against the night sky she saw dark silhouettes flying just above the wall. "Are they friend, or foe?"

Demon notched an arrow to his bow.

"Judging by the arrows they're shooting at the night watch, I'd say they're foe."

With that, he leaped into the air, drawing his arrow back as he rose to meet the attackers.

Freeze sighed. "Great. I get to kill the other half of my blood. I'll have to keep in mind that I'm more human than drake."

She flew into the air, following Demon as he sped toward the winged beasts that assailed the men on the walls.

Below her, the city was wakening to the call to arms. Men rushed out of buildings, many dressed in their night cloth, wielding whatever makeshift weapon they could get their hands on. Prefects in their black capes, as well as the city watch who were not manning the walls, gathered in the plaza before the western gate as the blue clad sentinels rushed into the city with no semblance of order.

Hopefully the sentinels are not in full route, Freeze thought with worry. The tough soldiers would be invaluable to the defense of the city.

Demon closed on the drakes. He loosed an arrow, shooting a rider off of his mount. Before the rider had hit the ground, Demon had another arrow notched and aimed. With a second twang, another rider met the same fate as the first.

Demon gained altitude, rising above two drakes that were circling together. He put an arrow through the eye of one drake, and positioned himself directly above the other as he drew his hunting knife. With folded wings, he descended upon the drake below him, slashing the tendons in its left wing as he darted by. The drake bellowed in pain. Its injured wing went limp, and trailed behind it as it crashed into the ground below.

Demon is quite talented at this, Freeze noted.

She was still chasing after her first drake, trying to follow it through the black of night. It was hard for her to keep track of it. She rose above the drake, silhouetting it against the lights being lit all over the city. She descended upon it with her katana raised. She cut the drake's wing halfway through as she passed, though she missed the main bone of the wing. It roared, and snapped its jaws at her receding figure, but to her surprise, it kept flying.

These are tough creatures, indeed!

She flew back up toward it, when an arrow seemed to appear out of the darkness, slamming into her armored shoulder. The steel head of the arrow glanced off her armor, etching a groove into the metal as it did.

"Elves at the gate!" She heard a human shriek the words in terror.

I could do much more good at that gate than I could here.

"Demon!" she called out as he put an arrow through the eye of another drake. It fell dead from the sky.

"I'm busy!" He loosed his last arrow into the heart of a passing drake. He descended with it, retrieving his arrow from its breast before the beast struck the ground.

"I'm going to the gate! I'll do more damage there. Good luck!"

He nodded to her as he pursued another drake. He dodged to the side as the elf rider shot an arrow at him before he returned an arrow of his own.

I need to rally the sentinel's first. I can't hold that gate by myself.

She swooped down upon the city, landing at the front of a group of sentinels.

"What in blazes???" the front runner exclaimed.

"Stop running!" Freeze urged them. "We can hold this city, but only if you stand and fight with us! Come with me to the gate!"

"We're not running, woman!" one of the sentinels barked at her. "The gate's a lost cause against what they're throwing at it, but sentinels don't surrender so easily. We're going to bleed them for every step they take into this city! To the rooftops boys!"

They rushed past her, loading bolts into their compact crossbows as they went. She was surprised to see that some of them were putting on woman's dresses while they ran to their defensive positions. She realized it was so they would look like non-combatants before they loosed bolts on the enemy.

What is being thrown against the gates of the city to make vicious men like these consider it a lost cause?

She took to the air, speeding toward the plaza and the main gate. The outlook was grim.

Prefects and city watchmen scattered in every direction as columns of elves marched through the gates practically unopposed. The men atop the wall shrieked in terror as they fled, dropping their bows in their fear.

"Hold!" Freeze shouted to no one in particular. "Hold here! You have a hybrid with you!" She flapped her wings to gather their attention. "Men of Shale! Show your valor! Show the strength I know you have! Rally to me! Let them come through the gate, for we shall slay them here in the plaza all the same! Rally to me!"

"All is lost!" a prefect wailed to her. "They bring a powerful magician against us, and men with wings!"

Men with wings? Does he mean the drakes? Or maybe he thinks Demon is with the elves?

"You have hybrids with you!" Freeze called out again. "There is no army that can turn you! Stand and fight!"

For her efforts, men were beginning to gather around her.

As others fled, they saw their comrades reforming; they too turned and joined with Freeze.

We have a few hundred, at least. Perhaps it is not enough to turn the elves from the gates, but it is enough to make the short devils pay dearly for it!

She pointed her sword at the lines of elves.

"Men of Shale! Charge!"

With a roar, the combined force of prefects and city watchmen surged forward. At the sight, still more men rallied, and joined the charge.

The elves, not yet fully through the gate, formed up as best they could to meet the charge. They locked their shields together, and held their spears ready to repulse the defenders.

Bolts whistled over Freeze's head, the deadly darts finding their marks among the elves, weakening their line.

There must be sentinels on the rooftops! We can win this!

"Slay them all!" she cried as the forces clashed.

The men of Shale threw themselves bodily against the enemy's lines, paying dearly at the tips of the elfin spears, but nonetheless pressing their foe back. With the spear wall broken, the elves drew short swords and prepared for close combat.

Freeze was in her element. She blasted elfin soldiers with her telekinesis while her katana danced through the air, seeking the weak points in the elfin armor with grim efficiency. She tore through the elfin line, her men following closely behind her to take advantage of the gaps she made in the elves.

Elves began to run in terror of her, and as they ran, the courage of the other elves waned.

They're going to flee! We'll chase them right out of that gate!

Freeze abandoned the elves already running, and turned her attention to the elfin right flank, which still fought hard. They too began to break as she devastated them with sword and magic. The routed elves started to clog the gates, preventing more elves from entering. Freeze knew that now was her chance to turn this battle into a slaughter.

She turned to her left, and watched in bewilderment as her men ran in terror, abandoning the battle and those they fought alongside with.

Why are they running? We were winning!

"Yes! Flee you dogs!" a tall man with white hair shouted after the fleeing men of Shale. He held a large, bloody claymore in his hands, and dead men littered the ground around him. He turned his head, and his eyes locked on Freeze. His scar covered face grinned at her almost casually. "Would you mind standing aside, miss? My elves need to get into the city."

She glanced behind her. She still had her center, and her right flank was mopping up the last of the elfin soldiers before her. If she could break the elfin left flank, she might still be able to turn this into a success.

She was about to attack the man, when suddenly she heard screaming behind her. To her astonishment, she saw a man with dark wings laying waste to her men. For a moment, she thought it was Demon, until she saw the longsword in his hand, and the armor that he wore.

That's a hybrid! But it's not one of us!

Her men broke, running desperately toward the safety of the city as bolts loosed by sentinels helped to cover their retreat.

The gate is a lost cause! I'll die if I have to fight that hybrid and all these elves.

She fell back with her men. She used her telekinetic powers to slow the advance of the elves, and to try to keep the hybrid at bay. The winged man didn't seem to handle her magic very well, and he withdrew from her.

Elves now poured unopposed through the gates. Their battle line quickly stretched all the way across the massive plaza. The elves marched toward the center of the city, taking crossbow bolts from the stubborn sentinels the entire way.

Where is Demon? We need him!

She looked up, searching the skies which were being lit by the many lights now burning in the city. She just barely saw him. There weren't any drakes flying with him; he had either slain them, or they had dispersed. However, there was someone else flying with him. A short man with wings on his back and a rapier in his hand chased Demon through the skies. Demon only had a few arrows left, and so he dodged, biding his time until he could get a sure shot.

"There's the plunder, you short little warriors!" the white haired man pointed his claymore toward the city as he called out to his elves. "Take as much as you want!"

The elves charged forward, crossing the plaza and entering the narrow streets of the city as still more elves began to march in columns through the gate.

Freeze worked to rally groups of prefects and city watchmen to join the beleaguered sentinels in the defense of the city. Even so, despite the terrible nature of their enemy, the sentinels had made good on their promise to bleed the enemy with every step taken into the city. Sentinels dashed along the rooftops, and through the streets, only engaging elves long enough to release a deadly salvo of crossbow bolts before the blue clad men would retreat back into the city to repeat the process. It was an irregular way of fighting, but Freeze was impressed by its effectiveness.

Despite the heroic efforts of the sentinels, the elves continued to press into the city, and more of them entered through the gate every moment. The elfin reinforcements soon pushed Freeze and the sentinels back and out of sight of the gate. She flew above the streets, lending her sword to the sentinels whenever she could, and attacking any group of elves separated from the main force.

Where are the walkers? We need them here!

She fought on, keeping her eye out for any more hybrids, but she failed to see any until she saw Demon standing on a roof with his quiver full of elfin arrows, which he rapidly loosed back at their makers.

She landed next to him. "What happened to that hybrid who was chasing you?"

He shot before he spoke. "He disengaged when one of my arrows took a piece of his ear off. I only had one more arrow, so I decided not to follow."

Freeze shook her head as she looked at the city before her in horror. Flames rose from buildings, and the screams of fleeing women and children could be heard above the sound of the elves looting the city.

"The little monsters!" Freeze shouted at the skies. "We'll kill them all! Along with their hybrids and whoever created them!"

With a twang, Demon slew an elf who carried an armful of looted jewelry.

His face was grim as he turned toward Freeze. "We can't hold this city, Freeze. If things don't change soon, there will be an elfin flag flying over the mansion. We're strong, Freeze, but we can't stop this army, and neither can the sentinels."

"I know, but we have to fight anyways. Just listen to that!" She motioned to the screams filling the night air. "I'll not stand idly by while that happens, nor will I retreat from those causing it. Even if I must die to protect those people, I will do it! I will fight to the last for this city, and as a member of the Royal Guard, I expect you to as well."

He nodded. "I'm with you to the end, Freeze. Let us show them what damage two of the Royal Guard can inflict."

As he finished speaking, a long howl from the direction of the main gate pierced the air.

Freeze shouted for joy. "That could only be Howl! The walkers are here! Come! Let us drive these elves back to their homelands!"

She leaped into the air, rising high above the city as she flew toward the western gate. She saw the two massive forms of Crash and Crunch sweeping elves away with their weapons, as light haired Silver blasted telekinetically and and launched bolts of fire. All of the walkers were there: Howl with his scimitar and his claws, Rocky with his war-hammer, Sting with his falchion blade and his deadly tail, and Mer with his short-sword. Their combined power scattered the rear echelon of the elves, sending the short soldiers fleeing in broken panic into the city.

Freeze smiled. Trake had hope once more.

Cearon had been waylaid more than he would have liked—even if it was his own choices that waylaid him. He had tried to avoid the elves in the city, but his hate for their kind had proven too strong. Seeing them looting the homes of Trake like they had once looted his home had been more than he could bear, and though Sky urged against it, Cearon fell upon any marauding elves he saw.

He slew them with sword and magic, rescuing all the civilians he could, and devastating all the elves he had power to devastate.

"One of them senses you," Sky warned. "The one they call Marcus. He's powerful. He is coming for you."

"Let him come! If he wants to die now, that is his choice!" Cearon said as battle rage flooded his senses.

"Now is not the time for revenge! Run now, while you still can!" Sky insisted.

Cearon bit his lip. Part of him wanted to fight Marcus, but he knew that Sky was right. He was tired and wounded—in no condition to fight Marcus and those who followed him.

"What do I do?" Cearon asked, breathless and feeling the fatigue from chasing elves.

"He will be between you and the east gate before you can get there. Most of his force is back at the battle, though. This is your best chance to break out. Now or never, young one! Strike your hardest and keep your head on your shoulders."

Cearon took a deep breath and ran toward the east gate, vaulting over obstacles and sprinting through alleyways with all the speed he had. Even with Cearon's quick feet, it was no use. When he rounded the last street corner to the gate, there stood Marcus with a dozen elves and a towering man in black armor.

Gourn! Perhaps now is the time for vengeance!

"Vengeance can wait," Sky told him. "For now, you must escape."

"Cearon, I am glad I caught you before you left," Marcus said with an arrogant smirk.

Cearon looked around at the rooftops and sensed no one else. "Where are the others? I figured you would pit my siblings against me."

"They have work to do. I haven't enough elves to take this city, so it falls on them to pick up the slack," Marcus said. "But you're weakened already; I could sense that from across the city. The Royal Guard has been giving you trouble, then?"

"I'm not going to waste time with petty words, Marcus," Cearon growled. "I have the Relic, and I have more than enough power to beat your pitiful entourage. Let me pass, or die."

"You arrogant little—" Gourn said angrily as he gripped the mace-and-flail looped on a small spike protruding from the armor at his hip.

"Calm yourself, Emissary," Marcus said with a raise of his hand. "Relic or not, boy, you don't have what it takes to escape. Four of your siblings are here in the city, along with me and some other tricks I have. Even if you get past me, you won't make it far."

"Let's see just how far."

"Cearon, I understand your anger," Marcus said sincerely. "I do. But trust me when I tell you that all you've suffered was necessary for the good of the Kingdom of Shale—for the good of the world!"

"You killed my parents in front of my eyes! You captured me and forced me to become a slave warrior! Where is the good in that, Marcus?"

"Keep a level head," Sky warned.

"The needs of the masses outweigh the needs of the few, Cearon! I needed you! The world needs you! Even as a boy, you showed great promise, but your parents would not part from you! I needed you at the head of my armies! But now you stand against me—stand poised to throw down all that I've worked for!"

"You've worked for nothing but evil, Marcus! How many young ones lost their lives in the Academy? Do you even know? Did you lose any sleep over their lives, Marcus? Did you weep as I did when Tiger-Eye was whipped out of his skin? You are no savior—you are a born tyrant!"

"Do not cross me, Cearon! I will do what I must to keep peace in the world! I will do what I must to keep this world from burning, no matter what the price!" Marcus's face was red from passion.

"I can't help but notice, Marcus, that the price you speak of seems to be having you as emperor!" Cearon spat venomously.

"If that is the cost, so be it. You don't know, Cearon … you don't know the peril this world is in. You don't see how close we are to watching everything we love fall to the hands of true tyranny. I am fighting so that what little freedoms we have we may keep! So the flames of the past do not return! Do you know who built this city? Or Castle Shale? Or Krone? Or any of the dozens of ancient buildings? I do, Cearon! Do you know what brought the Scourge? Cearon, I warn you: something far more terrible than the Scourge stands at our doorstep, poised to break in. The world will burn without me!"

"Enough!" Cearon drew his sword. "I will hear of your delusions no more! Stand aside, Marcus, or die by my blade."

"You may leave, Cearon, but not with the Relic. Give it to me, and you will have your freedom."

"Come and take it, old man."

"Tell me—has it begun to whisper in your mind yet?" Marcus asked.

"Not a word," Cearon bluffed.

"Please, Cearon—I know these weapons. I've watched them devour the sanity of men greater than you. It will lead you to ruin, Cearon. Its words will sound like wisdom, but its motivation is destruction. It will manipulate you into doing terrible things. Why do you think it was hidden?"

"He speaks lies," Sky said. "He wants the Sword for himself. He is mad with power; don't listen to a word he says."

Doubt began to gnaw at Cearon.

Sky is powerful ... very powerful. But is Sky evil? Can I trust him?

Cearon made up his mind. "Whatever he wants, Marcus, it's not what you want—so that means it's what I want."

"You doom us all, Cearon," Marcus said darkly. "It wants to see the world perish before the ancient flames!"

"I was the only one who fought *against* those flames!" Sky said indignantly.

"No, right now, it's just you who is doomed, Marcus," Cearon said. He sprang forward, his sword glimmering against the soft glow of the fires.

The elves charged, but with a wave of his palm, Cearon sent them flying in every direction.

The Emissary pulled his mace free and hurtled forward with the ground thudding beneath his heavy heels. The wind whistled around his mace-and-flail as he swung at Cearon, but Cearon was quicker, stepping back just far enough to let the flail pass by. He stepped in after it, thrusting his sword forward. His blade cut through the dark armor like a beam of light through shadow, and with a cry of anguish, the Emissary fell to his knees. Cearon kicked him hard in the chest, knocking the gargantuan man to his back.

"You are strong," Marcus admitted.

"More than you know," Cearon snarled. He stepped toward Marcus with his sword ready to thrust. A powerful wave of magic knocked him back and away from Marcus, slamming him into the wall of a house.

"I have studied magic long and hard," Marcus warned as he lowered his hand. "It will take more than the weakest part of the Relic Sword to overcome me!"

"Your blade will do you no good against him," Sky said. "You must defeat him with your mind."

Cearon sheathed his sword and prepared his tired mind for combat. He was still weakened from his previous battles, but he was confident he could overcome Marcus.

"Do not underestimate him," Sky cautioned. "Focus your attacks hard."

With a shout, Cearon thrust his hand forward, and a wall of fire leaped from his fingertips, spreading out until it filled the whole street as it rushed toward Marcus. At the last moment, it separated in the middle and passed harmlessly by Marcus.

"I said focus!" Sky shouted.

"You still know so little," Marcus said as he thrust his hand forward. A great wind swept past him, throwing his hair about in the torrent as it roared toward Cearon. The wind slammed into Cearon, pressing him back against the wall with a painful thud.

Marcus raised his other hand, and before the wind had even let up, a thunderbolt streaked from his palm, striking Cearon in the chest. Cearon screamed in agony as the electricity poured through his body, breaking any focus he still had.

"Get your guard up!" Sky roared. "Deflect his attacks!"

Before Cearon could recover, Marcus grabbed him with magic and pulled him away from the wall, back out into the street. Marcus sent another wave at Cearon.

"Block it!" Sky bellowed.

With a roar, Cearon barely mustered up the energy to block the invisible assault and then sent a wave back at Marcus, taking the magician off guard. Marcus flew back, smacking hard into the gate behind him.

Cearon ran forward and drew his blade as he jumped into the air, bent on passing the steel through his enemy's ribs.

"Not your sword!" Sky yelled. Marcus was quicker than Cearon had anticipated. A wave of flames surged forth from his hands, flying up at Cearon and instantly coating him with the red tongues.

With a cry of surprise, Cearon landed awkwardly and tripped, falling on his shoulder. With desperate concentration, Cearon extinguished the flames with his own magic before they could burn him.

"Get up! He's attacking!"

He rolled to his feet again and was instantly struck by a massive wave of telekinesis that hurtled him into a wooden door of a house. The door burst asunder against Cearon's momentum, and he tumbled wildly through the small home until he smacked against the stone wall with a sickening crack of skull against stone.

Cearon groaned. He slumped over and vomited on the floor. His head was swirling from the impact, and the agony of his aching skull broke any concentration he had left to muster.

I'm ... defeated. He could barely believe it.

"Oh, no." Sky's voice was filled with pity and sorrow. "Cearon, you must run! It's your only chance."

Cearon vomited again from his swirling head. He tried to pull himself up onto his feet; he fell. Once again, he tried to pull himself up. He managed to take two staggering steps before a lightning bolt struck him back down to the floor. With a charge of electricity still in the air, Marcus stepped through the doorway.

"Pathetic," Marcus said in disgust. "Even with the power of the Relic, you are still a weakling. Why did I ever think I needed you?"

"Come and find me here again once you've escaped," Sky's voice said.

"Now where's the Sword?" Marcus barked angrily. Cearon glanced down at the handle still clutched tightly in his hand.

"Well? Where did you hide it?" Marcus demanded.

"Somewhere you'll never find it," Cearon muttered with a grin despite his pain.

"I'll find it," Marcus said with his smirk. "I'll find it, because I have to find it. And you ... you will tell me where the other pieces are hidden, because you will have to tell me."

Cearon laughed at Marcus in contempt. "The Sword has a mind of its own, Marcus. You'll never find it unless it wants you to."

"We'll see who knows more about the Sword by the end of this."

A gruff voice spoke from behind Marcus: "Give me the assassin, human."

Marcus turned around, and there, standing in wolf form, was the werewolf Guard. His fur was matted with blood, none of which appeared to be his, and his scimitar had blood dripping from it, as did his mouth. A bloodied bit of cloth remained caught on one of his claws.

"He is my prisoner!" Marcus said defiantly. Before Marcus could blink, the bloody scimitar was pressed against his neck and a clawed hand was clutching him by the hair.

"If you wish to keep your blood, you will surrender him to me." A coldness settled in the werewolf's eyes as he spoke.

"Howl? Where are you?" Voices came from outside.

"Here come your friends to put you back on your leash, dog." Marcus spat on him in contempt.

Howl's eyes sunk into a look of rage; he tilted his head back and howled so loudly that the room reverberated with the sound. Marcus closed his eyes and cringed at the noise.

"What are you doing, you cursed beast? I'll kill you for—" As Marcus spoke, Howl moved his sword with a speed that barely could be seen with the naked eye, crashing the butt of the sword into Marcus's temple. The man was knocked out before he even knew he was hit.

Cearon watched his enemy crumple on the ground before him. Cearon thought about trying to run, but his world still seemed to spin.

"So, what is to become of me?" Cearon grunted. His head ached far too much for him to focus on any real magic use, and his body was too broken to put up any kind of fight.

Howl stood above Cearon and held the sharp end of his scimitar against Cearon's throat. "You come with us."

The unicorn walked into the small room with the manticore behind him, blood dripping from both their weapons and from the manticore's tail.

"There you are, Howl!" the unicorn said. "What possessed you to run like that? We nearly lost you!"

"We have him," was Howl's only response.

"You captured him?" the manticore asked in amazement.

"What happened to Marcus?" the unicorn asked, looking at his crumpled body.

"The assassin nearly killed him," Howl lied. "I arrived just in time."

"That he did," Cearon said with a grin.

"Send me from your side," Sky said in Cearon's head. "Find

me again when you are once more free. There is much we must do if Marcus speaks true." Cearon released the handle, and with a final test of his endurance, he sent the hilt flying out of the window of the small home. None of the hybrids noticed.

There is much strange magic about that sword—stranger even than I expected.

The gargoyle Guard landed in front of the door, his bow drawn and pointed at the air.

"What are you doing? We need your help now!" he shouted as he released the arrow, sending it whistling up toward the sky.

"What? Why?" the unicorn barked.

"Freeze didn't tell you??? They have hybrids with them!" the gargoyle cried out as a winged figure landed on the street.

"But ..." the unicorn began. "No ... we're the only hybrids!"

The winged figure drew a rapier from his sheath and extended his wings menacingly.

"Guard the assassin!" Howl roared as he charged into the street.

"Death-Talon." Cearon smiled. "We meet again."

"No time for small talk now, cursed one. I have business to attend to," Death-Talon said as Howl approached, scimitar drawn.

Death-Talon had a handsome face, with brown hair, an angular jaw, and amber eyes. His strong wings bore feathers like the griffin's. On the end of each finger he had a talon-like claw. He wore hardened leather armor and wielded a rapier with a basket hilt to protect his hand. Cearon noticed that his ear was bloodied and missing a chunk.

Howl attacked the lone figure with a fury, his scimitar but a blur streaking through the air as Death-Talon struggled to defend against the fierce onslaught, even with his quick rapier.

Howl slapped his sword aside and with his sharp claws, he raked Death-Talon across the face. Death-Talon twisted from the impact and slashed out at Howl while retreating. Howl blocked the blow, and after a victorious howl to the sky, he attacked again.

The manticore and the unicorn closed around Death-Talon as well. Death-Talon slashed out one more time at Howl before he leaped into the air and flew away with all speed. The gargoyle loosed an arrow after him with a spell of accuracy over it. Death-Talon tried to block it mentally, but despite his attempts, the gargoyle's spell guided it into his leg. With a cry of agony, Death-Talon retreated toward the city with the gargoyle in pursuit, pulling another arrow from his quiver.

"You know that creature?" the unicorn asked as he returned to Cearon, giving him a light kick to emphasize the point.

"Like a brother," Cearon said. "Though I am dead to him now."

"And to everyone else," the unicorn said, just before his foot stomped down on Cearon's jaw, knocking him out cold.

Chapter Twenty

Cearon awoke. His head ached, and his whole body seemed to scream with pain. He tried to roll over but found he couldn't move. A terrible screeching sound came from either side of him, and breathing was difficult. He let out a soft moan and cracked his eyes open. He saw the stars above him, along with dark trees against the night sky passing slowly by.

He looked down and saw his body bound in chains, which were in turn locked to wooden walls that surrounded him. He heard the squeak and groan of wagon wheels and the trudge of footsteps alongside.

"Where am I?" he asked no one in particular. "Sky? Where is Sky?"

"Who's Sky?" he heard someone whisper.

"I don't know," a voice whispered back. "Maybe he's delirious."

"What happened? What's going on?" Cearon asked.

"You're on your way to prison, dog," a deep voice said. The head of the sasquatch Guard came into view against the sky. "Try to struggle. I'd prefer to kill you here and now."

"Where's Sky?" Cearon asked again.

"He'll be dead soon, too," the hairy Guard said. "Oh, and you'll be happy to know we defeated your little friends in the city. Trake still stands as the king's city. Your plot failed."

"Not mine …" Cearon mumbled. "Not my friends. Enemies."

"Whoever they are, we sent them running like frightened animals, along with the elves they fought with."

"Good," Cearon grunted. "Can't let Marcus win ..." And with that, his consciousness passed back into darkness.

Howl walked alongside the wagon, his jaw set with anger. Some of the remaining sentinels who had not been cut down by the elves at Trake followed the cart in their characteristic blue cloth, watching the chained assassin closely. The walker hybrids all followed as well, while Demon and Freeze flew above. Jinx had flown back to Castle Shale after being revived by Mer. She was being sent to prepare the castle for the new prisoner and to hopefully smooth things over with King Leon.

Howl scowled at the ground as he watched it pass beneath his feet. He was angry at the assassin for killing Pyre—and likely Blade as well, who was missing. He was angry still at humanity for his constant mistreatment at their hand—even after the Battle of Trake. Many of the prefects and soldiers fighting along with the Guard had seen him attacking elves in his wolfish form, and though he had slain many enemies, they still had treated him like a wild animal.

The fools. Howl scowled all the more.

Most of all, however, he was angry that they were returning to Castle Shale. Jinx had been the voice of reason, assuring everyone she could calm the king and reminding them that with the assassin in the dungeons, the king would now need them to guard the halls more than ever to ensure that the assassin could not escape. Though Howl had disagreed vehemently, the others had relented, and so Howl was faced with the choice of setting off alone or returning to his cage to be with his friends. He had most reluctantly chosen friends.

He looked out at the forest passing by. How he longed to run through the trees—to explore the high mountains, the low valleys, the broad plains, the deserts, the coasts, the swamps, and all other terrain the Kingdom of Shale had to offer. He scowled again and continued his steady tramp back toward Shale Castle.

Cearon awoke; he wished he hadn't. His head was swirling, but not like before.

This isn't caused by any head injury. This is something different.

He opened his eyes and saw two mages standing in front of him, focusing their thoughts against him, trying to confuse his mind. He tried to focus back, to counter them, but the injury to his head stopped him with a flash of pain. He sat back and let his focus be lost. His arms and legs were chained to a cold dungeon wall. Just a few torches cast red, flickering light about the dark and dingy place, and grim-faced men stood around.

"He's awake," a voice said. Cearon looked over and saw someone he thought he recognized. She had deep blue eyes, and her bright red hair was cut short and drawn back into a ponytail. A familiar sword rested on her hip; the pommel bore a gem the same color as her hair.

I know I know her ... but from where?

A figure walked in—one Cearon recognized even in his state of mind.

"Marcus!" Cearon growled.

"You have good mind, Cearon. Lesser men would be completely lost to this treatment," Marcus said as approached.

Cearon focused hard to register what Marcus had said; it didn't add up in his chaotic mind.

He said something ... but ... what did it mean?

"Leave ..." Cearon started, but he forgot what he was going to say. "You are ..." Once again, he was lost. He closed his eyes and tried to push the magicians out of his head, but once more, the pain in his skull stopped him. He groaned with frustration.

"Isn't the head injury enough, Marcus? Why are the magicians necessary?" the red-haired woman asked angrily. She looked at Cearon with what he thought may have been pity.

Marcus laughed. "Let him think," he said to the magicians. They relented their treatment, allowing Cearon the privilege of basic thought.

"Where did you hide the Sword, Cearon?" Marcus asked.

"You will never know." Cearon looked at the red-haired woman. "Oh, it's you, Bloodmane. It has been a long time."

She only nodded in reply.

"I need that blade, Cearon," Marcus said. "You have no idea how much I need it—how much the world needs me to have it."

"Then go find it. If it wants you, it will let you find it."

Marcus glowered where he stood. "It does not want me, Cearon, because it knows the good I will achieve with it."

"That's not what he said ..." Cearon said in a singsong voice with a sly grin.

Marcus slapped him on the side of the head in retaliation; Cearon's damaged skull throbbed with agony in response. *He can slap me all he wants. I don't even really know exactly where the Sword is, anyway.*

"Where is it, Cearon?"

"I'll never tell you. You want it to rule people."

"And what do you want it for?" Marcus shouted. "Everyone wants it for the same reason!"

Cearon just smiled coyly and looked at Marcus through his bright orange eyes. Marcus stared at his eyes.

"Oh, but of course," Marcus said as realization dawned on him. "You want it as the key, don't you? You want to open the Forbidden Mountains ... those eyes of yours burn for it. You won't rest 'til you have released what was locked away so long ago."

Cearon just smiled more. "It's in my blood, so to speak."

"And in your eyes," Marcus said. He drew a curved knife from his belt. He walked up and held Cearon's head in place while he put the point uncomfortably close to Cearon's orange eye. "And if you tell me where it is, I may just let you keep them."

"Never."

Howl stood at the top of the dungeon stairs, listening to what was going on down below. Marcus had been granted authority by the king to interrogate the assassin with only a few of his own minions present.

Marcus used magic to get this privilege. He must have!

It was ridiculous. The king would not believe that it was Marcus's elves who had attacked Trake—and, even more heinous, that Marcus had his own hybrids helping his elves. Marcus had claimed that he had led his elves against another force of elves led by hybrids. King Leon would believe nothing else, even when Freeze and Demon swore they saw no elves fighting any other elves.

Howl couldn't stand these humans. They were fools, all of them but for the few clever enough to rule the fools, and Marcus was one of those few. *I will not sit back and let Marcus take control of everything.*

He heard the assassin screaming down below in the dungeons as they tortured him. He winced as he heard the screams. As much as Howl hated him for slaying Pyre and Blade, Cearon didn't deserve that. *Besides, I don't want him too weakened …*

"What's going on down there?" Jinx asked as she walked up, speaking gingerly through the war wounds that the assassin had inflicted on her. Her jaw was swollen and she had a bruised eye, but she had come out of that fight relatively unscathed in comparison to most.

"They're torturing him."

"Good," Jinx said. "It's less than he deserves for what he did to Pyre."

Howl didn't say anything; he just looked down at the door the screams were emanating from. *If only those were Marcus's screams. There's a man who deserves this.*

"What do you think happened to Blade? We should have at least found a body."

"I don't know," Howl said coldly. "Where's Shadow? Hasn't he disappeared as well?"

Jinx smiled. "I know where he is."

"Where?"

"He's hiding, closer than any of you think. He's better at stealth than I ever knew."

"I'd bet I could sniff him out."

"You'd lose that bet. But that's not why I'm here. I need to talk to you."

Howl turned back toward the dungeon door. "About what?"

Jinx looked past him, down at the door. "Why are you so focused on that door?"

"I have something I want to ask him."

"What?"

"Something that's been troubling me."

"You've been different lately," Jinx said seriously. "That's why I am here."

"I know I have been," Howl said dispassionately. "That's what's been troubling me."

"What's going on, Howl? What is bothering you?"

Is she using her powers on me? Why am I telling her this? "People," he said. "Humanity and all its problems. This kingdom, this castle—it's driving me mad, Jinx."

"Are you planning what Shadow thinks you're planning?" she asked.

"No. I won't do anything foolish. I just need to ask him something."

"What?"

"I … don't know yet. I … I just need to talk to him."

"He'll tell you nothing that will help you," Jinx said warningly.

"I know. I need to, though."

"No, you don't—" she countered.

He cut her off. "Leave me alone, Jinx. I need to think."

"Don't do anything foolish, Howl. I know you're a passionate man, just—"

"I am no man," Howl growled. "I will not be called human. I have nothing in common with these creatures."

"You have more in common with them than the wolf in you, no matter how feral you think you get."

"Maybe," was all Howl said before he looked back down at the door. *Leave me be, Jinx. I am the lord of the wild. I do not need to justify myself to you.*

"Do nothing foolish, Howl."

"Don't worry about me. I know what I am doing," Howl said gruffly. She sighed hopelessly, and he listened to her footsteps recede down the hall as her scent grew fainter and fainter.

When Marcus finally emerged, his hands had blood on them, and several of his guards followed him closely. One guard in particular caught Howl's eye. She had bright red hair and eyes bluer than any waters Howl had seen; they looked like two sapphires set in her slender, pale face. He instantly did not trust her.

Marcus went up the stairs, watching Howl closely as he massaged the bruise on his temple. Howl eyed him back as he leaned against the wall, his hand stroking the hilt of Agras Dol.

"Stay away from me, you animal," Marcus said as he passed. "Few who have wronged me live long after."

"Watch what you say to the wolf, manipulator, or it may not be the dull end of my blade to find your head next time."

Marcus didn't reply. Instead, he brushed by in a fury.

Clearly, things did not go as well as he had hoped down in the dungeon. As the red-haired woman passed, Howl caught her scent. *She is no human!*

"Guard yourself ... hybrid," Howl whispered to her as she walked by. She eyed him carefully, and her hand instinctively went to her sword. Howl gave a low growl as he morphed into his wolf from and snarled at her receding figure. When they were out of sight, Howl returned to normal.

He turned back to face the door. *Marcus is bold enough to bring his hybrids into the halls of the king. Something must be done—and soon.*

Howl gave a sigh. He knew what he had to do, but he felt reluctant. He wasn't sure if it was even what he really wanted. He closed his eyes and steeled himself. Slowly, he opened them and then walked down the stairs.

He entered the dungeons to see five of Marcus's guards standing around Cearon, with two magicians focusing their thoughts against him. Howl shook his head.

He looks pitiful.

Cearon's body slumped loosely against the chains, his head hung from his shoulders, and his body smoked. The air felt charged with electricity. *Marcus clearly used his magic to full effect to torture him.* Howl had not much love for the assassin, but this was simply cruel.

Howl walked up. "I wish to speak with him." The mages did not respond, but one of Marcus's guards spoke.

"None but Marcus speaks with Cearon."

"I have orders from the king," Howl lied. He gripped the shoulder of a magician menacingly. "I will carry them out."

The magicians looked at one another nervously and then at Cearon's feeble figure.

"What harm could he do?" one asked. The other nodded, and they relented.

"Cearon?" Howl asked as he pulled Cearon's chin up. He recoiled with horror. Blood leaked from beneath the shut lids of Cearon's eyes.

"You monsters!" Howl roared to the others, causing the guards to step away from him in fear.

"Who calls me?" Cearon asked feebly. "Is ... is it Sky?"

"No," Howl said, turning slowly back to him. "It is one of your enemies."

"You are the wolf," Cearon said, smiling faintly despite his situation. The chaos in his mind was once again arranging itself into order. "I know."

"How ..." Howl asked. "You cannot know my voice. Do you? You have only heard me speak as a werewolf."

"I have many eyes," Cearon said. "Eyes that Marcus cannot destroy."

How long will Marcus be gone? I must get what I came here for before he returns. "Who do you fight for?" Howl asked.

"I fight for myself, and I fight for those of my kind oppressed by your kind."

"By werewolves?"

"Humans," Cearon corrected.

"What do you mean? Are you not human?"

"Only half." Cearon grinned.

Realization dawned on Howl. That was how this man had defeated multiple Guard members at once, that was why this man was on this mission, and that was why Marcus was so cruel to him. He had once belonged to Marcus; he had once been one of his hybrids.

"My kind, too, are oppressed by humans," Howl said.

"They tend to do that."

"What mission are you on?"

"A mission of freedom."

"That sounds nice."

"Only if I could get out, but here I shall probably die, and my mission with me. Not much is nice about that. Do you think anyone will ever write of my tragic story?"

Howl paused for a moment. His mind was in turmoil. The lines between friend and foe were no longer distinct, no longer obvious. The only beings Howl truly felt loyal to were the Guard—but were those who ruled the Guard worth fighting for, or against?

He closed his eyes. He thought of the nature of humans; what he had seen was not to his liking. He thought of Marcus, sitting on the throne of Castle Shale with the Relic Sword in his hand.

"Will they write tragic stories of you?" Howl reiterated, opening his eyes. "No." Quick as lightning, he drew his blade and cut the head from the first mage, then whipped around and cut down the second.

"What?" Marcus's guards cried out as Howl descended upon them, cutting two down before any could even pull their blades. The rest were no match for Howl's deadly swordsmanship, and within moments, they all lay dead on the floor.

"You ... would help me?" Cearon asked, bewildered. "Why?"

"I will not see Marcus as king," Howl said. "And nor shall I be in service any longer to these filthy humans. They are not my allies; they are my enemies. Will you accept a companion for your journey—another soul on a mission of freedom?"

Cearon smiled broadly. "Gladly. Loose me from these chains. I can still run."

"Can you see, or do you need my shoulder?" Howl asked.

"Loose me, and you shall find out."

Howl looked at the chains holding Cearon captive. He raised Agras Dol above his head and with all his might struck down. His keen scimitar cut through the iron chains with ease, and after another cut, Cearon stood with only iron restraints around his wrists.

"We can get these off later," Cearon said, gesturing to each band in turn. "Now, we must get out of the castle. I won't stand a chance if I have to face Marcus now."

"He'll fall to my sword if he's unfortunate enough to cross us," Howl growled.

"Don't underestimate him. He has a mastery over magic that few in history could ever boast." Howl opened his mouth to give his thoughts on Marcus's magic, but Cearon cut him off. "We can debate this later. Now, we need to get out quietly, if possible."

"Put on one of their uniforms," Howl said, motioning toward one of the dead guards.

"It's covered in blood," Cearon said.

How did he possibly know that? But he was right: Agras Dol had spilled blood all over the uniforms.

"That's the idea," Howl said as he pulled the bloody coat off the guard. "You will look wounded. No one will stop a man who looks as if he's about to bleed to death. We'll say you escaped and are running amok in the castle. Everyone will scramble to search for you while we escape."

"You're a clever one. I think we'll work well together."

"For now, at least." Howl tossed the coat up to Cearon, who grabbed it out of the air. "Marcus's knives haven't seemed to slow you down much."

"No," Cearon agreed. "As powerful as Marcus is, he is a

fool." He pulled the blood-covered coat over himself. "Give me something to cover my face with."

Howl ripped off a stretch of cloth and gave it to Cearon, who tied it like a bandanna over his face, concealing both his eyes and his identity.

"How do I look?" Cearon asked.

"Like a guard about to die. Come with me. Lean on my shoulder, as if you can't walk." Cearon did, and together they made their way up the stairs. Howl cracked the door open and looked out; he couldn't see anyone. He stepped out with Cearon, and they began to make their way toward the gate.

Through the winding halls they traveled, drawing stares from all the guards they passed.

"The assassin is escaping!" Howl barked at them. "He's wounded this man! Get to the dungeons and detain him before he gets loose!"

Guards sprinted down the hall—most away from the dungeons in near panic. They all feared the assassin; they had heard his stories.

Farther the two went until they came into the courtyard. They moved through the lush gardens toward the wall gate when Shadow seemed to materialize out of nowhere from the shade of a tree, his leg still wounded from the battle before.

"Where are you going with him, Howl?" Shadow asked calmly.

"The gremlin," Cearon muttered darkly.

"He's a wounded guard, Shadow. He needs treatment—now," Howl said with as much authority as he could.

"When did you start caring about human guards? And when has treatment for wounds ever lain outside these walls? Don't play me for a fool. Why are you helping him?"

"Don't make us crush you, gremlin," Cearon said warningly.

"Shadow, I've always liked you, but don't you dare stand between me and that gate."

"You're betraying us, Howl. You're releasing our enemy."

"Our enemy sits on the throne in that castle!" Howl shouted, pointing back at Castle Shale. "And another enemy tried to have his hybrids kill us in Trake! I'm not the one doing the betraying, Shadow. I'm like you: I've been betrayed. But unlike the rest of you, I will not sit back and watch as my enemies take control. I will fight, Shadow, and if you will fight for my enemies ... well, then you are my enemy too." Howl drew his sword.

"I am not your enemy, Howl," Shadow said as he unbuckled his dirk and placed it on the ground. "I will not fight you. But think about what you're doing, Howl! He killed Pyre! He is our enemy more than any in that castle!"

"That's what they would have you believe, Shadow. He killed Pyre in self-defense. You know it. How many times could he have killed one of us? But he spared us whenever possible. He could have killed you in these very gardens if he had had a mind to! He's the only one who's shown us any compassion!"

"Don't do this, Howl. I don't want to hunt you."

"Then join us," Howl said.

"You know I can't do that."

"Then stand aside."

"Howl, you're making a mista—" Before Shadow could finish, Cearon raised his hand and threw the gremlin back against the tree.

"We don't have time for this!" he barked angrily, trying to ignore the searing pain in the back of his head. "We need to get past that gate, Howl! Let's move!"

Shadow looked up from where he had been knocked over.

"Don't do this, Howl!" Shadow said desperately. "Don't make us enemies."

"What's going on down there?" a guard on the wall called down after seeing Shadow blasted to the ground.

"I don't make us enemies, Shadow," Howl said. "I leave that entirely up to you."

"Come—we must go," Cearon said. The wall guards were now running their way. "We can escape through the culvert." He motioned toward where the stream that came from the castle moat passed under the wall. It looked as if iron bars blocked passage through it, but Cearon knew that below the water's surface, the iron bars had been filed away. After all, he had spent weeks working on them to get into the castle the first time.

"Howl!" Shadow cried out urgently. "Don't go!"

"I must go," Howl said. "Don't follow me, Shadow. Do that for both of us. Don't follow me." And with Cearon, he turned, abandoned the injured-soldier charade altogether, and sprinted for the culvert.

"Halt! Stop where you are!" the wall guards shouted before they began loosing arrows. Even in Cearon's beaten state, he had no problem deflecting unenchanted arrows.

"Hurry up, will you?" Howl called back to Cearon. Cearon was wounded, and Howl was very, very fast. Even well, Cearon would have had difficulty keeping up.

"Trying ..." was all Cearon muttered as he ran. He held his hands at shoulder level with the palms open as he deflected the barrage of arrows hurtling toward them.

"Call the Royal Guard!" a wall guard shouted. One began to ring a bell set into the ramparts of the wall.

"They'll be here in moments," Howl shouted. "Hurry!"

"Trying!" Cearon shouted back as he deflected still more arrows. His mind throbbed in agony, but he forced himself to continue. *It is either this or death.*

Howl reached the culvert. "There's iron bars here!" he called back to Cearon.

"Under … water!" Cearon called back, his mind reeling from the pain in his head. *My skull must have fractured when I hit the wall.*

"Hurry! The Guard will be here any moment!" Howl shouted, looking up at the sky, trying to spot any armored figure flying about.

Cearon roared as he threw forth a wave of magic with every ounce of his strength. It deflected the incoming arrows aside like dust before a shield and knocked the archers from their feet. Cearon lowered his hands and ran for the culvert, arriving just as the archers were beginning to notch their bows again.

"Where do we escape through?" Howl asked desperately, motioning toward the fast running current that rolled against the heavy iron bars.

"Follow me." Cearon dove headfirst into the water as deep as he could. He passed under the bars, and the strong current swept him away from the castle, away from the walls, and away from his enemies. He felt relief sink in as the water carried him to safety. He had escaped from the castle … again.

Hopefully, this will be the last time I ever need to do that— especially since they're bound to bar up the culvert again after this.

He rose to the surface and took a deep breath. He watched the town go by with his mind, thanking his luck that no guards pursued him along the banks. People traveling in boats looked Cearon over strangely as he floated down the river, now swimming with the current. He found a boat he liked—a fast-looking and small skiff that would be easy enough to man with just two people. He swam up to where it was moored against a small dock and hauled himself aboard. He pulled its mooring ropes loose as quickly as he could.

"What are you doing? That's my boat!" a townsman said angrily as he approached. Cearon looked up, giving him a full view of his blood-covered uniform. The townsman's eyes grew large. Cearon smiled to himself as he threw the last line loose and set the ship free into the current.

"He's taking my boat!" But Cearon was already away. The man tried to leap to his boat, but Cearon blasted him back with magic. No one else tried to take the boat.

With his mind, Cearon could see Howl in the water just a short ways back, swimming desperately toward him. Cearon grabbed a spare bit of rope and threw it out to him. Howl grabbed it and let Cearon pull him to the boat.

"Swimming is a bit hard with Agras Dol weighing me down," Howl said with a grunt as he knelt on the deck, motioning toward his scimitar.

"Of course," Cearon said, gingerly touching the back of his skull. He needed healing soon.

"So is that how you escaped the first time?" Howl asked, looking back at the quickly receding walls of the castle.

"Yes. Easier then. You weren't expecting it, and stealing a boat at night is child's play. I was spotted taking this one."

"Ah," Howl said with a dismissive wave. "We can just blend with the rest of the trade ships 'til we get to Lokthea, or anywhere in between. We don't look too out of the ordinary ... well, except for ... you know," Howl said, motioning toward his eyes.

"I'm already used to playing the blind man. Now, I just am the blind man. I would say that I will make Marcus pay for this, but I already swore I'd make him pay as much as I could for what he'd done to me. Not much more I can swear against the man."

"Eh, I suppose you could take vendetta against his children." Howl shrugged as he watched the people of Syienna bustling through the streets; many gathered around the banks of the river to fish, wash clothes, and get water.

"You mean Harold? Please—he's been one of my greatest assets ever since I broke into that castle." Cearon began working the sails.

"What? You mean he was with you from the beginning? I suppose that explains how you knew the castle so well."

"No," Cearon corrected. "I knew the castle because Frederick the Rogue Master told me all about it. Harold joined me after I … well, interrogated him. Roughly."

Howl got up and helped Cearon with the rigging. "He helped you after you beat information out of him? Strange person."

"That he is. But he's good to have around. The man knows potions better than anyone I've met. He's brilliant at them, and he's been more loyal to me than anyone I've ever known."

"Really?" Howl said as he tangled a line. Cearon reached over and untangled it. Apparently deciding he was doing more harm than good, Howl went to the rudder. "That is a strange friendship."

"Well, I did release him from a curse his father had put on him as a child. The poor man heard ringing in his ears all the time."

"Marcus cursed him? Why?"

"Relic Sword," Cearon said. "He made Harold swear never to tell anyone about it and put the curse on him to make sure he wouldn't. The second he told me where the map was, he started screaming in agony and clutching at his ears."

"That's horrible," Howl said, playing with the rudder to get a feel on how it moved the ship.

"Marcus is a cruel man. Men, women, children, even his own child, they're just tools to him. Things he can use to further his plans. He's the type of man who will kill your parents in front of your eyes and then try to make you his slave," Cearon said as he pulled a final line. The wind caught the sail, sending the boat skimming downstream.

"Where did you learn to sail like this?" Howl asked.

"I never learned. But I can see the ropes in here." He pointed to his head. "I can see how they strain and pull on each other, and I can see the wind, and where the sail needs to be to catch it. Sometimes, puzzles are simpler if you don't use your eyes."

"You'll have to teach me that sightless eyesight trick—looks as if it comes in handy," Howl said as he stepped aside to let Cearon take the rudder.

"I can teach you some. Much of it can't really be taught, though; you have to just pick it up. I was always a natural at it—the best at the Academy. It's why I was so good with a sword; it is much easier for me to watch where everything is and is going to be. It made me useful on the battlefield, too. I was supposed to be the commander in Marcus's little world." He smiled and even laughed a little. "But Marcus forgot that sometimes slaves rebel, and they won't hesitate to use all the things you've given them against you."

"So, Marcus, is he trying to build his own empire, then?"

"Yes, I suppose that's what you'd call it. He's enlisted men and elves, along with more dreadful things: warlocks, Druids, giants from across the Sapphire Ocean, and who knows what else."

"So warlocks are real!"

"Yes. Yes, they're real, all right. For the most part, secretive, not to mention delusional, but real."

"So the Rogues are Marcus's men, then—right?"

"No. They'd have been loath to tell me about the castle if they were in Marcus's employ. Marcus doesn't want me anywhere near him."

"So who do they work with?"

"Themselves. They are fighting, much like you and I, for the good treatment of their kind. Have you ever seen a Rogue up close? They have dark skin. They've not been treated well in the last two hundred years. Their homeland lies to the east. The Kingdom of Shale has long raided them, oppressed them, conscripted them for wars, and all-around stepped on them whenever convenient. Frederick has finally given them a leader to rally behind, so they've brought their quarrel here, to the lands of their enemies. The Rogues at this point are really the only substantial ally we've got."

"Maybe not," Howl said nervously. "I killed many of them at Bel."

"They don't know that," Cearon said quickly. "And I wouldn't be too quick to tell them, either."

"No problems there," Howl said as he sat down on the deck. "So, why are you after the Relic Sword, anyway? So Marcus can't get it?"

"No. Well ... yes and no," Cearon said. "I don't want Marcus to get it, but that's not the main reason I want it."

"So what's the main reason?"

"My memories from before I turned three are very fuzzy. Those are my human memories, before I was transformed— before I was crossed magically with the greater part of me."

"Hybrid," Howl said knowingly. "I don't know why I didn't figure it out sooner. Seems blatantly obvious even from the beginning, now."

"I remember seeing him," Cearon continued. "He was chained to the floor, his mouth bound shut, his talons nailed to the floor and his wings cut from his back. They spoke many incantations—the mages, that is—and I blacked out. When I awoke, my eyes were orange ... and I remembered, Howl. I remembered the things he had remembered. I saw deep into the past, saw the suffering of my kind. I saw the Scourge, I saw the sins of King Derek the Cruel, and I saw my retribution on his kind. Most importantly, I saw my kind locked away within the Forbidden Mountains."

"So why do you need the Relic Sword?"

"The human champion used the Sword to raise a magical barrier to lock us in the mountains. It's the only thing I know of that can lower that barrier."

"So you need it to free your kind?"

"Yes. The Sword is the key to their freedom—and to their

protection as they regain their freedom," Cearon said as he steered the light skiff around a large brig making its way downstream.

"So who, exactly, are your people?"

Cearon smiled. "Dragons."

Howl raised an eyebrow. "I was always taught they were just myth—that man imagined them while seeing drakes breathe on a foggy morning."

"I know. It's the lie humanity has told itself. Humanity swore to erase dragons—even from history, even from their own minds. The dragons burned Aetha to the ground after the humans had attacked the largest hatchery the dragons had, killing all the children, nurses, and eggs."

"You know this?"

"I remember it," Cearon said. "I remember flying over Aetha and watching sheets of flame erupt from my jaws. I remember watching people run in fear while rage burned within me for my lost son."

"So it was your kind who melted the city? Jinx was telling me about the strange destruction of the city."

"No," Cearon said thoughtfully. "No, my kind burned down wooden buildings built over the melted ruins of the stone ones, and burning humans out of stone buildings still undamaged enough to live in. I don't know who did that to the buildings." A long silence elapsed as the two pondered different things.

"I inherited no memories from my other half," Howl mused.

"Maybe it's a dragon thing," Cearon said. "We are incredible creatures."

"But how did the humans forget—and get everyone else to forget—the dragons?"

"Partially through spells, partially through lies, and partially by locking all the dragons up in the Forbidden Mountains ... well, most of them. I'm proof enough that there are still at least a few roaming around the world today." Cearon almost motioned toward what had once been his orange eyes to illustrate his point, until he realized they were destroyed. He wondered why his eyes didn't hurt very much. He had always imagined having his eyes cut would hurt terribly. *Maybe the throbbing at the base of my skull is just overshadowing it.*

"So, any plans from here?" Howl asked as he scanned the sky for any Guard members.

"Not really," Cearon admitted as he pulled the guard's bloody shirt off and tossed it into the water. He kept the bandana on. "I told Harold to meet at a camp outside of Trake. Hopefully he'll be waiting for me there. I also need to talk with Frederick; he may be my only hope for acquiring the pommel stone. The thing is hidden in Krone."

"You mean the kingdom's most powerful fortress, Krone? The one mysteriously cut out of a mountain?"

"The very same," Cearon said grimly.

"That … that will take some planning to break into there. I've heard those walls are protected by spells more ancient than any of the magic we know of."

"Hopefully by then I'll have enough of the Sword to get us past any of that. It's the one thousand soldiers and who knows how many mages I'm worried about. I'm skilled with a blade, but not that skilled."

"That will be a suicide mission for the Rogues. They'll march straight into the jaws of the kingdom."

"I know. I don't know what else I can do. I can't sneak in there; it's much too protected for that. But I suppose I'll have to cross that bridge as I come to it, won't I?"

"Not much else you can do," Howl admitted.

"Thank you, by the way," Cearon said seriously. "For freeing me from those chains. They would have killed me the moment they found out where the hilt was. You saved my life."

"Probably won't be the only time I'll do that, either." Howl grinned.

Cearon smiled. "Well, I won't complain."

"So where is our first destination?" Howl asked.

"Trake. I need to speak to Harold, and I need to speak with someone I recently met there ... well, sort of met. I spoke to him. He seemed to know what he was talking about, though—and, hopefully, with his help, we can bring Marcus's plans to ruin."

"And who is he?"

"I don't know"—Cearon shrugged—"but he told me to call him Sky."

Character List

Blade – The member of the Royal Guard intertwined with a griffin. He has bronze colored wings, talons on his fingers, and wields a longsword with expert skill. He is close friends with Pyre, and a dutiful soldier for the Kingdom of Shale.

Jinx – The member of the Royal Guard intertwined with a harpy. She has golden, feathery hair and similar wings. She is adept at magically bewitching people to do her will. She wields a spear, and is the closest to the mysterious Shadow.

Pyre – The member of the Royal Guard intertwined with a phoenix. He has orange and red wings. He is the only Guard member capable of wreathing himself in flames, and his armor is designed to glow with the heat of his fire. He wields a broadsword superbly, but is somewhat unaccomplished in magic. He is like a brother to Blade.

Shadow – The member of the Royal Guard intertwined with a gremlin. Shadow has dark hair, and often covers himself with dirt and soot to help him blend in. He wields a dirk, a blow gun with poisoned darts, and throwing knives. He has dark, leathery wings capable of flying nearly silently. He is the Royal Guard's assassin, and is well trained in stealth and ambush. He is an excellent practitioner of magic, and has many strange spells in his arsenal that he designed himself. He is famously shy, and often stumbles over his words.

Sinister – The member of the Royal Guard intertwined with a basilisk. Sinister has thin, blonde hair and red irises. He wields a longsword, and has a basic understanding of attack magic. He also is capable of paralyzing and incapacitating foes by staring them in the eye. He is well known for his selfishness and his treachery.

Howl – The member of the Royal Guard intertwined with a werewolf. Howl has dark hair and brown eyes. He wields a well crafted scimitar that he made himself out of enchanted steel. The words, "Agras Dol," which means Wild Heart, are etched into the blade in ancient lettering. When Howl transforms, short, gray hairs cover his body, his snout protrudes from his face like a wolf's, and his hands grow sharp claws. He is a brilliant swordsman, and is undoubtedly the fastest runner among the Royal Guard.

Silver – The member of the Royal Guard intertwined with a unicorn. Silver has shimmering hair as well as silvery irises. He wields a quick rapier, but the true danger to his foes is his spectacular ability at attack magic. Silver is the strongest magician among the Royal Guard, which is reflected in his arrogance.

Crash – The member of the Royal Guard intertwined with a sasquatch. He stands at well over six feet tall, and has short brown hairs covering his body. He is a man of great strength, and wields a battle-ax to terrible affect against his enemies. He is close friends with Crunch.

Crunch – The member of the Royal Guard intertwined with a troll. Crunch is not as tall as Crash is, but he is stockier. Crunch is close friends with Crash, and the two of them together can scatter grown men before them like pebbles.

Crunch wields a mace deftly, but has little experience in magic.

Freeze – The member of the Royal Guard intertwined with a drake. Freeze has received her name because of her somewhat icy demeanor. She has black hair, and brown, leathery wings. She wields a katana and has a strong understanding of telekinetic magic.

Sting – The member of the Royal Guard intertwined with a manticore. Sting has a thick mane, as well as a scorpion tail. Each of his fingers ends in a sharp claw, as well. He carries a falchion style blade which he uses in tandem with his claws and venomous tail.

Mer – The member of the Royal Guard intertwined with a merman. Mer has damp, greenish hair as well as green and blue tinted scales that cover part of his body and some of his face. Mer carries a straight short-sword, and is a master at healing magic.

Demon – The member of the Royal Guard thought to be intertwined with a gargoyle. Demon is the only archer among the Guard. He uses magic little, but what he does use, he uses to augment his arrows. He is a quiet man who only speaks when necessary, and is an agile flier.

Rocky – The member of the Royal Guard intertwined with a golem. Rocky is completely bald, as his skin is entirely made of stone. He is impervious to all but the heaviest of strikes, though his mobility is compromised as a result. He wields a war-hammer.

Marcus – The leader of the Order of Magicians who is well agreed to be the most powerful magician in all the land. He fought in the Battle of Elfin Folly along with the mercenaries from the east. Marcus is the illegitimate son of King Francis the Lecherous, who is the grandfather of King Leon the Meek.

King Leon the Meek – The eighteenth ruler in the Shale dynasty, King Leon the Meek is the timid son of King Harold the Brave. King Leon's father was assassinated by his closest adviser, Lord Arromat. King Leon has since developed an overly acute sense of caution and a fanatical obsession with safety.

The Hooded Man – A mysterious man with strange powers, he fights ferociously against the Kingdom of Shale. He searches for something known as the Relic Sword, a weapon of legend that has not been heard of since the terrible Scourge of old.

Harold – The son of Marcus, Harold has sided with the strange hooded man. A young magician of only marginal accomplishment in magic, Harold was often a disappointment to his father. However, Harold has proven his value through his mastery of potions.